TWO UTOPIAN NOVELS..........

2121

Morrison Bonpasse

AND

JESUS and JESUSA

Maria Maddalena

BonPasse Exoneration Services. (a Maine non-profit corporation)
P.O. Box 390
Newcastle, ME 04553 USA
001-207-586-6078
Morrison Bonpasse, Executive Director
morrison@bonpasseexonerationservices.org
www.bonpasseexonerationservices.org

2121 AND *JESUS and JESUSA*
Morrison Bonpasse

ISBN-10 0-9837985-8-3
ISBN-13 978-0-9837985-8-3

TABLE OF CONTENTS

FOREWORD to publication of
2121 and *JESUS and JESUSA*
together in one volume.

The two utopian novels, *2121* and *Jesus and Jesusa*, work together, though they can be read separately.

They are presented in this volume in the order in which they are best read: first *Jesus and Jesusa* and then *2121*. In *Jesus and Jesusa* the world's changes in the 21st century are accelerated by the activism of the twin Co-Popes, Jesus and Jesusa.

2121 describes the conviction of Chad Forbes for "chemical manslaughter" in 2117 in Portland, Maine. It describes the world of that era as it had evolved after the 2014 publication of the novel *Jesus and Jesusa*. Population growth is reversed, global warming is reversed, and wrongful convictions are reduced to less than .1% of all convictions. In the year 2121, Chad's case is resolved and his sister, Eleanor Perkins, has twin daughters in the 69-person utopian community, UtopiaDos, on the planet Mars. Baby steps for them, giant steps for humanity.

JESUS and JESUSA

Maria Maddalena

BonPasse Exoneration Services. (a Maine non-profit corporation)
P.O. Box 390
Newcastle, ME 04553 USA
001-207-586-6078
Morrison Bonpasse, Executive Director
morrison@bonpasseexonerationservices.org
www.bonpasseexonerationservices.org

Jesus and Jesusa
by Maria Maddalena (pseudonym)

ISBN-10 0983798567
ISBN-13 978-0983798569

TABLE OF CONTENTS

How the world changed – See 2093 Ph.D. Thesis of
Charlotte Amalie Perkins, The Global Social and
Political Impact of the Utopian Novella *Jesus and
Jesusa* as summarized in Appendix B of upcoming
book, *2121*, by Morrison Bonpasse

.

Foreword

The forward looking novella, *Jesus and Jesusa,* is published in 2014 as the first of a two-book combination with the novel, *2121*, to be published later in 2014, although ostensibly written in 2121. They are both utopian, with *2121* incorporating by "looking backward" the publication of *Jesus and Jesusa* into its story. Each can be read separately, but it's recommended that they both be read, and in order of their publication.

Both books present what may be called realistic utopias, as the societies they describe are believed by the author to be realistic, given what we know about science and human relations. They are optimistic in the sense that present a view of humanity as solving its problems of global warming, overpopulation and wrongful convictions, and emerging in the early 22nd century as a kinder, gentler and smarter species.

The alternatives, which usually seem more likely, are a diminished Earth and a diminished human population unworthy of its good fortune to have evolved this far.

List of Characters

(Dates are dates of birth unless followed by a hyphen and a date of death)

Primary Characters

Jesus, born as Jesus Prescelto, 2014-2089

Jesusa, born as Jesusa Prescelto, 2014-2089

Prescelto, Giuseppe, born as Giuseppe Altacelto –
    Father of Jesus and Jesusa 1979-2076

Prescelto, Maria, born as Maria Prescudo – Mother of
    Jesus and Jesusa 1978-2078

Other characters

Bakhita, Susanna - Pope

Benedict, Arnold – friend and roommate of Patrick
    O'Laughlin

Bush, John Ellis ("JEB") – 45th President of the United
    States. 1953

Donato, Guglielmo Donato - Cardinal in Vaticano.

Eggerickx, Sonja - leader of the International
    Humanist and Ethical Union (IHEU)

Francesco I, Pope 1936

Francesco II, Pope

Friday, Josephine – Dallas Police Dept. Lieutenant

Galvani, Allessandro – Scientist at Universita del Sigli
    di Salerno.

Lawrence, Budge – President Bush's liaison to the GTO
    (Great Transformation Org.).

More, Thomasina – Archbishop of Canterbury.

Obama, Malia – Sec'y General of the United Nations.

Obama, Natasha (Sasha) – Governor of the
    Commonwealth of Virginia.

O'Laughlin, Patrick – Convicted of attempted
    assassination of Co-Popes.
Pappalardo, Angelo - Scientist at Universita del Sigli di
    Salerno.
Scheck, Teresa – Attorney and priest.
Sediva, Elvira – Executor of the estate of Alessandro
    Galvani.

Chronology

2014 Births of Jesus and Jesusa

2020 Nuclear Explosion at Kahuta, Pakistan nuclear facility

2020 "Great Transformation" 50-year campaign begins

2021 Alexandria Treaty between Israel and Muslim/Arab neighbors.

2026 Adoption of a Single Global Currency: mundo.

2032 Graduation from Da Vinci School

2036 March along the Great Wall of China

2037 Graduation from Universitat Heidelberg

2038 Become co-presidents of International Humanist and Ethical Union.

2041 Global Religious Framework.

2042 Vaticano Council IV convenes. Jesus and Jesusa ordained as priests, then cardinals.

2044 Jesus and Jesusa elected Co-Popes.

2045 Temple Mount Accord

2054 Reunification of Roman Catholic and Eastern Orthodox Churches.

2084 Resignations of Co-Popes Jesus and Jesusa.

2089 Deaths of Jesus and Jesusa

Chapter 1 Births of Jesus and Jesusa

On May 30, 2014 twins were born, apparently fraternal boy and girl, to Giuseppe and Maria Prescelto of Paestum,[1] in the province of Salerno, Italia.[2] Giuseppe Altacelto and Maria Prescudo were married on New Year's Day, 2000 at the ages of 21 and 22, respectively. They grew up in neighboring towns, but didn't meet each other until matched by the online dating service, www.italianoamore.com.[3] To make a new start and escape the sexist naming customs, they melded their surnames to become Prescelto. Giuseppe was a mason and stone cutter with his primary work at the Magna Graecia site in Paestum, with its three magnificent temples. He recreated pieces of each temple as they would have appeared at their time of original construction between 600 and 400 B.C. The pieces were then exhibited in the Paestum Archeological Museum, alongside surviving real pieces, or re-cast lookalikes. Sometimes, the pieces were painted as they originally appeared.

Maria was an attorney, specializing in building and real estate law. Growing up, she barely knew of the Paestum temples and only visited them once, when out-of-town relatives came to visit.

Maria and Giuseppe became aware of their infertility around 2003 when they stopped using

1. This is the current Italian and historic Roman name for the site. The Greek name was Poseidonia.
2. Italy. Since 2014, many new words have been introduced into English primarily because of the decision of the Global English Standards Organization (GESO) in 2025 to use the native, local or real spellings of names of people and places. The practice is called RealName. GESO was established by the United Nations in 2018. If the native language didn't use the Latin alphabet, then the best transliteration was used, rather than a translation. This RealName usage is intended to respect the integrity of the named people and places.
3. As of 2014, not a real website.

contraceptives with the intent of raising one or two
children, preferably twins. Maria did not look forward
to pregnancy, and a single pregnancy was preferable to
two. After other methods of overcoming infertility did
not work, including medicines and sexual exercises,
Giuseppe and Maria were referred to Dr. Pappalardo's
Infertility Team at the medical school of the Universita
del Sigli di Salerno. This school had a distinguished
history as the site of Europe's first medical school,
Schola Medica Salernitana, which was most prominent
from the 11th through the 13th centuries. One of its
most famous graduates and teacher was a woman,
Trotula, who wrote medical texts on women's
medicine.

Dr. Pappalardo told Guiseppe and Maria that their
infertility was unusual in that it had a double cause:
his low sperm count and the production by her ovaries
of eggs which had an immunal rejection response to
his sperm. Still, Maria's uterus seemed healthy, and
Dr. Pappalardo heard Maria's request for twins, so the
doctor recommended that two fertilized eggs from the
same donors be implanted artificially. Two were
becoming available in late August, which timing was in
synch with Maria's menstrual cycle. The Presceltos
were told that the male and female donors were
graduate students at the Universita del Sigli di
Salerno. For reasons Dr. Pappalardo didn't explain, he
didn't want to freeze the eggs once they became
available.

Giuseppe and Maria agreed to raise the two
children until adulthood, and agreed not to seek the
identities of the biological parents, according to
standard practices of in-vitro fertilization. The
implantation of the two embryos was successful, and
Maria's pregnancy was easy and she was happy. As
was the normal practice for expecting parents, Maria
underwent pre-natal genetic testing, and the fetuses
were entirely normal.

After the birth of apparently fraternal twins, they were baptized in the neighborhood parish church. Without prompting from the scientific team, Giuseppe and Maria named them Jesus and Jesusa (Jay-sooz' a). They chose the English spelling for Jesus because Maria had become fluent in English during her one year in a high school in the United States through the American Field Service (AFS). The Espanol spelling was chosen for Jesusa, because it was the most common in their Google search for feminine equivalents for Jesus. Relatives and friends saw the children and called them "angelic," and "divine," but because such terms were commonly used to flatter the parents of attractive children, no further weight was given to such labels.

The friends and relatives were closer to the truth than they realized.

Chapter 2 Foreskin of Calcata – from Roma to Calcata to Roma

The story of Jesus and Jesusa began in Calcata, a small town north of Roma, Italia, and 230 kilometers northwest of Salerno. In January 1983, the town's sacred relic, the foreskin of Jesus of Nazareth, also called the "Holy Prepuce," was removed by an unknown person from a box under the bed of the village priest in Calcata, Don Dario Magnoni. Actually, it was in Calcata Nuova (new) because Calcata Vecchia (old) had been abandoned by most residents in the 1930s after the Government condemned the town due to risks of landslides of volcanic soil, especially during earthquakes. Nearly the entire population of about 400 people moved up the hill to the newly built replacement town. After the feared slides did not occur, some residents returned to Calcata Vecchia and others were attracted by the opportunities for rent-free squatting in abandoned homes. Most of those latter residents later purchased their squatter homes.

The foreskin had remained in the old church, which was named for Saints Cornelius and Cyprian. Pope Cornelius and Bishop Cyprian worked together for the Christian faithful in the third century. Cyprian was martyred by beheading in 258 A.D. Sometime before leaving for a church-related trip to Roma, Don Dario brought the relic from the old church to his bedroom in Calcata Nuova. When he returned from Roma the next week, he found his house had been burglarized. No money was taken, but the "Holy Prepuce" was gone.

As the body of Jesus of Nazareth had ascended, by Christian belief, into heaven, the foreskin from his Jewish circumcision was purportedly one of only two remnants of his body remaining on earth. The other is a section of his umbilical cord which is a relic at the Papal Archbasilica of St. John Lateran in Roma, said

14

to be the most important church of the Roman Catholic faith. It even outranks St. Peter's Basilica at the Vaticano. Of the two bodily relics, and several churches claimed to have a piece of the Holy Prepuce, the foreskin was the more famous or exotic, perhaps because of its sexual location.

While there were only a few relics of Jesus himself, there were hundreds of relics of the Apostles and other saints on display in Western Europa churches. There are skulls, arms, legs, livers, and other parts of most Christian saints everywhere. For many churches, these items were treasured links to the holy past, and the sources of miracles and, not incidentally, monetary contributions to the church.

There were about 30 churches which claimed to have one of the two or three nails which were used to fasten Jesus of Nazareth to his wooden execution cross, and many others which claimed to have a piece of the cross itself. The most famous relic of Jesus of Nazareth, and the one subjected to the most serious testing, is probably the Shroud of Turino which purportedly covered the body of Jesus of Nazareth after his crucifixion.

The Calcata foreskin relic had been in the town since 1527 when a Deutsch[1] soldier was captured in the town with the relic in his possession. He had participated in the "Sack of Roma," and was returning north to Deutschland when captured. He hid the relic in his cell and left it behind upon his release, perhaps fearing punishment if it became known he had taken it from Roma. The foreskin was rediscovered in the jail 30 years later in 1557. It was thereafter displayed in the church in Calcata, and Christian pilgrims were rewarded with indulgences for visiting the site. An indulgence was thought to assist Christians to reduce the spiritual punishment for their forgiven sins.

1. German

15

Before the Martin Luther-led Protestant divorce from the Church, indulgences were widely sold to raise funds.

The Calcata relic was one of several foreskins in Europe claimed to have belonged to Jesus of Nazareth. In the 12th century, the Abbot of Charroux Abbey in western France asked Pope Innocentius III to decree that the abbey's "Holy Prepuce" was the genuine article. The pope declined to decide and the relic disappeared. In 1856, a workman at the ruins of the Charroux Abbey claimed to have re-discovered the "Holy Prepuce" which had been hidden in the ruined abbey's walls. The owners of the relics in Calcata and Charroux, and other places, argued for the bragging rights for the authenticity of their relics.

The Church found the issue sufficiently embarrassing and distasteful that in 1900, an order was issued that any Catholic speaking or writing about the "Holy Prepuce" would be excommunicated. That order didn't stop the controversies and curiosity, so in 1954 the punishment was increased to the higher level of excommunication and shunning. One reason for the continued interest was that January 1 was still celebrated by Catholics as the "Holy Day of Circumcision." To reduce that attention, the Vaticano Council II, 1962-65, changed the name of the holiday to "Octave of the Nativity."

Still, the issue of a foreskin relic continued to surface from time to time among theologians until the relic disappeared from Calcata in 1983. Interest in the foreskin was rekindled by the 2009 publication of the book, *An Irreverent Curiosity*, by David Farley of the United States.

Chapter 3 Cloning the Foreskin

In the 1950's James Watson and Francis Crick, with the inspiration and initially unrecognized assistance of Rosalind Franklin, presented to the world the structure of DNA, the key to the design and propagation of life. Speculation began in the ensuing decades about how DNA could be used to artificially recreate cells, and then organs and finally people, which was described in several science fiction books. Gradually, reality caught up to those books. A big forward step was the cloning of the Scottish sheep, Dolly, in 1996 from a cell taken from a female sheep's mammary gland.

Pope Ionnes Paullus II[1] was advised in 1982 that scientists could, in the foreseeable future, take the DNA from the only known purported remnants of the body of Jesus, his foreskin or his umbilical cord, and use that DNA to recreate a human being. Pope Ionnes Paullus II saw potential danger to the church, and Christianity, too, that the relic could be stolen by others, so he is thought to have taken the prudent step of having the foreskin relic removed in 1983 from the church in Calcata and brought to the Sacred Archives in the Vaticano for safekeeping. It was a secret operation, and speculation arose later that the local priest and/or others had stolen the relic, but no one in the town knew the real story.

At the Vaticano, controversy swirled about the future of the Catholic Church and what role the Holy Prepuce or Holy Umbilical Cord could play in the Church's revival. The use of the Holy Umbilical Cord was rejected by scientists because its container for

1. Pope John Paul II, (1978-2005). He was the third longest serving pope, after St. Peter (Petrus) (33-67) and Pope Pius IX (1846-1878).

several centuries was made of lead, which was thought to have caused damage to the cells of the Cord.

In November, 2011 Cardinal Guglielmo Donato, the newly appointed President of the Pontifical Commission for Vaticano City State, authorized a Catholic scientist to remove a .5 centimeter square of the foreskin relic and evaluate whether the DNA in that fragment could be used to recreate a human being. The scientist, Angelo Pappalardo, of the Universita degli Studi di Salerno, recruited four others for his team in this project. All were sworn to secrecy.

After six weeks of analysis, the team agreed that it was possible to recreate a human being from the DNA in the Holy Prepuce. However, they also agreed not to tell Cardinal Donato the truth. They were scientists first and Catholics second, and they believed that Pope Benedictus XVI, who succeeded Pope Ionnes Paullus II in 2005, would suppress any report of feasibility that the team might issue. Further, they feared for their own safety if they told the Vaticano the truth. If a Pope could authorize a burglary, who knew what he could authorize.

After the report of "no feasibility" was sent to Cardinal Donato, the team of five was not sure what to do. The team had kept the .5 cm square sample, after telling the Vaticano that it had been consumed in the analysis process. Professor Pappalardo then proposed that as scientists they must pursue what they believed to be possible. He recommended that sufficient DNA be extracted to clone not one but two human beings: with one of each sex. The sexual change could be achieved by taking one of the cloned embryos and switching "off" the Y sex chromosome and doubling the X sex chromosome so as to create a female.

He argued, "In this world of gender equality, it would not be fair to produce just a male child from the Jesus foreskin." Prof. Pappalardo proposed that an infertile and married woman volunteer, who is seeking

18

to have children, be found to bear the two children and raise them to adulthood. The other four scientists appeared to be astonished, but agreed that it was possible and that it would advance the science of reproduction, if not the Catholic religion. One member, Alessandro Galvani, expressed optimism but with doubts about the chances of success. He said "I very much want this to work, but no one has ever successfully cloned cells which are this old."

The five members of the team agreed unanimously to proceed with the project. It was agreed further that members of the team would tell no one else of the source of their human DNA, including the prospective mother and father.

The actual cloning was predicted to take approximately four days, after soaking the foreskin sample in a special solution for a week. After the prospective parents were identified, interviewed and approved for the project, "Cloning Day," was set for August 26, 2013, with implantation scheduled for August 30.

Chapter 4 Childhood and college

As Jesus and Jesusa grew, they were clearly happy children and seemed to enjoy every minute they were awake. They didn't need to be taught to share. Gradually, it became more evident that they were different from other children. They spoke in measured cadences, in order that everyone could understand them. They were extraordinarily polite. They were very interested in their father's work at Paestum, to the point of knowing almost as much as he knew. In their teens, the twins were said to have had "wisdom beyond their years." They had an unusual affection for each other as well. Unlike most twins and siblings they showed no signs of conflict with each other.

The education at their primary school was based on the Reggio Emilia approach which stressed the dignity and integrity of the students, even at that young age. That method arose after World War II through the work of educator Loris Magaluzzi in Reggio Emilia which is 350 kilometers northwest of Roma. He was motivated to educate students who would not so willingly surrender individual freedom to future governments, as he had seen happen in Fascist Italia and Deutschland.

Jesus and Jesusa had no violent conflicts with fellow students at school. Whenever there was a controversy or argument between Jesus or Jesusa and another student, it would be settled with an unusual turning of the other cheek or another signal of peace. The other student would cease arguing in every instance. For example, one student bully, Sylvio, took a book from Jesus, who simply said, "If you want it, it's yours. Learn from it. Then give it to someone else and share what you both learned with me. Go. Take it, now." Sylvio was stunned. He never planned to read the book, as the theft was only a prank. Secretly, he returned the book to Jesus the next day, by placing it into his book bag when Jesus had left it for a few moments. The next time they saw each other, Jesus smiled, and Sylvio looked down at the floor.

On another occasion, while playing football, another player intentionally tripped Jesus who fell forward onto his face. The referee didn't see the violation, but other players and his coach saw it and urged Jesus to file a complaint with the school of the errant player. Jesus declined, saying, "Let it be. That player knows what he did, and his teammates know what he did. Let's play the kind of football we know that we can play. We are better than they are." After the halftime break Jesus's team members felt energized by Jesus's forbearance and they outscored their opponents for the win.

Jesusa had different problems. She was beautiful, but cared little about spending time on her hair or skin or wearing jewelry. Sometimes a jealous girl would mock Jesusa for her appearance and Jesusa might respond, "I am here on this earth to help others and not to enhance my own looks." For a 12-year old, this was extraordinary.

Recognizing that their children were special, Giuseppe and Maria enrolled them in 2028 in the Da Vinci School, a secular humanist private boarding school run by the Italian Secular Humanist Foundation, a member of the Global Secular Humanist Movement. The school was in the former Benedictine Abbey in Santa Maria di Castellabate, about 70 kilometers south of Salerno. They wanted their twins to learn about the world through the lens of every religion and not just one.

The Da Vinci School was founded in 1978 by a disciple of A.S. Neill at Summerhill in the United Kingdom. The emphasis of the school was on student initiative and responsibility, and this program was well-suited to Jesus and Jesusa.

For their senior year project, they chose to study wrongful convictions and the death penalty. Italia has an honorable place in the pantheon of countries leading the world toward the abolition of capital punishment. In 1786, one of Italia's predecessor countries, the Duchy of Toscana[1] with its capital in Firenze,[2] was the first modern state to abolish the death penalty. Subsequent Italian governments, especially the Mussolini Fascists in the years 1922-43, legalized the punishment, but used it infrequently, and it was finally abolished in 1948. The last executions were of three civilian murderers by firing squad in 1945.

In 1994, Italia proposed at the United Nations a worldwide moratorium on the use of capital punishment. The resolution lost by eight votes. In 2007, Italia led the European Union to propose a similar resolution, based in part upon the U.N.'s own 1948 Declaration of Human Rights. It passed by a vote of 104 to 54 with 29 abstentions. Subsequent efforts in 2008 and 2010 were approved with similar votes.

The project for Jesus and Jesusa was on two levels. First, they studied the conviction, and execution by crucifixion, of their namesake, Jesus of Nazareth, for treason against the Roman Empire. It was a wrongful conviction, because he had argued for the separation of church and state, and not the overthrow of the Roman occupation of Israel, when he said, "Render unto Caesar the things that are Caesar's, and unto God the things that are God's."[3] He also said, "My kingdom is not of this world."[4] To the Romans, a man who was said to be the King of the

---

1. Tuscany.
2. Florence.
3. Book of Matthew, 22:21.
4. Book of John, 18:36

Jews, and who spoke of his "kingdom" was enough of a threat to warrant execution, and crucifixion was the standard method used in the occupied territory of Israel. In other parts of the Empire, even more cruel methods were used, such as being eaten by lions in the Colosseum.

At one point in their research, Jesus mused to Jesusa, "Have you ever wondered what symbol Christianity would now be using if Jesus had been simply imprisoned or executed in some other way, such as stoning or to be killed by animals or gladiators in the Colosseum? Perhaps a statue of a lion?"

Jesusa responded, "You know, men are weird, sometimes. I never would have thought of that question, but come to think of it, it's an interesting idea. Symbols are very important and the more elegant and simple they are, the more powerful and persuasive. Where would Christianity be without the cross?"

The second level of their interest in wrongful convictions began with the case of Derek "Rocco" Barnabei who was executed in the U.S. State of Virginia in 2000 for the 1993 murder of his 17-year old friend and occasional sexual partner, Sarah Wisnosky. Twenty-six at the time of Sarah's death, Barnabei was born in 1967 in the U.S. to Italian parents, hence the interest in Italia in his case. Barnabei was seen with Wisnosky on the night she disappeared, and he had driven the next day to his home in New Jersey. However, that trip was pre-planned, as hc had told friends, to help his mother celebrate her birthday. Wisnosky's body was found in the Lafayette River in Norfolk. Derek asked for DNA testing, which was not finally performed until a few days before his execution. It showed his DNA in her body, but that was not a surprise as he had already acknowledged having consensual sex with her the day before her murder. Similarly, his DNA was under one of Wisnosky's fingernails, but not under a fingernail which also had her blood, presumably from the fatal assault. Barnabei passed a polygraph exam which he voluntarily took after his arrest, but the report of that test was lost by the police. While on death row in August, 2000 Barnabei offered to take another polygraph examination, but the State of Virginia did not grant the request. The case for his innocence was strong enough that there was a worldwide campaign to stop his execution so that the investigation of his case could continue. Pope Ionnes Paulus II wrote to Governor Gilmore of Virginia to urge that the execution be stopped. However, on September 14, 2000, Barnabei was killed with a lethal injection. His last words to his family were "I am truly innocent of this crime...Eventually the truth will come out." On his gravestone is the message, "The fight goes on," and his mother continued that effort.[5]

After much study and discussion, Jesus and Jesusa prepared a report and a video about the Barnabei case and wrote to Governor Natasha (Sasha) Obama to ask her to appoint a panel to re-investigate the case. Jesus and Jesus also asked the International Criminal Court to investigate the case for violations of Crimes against Humanity.

"Do you think anyone will care?" asked Jesus of Jesusa.

"Probably not," she replied. "Maybe, maybe not, but it was good to try. The fight goes on."

To their surprise, Governor Obama did appoint a committee of five people, including two lawyers, two private investigators and a DNA expert to investigate the case. After eight months, the Committee unaminously concluded in 2033 that Barnabei was

---

5. The website about the case is at http://www.barnabei.com. His case is one of 18 described in the book by Richard Stack, *Grave Injustice – Unearthing Wrongful Convictions.*

wrongly convicted and recommended that the Governor posthumously pardon him and pay compensation to his family. This was not a declaration of innocence, but an acknowledgment that the judicial process had failed in the Barnabei case.

A similar conclusion was reached 66 years earlier when Governor Michael Dukakis issued a declaration in 1977 that the Massachusetts justice system had failed Nicola Sacco and Bartolomeo Vanzetti who were executed by electrocution in Massachusetts in 1927 for robbery and murder. Sacco and Vanzetti were both born in Italia and had emigrated to the United States, and their cases had aroused even more international protest than the subsequent Barnabei case.

In June 2032, at the age of 18, Jesus and Jesusa Prescelto graduated from the Da Vinci School. They chose this day to drop their surname and be known only by their first names, or their mononym. In music history, they had learned how the New Jersey singer, Madonna Louise Ciccone, born in 1958, renamed herself "Madonna." Similary, Cher was born as Cherilyn Sarkisian. Jesus and Jesusa felt that perhaps they had a mission on earth and their mononymous names were closer to their destiny. At some level, they knew they were not Presceltos, but Giuseppe and Maria did not take offense at the change because they knew that their children were special.

At school, Jesus and Jesusa wore traditional uniforms, with blue pants and white collared shirts and ties for boys, and blue skirts and blouses and ties for girls. The boys' ties were blue with white prints of Leonardo Da Vinci's "Vitruvian Man," with a naked man inside a square figure and a circle. The girls' neckties had print outlines of the Mona Lisa, as painted by Da Vinci.

In an effort to begin moving the school to less sexist clothes choices, Jesusa asked the Head of School if she could wear pants, with a blouse and the

Mona Lisa tie. At first the school resisted, but the teachers knew how determined Jesusa could be for a cause she felt was just, so she was allowed to wear pants like the boys. Soon, other girls followed suit and they asked for a schoolwide vote on their uniforms. The choice was either to continue the current system or change to pants and a blouse for everyone, together with a new school tie that had both the "Vitruvian Man" and the Mona Lisa images. The school agreed to the vote, but the Head of School said the rules could be changed only by a 75% vote.   With the social media buzzing, Jesus and Jesusa were able to secure an 82% vote for the change.

When not in school, the twins saw that they had similar tastes in clothes and that they often fit into the same clothes. Jesusa's body became more feminine, but her breasts were modest and her hips were not much wider than her brother's. Neither liked collars, so they cut them from their shirts, when they couldn't purchase shirts without them. They also removed shirt pockets as Jesusa didn't use them as such use would bring further unwanted attention to her breasts. Since Jesusa couldn't use the shirt pockets, Jesus agreed that it was unfair that he should use such pockets, so they removed them from all their shirts. They both wore pants.

Jesusa said to Jesus, "Why should my clothes show more of my skin than yours? What's up with that? In this day and age, which gender is the initiator of contacts and which is the initiatee?"

The words "initiator" and "initatee" were awkward for her, but they were the only words she could think of that avoided stereotypes. Using "predator" and "prey" made relationships sound barbaric, and "aggressor" and "aggressee" sounded violent. "Aggressee" seemed to be a euphemism for "victim."

When they found that they fit into each other's clothes, they began purchasing two of everything. At first, they wore the same clothes when appearing together at parties, but gradually they were wearing the same clothes most of the time. The practice was noticed and a few photos made it to Facebook where they went viral. Soon, many couples, gay and straight, began dressing in the same style clothes, even if they weren't the same size.

Their intellectual and spiritual passion was to learn more about the religions of the world, in the hope that there was common ground among them. From the Bellagio Center Foundation, they obtained a travel grant for 15 months, until their delayed entry into the multinational campus program at the Universitat Heidelberg in Deutschland. Staying at student hostels, they traveled to Espana, Africa and South Asia where they stopped to work at Mother Teresa's Nirmal Hriday (Home for the Dying) in Kolkata.[6] Jesus and Jesusa had never been close to anyone dying before, and their six months in Kolkata were among the most important of their lives. Dying with dignity was better, they came to see, than a painful struggle to breathe each additional breath.

They had learned English and Arabic at the Da Vinci School and those two languages, together with the Latin-based Italian, allowed them to talk easily with most people they encountered. English was the first or second language of approximately 1.5 billion people. When their learned languages were insufficient, Jesus and Jesusa used their "Lingua Mundas," the near-instantaneous computer translators. The devices were small enough so Jesus and Jesusa usually carried five or six in their purses or bags, in the event that others needed them for a group conversation. In a conversation, a person would

---

6. Formerly spelled by the British as Calcutta. The city has no connection to the Italian town of Calcata.

hear in his/her earphone the translations of what participants were saying.

Their first year at Heidelberg, beginning in the fall of 2033, was spent at the Deutschland campus, with subsequent years in Johannesburg, Boston, and Beijing. They studied as much science as possible, together with courses about ethics, justice, religion and utopias.

Transportation to these international campuses used to be an ethical and cost problem for colleges, most of which had joined the "Fossil Fuel Divestment" campaign and the "Campaign Against Carbon Capitalism." With every country, there was now enough alternative energy to keep buildings warm or cool, as needed, and power the enormous computer and lighting systems, but fuel for air travel was a problem. Fortunately, environmentally sound jet fuel became available with the development of syn-gas (for synthetic gas) which was derived by a process of recombining carbon dioxide and water, when exposed to metal oxides under intense heat provided by concentrated solar reactors. The syn-gas was then converted into kerosene for aviation and other fuels, such as diesel and gasoline as needed. When those fuels were burned, they created carbon dioxide, but no more than was recombined at the beginning of the process. So the process was CO_2 neutral. Although being CO_2 neutral was not good enough to warrant burning wood and biomass, necessity sometimes overcame environmental preferences, so the syn-gas program was a global exception. The syn-gas process became commercially competitive with fossil fuel sources around 2021. One innovative oil and gas refiner, Earth Fuel, Inc., switched completely to syn-gas and used that switch for its major marketing push.

Among the incentives for the development of syn-gas was the clarification that global carbon taxes, which were generally implemented in the 2020s, were to be applied only to fossil fuel carbon, e.g. coal, oil, natural gas, and not to synthetic carbon-based fuels, and not to wood and other bio-sustainable fuels which were used out of necessity. The goal of the carbon taxes, even if applied after so much carbon had already been pulled from the ground, was to require that the carbon extracting industries pay for the cost of sequestering the carbon from the atmosphere and returning it to underground storage.

Also, the previous tax subsidies, worth approximately 200 billion mundos annually, for fossil fuel development were withdrawn and either devoted to reducing national debts or applied to green energy development.

The newer planes needed less fuel because of the increased efficiency of the solar collectors on their upper surfaces. Using a unique combination of composite graphene and aluminum alloy, the planes' solar collectors were able to collect 20% of the energy they needed for propulsion and internal electrical needs. As planes usually flew above the clouds, and increasingly flew during daytime, this source was more intense and reliable than on the ground.

Another technological boost for movement away from fossil fuels came from the development of solar-powered hydrogen crackers, which led to cheaper availability of hydrogen for hydrofusion plants and, in greater quantity, for fuel cells.

Together with the global boycotting of the stock of fossil fuel companies, the development of syn-gas and cheaper hydrogen cracking ensured the global cessation of further exploration for in-ground fossil fuels. Existing wells continued in operation until exhausted, but the old wells were not updated with new extraction technology and new wells were no longer drilled.

Sometimes, Jesus and Jesusa would share "Eureka!" or "Ah Haaa!" moments which would clarify their understanding of the world, and solar energy was one of them. In an "Energy 101" class at Heidelberg, their professor circulated a list of "Key Points" about solar energy. They recalled two examples and posted them on their shared Facebook page. They also had their own separate Facebook pages.

- More solar energy hits the earth every two hours than all the energy, 750 exajoules,[7] humanity consumed during 2033.
- Those 750 exajoules could be supplied by solar collectors occupying about 600,000 square kilometers[8] of land (i.e. a square 774.6 kilometers on each side, or the distance from Portland, Maine to Baltimore, Maryland).
- More solar energy hits the earth every hour than the energy in all the earth's annual oil and coal production combined in the year 2014.

Making international travel easier was the use of United Nations passports, which were now held by about a billion people. Originally, the UN documents were introduced as a way to raise funds for the organization, but their popularity ballooned when people saw them as a way of declaring their solidarity with other peace-minded people. The message was

7. A joule is the work required to produce one watt of power for one second, or one "watt second," which is 1/3,600 of a kilowatt hour. An exajoule is one quintillion (1018) joules.
8. This land area is slightly larger than the island of Madagasgar with its 587,041 square kilometers, and substantially smaller than Texas and Afghanistan with their 695,662 and 652,230 sq. km, respectively.

that UN passport holders considered themselves citizens of the Earth first, and citizens of countries second, and then citizens of states, provinces, cities and towns.

During the long flight to South Africa, Jesus and Jesusa watched the classic 2006 documentary film, "An Inconvenient Truth," by the former U.S. Vice-President, Al Gore. The movie saddened them because they hadn't fully understood that many people in the world already knew in 2006 about the dire fate of the world. Further, the movie didn't shake the world's decision makers as it should have, even though Al Gore won the Nobel Peace Prize in 2007, together with the United Nations' Intergovernmental Panel on Climate Change. As Jesus and Jesusa both understood English well, they chose to listen in Afrikaans, the official language of South Africa which they were seeking to learn. Using the subtitle option, they also saw the words at the bottom of their screens as they were listening to them. The oral translation and written subtitle options were added to all new movies, and retroactively to many, beginning in 2021 in order to increase viewers' understanding. It had been found that many moviegoers couldn't hear the words in movies, even when they filmed were in their own native languages. A typical problem was that of the U.S. moviegoer who would watch a movie made in England and not understand most of the dialogue because of unfamiliar accents and words. The default subtitle option was the intended language of the film. As part of the global campaign for literacy and education, it was important that movies, especially documentaries, be easily understandable.

At the Johannesburg campus in 2034-35, Jesus and Jesusa studied two major South African figures who contributed to the transition to the "Great Transformation" in human life: Mahatma Gandhi and Nelson Mandela. Born in India and educated in

England, Gandhi's first work as a lawyer was in South
Africa where he developed his ideas about peaceful
resistance to unjust laws, and about his vegetarian
diet. In South Africa, the people of color were
discriminated against, although not to the extent of
the subsequent apartheid regime during approximately
the years 1948-94. In 1915, at the age of 46, Gandhi
returned to India and led efforts for independence for
British colonial India, which then included what is
now Pakistan and Bangladesh, and for the rights of
women and the "untouchables." Importantly, Jesus
and Jesusa learned of Gandhi's heartbreak at the
religious strife which broke out after independence for
India and Pakistan in 1947. People killing each other
because of their religions perplexed and frustrated
them, and seemed counterintuitive.

"Isn't religion about affirming the best in
humanity?" asked Jesusa of Jesus.

Nelson Mandela was born in 1918 to tribal royalty
and, like Gandhi, was educated in the law. He was a
political activist in the struggle for Black African
justice and political representation in South Africa.
Influenced by Gandhi's work in South Africa,
Mandela's initial work was nonviolent, but as the white
minority moved South Africa toward extreme
apartheid, and as nonviolence failed to achieve the
goals of fair representation for black South Africans,
Mandela joined the Communist Party and actively
supported acts of sabotage. It was for those acts that
he was convicted in 1964 of conspiracy to overthrow
the government, and was sentenced to life
imprisonment. Almost 20 years of that sentence was
served in the notorious Robbens Island prison. His
stature, his continued thirst for knowledge, and his
ability to communicate with people of all political
beliefs led to the increasing recognition of his
leadership of the Black African movement. In 1990, he

was freed from prison and later became the first elected Black president of the Union of South Africa.

Jesus and Jesusa met with Mandela's family and supporters, which prompted them to discuss their futures. The Mandela children were struggling with their roles which birth thrust upon them.

"What do you think we should do?" asked Jesus to Jesusa, knowing that they had already pledged to each other that they would work together to improve the world in some way.

"We don't know, yet," said Jesusa. "But, we do know that we have been inspired by nonviolence and communication. We'll just have to keep exploring options."

The "Great Transformation" was a global political and social movement which began in 2020 primarily to save the planet Earth from humanity. It was triggered by two disasters of that year. First was the South Pacific typhoon, Chanthu, which caused 45 million deaths and 2.1 trillion U.S. dollars of damage. Next was the nuclear explosion in Kahuta, Pakistan which killed 80,000 people. After those disasters, people around the world said to each other, "Enough is enough." That is, the foibles of mankind were now coming intolerably close to causing the extinction of humanity, and it was time for well-meaning people around the world to work together to transform the future.

With funds contributed from several global foundations and from a global "kickstarter" campaign, a new networked organization, Great Transformation Organization, was created with a website, www.greattransformation.org.[9] It became known as GTO. The organization sought to bring people together to find common ground to solve problems. Among

9. As of 2014, not a real website.

other programs in its 50 year campaign, the GTO
promoted solutions to these problems:
- global warming. For too long, said the GTO leaders,
    governments had ignored the warnings about
    global warming. It was time to stop global
    warming by reducing the concentrations of carbon
    dioxide and methane in the atmosphere to pre-
    Industrial Revolution levels.
- demilitarization. This campaign combined the
    reduction of nuclear weapons, pursuant to the
    Non-Proliferation Treaty, with the efforts within
    countries, led by Costa Rica, to eliminate military
    expenditures entirely. These countries had police
    forces to provide security and suppression of
    crime, but no need for the expensive toys of the
    generals and admirals.
- education. In order for the Great Transformation to
    be successful, the global public needed to be
    educated. Literacy needed to be brought to 100%
    and every human needed to understand basic
    information about science, life and Earth. It was
    not enough that everyone could read. Reading
    rational information about the true "facts of life"
    was critical.
- communication/computers. Every human being with
    the ability to speak and think needed to be
    connected to the global electronic/computer
    network through one or more devices, beginning
    with a smart phone.
- judicial resolution of international disputes. GTO
    urged the universal use of the International Court
    of Justice to resolve disputes among countries,
    such as territorial disputes.
- civil dispute resolution. At the non-state level, the
    GTO encouraged the submission of all disputes to
    civil forums, such as mediation, arbitration,
    courts, and legislatures. The GTO called for the
    end of the misclassification of "terrorism" as an

end rather than a means. That is, if people sought
to terrorize others for the purpose of causing fear
for its own sake, that was to be dealt with as a
common crime, and not as an act of war against a
country. If people used violence to achieve political
ends, such violence had always been classified as
criminal. If terror was part of that violence, then
the level of the crime and the eligible punishment
was increased.

- population stabilization and reduction. The GTO
  sought the reduction of unexpected and unwanted
  pregnancies, as part of the effort to stabilize and
  reduce the size of the human population.
  Conservatives sought to save money from the
  anticipated reduction in the need for government
  services, and liberals sought to enhance the lives of
  young women.

- reduction of use of incarceration as criminal
  punishment. Conservatives sought to reduce
  expenditures that could be better used for
  reduction of government debt, and to enhance the
  value of personal liberty; and liberals sought to
  reduce the unequal treatment of minorities by
  judicial systems around the world. Legalization of
  recreational drugs was part of this campaign.

- adoption of a Single Global Currency. The people of
  the world wanted stable money, and no longer
  could tolerate the absurdities of the multicurrency
  system.

- better nutrition for all humanity. This was to be
  achieved by eating foods lower on the food chain,
  with less cooking, and by severely reducing the
  consumption of meat and fish.

- fair and free elections. The GTO sought publicly
  funded elections around the world, pursuant to its
  faith that if the people of the world were informed
  with the truth from unbiased sources, they would
  vote for what is best for themselves, their families

and the Earth. It was no longer tolerable that the
results of elections depended upon the bank
accounts of those seeking office.
The Great Transformation Organization was the
rallying point for people around the world, formerly
called the "silent majority," who simply wanted a better
world for their children, and were fed up with the old
solutions, or with pleas that there were no solutions.

The ideas embraced by the GTO had been
proposed by others, but the new organization brought
to the table what it called "FORTHINK," which was
short for "Forward Thinking." The supporters of GTO
were called "forthinkers." The key to this concept was
that the future counted as much as the present when
considering action and funding. One aspect of
forthinking was the consideration and payment of
external costs whenever considering actions and
funding. For example, GTO forthinkers successfully
argued that a builder of a building which was to
replace another nearby building had to provide a plan
for the demolition or re-use of the former building,
rather than leaving the old building to deteriorate and
impose visual and other costs upon its neighborhood.
The biggest boost for forthinking was the campaign in
the early 21st century to legalize recreational drugs.
Reform advocates compared the total costs of
prohibition, including the forward external costs of
incarceration, with the benefits, including taxation, of
legalizing drugs. When compared directly, the benefits
of legalization outweighed the costs by a ratio of 5:1.

Forthinking encompassed a new, while
resurrecting the old, way of looking at debt, which was
that it should be avoided, except in unavoidable and
unpredictable circumstances. Borrowing for purchases
of consumer products and services did not fit either
category. In the 21st century, before the universal
availability of health insurance or coverage, the best
justification for personal borrowing was the payment

of unanticipated health costs. That justification no longer existed after the adoption of publicly funded universal health care. Similarly, liability and property insurance protected against most other unanticipated costs. On the national scale, money could be borrowed to finance wars, as the U.S. did for during World War II, but during the GTO period, and thereafter, there were no large scale wars.

Until modern times, borrowing was discouraged. The Bible disdained debt and excessive consumption, e.g. "The rich ruleth over the poor, and the borrower [is] servant to the lender."[10]

Shakespeare presented Polonius in Hamlet, who said to his son, Laertes,

"Neither a borrower nor a lender be;

For loan oft loses both itself and friend,

And borrowing dulls the edge of husbandry."[11] Benjamin Franklin summarized the pre-industrial era view of debt with his saying, "Rather go to bed supperless than rise in debt." The recommended way to finance a purchase or a project was to save for it, instead of paying interest for years afterwards. At 4% interest, a 10,000 mundo loan for a five year term would cost 1,049 mundos, or more than 10% of the original loan amount, in interest.

By the mid-20th century, John Maynard Keynes had persuaded a generation and its successors that it was good policy to borrow money to prime the pump of an economy. However, what people, voters and nations forgot was that the periods of borrowing needed to be balanced with periods of saving. The ease of borrowing by nations was communicated to citizens who overloaded themselves with debt for education, consumer products, and homes.

10. Proverbs 22:7.
11. Act 1, Scene 3.

The tide against debt turned when the adoption of a Single Global Currency, managed by the Global Central Bank within the Global Monetary Union, led to near-zero inflation, which reduced global interest rates. When debtors and citizens realized that they would be paying off debts in the future with money that was maintaining its value rather than being devalued through inflation, the enthusiasm for debt diminished. Forthinkers persuaded the world that such borrowing for the present was not worth the future cost.

Another benefit of the mundo was that the world no longer needed the U.S. to finance the expansion of the global money supply through its own trade and government fiscal deficits. Without that need, purchasers of U.S. debt were less willing to lend money to the U.S. That caused interest rates on government debt to rise, which also led to decreased U.S. borrowing.

During his term, former President John Ellis Bush ("JEB") lauded the creation of the GTO and supported most of its objectives. He said, "We have to learn from our new techniques for educating people about the real world and reversing global warming. He appointed his Phillips Academy classmate and businessman, Budge Lawrence, as special liaison to the GTO.

Another connection to the Great Transformation was President Bush's close relationship with Pope Francesco I[12] who saw the need to change the views of his church and the world toward global warming and

---

12. Known as Pope Francesco, he was not designated as Pope Francesco I until after the election of his successor who chose the name, Francesco II. Both were named after St. Francesco of Assisi, 1182-1226, who was born with the name Giovanni di Pietro di Bernardone. Giovanni's father was on a business trip to France when Giovanni was born, and upon his return, the father called his son, Francesco, which is Italian for the "Frenchman."

non-proliferation. Brought up as an Episcopalian, Bush had converted to Roman Catholicism, the religion of his Mexican-born wife.

During the next few years, and into his second term, Bush helped move the United States toward acceptance of its new role in the world which was as an equal member, albeit large, of United Nations rather than as the world's policeman. Further, he spoke of the U.S.'s large responsibility for global warming because of the disproportionate proportion of U.S. generation of CO_2, as compared to the rest of the world. With only 4% of the world's population, the U.S. was still generating 17% of the world's carbon dioxide, and its historical proportion was even larger. "It is time to reduce the net U.S. share," said Bush, "to less than four percent and then to zero." Subsequent U.S. presidents and governments continued to pursue those goals.

For their next academic year, 2035-36, Jesus and Jesusa went to Boston and Cambridge. They studied at Harvard, the U.S. affiliate of Universitat Heidelberg. While there, they studied the 19th century utopian communities at Fruitlands in Harvard, Mass., and Brook Farm in West Roxbury, Mass. These were communities which arose in response to the unhealthy conditions of the Industrial Revolution in the U.S. They faded away for the same reasons as all the other utopian communities: they asked too much from the people who lived there. It was a mistake to ask people to depart too far from their human nature.

One earlier group, the Shakers, were as much religious as utopian. They were a spinoff group from the Quakers in England and from the beginning they stressed the leadership role of women. One of the first Shaker preachers was Jane Wardley, who was followed by Ann Lee, who claimed to be the Second Coming of Christ, despite the gender difference. Formally called the United Society of Believers in Christ's Second

Appearing, Ann Lee led a group of eight Shakers to the U.S. in 1774. By 1790, the group had established written agreements whereby new members contributed all their property and their future labor to the Society. They also pledged to remain celibate. When married couples joined, their marriages were essentially terminated as they were required to live in separate dormitories. The population of Shakers grew rapidly through recruitment, and many Shaker communities were established in the eastern U.S.

What attracted Jesus and Jesusa to learn more about the Shakers was their belief in the equality of men and women. Their work roles might be different, but their essential equality was respected. Jesus and Jesusa saw that the Shakers spread faster than other sects not by reproducing with children, but by communicating a message of hope and faith. Later, it became clear that there was no Second Coming, and the Industrial Revolution reduced the costs of many products which competed with those manufactured by hand by the Shakers. With less faith, and less prosperity, the Shakers foundered. As the sexual repression of the Victorian era was subsiding in the late 19th century, the celibacy of the Shakers seemed less attractive for future members, just as the Roman Catholic Church's celibacy rules for priests and nuns led to the declines in their numbers until the Vaticano Council III eliminated the celibacy requirement in 2023 and permitted women to become priests, bishops, cardinals and even popes.

Only two hours from Boston was Hartford, Connecticut with one of the homes of Harriet Beecher Stowe, the author of *Uncle Tom's Cabin*. Joined with the home was a museum with a small collection of works by Charlotte Perkins Gilman, who was a grandniece of Stowe, through Charlotte's father Frederic Beecher Perkins. Gilman, who acquired that surname upon marriage, was a feminist writer, speaker and suffragette. She wrote the utopian novel, *Herland*, which first appeared in Gilman's magazine, *Forerunner*, in 1916. It wasn't published as a standalone book until 1979. The book describes a society of women, who have been without men for about 2,000 years and reproduce themselves asexually. They knew nothing of war or violence and certainly suffered no domination by men. Jesusa was especially interested in Gilman's personal independence from convention and the manner of her death. Gilman was diagnosed in 1932 with incurable breast cancer. She publicly advocated euthanasia for the terminally ill, and in 1935 she committed suicide with an overdose of chloroform. Her suicide letter was clear, "When all usefulness is over, when one is assured of an unavoidable and imminent death, it is the simplest of human rights to choose a quick and easy death in place of a slow and horrible one."

Another utopian community which interested Jesus and Jesusa was in New York, but *Walden Two* was fictional and its author, B.F. Skinner was from Harvard and Boston. Skinner died in 1990, but the twins were able to talk with some of his former students who were now professors. They discussed Skinner's 1971 non-fiction book, *Beyond Freedom and Dignity*, which argued for the "cultural engineering" which later became part of the global Great Transformation campaign. The idea was that the study of psychology had become sufficiently advanced, especially operant conditioning, that appropriate positive reinforcements for desired behavior could be established by governments.

The contemporary criticism of *Walden Two* was that the design of the reinforcements seemed to come from one person, the fictional T.E. Frazier, who could be therefore characterized as a dictator. Instead, it was said to be perfectly legitimate for a democratic government to decide what behaviors should be rewarded with positive reinforcement and what behaviors should be discouraged.

The other intellectual focus for their Boston term was the issue of wrongful convictions which they had studied in their senior year at Da Vinci School.   Near Boston was Middlesex County where Kenny Waters and Dennis Maher were separately wrongly convicted of murder and rape, respectively, in the 1980's. They were both exonerated through DNA testing after 18 and 19 years in prison. The Waters case became widely known when it was the subject of the 2010 docudrama movie, "Conviction."

Jesus and Jesusa met with the current District Attorney for Middlesex County who proudly told them that there had not been a wrongful conviction in the county since 2021. That conviction, for murder, was vacated six months later after an internal investigation by the County's own Conviction Integrity Unit. It was determined than a technician in the DNA laboratory had a romantic relationship with the investigating police officer which led him to alter the DNA-test results.

Jesus and Jesusa visited prisons in Massachusetts, including the facility at Shirley which was on the site of a former Shaker village. They learned that the DNA revolution had led to a dramatic change in the U.S. justice system by providing irrefutable proof that innocent people were being convicted. In the past, this truth was known by many defense lawyers and some prosecutors, and certainly by those innocent victims of the system who went to prison and were sometimes executed. The DNA revolution forced the truth upon lawyers and people within the justice system and upon the citizens who were served by, and sometimes judged by, that system.

In 2014 a National Commission on Forensic Science was established to extend, as much as possible, to other forensic sciences the precision which had been achieved with DNA. In 2015, the Commission issued a sweeping report which highlighted the deficiencies which had sent thousands of innocent people to prison and allowed others to be "wrongfully free," and therefore free to commit more crimes. New standards were proposed for scientific proof in many areas including: arson, ballistics, fingerprints, lie detector tests, tire tracks and eye witness identifications. The Commission forecast that the adoption of its proposals would reduce the wrongful conviction rate in the U.S. to less than .1%. The Commission compared this goal to the previous estimates of wrongful conviction in the range of 1-5%. The Commission recommended that these standards be implemented as soon as possible, beginning with a five year campaign, and that all the cases of the people who were convicted by use of the earlier, less rigorous, standards be thoroughly re-examined.

A first step was to send to every inmate in the country an invitation to declare his or her innocence on any of several levels:
1. Completely innocent, with no involvement in the crimes for which convicted.
2. Innocent by reason of being a juvenile, under the age of 18, at the time of the offenses.
3. Partially innocent, but convicted and sentenced as if the sole perpetrator.

The plight of the guilty, but grossly and unfairly oversentenced, had to wait for their justice in another campaign.

Approximately 160,000, or 9% of the total inmate population claimed "Complete innocence" and their claims were addressed first, and were posted on the National Registry of Claims of Innocence website, www.registryofclaimsofinnocence.org.

The Commission recommended that where the previously deficient forensic science was an important basis for convictions, those convictions should be set aside and the inmates either be freed or scheduled for a new trial, with or without bail.

Jesus and Jesusa met with a few of the approximately 95,367 inmates who were released from prison in the 2020s and 2030s through the implementation of the Commission's standards.[13] The eradication of wrongful convictions became one of the primary concerns of Jesus and Jesusa, and that concern continued with them for the rest of their lives.

When visiting the State House in Boston in April, they came across the large, but simple, statue of Mary Dyer who was executed by hanging on Boston Common in 1660 for preaching Quakerism, including the view that men and women were equal before God. It was her second conviction and death sentence, but the first was waived in favor of permanent exile. She intentionally returned to Massachusetts to preach and protest. Like all convictions for religious beliefs, and like that for Jesus of Nazareth, Dyer's convictions were wrongful, which made her execution especially heinous.

Said Jesusa to Jesus, "A cousin of the Bush's, Dorothy Bush Rafferty, told me yesterday when I met her at Harvard, that she would give us an introduction to her distant cousin, former Texas Governor Prescott G. Bush. Let's go to Texas and meet him and thank him for leading Texas to abolish the death penalty in 2024. I remember that when he became governor in 2022, he refused to sign any execution warrants, which meant that the infamous Texas count of those executed since 1982 stopped at 629. More importantly, we can seek his assistance for the final stretch of the global campaign to abolish the death penalty."

13. See the National Registry of Exonerations at https://www.law.umich.edu/special/exoneration

The last U.S. state to execute a convicted defendant was Missouri in 2028. After that, it was clear that any future effort to any of the remaining five states with death penalty statutes to actually execute someone would be declared by the U.S. Supreme Court to be "cruel and unusual punishment," which was prohibited by the 8th Amendment to the U.S. Constitution. Except for some rigid literalists in law schools and a few judges, no one interpreted "unusual" to mean infrequent when the 8th amendment was ratified in 1791 with all ten of the first Amendments, also called the "Bill of Rights." Instead, it meant infrequent at the time of the current litigation.

The only remaining countries with the death penalty were Afghanistan, Bangladesh, China, and Iran.

Jesus and Jesusa had known of Bush's efforts since their senior year project at Da Vinci School. Bush was elected as Governor when voters rejected the harsh, vengeful justice approach of the previous governor. Bush campaigned for a "kinder, gentler" Texas, which was a phrase made famous by his grandfather, George H. W. Bush, in his 1988 acceptance speech for the Republican nomination for president when he said, "I want a kinder, gentler nation."

Jesus and Jesusa flew to Texas and met former Governor Prescott Bush at his home, where he explained how he had come to the decision to try to abolish the death penalty. He was brought up as a Roman Catholic and he learned that Pope Ionnes Paulus II had issued an encyclical, "Evangelium Vitae" (The Gospel of Life) in 1995 which stated that capital punishment was appropriate only in cases of absolute necessity, which meant almost never.

As a teenager he had a friend whose father had been sentenced to death for a murder he denied

committing. Prescott remembered how the family was
preparing for a funeral, when the execution was
canceled about 12 hours before the scheduled time.
Apparently, a new witness had come forward to say
that another man committed the crime and that
witness had passed two polygraph examinations. As
the other man was in prison for life for other crimes,
he agreed that the new witness's story was correct.
The bargain was that he would plead guilty to that
crime in return for a promise by the state not to seek
the death penalty.

Thus, said the ex-governor, "My friend's father was
home for Christmas in a car instead of a box."

During the campaign for Governor, Prescott
learned that Texas was second only to China in the
number of criminals who had been executed
since 1982, the year that Texas resumed executions
after a judicial moratorium. Texas was even "ahead" of
Iran and Iraq.

Bush continued, "This second place so-called
achievement was not going to help me present Texas to
the global investment and business communities as a
progressive and modern state. In fact, a global boycott
was planned against Texas in 2023 by the World
Coalition Against the Death Penalty. My opponent
said, 'Go Ahead. Make My Day. Boycott Us,' but the
people of Texas didn't agree with that position."

Jesus asked, "Will you join the ongoing effort to
persuade China and the other three countries to
finally abandon the death penalty. He responded,
"Sure. Just tell me what I can do."

They returned home in June 2036 to Salerno for
summer vacation. While they were in the U.S., they
saw that many Americans still quoted prices in U.S.
dollars, even though the mundo was ten years old, and
now used by 142 U.N. members. The mundo
purchased about what 1.5 dollars used to purchase.

Maria met them at the airport in Napoli. "You both look different," she said. "Did you eat too much American pizza?" That was a family joke, of course. Giuseppe prided himself on his pizza, as did many Italians. That summer the twins worked at the Paestum archeological site as guides. It was an excellent opportunity to continue to learn about the Greek and Roman gods to which the three surviving temples were dedicated. At different times, two of the three temples were built for Hera, the wife and sister of Zeus, head of all the gods. She was the Greek goddess of women, fertility and childbirth.

The apparent dominance of a woman god at Paestum is likely a product of archeology and history. The name "Paestum" is Latin for Posiedon, who was Hera's brother and god of the sea. It's likely that there was a temple to the city's namesake god, even if it hasn't survived or been unearthed.

During that time, Jesus and Jesusa also had time to think about their upcoming studies in China and the potential for their activism there against the death penalty.

That fall, they took the trans-Siberian railway to China for their studies at Beijing University for the 2036-37 academic year. In a sense, the Communist regime since 1949 was a utopian experiment in government without capitalism and private property. Like other utopian communities, it subsequently conformed to the global norms. Five religions were allowed, along with atheism and a Confucian belief system: Taoism, Buddhism, Islam, Protestantism and Catholicism. Beginning in the late 1970's Chinese leaders moved the economy toward capitalism and allowed direct foreign investment. When the controls on the economy were relaxed, the controls on belief systems and religions were also relaxed. By 2040, the Chinese Catholic Church was allowed to re-affiliate itself with the Roman Catholic Church due to changes within China and within the Roman Church.

Jesus and Jesusa soaked up as much as they could about life in China, as the country constituted about 15% of humanity. It was a higher percentage in the late 20th century, but the Chinese leadership realized that population growth was a drag on economic and social growth, rather than an accelerant. With a one-child per family policy, with some exceptions, the Chinese population was stabilized at 1.5 billion in 2028 and it began its decline thereafter.

During the fall, Jesus and Jesusa met with leaders of the China Campaign Against the Death Penalty (CCADP), but were frustrated that there was no concrete plan for action. They had proposed walking atop sections of the Great Wall of China to dramatize the Chinese position as the largest and most frequent user of the death penalty, among the four remaining countries using that punishment for crimes. During the previous decade, China killed an average of 45 of its citizens each year. However, the CCADP voted down the idea, despite some support among the members.

Jesus and Jesusa decided to begin a walk on their own, beginning on Wednesday, February 18, the beginning of the Chinese year 2588. As the year of the Snake, a walk and march along the winding Great Wall seemed symbolic. Jesus and Jesusa would argue to the media, who were certain to come to join their trek, that the Chinese could no more avoid the global movement toward abolition of the death penalty than their Great Wall could keep out invaders – which it didn't.

Jesus and Jesusa took a MAGtrain to Shanhaiguan, where the Great Wall begins at the

Bohai Sea across from Korea,[14] on February 10, and began their blogs on Facebook and Qzone, its Chinese equivalent. Their primary Chinese partner was Zhao Zuohai who had been convicted of murdering a man during a fight in 1998 and was sentenced to death. It was claimed that torture was used to extract his confession. Fortunately, through court appeals, and because the purported death arise from a fight, Zhao Zuohai's sentence was reduced to 29 years.

In 2010, the purported murder victim, Zhenshang Zhao, returned alive to his village and Zhao Zuohai was exonerated, and the inadequacies of the Chinese justice system were exposed. The case bore an uncanny resemblance to the case of the brothers Jesse and Stephen Boorn who were convicted in Vermont, USA for murdering their brother-in-law, Russell Colvin in 1812. The Boorns were convicted and sentenced to hang. Fortunately, appeals took longer than usual, because in 1819, the purported victim was spotted in New Jersey. Colvin was enticed into going to New York City and then tricked into a stagecoach which took him to Vermont instead of his intended return to New Jersey. Upon his arrival in Vermont on December 22, it was clear to waiting observers that he was, in fact, Russell Colvin, and that he was not dead. The hanging of the Boorn brothers, scheduled for January 28, 1820, was canceled.

The Boorn case had been heralded as the first wrongful conviction case in the U.S., but that was unhappily not the case. The brothers were preceded by the convictions and executions of 20 witches in Salem, Massachusetts in 1692-93, and the Mary Dyer execution in 1660. There were many more. Nonetheless, the Boorn case was dramatic and the

---

14. North Korea and South Korea were reunited in 2029, after the death of the last surviving member of the hereditary rulers, the Kim family.

innocence of the brothers was very clear, so the label of "first" stuck.

A major difference between the Zhao Zuohai case and the Boorn brothers was the 190 year interval. When the media learned of Zhao Zuohai's participation in the upcoming march by Jesus and Jesusa, and the U.S.-based media introduced the Boorn case to the news, the embarrassing comparison was presented to the world. Still, China insisted on its right to execute its criminals.

Jesus, Jesusa and Zhao Zuohai started on their trip at "Old Dragon Head" where the Great Wall of China met the Bohai Sea in Shanhaiguan. In the beginning, the media representatives were planning only to meet the marching party in the evenings, when they set up their camp tents. After two days, there were millions of "followers" on Facebook and Qzone, and about 100,000 were joining every few hours. On the third day, the representatives of several media organizations began walking with them, and Chinese citizens joined, too. Some joined for the duration and some joined for a day. Many others brought food and water to the marchers, who completed approximately 25 kilometers a day. At that rate, they would walk the approximately 500 kilometer distance to Mutianyu, about 70 kilometers from Beijing, in about 20 days.

On the 10th day, February 28, Jesus and Jesusa held a media conference, and the world was watching. By this time, Afghanistan and Bangladesh had announced that they were abandoning the using of the death penalty. The leaders of those countries could see the writing on the wall, and neither wanted his/her country to be the last. That dishonor would await either Iran or China.

At the media conference, the CNN reporter asked, "Your blog states that the goal of this march on the Great Wall to Beijing is to bring a global end to the death penalty. Do you think that's realistic?"

Jesusa answered, "We began our march on February 18, and already two of the remaining four countries have finally abandoned the death penalty. As the saying goes, 'Better late than never.' We have approximately ten days to go on this march, and we are down to two countries. We'll see."

The *South China Morning Post* reporter asked, "Are you not afraid that the Chinese government will arrest you?"

Jesus answered, "That would be interesting, wouldn't it? I don't believe we are doing anything wrong." Later, Jesus took the reporter aside for an 'off the record' discussion, and said,... "Here's the headline around the world, 'China arrests Jesus and Jesusa.' What are they going to do to us, crucify us? They probably would simply put us on a plane, but that would be an act of fear and cowardice. China has for centuries claimed to lead the world with its ethical views. Being the only country, or only one of two countries, to continue a practice roundly condemned by the rest of the world does not sound like leadership to me."

In Iran, there was hope that that country would not be the last. Building on the sharia law custom that the family of a victim can forgive a criminal and thereby lead to a far lesser sentence, if any, the women of the families of the victims of the inmates on death row became re-energized by the Jesus and Jesusa march. The women obtained affidavits from 90% of the families of victims asking that "their" perpetrators be forgiven and not be subjected to the death penalty, i.e. killed. They also ask that the death penalty be abolished entirely in Iran. Like China, Iran was a country that had always aspired to moral leadership, in the Muslim world, and on this issue it was clearly lagging.

On March 1, the Iranian Supreme Leader, Sayyed Ali Khomeini, announced that Iran would no longer execute any criminals. As the number of Iranian executions had declined over the years from 2-300 annually to less than 20 in 2037, the trend toward abolition was being led by the people running the criminal justice system. Clearly, the death penalty was far less acceptable to the people of Iran, especially to young people.

That left China as the holdout, and a classic example of political inertia. Most Chinese opposed the death penalty, and everyone knew that its application had been less frequent since the 2020s, with only 33 executions in 2036, and none of those was in public. However, no Chinese leader wanted to step forward and push the button on this outdated policy. The policy was not only at odds with all of the other members of the United Nations; it also conflicted with other Chinese goals, such as the desire to reunite with Taiwan. Reunification negotiations between the People's Republic of China and Taiwan had begun in 2030, but had stalled on the issue of the death penalty, which Taiwan had abolished in 2021.

The march by Jesus and Jesusa continued to attract Chinese marchers and global interest by all the available broadcast media. On Day 13, Jesus and Jesusa held an impromptu media conference and called on people opposed to the death penalty around the world to march with them. Supporters could show their support by marching around the Chinese embassies in their respective countries. This tactic multiplied the global coverage of the campaign as crowds of over 100,000 encircled 145 Chinese embassies. There was local media coverage at each one, along with 14,500,000 cell phones, tablets and Google glasses.

One Chinese leader had the stature to respond to the invitation by Jesus and Jesusa. That was Sun Sui-Zhang, a great, great granddaughter of the founder of modern China, Sun Yat-Sen. Quietly, she joined the

Jesus and Jesusa march at Simatai and introduced herself to the twins at the end of the day's march.

Sun Sui-Zhang said, "It is an honor to join you, but I fear that if you proceed to Beijing and try to assemble at Tiananmen Square for a rally, you will harden the will of those who resent foreign pressure. The resentment of foreign interference goes far back in Chinese history and is part of our cultural DNA. In fact, the Great Wall itself is a monument to our desire to block foreign intrusion."

Responded Jesusa, "Thank you so much for coming. We, too, are concerned about causing unproductive resistance. How can we negotiate a way forward that respects the will of the world, together with the pride of the Chinese?"

Sun Sui-Zhang was pleased that Jesus and Jesusa were more interested in a peaceful resolution than they were in scoring points or forcing a confrontation at Tiananmen Square. She proposed, "What do you think about this proposal? I will ask the Party leadership to enact a moratorium on executions for six months, while the issue is studied. In return, you would agree to stop your march in Mutianyu, outside Beijing, next week, and ask your supporters around the world to peacefully stop their protests at midnight on March 7th."

Jesus and Jesusa saw merit in the proposal, and the opportunity for both sides to save face and achieve their goals. Sun Sui-Zhang returned to Beijing and secured the agreement of the leadership, and talked by phone with Jesus and Jesusa. The last execution, of a man who had murdered his wife, was on Friday, March 6. The execution was by lethal injection. Sun Sui-Zhang then returned to the Great Wall on March 9 as the 10,000 marchers stopped outside Mutianyu. The next day, Jesus, Jesusa and Sun Sui-Zhang held a media conference to conclude the march, as had been pre-announced around the world.

The Chinese government was true to its word and there were no more executions. Six months later, the formal abolition was announced quietly on the government's website. Henceforth, March 6 was designated as the day of global celebration of the end of the death penalty. The next goal for some forthinkers was the end of killing of all other animals, starting with mammals.

Jesus and Jesusa returned as global heroes to Universitat Heidelberg for the last part of their senior year in May, 2037. Graduation was scheduled for Saturday, August 29 at the Heidelberg campus.

Back in Salerno, early in the summer of 2037, Professor Emeritus Pappalardo, and the two other surviving members of the Salerno fertility team, visited Giuseppe and Maria Prescelto and told them about the origin of their children. From the available information on the internet, Dr. Pappalardo and the team had been watching the development of Jesus and Jesusa. First, of course, they were stunned to see the names that Guiseppe and Maria had given to them – without knowledge of their origin. Second, they were impressed with the twins' spiritual growth. Third, they were concerned about what the knowledge of their origin would do to the twins, their family, and their role in the world.

The fourth issue was the question of publicity. During the 23 years since the births of the twins, there had been several efforts at cloning humans from long dead tissue, but no one had successfully used the technique secretly used by the Salerno team. In fact, the Salerno team had tried to reproduce its own work with other human tissue from deceased members of their own families, but it hadn't worked. Some team members still wondered whether they should have conducted their live experiment, just because they thought they could do it. They wondered why the Jesus and Jesusa project worked, whereas the others did not. Still, the opportunity had arisen in 2013 to change science and the world. Yet the team members were sworn to secrecy, as they agreed, until the twins turned 21 or graduated from college, whichever came later. The team's plan was to write a scholarly paper about what they did, but keep the names of the twins secret, unless the twins agreed. It was a plan that was out of touch with the modern reality of communications, including social networks.

Jesus and Jesusa were coming home before the beginning of the final two month college session in the summer of 2037 and their parents decided that this was the time to tell them about their origin, beyond what they already knew.

The twins knew they were special, but they didn't know why. They used to be the objects of jokes about their names, but they were not the first children to feel the sting of the cruelty of their peers.

Maria began the conversation, "You know, as we have told you, we went to a fertility clinic in order to have children as pregnancy was not coming to us the traditional way – although we had fun trying."

"Yes, Mom," said Jesusa, "but you know how it still embarrasses us to hear about you and Dad having sex. After we were born, that was the last time, right?"

"Ok, good joke," said Guiseppe, "but No. Your mother and I have always had a good sexual relationship. But that's not why we asked you to sit down with us here. We had a visit last week from the medical team at the fertility clinic. They told us who were your real parents, or parent."

"What do you mean, 'or parent' " asked Jesus.

"Well, that's what we're getting to," said Maria. "The DNA of the two eggs which were implanted into my uterus was actually cloned from the body of a single man."

"Wow!" said Jesus, "Why would someone want to do that?"

"Well," said Guiseppe, "because that single man has been dead for 2000 years."

"Like who?" asked Jesusa.

"Like Jesus. That Jesus," responded Maria.

"How could they do that? That's ridiculous. What have you two been smoking or drinking?" said Jesus.

"In a way, I wish that were the explanation, but here's what we were told," said Maria. "Have you ever heard of the 'Foreskin of Calcata' which was purportedly a portion, or entirety of the actual circumcised foreskin of Jesus?"

"No," said both Jesus and Jesusa, and Jesusa continued, "but I just figured it out, as we're familiar with the church relic game."

"Well," said Maria, "before the foreskin disappeared from Calcata in 1983, "a scientist took a sample and brought it to the Universita del Sigli di Salerno for further study and preservation. It was from that sample that the cells were removed and cloned. Originally the idea was somehow to enhance the Catholic Church, but later it became simply a matter of scientific curiosity – to see if it could be done."

"Wow," said the twins in unison.

Said Jesus, "Part of me wishes that you had told us earlier, and part of me wishes that you had never told us."

Jesusa was similarly perplexed, "Now what do we do? This news will either make us circus curiosities or it will give us some gravity to do what we want to do. Maybe this is a blessing."

With their knowledge of religion and of people around the world, Jesus and Jesusa knew that the news of their origin would be of great interest and importance, but they sought to keep it secret, while they had some time to think about it. The four family members agreed to try to keep it secret, but the story was already out of their control.

On August 26, the Salerno team published their article, "Nature-Nurture in Human Cloning," in an academic publication, *The Journal of Human Genetics.* Without giving the names of the twins, the article did speculate about the relative importance of their genes as compared to their upbringing.

The article added new information about the authenticity of the "Holy Prepuce" with carbon-14 analysis. With a margin of error of 50 years, the Salerno team established that the foreskin was 2000 years old, so it could have belonged to Jesus of Nazareth.

One potential problem for the team was the lie that Professor Pappalardo had told Cardinal Donato about the impossibility of the cloning, and the consequent abandonment by the team in 2013 of the foreskin cloning effort. The Cardinal was now deceased and the Salerno team did not know who else in the Vaticano hierarchy knew about the secret effort. The team agreed not to approach the current Vaticano hierarchy about the upcoming article. Because the Church never officially acknowledged that the Vaticano Swiss Guards had taken the foreskin from Calcata in 1983, the origin of the tiny foreskin section which was used to clone Jesus and Jesusa was a delicate matter.

The Salerno team decided to lie again in order to protect themselves and the Vaticano hierarchy from embarrassment. A cover story was invented, which was surely not the first fabrication in the long history of the foreskin of Calcata.   The article briefly stated what the team told the Presceltos, which was that Dr. Pappalardo's predecessor at the University had been to Calcata in the early 1980s and had been authorized to cut a section of the foreskin for carbon-14 analysis. The results of that carbon-14 analysis were never revealed, until the current article. When the Pappalardo team found the foreskin section in the laboratory in 2013, they decided to conduct the cloning experiment. The team calculated that the Vaticano would know otherwise, but would be reluctant to officially acknowledge that it had taken the Holy Prepuce from Calcata in 1983. At the time of the burglary, the Vaticano had denied any knowledge of the relic's whereabouts.

When the article was published, so much attention was paid to trying to identify the twins, that the questions about the details of the cutting of the section from the foreskin were not asked.

Despite the team's efforts at anonymity for Jesus and Jesusa, there were calls from journalists to their parents' home on the 27th and to their college dormitory rooms by the 28th. Because the article described the creation of twins of both sexes, and that their names were religion-based, and because it said, "... the twins seem to be endowed with wisdom beyond their years," it wasn't long before the social media focused on Jesus and Jesusa.

The twins knew they had to present the truth, as they knew it, but they begged the reporters for time.

They scheduled a media conference in Salerno for Monday, the 31st and asked reporters not to ask them questions until then. Of course, that didn't prevent the Heidelberg graduation from being one of the most widely publicized college graduations in history. Even without the participation of the twins, the story went viral around the world.

Chapter 5 Coming out and Humanism

At the media conference on Monday, August 31, 2037, the twins began to feel the full impact of who they were and what they represented.

The conference began with Professor Pappalardo describing the work he and his team did to clone cells from the foreskin of Calcata. Two other members of the team were with him, including Allessandro Galvani. No one asked, and Prof. Pappalardo did not explain, when the piece of tissue was lifted from the relic. The relic was famous, but no one compared the year of the birth of Jesus and Jesusa, 2014, with the year, 1983, that the relic was stolen from the home of the priest in Calcata.

"Are you the Second Coming?" asked one reporter. Jesusa responded, "We are here to serve others. As Jesus of Nazareth said, I think it's in Mark, Chapter 10, 'Whoever wants to be a leader among you must be your servant, and whoever wants to be first among you must be the slave of everyone else. For even the Son of Man came not to be served but to serve others and to give his life as a ransom for many.' "

"Which of them was the Messiah?" asked another, to which Jesus answered, "If one of us is, then we both are."

A Muslim reporter asked about their potential roles as Muslim prophets, and Jesusa answered, "We are here for all humanity and all religions. We would be honored if the people of Islam were to consider us to be prophets."

The reporter continued, "But, you are a woman. There are no other women Muslim prophets."

Jesusa was ready, "There were only two women prophets in Judaism and Christianity: Miriam and Deborah, and very few people know anything about them. They were in the past. Whether there were two women prophets in a religion more than a thousand years ago or zero women prophets doesn't seem to make much difference today. We are now in the 21st century, and women are largely free from the shackles of their history. If Islam chooses to reject me because I am a woman, then it will decline further as a religion, just as did the Roman Catholic Church until it opened its doors fully to women. We need to combine the glories of Islam in medieval times when it led the world in science and math, with the need today to embrace men and women equally."

After the media conference, Jesusa said to Jesus, "Did you talk with the members of the medical team, in addition to Professor Pappalardo?"

"Yes," said Jesus, I talked with Dr. Galvani. He seemed very interested in our schooling, our interests and our lives in general."

"Was he the man with the brown hair and short goatee?" asked Jesusa.

"Yes, that was he," answered Jesus.

"Well, did you notice what he looked like?" continued Jesusa.

"What do you mean?" responded Jesus.

"I mean, did you notice that he looked like us?" pressed Jesusa. Did you notice that his eyes were brown. His hair was brown. His nose looked like ours. And so did his unusual ears. His eyebrows were curved like ours and he has a dimple on his cheek."

"Forgive me, Sooz, but last month at the museum in Darmstadt, you looked at the seldom-seen painting, "Arrest of Jesus" by Heinrich Hofmann and you thought that the Jesus in the painting looked like us. And that painting was finished in 1854!"

"Ok. Point taken, but I still think that Prof. Galvani looks like us, or what we will look like in another 25 years. Also, he kept staring at me, and when he wasn't staring at me, he was staring at you. Oh, well."

At age 23, they were not the youngest people to ever experience the thrill and fear of international youthful fame and the temptations and challenges that come with it. Shirley Temple was famous at age five in 1933 and continued to live a productive life. Princess Diana of England struggled with her fame, but morphed into the world's best-known supporter of what became the 1999 International Mine Ban Treaty, before her accidental death in 1997. Austrian Crown Prince Rudolph was heir to the Austro-Hungarian Empire, and all its apparent power and wealth, but he committed suicide at age 31 in 1889. To him and his lover, life was not worth living. The 20th century was littered with rock-and-roll stars who lost their balance and lives quickly, such as Janis Joplin, Jim Morrison, and Michael Jackson in the 21st.

However, Jesus and Jesusa had already developed perspectives on life and humanity and they chose, not unlike some of their peers, to use their fame to change the world for the better. They spoke of peace, and sustainable humanity on Earth, and of the need to severely reduce military budgets. They campaigned for an International Peace Day as part of the general campaign for an International Holiday Treaty. That treaty later became international law in 2040, upon the ratification by 50 countries. Jesus and Jesusa added their voices to the movement to provide family planning services to all men and women around the world in sufficient volume that every child born was a wanted child. While global population growth was slowing down and would soon stabilize, it was still over 8.5 billion.

They visited religious leaders around the world and asked that those leaders encourage their members to seek and find common ground with members of other religions, rather than exploit their differences. They had developed a following, similar to that of the Dalai Lama who, like themselves, was placed by the decisions of others into the forefront of his or her religion.

With all their speaking and traveling, they had little time for their relationships with friends and peers, and thus they had few. It seemed that they were, like their namesake, giving their lives for their fellow humans. They despaired that the human population was destroying their Earth with its fecundity and its toxic gasses and substances.

The burden of their heritage and names haunted them and they decided not to pass that heritage on to others, at least not biologically. Jesus had a vasectomy and Jesusa had a tubal ligation, and they made their decisions public. "It was time," they said, to care about the Earth and for the long term future of humanity." They were not asking, they said, for everyone to have themselves sterilized before having any children, but they recommended the operation for all who had made that decision, with or without children.

The major religions of the world took notice of these courageous twins, for they understood the meaning of sacrifice, and sacrifice was part of the core of those religions. Now, the questions came more frequently from the Jews, "Are you the messiahs?" And from the Christians, "Are you the Second Coming of Christ?" Such questions and hyperbole annoyed Jesus and Jesusa because they focused on their perceived divinity rather than their ideas.

However, like others born into outsized roles, such as the heirs to the British crown, they understood the reality of their fame. They knew that scientists created their first cells from the skin tissue of a long-long-deceased human who most likely was not the man called Jesus of Nazareth. They also knew that the primary reason that anyone listened to them was because, like their namesake, of the claims of their unusual births. It was a dilemma of dilemmas.

They knew they loved each other, but they kept that physical relationship secret and infrequent. When traveling together, they always had separate rooms. They thought that the public would never tolerate their sexual relationship. They knew that incest was prohibited in civilized societies as a pre-modern way to prevent unwanted genetic mutations. However, even though their sterilizations doubly assured the prevention of such mutations, the taboo was too strong to test openly.

Jesus found himself to be part asexual and part bisexual. He had quiet relationships with men and women, but his closest friends knew that his first love was for his sister. Similarly, Jesusa was bisexual, but mostly loved women, except for Jesus.

As their fame and influence spread, they understood that it was not what their namesake said and did that led to the creation of a religion in his name. It was the mythology of who he was and what his followers, especially Paul, said about him after his crucifixion. Further, it was his sacrifice and the sacrifices of his followers which gave momentum to Christianity.

Jesus and Jesusa looked for the best opportunity for their unique voice. At an environmental conference in Istanbul in May 2038, they met the former leader of the International Humanist and Ethical Union (IHEU), Sonja Eggerickx, and they explored their mutual interests. She encouraged Jesus and Jesusa to join and take a leadership role in the IHEU. Jesus and Jesusa wanted people to focus on Earth-oriented values and discard the mythology in many religions of where founders of religions came from, or where their bodies went after death. To them, fertilized eggs become embryos in mothers' bodies and people are born, and when they die, their bodies are all that remain, and not for long.

"In this respect," they would say, "we are no different from the other mammals on this earth." Further, they would remind their audiences, "From dust unto dust..."

They knew about the IHEU from their studies and they remembered learning that the brother of Aldous Huxley, author of the dystopian novel, *Brave New World*, was Julian Huxley who was one of the founders of the IHEU. The Huxley family was distinguished for many reasons, and the brothers were the grandsons of Thomas Henry Huxley, a friend and supporter of Charles Darwin.

In the fall of 2038, Jesus and Jesusa were elected co-presidents of the IHEU and the organization prospered. Many new members cited the "children of Jesus" as the reason for their support of humanism. "If a child of Jesus can dismantle the mythology of Jesus's purported birth and death, then it's safe for all of us," wrote one new member on an IHEU blog.

As Jesus and Jesusa were seeking to promote a better life for all humans on earth, their earlier interest in utopias blossomed into support for advocates of a future, more rational society. They joined in the endorsement of the "Great Transformation," the 50-year campaign which was announced in 2020. The number of people who openly declared themselves to be atheists or humanists grew dramatically after their election.

One of the co-presidents' first priorities was to seek out other organizations and religions and find common beliefs and philosophies with them. They chose, however, to stay with traditional humanism rather than extending the philosophy to transhumanism, which was the belief that with science and technology the abilities of humans could be expanded beyond the norm. A founder of transhumanism was the same Julian Huxley who helped found humanism. He wrote in 1957, "The human species can, if it wishes, transcend itself - not just sporadically, an individual here in one way, an individual there in another way, but in its entirety, as humanity."[1] Jesus and Jesusa believed that while the elites and wealthy of the world could avail themselves of the genetic technology to lengthen their lives and to expand the powers of their minds, such efforts could not be endorsed while there was no feasible way to extend those benefits to everyone.

The beliefs of the members of the IHEU were summarized in its 2002 "Amsterdam Declaration,"[2] as subsequently modified by the 2018 Geneva Declaration which eliminated references to established religions. Written in "British English," it states:

Humanism is the outcome of a long tradition of free thought that has inspired many of the world's great thinkers and creative artists and gave rise to science itself.

The fundamentals of modern Humanism are as follows:

1. Humanism is ethical. It affirms the worth, dignity and autonomy of the individual and the right of every human being to the greatest possible freedom compatible with the rights of others. Humanists have a duty of care to all of humanity including future generations. Humanists believe that morality is an intrinsic part of human nature based on understanding and a concern for others, needing no external sanction.

2. Humanism is rational. It seeks to use science creatively, not destructively. Humanists believe that the solutions to the world's problems lie in human thought and action. Humanists believe that science rather than belief will uncover the truths about the origins of our

1. Julian Huxley, *In Bottles for New Wine*, 1957, at http://www.transhumanism.org/index.php/WTA/more/huxley/
2. See the IHEU website, http://iheu.org/humanism/the-amsterdam-declaration/

universe and life on earth. Humanism advocates the application of the methods of science and free inquiry to the problems of human welfare. But Humanists also believe that the application of science and technology must be tempered by human values. Science gives us the means but human values must propose the ends.

3. Humanism supports democracy and human rights. Humanism aims at the fullest possible development of every human being. It holds that democracy and human development are matters of right. The principles of democracy and human rights can be applied to many human relationships and are not restricted to methods of government.

4. Humanism insists that personal liberty must be combined with social responsibility. Humanism ventures to build a world on the idea of the free person responsible to society, and recognises our dependence on and responsibility for the natural world. Humanism is undogmatic, imposing no creed upon its adherents. It is thus committed to education free from indoctrination.

5. Humanism recognises that reliable knowledge of the world and ourselves arises through a continuing process of observation, evaluation and revision.

6. Humanism values artistic creativity and imagination and recognises the transforming power of art. Humanism affirms the importance of literature, music, and the visual and performing arts for personal development and fulfilment.

7. Humanism is a lifestance aiming at the maximum possible fulfilment through the cultivation of ethical and creative living and offers an ethical and rational means of addressing the challenges of our times. Humanism can be a way of life for everyone everywhere.

8. Humanists recognise the rights of other animal species to live as they have evolved without human predation. While understanding that humans ate other animals for centuries, humanists seek a return to vegan diets for themselves and the world. Humanists support

the extension of the imperative "thou shall not kill," to all animals, except where necessity requires.

Our primary task is to make human beings aware in the simplest terms of what Humanism can mean to them and what it commits them to. By utilising free inquiry, the power of science and creative imagination for the furtherance of peace and in the service of compassion, Humanists have confidence that people have the means to solve the earth's problems.

Paragraph 8 was added at Geneva in recognition of the increased understanding that humans are one animal species among many and that humans deserve no special rights or privileges. Humans were never, by nature, predators, and they should return to their original sources of food for their own benefit and the improved welfare of the Earth and its other animal species.

In 2039 Jesus and Jesusa circulated these principles to the leaders of all major religions and asked, rhetorically, "Are we not all humanists?" They asked for comments and contributions for a new IHEU declaration of principles. They asked, "Please tell us what parts of this declaration conflicts with the principles of your religion, and secondly, what you would add." The final result was the 2041 Global Religious Framework which began with the "basic statement" of human ethical and moral beliefs followed by 26 appendices where each of the major religions presented what was unique about that religion and which was not accepted into the "basic statement."

Chapter 6 Co-Popes in the Church

In January, 2039, Jesus and Jesusa met with Pope Francesco II, who succeeded to the papacy in 2027 after the abdication of Pope Francesco, now called Pope Francesco I, on his birthday, December 17, 2026 at the age of 90. Formerly called Cardinal Agapiti Ndimbo, Pope Francesco II was from Tanzania and was the first Black pope.

"Welcome to the Vaticano," said the Pope. "We have much to talk about."

"Thank you very much," said Jesus and Jesusa, together. "We've been looking forward to this day," continued Jesusa, "for several years."

"What can we do, together, to serve humanity?" asked Jesus.

If Pope Francesco II knew anything about the actual source of the cloned section of the Holy Prepuce, he said nothing to Jesus and Jesusa. They, in turn, knew nothing more than what was said at the 2037 press conference and in the article by Professor Pappalardo and his team.

The Pope told them of his plan to convene a Vaticano Council IV in 2042, 20 years after the convening of the reform Vaticano Council III, which had endorsed the ordination of women, the abandonment of celibacy and the welcoming of marriage for all priests.

He then interrupted himself, "Before I continue with the planned changes in the church," he said, "I want to hear about your views on the moral issues relating to human food consumption."

Jesusa responded for herself and Jesus, as this was one of her areas of specialization, "Ok. I'll start. For the next two or three hundred years, until the human population returns to an equilibrium or sustainable level of one or two billion, we have to reduce our ecological burden on the Earth. One way is

to eat foods lower on the food chain. For example, a
single hectare[1] of land planted with potatoes can feed
29 people for a year. However, if that same hectare is
planted with grass for cattle, the resulting meat will
feed only one person for a year. If sheep are the
grazing animals, there will be meat for two people.
You can see how the eating of meat consumes at least
ten times as much land as the eating of grains and
vegetables. Of course, there are variations by country
and continent and by level of economic development.
We cannot develop any scale of morality that favors
the rich, who have been the people historically who
could afford to eat meat."

"Agreed," said Pope Francesco II. "It's been
generally forgotten that we ask Catholics to abstain
from eating meat on Fridays, in deference to the
memory of the death of Jesus of Nazareth on Good
Friday. What we could do is remind Catholics of that
request for abstinence and ask that they abstain from
eating both meat and fish on two other days a week, as
a means of respecting the animals which support us
on the other days. It also shows respect for our Earth.
Someday we can ask people to live without meat and
fish every day of every week, but we must pace
ourselves."

"That's excellent," answered Jesus. "If all
Catholics, and an equal number of non-Catholic
Christians and Humanists responded to your requests,
the reduction of meat consumption would achieve
three goals. First, it would permit those who needed to
eat more meat-based protein, but for whom supplies
were costly and limited, to eat that meat. Second, it
would reduce the pressure to use increasing amounts
of land for grazing of animals for food. Third, it would

1. A hectare contains 10,000 square meters and typically
measures 100 meters by 100 meters. It is equivalent to 2.47
acres.

decrease, or at least not lead to further increases of, greenhouse gasses, including methanol, from the animals' waste products."

Continued Jesusa, "Our goal is to gradually eliminate the consumption of meat and fish that requires the killing of animals. While some vegan purists also do not eat products of animals, primarily milk products such as milk, cheese, and butter, we don't think it's necessary or feasible to go that far. The key is that we believe we can respect and care for animals while still eating their eggs and their milk products.

The sheer scale of the killing of animals for food is breathtaking – pardon the pun. Approximately 20 billion chickens and 250 million cattle, 700 million pigs, and millions of ducks, goats, and sheep are killed every year for meat. That carnage should decline dramatically, and finally stop. Putting it in human per capita terms, on average each North American and Western European killed and ate approximately 30 animals last year, and that doesn't count the fish. Actually, the lives of fish are so minimized in our civilization that they are not individually counted by anyone except the sportsfishing people. Their killing of fish by painfully hooking their mouths onto bait, which is often composed of dead fish, is even more hideous than killing them for food.[2] Fish do have brains and they do feel pain.

It's not that eating meat and fish has always been wrong. There certainly were times when humans needed to eat meat, either from hunting or fishing, or from domesticated animals. Now, however, in the 22nd century, most humans do not need to eat meat because their essential nutrition is available from the

2. The slogan of the Fish Liberation Organization (FLO) was "Let's get fish off the hook." See www.flo.com. [As of 2014, not a real website.]

other food groups, and from our manufactured a-food; and that's what tips the scale in favor of vegetarianism.

It was once thought that animal protein was necessary for an active human life, but nutrition science proved that to be wrong. Many famous people, including athletes, have been vegetarians. They include Christine Lagarde, who helped bring the world to a Single Global Currency, Leonardo da Vinci, Steve Jobs, Martina Navratilova, and Albert Einstein. Your predecessor, Pope Francesco I became a vegetarian, even though he was from the beef eating and beef producing country of Argentina.

We ask that you declare not that it's immoral to eat meat, at least not yet, but that one core of our morality is the preservation of the Earth, and the moral course of action is to reduce the eating of meat."

The Pope agreed, "Our church used to have absolute rules. This sounds more like 'moral relativity.' You can be good if you reduce your meat consumption. You can be better in the eyes of the Church if you eliminate meat consumption. Few of us can be perfect, but we can try to get as close as we can."

Moving beyond the subject of food, Pope Francesco II was planning to recommend the de-mythologization of the Catholic Church, meaning that the Church would abandon the long-held views in such impossible myths as the virgin birth of Jesus of Nazareth, his ascension into a heaven that does not exist for him or anyone else, and the existence of a personal God. Also to be abandoned were the claimed miracles of Jesus of Nazareth and some of his followers.

Said Pope Francesco, "Jesus of Nazareth was a wonderful man," but he didn't restore Lazarus or anyone else from the dead, and he didn't walk on water. Instead," the Pope continued, "I will urge the Church to focus its mission on what Jesus of Nazareth

actually said and did as a human being." The
messages of love and forgiveness from Jesus of
Nazareth were especially important to Pope Francesco.
For these dramatic changes he believed he had the
support of most of the Cardinals, especially, of course,
from those he had most recently appointed.

The pope said, "The Golden Rule seems a good
place to start. Jesus said, 'Do to others whatever you
would like them to do to you. This is the essence of all
that is taught in the law and the prophets.'[3]"

Jesusa responded, "We agree. And what's
incredible is that the Golden Rule is part of the
philosophy of almost every religion and non-religious
values groups. There are similar texts in
Confucianism, Buddhism, Judaism, Islam, ancient
Roma, ancient Graecia, Hinduism, you name it."

The Pope continued, "One of my favorite messages
from Jesus - not you, of course, the first one - is about
the need to seek truth. I recall from my seminary days
learning that Jesus urged his followers, 'And so I tell
you, keep on asking, and you will receive what you ask
for. Keep on seeking, and you will find. Keep on
knocking, and the door will be opened to you. For
everyone who asks, receives. Everyone who seeks,
finds. And to everyone who knocks, the door will be
opened.'[4] And, of course, 'the truth shall set you
free.'[5] "

Despite the ordination of women, the population of
the Catholic Church was continuing its long decline,
as education in sciences continued to grow. Polls had
shown to Pope Francesco II that former Catholics and
potential Catholics viewed the myths of the traditional
Church as the barriers to their future religious
participation. Most of the new women priests and

3. Book of Matthew 7:12
4. Book of Luke 11:9-10
5. Book of John 8:32

bishops and supported this de-mytholization change, and they were lobbying their cardinal superiors.

"Let's talk," said the Pope, "about your interest in joining the priesthood of the Catholic Church."

"Yes," said Jesus, "we've thought for a long time that we belong in the Catholic Church, given the special circumstances of our births. As co-presidents of the IHEU, we can communicate the messages of Jesus of Nazareth, although we present them in humanist ways. If we were simultaneously officers of the Church, we believe our messages could be more powerful and authentic."

"Of course," replied Pope Francesco II, "it would be a novel step to instantaneously pronounce you as priests, and not everyone in the hierarchy would approve. However, we must take innovative steps if we are to stay relevant, and move humanity in the right direction."

"I just remembered," recalled Pope Francesco II. "One ironic item to discuss is the circumstance of your own birth. Some people believe that you are both the children of Jesus of Nazareth. Should that claim be added to the myths which the Church is about to abandon?"

Jesus responded, "That's a good question. Jesusa and I have always wondered about our birth. As Winston Churchill said about the circumstances of his own birth, when he was born eight months after the marriage of his parents, Lord Randolph Churchill and Jennie Jerome Churchill, 'Although present on the occasion, I have no clear recollection of the events leading up to it.' In other words, we are not responsible for the information about our births. We have always minimized the idea of the cloning from the 'Holy Prepuce' relice, and surmised that someone was mistaken about some aspect of the story, but we never launched our own investigation to explore the truth."

"Right," affirmed Jesusa. "As we never claimed parentage from Jesus of Nazareth, we never were part of our parents' story. Like Churchill, we were not in a position to affirm or deny the story. We've been skeptical, like most people. We've been reluctant to call it a myth, during our parents' lifetime, as it was what they were told and no one has totally disproved the idea. I think that Churchill's position was correct. Let's set aside the story with humor and a dose of skepticism."

"I agree," said Pope Francesco. "My staff thought this might be a problem for me and you, but I don't think so."

At the conclusion of their visit, Pope Francesco II announced to the media in the press room the simultaneous ordination of Jesus and Jesusa as Catholic priests, together with their immediate elevation as cardinals. Jesusa thus became the sixth woman Catholic Cardinal.

Pope Francesco II immediately addressed the question about Jesus and Jesusa that journalists and some cardinals, bishops and priests were likely to ask, which was, "What about the origin of Jesus and Jesusa? Was that a myth, too?" With the prior approval of Jesus and Jesusa, after their quiet discussion earlier in the day, Pope Francesco II said that the foreskin of Calcata was most certainly not a fragment of the body of Jesus of Nazareth. This myth, like so many others in the Church, needed to be cast away and replaced with reality. He then added the obvious, which was that Jesus and Jesusa were not in any way related to Jesus of Nazareth – except one, which was that they were almost divine people, and the Church was honored to have them.

The Pope explained how the IHEU and the Catholic Church would be working together over the next three years to promote their mutual interests. By this time the IHEU claimed over two billion members or passive sympathizers, which put it at about the same size as all of Christianity. For the Catholic Church to align with such a large group would help the Church survive into the next centuries.

Combining their roles as co-presidents of the IHEU and as Cardinals of the Church, Jesus and Jesusa reached out to the Jews of the world and traveled to Israel and other Jewish centers. They actively, but quietly, sought recognition as messiahs, but that was not yet attainable. Since ancient times, many men and one woman, Eve Frank, 1754-1816, sought recognition as the Messiah who would usher in a new era of justice, peace and plenty. In short, a Messiah would transform the lot of humanity, or the Jewish people at least, into a real utopia. Aside from earning a Wikipedia entry to the List of "Jewish Messiah Claimants," Jesus and Jesusa did not make much progress.

Similarly they went to Medina and Mecca and sought the support of Islamic leaders for both of them to be recognized as prophets in the Muslim faith, just as Jesus of Nazareth was recognized as an Islamic prophet.

In 2042, Jesus and Jesusa joined other Cardinals at the Vatican Council IV and lobbied their peer Cardinals to join in declarations that the source of Christian faith was not in the divinity of Christ, just as they were not divine, but in the messages that he left with his disciples.

In 2043, the Vatican Council IV released its determinations, the most important of which was the de-mytholization of Catholicism. The Catholic Church was to be a humanist church. There were dissenters, to be sure, but now the Church would move forward to assist its members in the real moral issues of the day which related to the care of the Earth and the need to reduce the size of the human population, and increase the spiritual and physical welfare of all.

Supporting that focus on the true moral issues facing humanity, the Vaticano Council IV endorsed Pope Francesco II's proposal for the Vaticano to abandon its status as a political unit. There was no modern reason for the Catholic Church to be the only religion in the world which also was a political state. The change meant large financial savings for the dismantling of the Vaticano diplomatic corps, including its mission to the United Nations. Instead of being a state, the territory of the Vaticano would be included within Municipio I, one of the 15 municipalities of the City of Roma. The approximately 900 citizens of the Vaticano City became citizens of Roma and Italia. A pope had one vote, like every other citizen of Roma, and s/he could run for City Council or Mayor if s/he chose. These changes were subsequently negotiated with the Government of Italia as amendments to the 1929 Lateran Treaty. This change was not as radical as might have seemed to those without more knowledge of Italian history. After the formation of the modern Italian state in the mid-19th century, the Papal States ceased to exist and the pope had no temporal authority from 1870 to 1929. At that latter date, Dictator Benito Mussolini negotiated the Lateran Treaty to settle the long simmering dispute between Italia and the Church. Thus, the abolition of the Vaticano state meant a return to the status quo from 1870 to 1929.

Pursuant to the Council's determination, Pope Francesco II announced that the Catholic Church would be formally joining the IHEU.

He also announced his intention to abdicate in 2044 and retire to a monastery in Tanzania, where he could pray for the return of the snows to Mt. Kilimanjaro. He took the unusual step of designating Jesus and Jesusa as his nominees to become co-popes. He expected the College of Cardinals to convene later that year to confirm his selections.

That fall, the College convened at the Vaticano. Pope Francesco reaffirmed his earlier announcement and told the conclave that he planned to abdicate, but that he would not do so unless the Cardinals agreed by sacred pledge to elect Jesus and Jesusa as co-popes. There was considerable debate, the content of which leaked to the public, despite efforts to keep it secret. The conservatives wanted a man to become the next pope, and then to roll back the reforms of Vatican Council III. The liberals saw that the downward sprial of the population of the Catholic Church would continue if their theology continued to sponsor myths as real and as a core of religious belief. They also supported the change in the political status of the Vaticano. They reminded the conservatives of the words of Jesus of Nazareth, "Render unto Caesar the things that are Caesar's, and unto God the things that are God's."

Finally, the Cardinals acceded to Pope Francesco II's wishes. The white smoke was sent up the chimney, but for the first time it was not created by fire. It would have been easy to get a permit to have a small fire to create the traditional white smoke, formerly with dry straw together with the used paper ballots, but now with chemicals. Instead, Pope Francesco II decided to have the white smoke created entirely by electricity, using the technology of electronic cigarettes which were banned worldwide in 2025. The black smoke, generated for the previous votes to indicate an inconclusive balloting, was also created electronically.

Jesus and Jesusa thus became on October 15, 2044, the first co-popes, and Jesusa was the first woman pope. Also, at age 30, they were the youngest popes in modern church history, since the papacy of Pope Ionnes XII who became pope at the age of 18 in 955 A.D.

Breaking with recent history in many ways, Jesus and Jesusa chose to keep their names and administer the Church as Co-Pope Jesus and Co-Pope Jesusa. The last pope to keep his name upon elevation to the papacy was Pope Hadrianus VI, 1522-1523, who was born in Holland as Adriaan (the Dutch equivalent of Hadrianus) Floriszoon Boeyens. That was more than 500 years earlier, and the next most recent was 500 years before that, when Giovanni (the Italian equivalent of Ioannes, or John in English) Fasano Phasianus became Pope Iohannes XVIII from 1003 to 1009. The first pope to change his name upon his elevation to that office was a Roman named Mercurio who became Pope Iohannes II in 533.

The tradition of changing one's name when becoming pope was analogous to the Western tradition, particularly in the U.K. and U.S., of a woman changing her surname to her husband's upon marriage. That tradition was almost completely abandoned by the late 21st century. In the Catholic Church popes were thought to be married to the church, hence the practice of changing their names.

Chapter 7 World Tour and Common Ground

In May of 2045, the Co-Popes began a world tour going eastward, beginning with Istanbul. There, they signed an agreement authorizing the mutual exploration of re-unification of the Roman Catholic Church with the Eastern Orthodox Church, from which it split in 1054. The agreement specifically set 2054 as the target date for re-unification, which would mark the end of the 1,000 year schism. This agreement was a followup to the historic meeting in 1964 between Pope Paulus VI and Ecumenical Patriarch Athenagoras in Jerusalem. That led to the Pope's rescission of the excommunications which were ordered in 1054 by Pope Leo IX.

Jesus and Jesusa then traveled to Jerusalem, but via an indirect route. They first took a MAGtrain to Aleppo, Syria, and then a car to the three peaks of Mount Hermon, a symbol of the earlier divisions and wars among the Syrians, Lebanese and Israelis. Thanks to the 2021 Alexandria Treaty among the Israelis and their Muslim neighbors, Mount Hermon and the Golan Heights had been returned to full Syrian sovereignty, except that its military was not allowed in the territory.

The Alexandria Treaty was a long time in coming, if one considers the 1967 U.N. Resolution 242, or even Resolution 394 of 1950, as the beginning of negotiations. The basic formula was that Israel returned nearly all of the West Bank and all of Gaza to the Palestinian State in return for Palestinian recognition of Israel. Many of the illegal Israeli settlements in the West Bank were simply acknowledged to be entirely within, and governed, by Palestine. After considerable education and public relations by the Palestine government, the Jews in those settlements were persuaded that the Palestinian laws were fair and that they would be fairly

79

administered, regardless of religious orientation, as was required in the Alexandria Treaty. An added incentive to accepting Palestinian citizenship and authority was that the Palestinian tax rates were substantially lower than in Israel. A few of the larger settlements and those close to Jerusalem were determined to be subject to Palestinian property and commercial law, but their residents were dual citizens of Israel and Palestine with respect to civil liberties. Each country was free to establish its capital wherever it wished and each country was required to protect the religious freedom of its citizens.

A relatively new issue for the Israelis and Palestinians was the abolition of the Israeli nuclear weapons program. This became feasible after Iran agreed in 2015 to stop entirely its nuclear energy program which could relate to military use. Pursuant to the Alexandria Treaty, Israel then became nuclear-free, just as had been achieved in South Africa in 1989, when that country's government was persuaded to abandon its program, which had already produced several atomic bombs. In 2003, Libya voluntarily renounced its nuclear weapons program. In return for Israel's abandonment of its nuclear weapons, the military budgets of its neighboring countries were slashed.

From Mt. Hermon, the Co-Popes walked the approximately 320 kilometers to Jerusalem, stopping at sites along the way where Jesus and several prophets of Islam had preached. They walked along the Jordan River and swam in the Sea of Galilee. Arriving in Jerusalem they spent an equal amount of time at Christian, Jewish and Muslim holy sites and in meetings with the leaders of the three faiths.

At the Temple Mount, a place holy to the three faiths, the Co-Popes signed an accord with several Jewish and Muslim leaders. There were only 15 million

Jews in the world,[1] but Israel was primarily a Jewish country and the Temple Mount was in Israel. The Jews were represented by leaders of the Conservative, Orthodox and Reform branches, with the Reform leader coming from the United States.

Representing Islam were four Sunni leaders from Indonesia, Nigeria, Pakistan and Saudi Arabia and one Shia leader from Iran. Since 2042, approximately 1,400 years after the beginning of the Sunni/Shia schism which began in the leadership struggle after the death of the prophet Muhammed in 632, these leaders and about 20 others had been negotiating in Mecca to end that schism. Jesus and Jesusa encouraged the Muslim leaders at Temple Mount to continue those negotiations and come to an agreement, just as the leaders of Christianity had done. The perils facing the Earth were too great to waste time and energy in divisive theology, based on differences among Muhammed's successors so long ago.

Another reason for the two Muslim denominations to merge was that the rapid growth of the early 21st century had stopped and reversed, primarily due to the perception that Islam was hostile to women. The "honor killings" were primarily of women whose only crime was love for a man, and much less frequently a woman, they loved in preference to the persons chosen for them by their families. There were an estimated 8,000 such killings in 2010, but the publicity generated by the increasingly universal social media, caused widespread revulsion at the practice and at Islam in general. By unifying the two major denominations, their leaders hoped to show that the

---

[1]. Before six million Jews were murdered in the World War II holocaust, the global Jewish population was approximately 15.5 million, of whom 9.6 million lived in Europe. Thus, the holocaust saw the loss of 39% of the world Jewish population and 63% of the European Jewish population.

way forward was through reasonable discussion rather than hatred of those with whom there were disagreements.

Also invited and signing to the Temple Mount signing were the leaders of the ten largest Christian denominations, including the Eastern Orthodox, Protestants and Anglicans. Based on the 2041 Global Religious Framework, the accord presented the goal of merging their faiths into a single faith based not on the divinity of any of their ancestor leaders, but on the views of humanity they held in common. The Accord, later known as the Temple Mount Accord of 2045 also expressed a desire to join with the faiths of Asia and Africa and with interested secular humanists. It is presented below:

We leaders of several religious faiths proclaim our mutual interest in bringing humanity together toward several common beliefs:

1. Our religions arose from times when little was known about ourselves and about our universe.
2. The world now faces unprecedented environmental challenges which we must face together.
3. We share common values of justice, social justice, fostering community, kindness, trust, and curiosity.
4. We shall work together to discourage violence and injustice as actions incompatible with our shared understanding of religion.
5. Our differences, and the differences among our members and fellow citizens must be resolved through discussion and dialogue, rather than hostility and violence. Where there are differences which cannot

be yet resolved, and which do not
conflict with our common values,
we pledge to set those aside and
not permit them to interfere with
those common values and
interests.

6. We call for a global religious
enclave to be held in 2047 to reach
further understanding or our
common beliefs and interests, for
the benefit of our members or
congregants. The primary goal of
that enclave would be establish a
global common core of beliefs
which all humanity could share,
while simultaneously maintaining
local traditions which are not in
conflict.

Jesusa said at the media conference afterwards,
"When Jesus of Nazareth said, 'Every kingdom divided
against itself is brought to desolation; and every city or
house divided against itself shall not stand,'[2] he could
have been speaking to us today. We humans must
overcome the divisions among us, and together protect
our Earth."

One result of these efforts to bridge the gaps
among religions was the near elimination of sectarian
violence within the Muslim world, and from that world
toward the Western world. The other contributing
factor was the dramatic reduction in population
growth, which, in turn, reduced the previously large
numbers of unemployed or underemployed young and
disaffected Muslim men. Further, the increased
equality of Muslim women led to more open
expressions of sexuality which had been repressed in
that religion for hundreds of years. That change, too,

2. Book of Matthew, 12:25.

further reduced the frustrations of Muslim men which previously were directed at Westerners and women.

They then went to Kahuta, Pakistan to bring a message of peace to the survivors of the 2020 nuclear explosion. The twins were six years old when the world suffered its third atomic bomb explosion in a populated area. Over 80,000 people were killed, and another 90,000 were seriously injured. Kahuta was one of Pakistan's nuclear weapon development sites, and scientists later determined that the explosion was an accident due to a timing device that was erroneously activated. At least that is what the Pakistanis said. In fact, it may have been that the bomb exploded when someone was trying to steal it. In any case, it was another painful reminder that the Earth needed to rid itself of nuclear weapons.

Learning about the 2020 Kahuta bomb when Jesus and Jesusa were at the Da Vinci School had a significant effect on their decisions to work for world peace and religious tolerance and unity for the rest of their lives.

At Kahuta, they visited tombs of the thousands of unknown dead and visited with the survivors of the explosion which was only 25 years earlier.

Continuing eastward, the Co-Popes flew to India and met with Hindu leaders. They bathed in the Ganges River, which fortunately had been substantially cleaned up since it had been classified in the early 2000s as one of the world's most polluted rivers. They witnessed a solar cremation at one of the country's 23,000 solar crematoria. The use of these crematoria was credited with contributing to the reversal of Indian deforestation and the slow restoration of India's forests. Prior to the "Great Transformation," cremation was not favored by several religions, including the Baha'i's, but the Hindus led the world toward making the practice nearly universal. The next most popular means of disposing of the bodies of the dead was to bury them, without protection from solid materials, so their bodies would decay into the soil and thus regenerate in future plants and animals.

Jesus and Jesusa visited 'Sabarati Ashram,' one of the homes of Mahatma Gandhi, whose life work they had studied during their Johannesburg college year in 2034-35. Now, they were especially interested in his, and Hindu, respect for animals. They had read the famous quote, though incorrectly attributed to Gandhi, "The greatness of a nation and its moral progress can be judged by the way its animals are treated."[3] They had supported the "Respect Animals Movement" (RAM) and had long ago stopped eating meat and fish.

In a light moment, the twins were presented sets of ten Nehru shirts with their trademark short upright collars, which were similar to the collarless shirts which Jesus and Jesusa favored since their "Cotton Revolution" back at Da Vinci School.

Next, Jesus and Jesusa flew to Thailand to meet with Southeast Asian Buddhist leaders. "We must do what we can to save humanity," said Jesusa, "and working together with a common spiritual vision will help all of us do that work." The Buddhist leaders expressed optimism that the 2047 global conclave would be successful.

For Jesus and Jesusa, traveling to Beijing was a return "home" as they had spent almost a year there as students, and activists against the death penalty.

---

3. This was one of many times in which wise statements were attributed to people, but for which there was no reliable source. Others who denied making widely quoted statements attributed to them were Senator Everett Dirksen ("A billion here, a billion there, and pretty soon you're talking about real money.") and Margaret Mead, ("Never doubt that a small group of thoughtful, committed citizens can change the world; indeed, it's the only thing that ever has.") and William Sutton, ("I rob banks because that's where the money is.")

The Communist Party was no longer the only political party, as the country's politics had evolved into a multi-party system. Nonetheless, atheism was still more of an official religion than in any other country, although it had substantially evolved into humanism. Jesus and Jesusa assured their Chinese hosts, "We look forward to talking to everyone here, including atheists and humanists. If atheists care enough about their belief system to label themselves in some way, then they must have come to some recognition of their values, and we can talk."

Next, they flew to Lima, Peru and visited the major countries of South America traveling south along the Pacific coast and then back north along the Atlantic, and then to Cuba. South America still had the largest percentage Catholic population of any of the continents. From Beijing, they had considered going from Beijing to North America via the China-TransSiberian-Alaska MAGtrain, which was just completed in 2039, but that route took them too far out of their way.

Cuba was a special destination because of the powerful example of reconciliation between that country and the United States. In 2034, the United States unilaterally announced that it was giving up its perpetual 100-year old lease of the 116.5 square kilometer Guantanamo Naval Base, which had also been the site of the notorious prison camps for alleged Muslim fighters after September 11, 2001. In 2018, after the departure from the Cuban government of Raul and Fidel Castro, normal diplomatic and commercial relations were established between Cuba and the United States, including the payment of compensation for private property expropriated in 1959. The restoration of the Guantanamo base to Cuba capped 16 years of increasingly cordial relations.

In Havana, Jesus and Jesusa dedicated the renovated Havana Cathedral of Mother Mary, formerly called the Cathedral of the Virgin Mary. As with other churches and places with references to the now-discarded myth of a virgin birth, the name of the Havana Cathedral was changed. The mother of Jesus of Nazareth was still much revered in the Catholic Church for the values that she instilled in her son, but most Christian churches followed the lead of the Roman Catholic Church which proclaimed at its Vaticano Council IV that it no longer needed to rely upon myths for its spiritual strength.

Before heading to Western Europe and Roma, the Co-Popes flew to Miami for a New Year's Eve celebration and Mass. The Church continued the rituals of Mass with the sharing of bread and wine as symbols of the bodily and spiritual sharing of the sustenance for humanity.

Not everyone in the Catholic Church welcomed the changes brought by Vaticano Councils III and IV and by the ascendancy of Co-Popes Jesus and Jesusa. Before the trip began, Church leaders in the U.S. advised against coming to the U.S. for fear of an assassination attempt by disgruntled Catholics or from anyone who disapproved of the Co-Popes, or their presumed sexuality or their views. Too many such people still had weapons. There was some relief when the trip to Miami concluded without serious incident, aside from some heckling and threatening words on the Internet. "See," said Jesus to Jesusa, "despite some bitterness in the U.S. about its relative decline in the world, and despite some Catholic opposition to what we have done and what we symbolize, our messages of love and optimism are still welcome here." Officials in Dallas cringed when they heard of that comment, with its echo of the 1963 statement by Mrs. Connolly, the Texas governor's wife, to John Kennedy just before her husband and President Kennedy were shot, "Mr. President, you cannot say that Dallas doesn't love you."

As children, Jesus and Jesusa had learned about President John Kennedy, as his name was given to several streets in Italia and to a building at their school. When at the University of Heidelberg, they had traveled to Berlin and saw a video of Kennedy's trip to that city in June, 1963. Given their interest in John Kennedy, Dallas was added to their itinerary, before going to New York and then to Notre Dame Cathedral in Paris and then home. Traveling to Dallas was not the preference of the Co-Popes' security team.

In Dallas on Tuesday, January 3, 2045, the trip into the city started well, just as it did for the Kennedy's in 1963. Fifteen minutes later, reality loomed in the form of a drone that was flying toward the popemobile while on the way to the Dallas Book Depository and Dealey Plaza. "What's that?" said more than one visitor to the city who heard or saw the drone. A policeman called in a "red alert" message that a drone was flying toward the papal route. No one knew whether it was armed or whether it was a journalist's effort at getting a better look at the motorcade, but the Dallas Police treated the "alert" as seriously as they could – in the twelve seconds they had left before its possible intersection with the papal route.

Taking a slightly different route than the 1963 Kennedy motorcade, the Co-Popes traveled west on Elm Street and came into Deavey Plaza where Kennedy was shot. Coming from the north, and just after passing through the intersection with Houston Street, the drone fired six 9 mm caliber shots into the popemobile before crashing into it a 130 km/hour. Hitting the windshield, the drone further injured the driver, who had already been hit by two of the bullets, and the car burst into flame. Three other bullets hit the bulletproof glass protector between the driver and the Co-Popes.

The sixth bullet went through the front seat and hit Jesusa's left hand as she was ducking behind that seat. "Oh, my God!" she screamed. The popemobile crashed into a building on Elm Street whereupon police and EMTs descended upon the vehicle and removed Jesus and Jesusa and drove them to the new Parkland Hospital. It was built in 2015, replacing the hospital where John Kennedy was taken and died.

The wound to Jesusa's hand was serious, in the sense that any bullet traveling through a human body is serious, but not life-threatening. There were no broken or shattered bones and no nerves were severed. The radial artery was cut, and it was repaired after the loss of half a liter of her blood. She stayed in the hospital for a day and then she and Jesus continued their tour to New York City, where they addressed the United Nations.

As with others who had survived assassination attempts, such as Theodore and Franklin Roosevelt and Ronald Reagan, the stature of Co-Popes Jesus and Jesusa was enhanced by the near-miss in Dallas. It was even noted that Jesusa's wound was likely in the same location as the nail in the left hand of Jesus of Nazareth.

Jesusa spoke first, and began by saying, "Let us be thankful that the Great Transformation has, so far, brought us back from the brink of nuclear and environmental disaster. However, we have much to do to improve the status of humanity. We must continue to encourage humanity's best traits and discourage our worst.   There is goodness in all of us. We know from our history that we, men and women alike, have within us the emotions of hate and murder. We know that those emotions can be stirred up by demagogues, whether they are government officials or media celebrities. Our challenge is dampen those dangerous emotions and to foster the good emotions within us, such as love, happiness, curiosity and hope.

We can improve the behavior of humanity by positively reinforcing good behavior or non-violent behavior and negatively reinforcing bad behavior. This may sound like it came from the 20th century utopian classic, *Walden Two*, because it does. If we know that exposing people, especially young people, to violence in the media causes them to be more violent, then we should take reasonable steps toward reducing that exposure. The primary lesson of that book about the behavioral transformation of people's behavior should not be cast away because of its elitist, anti-democratic flavor. Instead, let's replace the Walden's leader, T.E. Frazier, with democratically elected representatives.

Reinforcing good behavior could involve the teaching of Emotional Education, where students learn about emotions and how to present those emotions to others in positive, constructive ways. It could involve teaching the techniques of mediation and negotiation and support of Peace academies in every nation. Prizes and medals should be given to those who peacefully resolve conflicts, instead of, or in addition to, bestowing awards on military people who kill other people.

To discourage violent behavior, movies, television programs, video games and other media should be assessed a tax roughly equivalent to the external costs of the excess or gratuitous violence as can be fairly allocated. As such an amount is extremely difficult to calculate, a fair estimate would be to double the cost factor where realistic violence exceeds normal frequency in real life, and to triple or quadruple the cost where the violence is unrealistic and excessive. As is sometimes said, the devil is in the details, but some means must be found to discourage such media violence.

The names of the people and corporations who produce such depictions of violence should be exposed for all to see. Just as Transparency International (www.transparency.org) has, for 50 years, beginning in 1995, been publishing its Global Corruption Index, the supporters of non-violence should publish an annual list of the purveyors of violence. Consumers should be encouraged to boycott, or otherwise stigmatize, those purveyors.

Violence in sports can more easily be discouraged, by simply changing the rules. The "no-brainer" place to start, and please pardon the play on words, is to stop the practice of allowing football (formerly called "soccer" in the U.S.) players to "head" the ball. It would also be a "no-brainer" to ban blows to the head in boxing, but that problem can be eliminated by entirely prohibiting boxing, with or without gloves. All related extreme sports and martial arts should no longer be taught to children or tolerated. In brief, any so-called sport which involves the infliction of pain or injury to another person should be banned. On the other hand, wrestling and judo and related sports are tests of skill and strength, and don't involve the intentional infliction of pain; and they can be allowed to continue.

From my days as a student in Boston, and in support of the positive reinforcement of B.F. Skinner and *Walden Two*, I give you now the lyrics of a great songwriter and singer, Johnny Mercer, who wrote and sang the song, "Accentuate the Positive." Now I sing my favorite lyrics:

> You've got to accentuate the positive
> Eliminate the negative
> And latch on to the affirmative
> Don't mess with Mister In-Between
>
> You've got to spread joy up to the maximum
> Bring gloom down to the minimum
> Have faith or pandemonium's
> Liable to walk upon the scene

Let us move forward in that spirit, with song and with a sense of humor. Bless you."

Jesus spoke next, beginning with his recent shock that someone or some group appeared to try to kill him and his sister.

He said, "We had received threats before, but this was the first time that shots had been fired at us. It was a reminder that we still have a long way to go to tame humanity's worst instincts, and correct the damage we have done to the Earth.

Supporting my sister's comments, I emphasize that we support the humanist approach of rewarding behavior that all humans are already programmed to show – unless detoured by behavioral messages of violence. Non-violence is not a complex message. Some of humanity's greatest leaders have advocated and practiced non-violence, including Jesus of Nazareth, Mahatma Gandhi and Martin Luther King, Jr. Please note that it doesn't take great education or intelligence to understand non-violence and the need to present our humane virtues. One of the many American victims of police brutality, Rodney King (no relation to Martin L. King, Jr.) famously said during the 1992 Los Angeles riots that followed the acquittals of his assailants, "Can we all get along?"[4] This is not a complex message.

We are not advocating massive transhumanist changes to the human genetic code. While there have been promising scientific advances in showing how electrical impulses and ingested chemicals can alter human behavior, we are not yet at the point where such technology is available to everyone.

4. King's was often misquoted as saying, "Can't we all just get along," but the meaning is nearly the same as the correct version. See the Wikipedia entry at
http://en.wikipedia.org/wiki/Rodney_King

I don't have the musical ear of my sister, but we do share a dream for humanity. That dream was well-stated by Martin Luther King, Jr. in Washington, D.C. in 1963, and I wish to borrow his cadence with my paraphrasing, to say:

> I have a dream that one day the
> sons and daughters of former
> antagonists will be able to sit down
> together at the table of
> brotherhood.
>
> I have a dream that one day even
> our least democratic countries,
> previously sweltering with the heat
> of injustice, and sweltering with
> the heat of oppression, will be
> transformed into oases of freedom
> and justice.
>
> I have a dream that all of our
> children will one day live in a world
> where they will not be judged by
> the color of their skin but by the
> content of their character.
>
> I have a dream today!

We have other dreams, too. That our planet will recover from the damage our forebears have caused and we will again live in harmony and equilibrium with our Earth. Bless you all."

The next day Jesus and Jesusa visited the World Trade Center site, the September 11 museum, and the apartment lobby where John Lennon was murdered. Jesus spoke to the group of reporters of the dangers the world faces if we allow the feelings of hate within all of us to overcome the feelings of love. He said, "I'm sorry to say that religion and religions played a role in that situation by encouraging people to believe that their way was the only way and that those who chose other ways were apostates and enemies. We are now moving away from such dangerous thoughts, but they are still present – as we saw last week in Dallas."

That afternoon, the Dallas police contacted the Popes' entourage to advise that they had arrested a suspect in the attempted murder of Jesus and Jesusa in Dallas. His name was Patrick O'Laughlin and the apparent motive arose from his opposition to the changes in the church since he was a child. When Jesus heard about the call and the arrest, he pulled aside his aide, Father Turkson, and said, "Please contact the Dallas Police Dept. and request that a videocall be arranged among me, Jesusa and O'Laughlin for later in the evening. Let's say, nine o'clock. We'd like to talk with Mr. O'Laughlin."

"But, your Holiness, this is a highly unusual request," said his Ghanian aide, who continued, "I understand that Americans try to keep victims away from accused perpetrators until after the trials."

"Thank you, Father Turkson, but I'm somewhat familiar with the American justice system," replied Jesus. "It's come a long way since they executed innocent people, including Derek Barnabei, the American of Italian heritage, in 2000. However, they have more to do before the U.S. justice system is as good as its lawyers claim. Let's take an active role in this case, even if the lawyers, prosecutors and police don't recommend it."

After dinner, the connection was made. O'Laughlin was in Dallas with his attorney, Craig Watkins, Jr.

"How do you do, Mr. O'Laughlin," began Jesusa. "I'm Pope Jesusa and this is Pope Jesus, but please address us by our familiar names, Jesus and Jesusa."

"How do you do, your holinesses. Sorry, that's what I was advised to call you," replied O'Laughlin.

Jesus reassured him, "That's OK. Please address us as Jesus and Jesusa and we will call you Patrick."

Jesusa stepped in, "Look, Patrick. We have heard of assassination attempts in the U.S., and one of our predecessors, Pope Ionnes Paulus II was shot and nearly killed in 1981 in Roma. He forgave his assailant, Mehmet Ali Agca, who was released after 19 years. Do you think we should forgive you?"

O'Laughlin had been eager to speak, "I do, but I don't. You see, I had nothing to do with the firing of those shots at you. I was flying that drone, but I had no intention of hurting you, let alone killing you. I'm innocent. Why should I ask for forgiveness for something I didn't do?"

"That's a good question," Jesus said.

Attorney Watkins added, "I understand that you have been interested in wrongful convictions, and I hope that this case doesn't become one like the Barnabei case. It seems to have that potential, however."

"Ok," said Jesusa. "We just assumed that we would be talking with someone who might be willing to talk with us about what he did. However, it appears that, once again, assumption can be a problem. It looks like we cannot help you right now, beyond wishing you good luck in your efforts to achieve justice; but let us know if you need help."

"Wait," said Patrick. "It's true that I dislike some of the changes in the church. In fact, I don't think that we should have a woman pope or co-pope, or whatever. No offense to you personally, Jesusa, of course, but it's wrong. It's not how I was brought up."

"Well, I can understand, Patrick," said Jesusa. "It wasn't how I was brought up, either. That is, I never expected to see a woman pope, or even a co-pope, but that doesn't mean that when the opportunity arose I should have refused it."

"Nope, I suppose not," said Patrick. "Another thing. Why do you talk with Muslims? They're terrorists."

Responded Jesus, "Only a few people in any society are hardwired true criminals. There was a time, earlier in this century, and before, that some Muslims saw violence as the only way to show their frustrations with the high Muslim unemployment and Western secular or Christian wealth. We think the better answer to unemployment is birth control for men and women who want it.   Well, that's a bit oversimplified, but a high birth rate, coupled with dramatic reductions in death rates, was a reason for the large proportion of young Muslims, and hence, their unemployment. With so many young people, there were not enough wise elders around to counsel them toward peaceful solutions. Back to your question. We think it's important to talk with everybody who wishes to talk with you, especially with those of different views. Hence our call to you this evening."

Jesusa looked at the clock on the ceiling, "Patrick, it's getting late here in New York. We have to go, as we leave tomorrow morning. Good luck to you. If the system works and you are telling us the truth, you should be found innocent. In fact, your case shouldn't even go to trial, but bigger mistakes have been made. Thanks goodness the death penalty has been abolished. Keep in touch. Let us know if we can help. If you have any idea of how your drone happened to shoot at us and almost kill us, please tell the police. We have to go."

"Ok. Thanks. Bye. Ciao," said Patrick.

The next day, they flew to London to meet with the Archbishop of Canterbury, Thomasina More, who had been the church's leader since 2034, the 500th anniversary of its separation from the Catholic Church. Before their world tour began in May, the Co-Popes had begun negotiations with the Anglican Church, together with its U.S. partner, the Episcopal Church. By the time they arrived in London, it was clear that negotiations were proceeding satisfactorily and that a reunification of the churches was probable in 2046. Jesus and Jesusa then met with King William V and then left for Paris and finally Roma.

The assassination attempt in Dallas caused worldwide revulsion at the widespread availability of guns and weapons in the United States, and spurred that country finally to enact more stringent rules for guns, including an amendment to the U.S. Constitution which provided that the States and the Federal Government "could regulate the manufacture, sale and possession of firearms and ammunition as was necessary to promote the general welfare."

Chapter 8 2045 to Resignation

Upon their return to Roma just before Christmas, 2045, the Co-Popes sought renewal and growth within the Church. They recognized that some conservative Catholics had left the church because, as they said, "The Church has left us." However, the way forward was to recruit people who sought a little more than the pure rationality of the IHEU, from which they had resigned as co-presidents. They could have continued as co-presidents of both organizations, but they realized that they needed to focus on one, and the spiritual attraction of the Roman Catholic Church led to their choice.

It was similar to the choice Robert E. Lee made when the southern states formed the Confederacy and seceded from the northern states. As a loyal solider of the United States Army for 32 years, since 1829, it was a wrenching decision to transfer his loyalty to the State of Virginia and the Confederacy. He did this, even after being offered by President Lincoln the command of the entire U.S. Army. Sometimes, two masters cannot be served.

Jesus and Jesusa were familiar with Lee's decision, from their studies in Boston, but they sought not to suffer the disastrous consequences which befell him. The Catholic Church was now a smaller organization than the IHUE, but it had a rich history and a profound responsibility to bring its members into the 21st century.

There had been many reforms, and many details needed to be resolved.

Over the next 20 years, the Church finally pulled itself away from the moral and financial disasters of child abuse which had been brought on by the now-abandoned policies of celibacy for priests, and prohibitions against women and homosexual priests. It was estimated by a special commission that fully one-third of the entire wealth of the Catholic Church, including its art and real estate, was consumed by compensation to the people injured by those earlier policies. Much property had to be sold, and much was given to governments and non-profit organizations as the Church could no longer afford to maintain them.

In April, 2046, Jesus and Jesus were advised by email[1] from Attorney Watkins that Patrick O'Laughlin was convicted of two counts of attempted murder and was sentenced to life in prison. Watkins apologized for not asking them to help during the trial, by submitting a video victim statement. He said he thought that the trial was going so well that he felt that he didn't need their help. The prosecution didn't need them as witnesses, as the entire event of January 3 was recorded on several video devices.

Jesus asked Jesusa, "What should we do? I know I can be naive about people and gullible too, but O'Laughlin didn't seem so angry that he would have tried to kill us. I believed him when we talked by videophone."

Jesusa agreed. "Let's ask Mother Scheck, the lawyer priest who helped set up the original interview among you, me and Patrick O'Laughlin, to look into the case and see if she can help. Perhaps she can conclusively find that he really did send the drone to kill us, or she can help exonerate him. She's a tough person. She went to the University of Texas Law School when she was a nun. Just after she became an attorney, the Vaticano Council III decreed in 2023 that women could become priests. One unanticipated consequence of that decision was that the role of nuns was thrown into uncertainty. As Sister Teresa Scheck, she had done considerable research on how American male-only colleges had become co-educational and the

---

1. jesusandjesusa@vaticano.org. [As of 2014, not a real email address.]

effects of those changes on the diminishing number of women's colleges. Similarly, the equalization of women in the U.S. military led to the dismantling of women-only units. Sister Scheck proposed in 2028 the very simple solution that all nuns be automatically ordained as priests except for those who wished to continue their careers or lives as nuns.

Similarly, monks had always been able to work as priests, or they could elect to be solely members of monasteries. In 2030, there were 555,000 Roman Catholic nuns and 108,000 monks, worldwide. Both populations were significantly less than 100 years earlier. In 2030, Pope Francesco II issued a papal "bull" that adopted Sister Scheck's proposal, which had been endorsed by all the major orders of nuns. Henceforth, she was known as "Mother Scheck." The previous title for the managing nuns of convents, "Mother Superior," was changed to "Bishop."

Jesus and Jesusa talked with Mother Scheck and she agreed to work on the O'Laughlin case full-time for the next six months.

In 2047, the one-month global religious conclave was held in Arusha, Tanzania, as was planned in the 2045 Temple Mount Accord. Arusha is about three hours from Mount Kilimanjaro, which became an international symbol of global warming when it lost its last snowpack in 2023. Attending the conclave were leaders from the major religions of the world, together with the IHUE and other humanist organizations. Giving the welcoming address was Pope Emeritus Francesco II, who lived in the nearby Franciscan monastery.

At its conclusion, the draft "Kilimanjaro Accord" was issued and distributed to the members of participating organizations and through the media to everyone in the world. The draft agreement combined the Temple Mount Accord of 2045 with the IHUE's 2018 Geneva Declaration. Paragraphs were added to emphasize the need for mutual education about other faiths and mutual tolerance. A protocol was established for a World Values Forum (WVF) which would meet semi-annually to discuss how the world's faiths can reach common moral and ethical ground on specific issues, such as marriage and death. The WVF was intentionally designed to parallel the older and richly endowed World Economic Forum which began in 1971 in Davos, Switzerland.

The Kilimanjaro Accord was ratified by all the major religions of the world, and by the IHUE. The signing ceremony was scheduled for December 10, 2048, the 100th anniversary of the adoption by the United Nations of the Universal Declaration of Human Rights. Article 18 of that Declaration, was especially applicable. It reads:

> *Everyone has the right to freedom of*
> *thought, conscience and religion;*
> *this right includes freedom to*
> *change his religion or belief, and*
> *freedom, either alone or in*
> *community with others and in*
> *public or private, to manifest his*
> *religion or belief in teaching,*
> *practice, worship and observance.*

One of the intended effects of the reconciliation among religions was the nearly complete elimination of religion-based violent acts. No longer were the clergy of any religion calling for any harm to be caused to any member of any other religion. The common ground was mutual tolerance.

During the reign of Co-Popes Jesus and Jesusa, the Catholic Church supported the "Great Transformation" until its formal pre-determined end in 2070. In its place, the "Great Transformation II," also scheduled for 50 years, was proposed by the United Nations Secretary-General Malia Obama and later ratified by the General Assembly. Obama had been

Secretary-General since 2045, and this was her last major project. She had long since exceeded her original goal of serving the U.N. for longer than her heroine, Eleanor Roosevelt, who served nine years from 1946 until 1953 and again from 1961-62, and was substantially responsible for the U.N. passage of the Universal Declaration of Human Rights in 1948. The Catholic Church, as the Holy See, rather than in its former status as the city-state, Vaticano, was a co-sponsor of the Universal Declaration.

The "Great Transformation II" sought by the end of 2120 these goals:

1. Through the continued reduction of the greenhouse gasses, the reversal of global warming. One flake of sought-after evidence of that reversal would be the return of a snow pack, year-round, to Mt. Kilimanjaro, perhaps before the death of Pope Emeritus Francesco II.

2. The continued reduction of the human population to 6 billion, which was the level last seen in 1999. Further reductions in the population should continue until approximately reaching one billion, which was the population around 1800. The United Nations Demography Office predicted and advocated for the following milestones in global population:

Year	Population
2100	6 billion
2125	5
2150	4
2180	3
2220	2
2300	1

   Alternatively, a team of scientists was to be assembled to determine the level of human population whereby

humanity can exist in equilibrium with
other species on the Earth. It's been
predicted that such a number would
be between the 1800 population of one
billion and the 1925 population of two
billion.

3. The continued reduction in the
incarceration of people, through the
reduction of crime, especially violent
crime, and the use of alternate
methods of punishment.

Back in Texas, Attorney Scheck read all she could
from the online records of the O'Laughlin case. Then
she contacted the "Free Patrick Committee" which was
led by Patrick's former roommate, Arnie Benedict.

She asked him, "Arnie, or do you prefer to be called
Arnold? Why does the committee want to see Patrick
freed?"

" 'Arnie' is good," he answered. "We think Patrick
should be freed because he didn't mean to have the
drone actually fire a weapon."

"How do you know that?" asked Scheck.

"Well, I just know. As Patrick testified at his trial,
he was just trying to scare the City of Dallas and
Texas, and even the United States, into doing
something about gun control. Weirdly, he didn't like
having Co-Popes, either, so scaring them seemed okay,
too. He had created his drone for hunting feral pigs,
which is why it had an infrared sensor on it. But he
didn't want to kill the popes."

Then Arnie introduced Scheck to his wofriend,
Jane Joplin. Mother Scheck thought it curious that
Joplin was Patrick's wofriend before the attack on the
popes and the trial. Also, Arnie told her that he, too,
was skilled with building and flying drones and that he
and Patrick had worked together on the drone involved
in the attack on the popes. Arnie was not asked to
testify at Patrick's trial.

Mother Scheck then traveled to the Coffield State Prison in Tennessee Colony, near Dallas to visit Patrick O'Laughlin. After introductions, she asked him, "Why did you send that drone toward Co-Popes Jesus and Jesusa?"

"Well," began Patrick, "I didn't like the Co-Popes, and don't think they should have been popes, especially the woman. But I didn't plan to hurt them. My plan was to scare them, and maybe then they would resign."

"Did you really think they might resign?" asked Scheck.

"Well, not really. But my other idea was that I was getting sick of too many people having drones and not knowing what they were doing. There have been several crashes recently. We ought to be certified and licensed. I know it sounds funny, because I had drones, but I knew what I was doing, and I needed drones for my work of finding and killing feral pigs for farmers in Texas. Those pigs were ruining lots of cash crops."

"So what's the connection?" asked Scheck.

"Well, I figured that if a drone got close to the Co-Popes, Texas might take seriously the need to regulate them, before somebody got hurt."

"Interesting. Did you explain that to your jury?" asked Scheck.

"Well, I started to, but the damn prosecutor cut me off and said what I was saying was irrevelant, irrelevant, or whatever," said Patrick. He continued, "Then a juror asked a question about what I said by sending a note to the judge, but the judge told the court that he would not allow the question. She said that my political views were not on trial, just my conduct. I think she misunderstood the question. In any case, my lawyer then blew it off, and questioned me about something else."

Attorney Scheck wished that she had been Patrick's attorney at the time, because she would have argued to have Patrick continue that part of his testimony. She asked Patrick, "If you didn't intend to kill the Co-Popes or even hurt them, why do you think the drone fired at them."

Patrick responded, "That's a good question. You might even call it the 64,000 mundo question. I don't know. I didn't push the trigger. At least I didn't think I did, and I had no intention to do that. But when the guns were fired, I panicked and pressed the "crash" button, which shut off the engines and inadvertently sent the drone into the popemobile."

"But you don't know?" asked Scheck, stumped.

"Funny thing was, Arnie and I had talked about installing an automatic firing mechanism, based on the heat of the pigs, but I said it wasn't a good idea, and I wouldn't add such a mechanism to our drone."

"Could Arnie have installed it without your knowing?" asked the priest attorney.

"Well, I asked him that question at some point after the trial, and he said he didn't," said Arnie, with less confidence. "Before the trial, I thought of it, but I assumed that Arnie would have told me, because we were close friends. Then I saw after my trial that Jane didn't move out of our suite with Arnie. She stayed there and hooked up with him. Made me wonder a little."

"What would such a switch look like and what parts would it have had?

"It would be a switch connected to the wires from the pyroelectric crystals of the infared sensor to the videocam. The switch would have a voltage sensor which would be triggered when the infared signals increased, like when the drone got close to the pigs. Come to think of it, that sensor wouldn't have to have gotten as close to the popemobile, because its engine was hot."

"Ok, thanks," said Attorney Scheck. "I'll check with the police and have a look at the remains of the drone in the evidence room."

Mother Scheck then went to the Dallas Police Dept. and met with Lieutenant Friday who was the officer who testified at Patrick's trial about the drone and its capabilities.

Attorney Scheck asked Lt. Josephine Friday, "Were there any parts that you didn't understand or were able to identify?"

"I don't think so, but let's go take another look."

In the evidence room, they spread the pieces out on the table.

"What's in that clear red bag?" asked Scheck.

"Right! I forgot about that," said Lt. Friday. She then said, "There was a voltage sensor with wires to nowhere, which we couldn't figure out."

"Would the wires have been long enough to reach the electronic trigger mechanism of the gun?" asked Attorney Scheck.

"Don't know. Let me check," answered Friday. "First, let's look at the schematic I drew of the reconstructed drone. Okay. Here's the electric trigger and here's the infared sensor. Yup. The wires were long enough."

Then, both women looked carefully at the area around the electronic trigger and found two tiny soldering points, one for each wire.

"Looks like the voltage sensor could have triggered the firing and the voltage sensor responded to the strength of the infared sensor. Never seen anything like this," said Lt. Friday.

"Me neither, of course," said Attorney Scheck. "I'm going to go back to ask Arnie Benedict a few more questions. You could come, but I think it would be better if I went alone. I'll even wear my clerical collar."

Mother Scheck called Arnie and arranged a followup meeting at a local coffee shop that he chose.

Scheck began, "As I mentioned on the phone, I've learned more about the drone since I talked with you yesterday. What can you tell me about an automatic trigger in the drone?"

Arnie struggled to respond. "Okay. You know. I thought we could get through this and get Patrick out of prison without my having to admit what I did. I didn't mean to hurt anyone. I just installed the automatic trigger to show Patrick how it would work with feral pigs. I didn't know that he was going to fly the drone toward the Co-Popes when they came to Dallas. More importantly, I forgot to de-activate the automatic trigger after I installed it. I thought Patrick was going to hunt feral pigs that night, but he didn't. Instead, the next day, he flew it toward the Co-Popes. I guess I'm in trouble now, right?"

Relieved the exoneration of Patrick was in sight, Scheck was sincerely concerned about Arnie's plight and said, "You need to retain an attorney, and he or she should help you to do what's right for you and for Patrick. He should not be in prison. And another thing. What Jane decides to do is important, too. Right now, it looks like you set up Patrick in order to get his wofriend."

"No, that wasn't it at all," responded Arnie. "It's true that I was attracted to her, but my leaving the electronic trigger activated was an accident. I'll be happy to take a polygraph or a polyvoicegraph test. Jane agonized about our relationship, and she went to Patrick to ask for his permission and he said it was okay for her to be with me. He said to her, 'It looks like I'm here for life, despite Arnie's efforts to get me out of here, but you have to move on with your life. If you love Arnie, go for it.' "

With the support of his new attorney, Arnie later took both tests and passed both of them. His attorney contacted the Dallas Prosecutor's Conviction Integrity

Unit and there was a meeting, together with Patrick's lawyer, to discuss the options.

The result was a plea bargain for Patrick to plead guilty to criminal assault for intending to fly his drone close enough to the Co-Popes to scare them. His prison sentence was reduced to time served. Like many people wrongly convicted of crimes they did not commit, Patrick did something wrong, but just not as wrong as the crime for which he was convicted. Unfortunately, by pleading guilty to a felony, he waived any right for compensation for the wrongly convicted. Arnie plead guilty to reckless endangerment and was sentenced to two years of community service.

Upon hearing the news, Jesus and Jesusa called Patrick and Arnie separately and forgave them both.

Said Jesus, "We invite you both to come to Roma at a time of your choosing." They agreed on a visit in two weeks, during which time they would sit down for at least one frank discussion.

In 2071 the Co-Popes traveled to England to celebrate the 25th anniversary of the 2046 reunification of the Roman Catholic and the Anglican Church, together with the U.S. Episcopalian partner. Greeting Jesus and Jesusa at Buckingham Palace was 30-year old Queen Georgiana, who had become queen the previous year upon the abdication of her father, King George VII. Georgiana sought some private spiritual guidance with Jesusa. They went to a private place and the queen asked, "What do you think about inherited titles? Does the practice seem right to you?"

Jesusa answered, "It's an interesting question, as the unusual circumstances of Jesus's and my births was said to have influenced our subsequent election as Co-Popes. It could have been argued that we inherited our positions. In our travels, we have met several monarchs who have indicated their discomfort with their inherited status. A few years after our 2045 world tour visit to Thailand, the queen there abdicated, but made her abdication conditional upon the abolition by the Thai parliament of the monarchy. What do you think?"

Georgiana thought for a moment and then answered, "Inherited status doesn't seem right to me, and being selected at birth for a position in the government, even if not as large a role as it used to be, seems unfair. The status we inherit should be equal to everyone else. Also, this really isn't the kind of work I want to do. I could abdicate, but that would just leave the problem for someone else to resolve. If you look at the course of history, it's easy to see where the future of monarchy is going – nowhere."

Jesusa responded, "It sounds like you know what you should do. Here's the private phone number of the former Thai queen, Suvahana. Maybe you would want to call her. Good luck. We should now rejoin the others."

Jesus and Jesusa, and Queen Georgiana participated in the 25th anniversary service at Canterbury Cathedral, which was conducted by Archbishop Chad Mercia.

Over the next few years, Pope Jesusa and Queen Georgiana talked by phone about the issue of a monarchy and in April, 2076, Queen Georgiana told Jesusa of her plan, which was very similar to that executed by Thai Queen Suvahana in 2048. Later that year, she had several discussions of her plan with her family, including her father, the former King George VII, who disagreed strongly with the plan, and with Prime Minister Diana Thatcher. Queen Georgiana scheduled an address to the nation for July 4, 2076.

She said to the people of the United Kingdom, "It is time to recognize the truth of what the American colonists told us 300 years ago in 1776, that all people are created equal, and there can be no exception for a few families blessed to inherit titles and countries. Therefore, I am today announcing my plan to abdicate as Queen next April 23, 2077, St. George's Day, conditional upon the enactment of legislation by the Parliament to abolish the monarchy and our system of nobility. Over the next several months, I am confident that Prime Minister Thatcher's government and I will work out a reasonable path forward on these matters."

Jesus and Jesusa were impressed by Queen Georgiana's determination which led to the end of the British monarchy in 2077. She and her husband, still in their 30s, went to work for the World Wildlife Fund.

The Co-Popes continued their reigns but at a slower pace. The major reforms were over, but the continued decline in the numbers of priests and, more importantly, members or congregants in the Catholic Church, forced the Co-Popes to be in forever downsizing mode. It was not a happy process. They were in reasonable health, but it was time for a new generation of leaders for the Church.

Finally, in May, 2083 they announced that they would resign the next year on May 30, 2084, which would be their 70th birthday. At that time, their 40 year reigns would be the longest in Church history. Until the Pope Benedictus XVI resignation in 2013, there had not been a papal resignation since Pope Gregorius XII in 1415. That resignation came after he convened the Council of Constance which ended the Avignon Exile. Thus, in the last 500 years, there had been only three resignations before those of Jesus and Jesusa, with all of them in the 21st century: Pope Benedictus XVI in 2013, Pope Francesco I in 2026, and Pope Francesco II in 2044.

At the recommendation of Co-Popes Jesus and Jesusa, the College of Cardinals elected Cardinal Susanna Bakhita of Sudan as Pope. She earned the respect of Pope Francesco II and her peer cardinals with her successful efforts to bring equality for women in Africa and the complete ability and right to control their reproduction. This work included reaching consensus with the Muslims to whom she brought the message from the Qur'an that Islam supports families, and that the best families come when parents want children and less to when they arrive by accident. She cited the statement from the Qur'an, "You should not kill your children for fear of want"[2] and interpreted that as meaning that good Muslims prevented children from being conceived where they could not be properly fed, educated and loved. This approach was most effective with poor Muslims. Rich Muslims needed no religious affirmation, as they were already having smaller, less than replacement size, families for other reasons. Most importantly, Cardinal Bakhita did not preach this message directly to Muslims. Instead she met with women of all faiths and together they developed consensus that was said to arise from all the religions of Africa. Afterwards, the messages were communicated by social networks and other people-to-people media.

Pope Bakhita became the first unitary woman pope and the first from Africa.

2. Qur'an (17:31, 6:151)

Chapter 9 Aging and Death

Jesus and Jesusa retired as popes emerita to their childhood home in Salerno. Their parents, Giuseppe and Maria, had died a few years earlier and the twins inherited their home. Giuseppe died of pneumonia in 2076 at the age of 97. Called "the poor man's friend" because it delivers a dignified painless death to its sufferers, pneumonia came at the time that Giuseppe was becoming bedridden due to arthritis and related joint and bone ailments. Always an active man, Giuseppe had long agreed with Maria that he did not want to live as a burden to others, and especially to his wife.

Maria continued for three more years, with failing health. She had stated to her children that she wanted to live to be 100, but that was enough. Three months after her 100th birthday in 2078, Maria died with the assistance of her doctor and a humane dosage of drugs. She drank the medicines and said to Jesus and Jesusa, "Good-bye and thank you. You have made me very proud. I love you both."

After their mother's death, Jesus and Jesus kept the family home and used it for occasional vacations, until their retirement in 2084. It was modest, but more comfortable for them than the vast papal retreat at Castel Gandolfo, to which Pope Benedictus XVI had retired. Pope Francesco I had returned to Argentina to his former home, and Pope Francesco II retired to Tanzania.

Although their energy was diminished, they still tried to respond to the requests for help from inmates claiming wrongful conviction. The letters from Italian inmates were referred to the Italia Innocence Project at the Universita degli Studi di Milano, and the others were referred to the Global Innocence Network (GIN) which was headquartered in New York. Fortunately, the numbers of such requests were declining as the estimated percentage of wrongful convictions was close to the Great Transformation Organization goal of .1%.

As was the experience of other cloned mammals, the bodies of Jesus and Jesusa declined faster than others, after the age of approximately 65. Earlier in their lives, they made a pact to leave this world together, just as they had come into the world together. If they had a choice, and were not otherwise taken by accident or paralyzing disease or assassination, they would commit suicide together. In March, 2089, Jesus had a stroke, causing a fall in the garden and he was partially paralyzed. In April, Jesusa was diagnosed with a new form of dementia, i.e. one that defied the previously developed cures for Alzheimer's disease and other related illnesses.

They knew their time to die was coming, and it did not scare them. They decided to take their lives on their 75th birthday, on May 30, 2089, in the presence of their closest friends. Jesusa would quote one of her heroines, Charlotte Perkins Gilman, who wrote in her own suicide note 154 years earlier, "It is the simplest of human rights to choose a quick and easy death in place of a slow and horrible one."

Instead of using a helium "exit bag" which imposed some obligation on those accompanying suicides during their last moments, Jesus and Jesusa chose to drink a suicide medicine in their bedroom. With the help of a doctor, and the previous successful experiences of millions around the world, they chose red wine with codeine, pentobartitol, and seconal.

They toasted each other and their friends, and then "to the eternal survival and goodness of humanity." Pursuant to the requests of Jesus and Jesusa in their wills, their bodies were cremated at the solar crematorium in Salerno and their ashes were combined. The co-mingled ashes were then taken to the Vaticano and entombed in the Sacristry together with most of their predecessor popes and not far from the "Holy Prepuce," formerly of Calcata.

Chapter 10 Post Script

Elvira Sediva, attorney, and the executor of the estate of Alessandro Galvani, had heard the rumors that Jesus and Jesusa would commit suicide at some symbolic time. Working as an attorney in Salerno, Elvira knew much about the twins, but her interest in the retired co-popes became more focused in 2076 upon the death of her client, Alessandro Galvani.

Galvani had created a "Last Testament" as part of his will and it was to be communicated to the executors of the estates of Jesus and Jesusa upon their deaths, and later to the public. Galvani's last statement read as follows:

> In 2013, I was a member of the team of five scientists, headed by Professor Angelo Pappalardo, which created the two cloned embryos which were implanted into the womb of Maria Prescelto of Salerno in August of that year. Her two children, Jesus and Jesusa Prescelto, were born on May 30, 2014.
>
> As a member of the team, I was devoted to its success. We were competing with other universities for prominence and for grants from international foundations.
>
> The team extracted DNA from the "Holy Prepuce" and my fellow team members were optimistic that the DNA could be successfully altered to produce a male and female being after being inserted into two donor ova. However, I was very confident that the procedure would fail. Therefore, at a critical time, I substituted my own stem cells to the

project before the gender differentiation stage. Their nuclei were successfully implanted into the two ova, and the nuclei of the donor eggs were removed.

The team was surprised at its success and I was criticized at the time for my pessimism. In fact, I wanted the project to succeed for the institutional reasons mentioned above, but also because I was hopeful that the resulting human beings would be helpful in improving the world. Regarding that latter goal, my hopes were greatly exceeded.

Jesus and Jesusa are excellent co-popes and have done much to save humanity from itself and I didn't want to do or say anything during their lifetimes which would impair their work to move the world to a more reason-based level. When asked, they always tried to deflect questions about their origin, and preferred to restate that they were humans, born of humans. As they chose not to reproduce themselves, there are no children which would be affected by my posthumous revelation of the truth about their origin.

This statement is also about the truth of the science of cloning humans. The truth is that our "Salerno team" did not successfully clone a human using the DNA of a 2,000 year old fragment of skin.

Date: July 6, 2063
Alessandro Galvani /s/

In early June, 2089, a few days after the deaths of Jesus and Jesusa, Attorney Sediva hand-carried

Alessandro Galvani's "Last Testament" to the executors of the estates of Jesus and Jesusa. The executors and Sediva worked on a joint public statement which was released a month later. The release stated,

"It has come to our attention that the circumstances of the births of Jesus and Jesusa were not as they and their parents were told 52 years ago upon their graduation from Universitat Heidelberg. The human cells from which their embryos came were actually from a member of the team of scientists which was working on the cloning project. His name was Alessandro Galvani, and his "Last Testament" is attached to this release. He died in 2069, and by the terms of his will, he mandated that his statement be released only after latter of the deaths of Jesus and Jesusa, without knowing, of course, that they would die on the same day.

All their lives, Jesus and Jesusa distanced themselves from the claims of their origin and, instead, proclaimed themselves humans born of humans, like everyone else.

We believe that this new information changes nothing about the work of Jesus and Jesusa to improve the world and assist in the Great Transformation of the role of humans on Earth from agents of destruction to participants in rebirth and equilibrium."

The sky did not fall when the truth became known around the globe in seconds. Most of the people in the increasingly sophisticated world knew that there was something amiss with the nearly miraculous story. However, belief in the births cloned from the Holy Prepuce did not hamper the work of Jesus and Jesusa, and even contributed to their sense of humor and perspective.

Afterword: The Global Impact of the book, *Jesus and Jesusa*

The novella, *Jesus and Jesusa*, changed the course of world history in ways reminiscent of other books, such as the *Communist Manifesto, On the Origin of Species, Uncle Tom's Cabin,* and *Silent Spring.*

By reading this novella, which showed what could happen in the world from 2014 onward, the realm of the possible was opened for humanity to see, and it paved the way for progressive change.

For more information, see the summary of the 2093 Ph.D. Thesis of Charlotte Amalie Perkins, The Global Social and Political Impact of the Utopian Novella *Jesus and Jesusa* as presented in Appendix B of the book, *2121,* by Morrison Bonpasse, to be published in 2014. *2121* is a utopian novel about the world through 2121 A.D. as it should be or could be.

2121

Morrison Bonpasse

BonPasse Exoneration Services
(a Maine non-profit corporation)
P.O. Box 390
Newcastle, ME 04553 USA
001-207-586-6078
Morrison Bonpasse, Executive Director
morrison@bonpasseexonerationservices.org
www.bonpasseexonerationservices.org

2121

Morrison Bonpasse

ISBN-10 0-9837985-7-5
ISBN-13 978-0-9837985-7-6

TABLE OF CONTENTS

FOREWORD (2014)

2121 is a utopian novel in the sense that it presents the view that humans are capable of being civilized to each other, and being beneficial custodians for the Earth. Written also as a history "looking backward" from the year 2121, it presents not a life of perfection, but, to use the State of Maine slogan of the early 21st century, "The Way Life Should Be." Another commonplace definition of a utopia might come from selected lines from John Lennon's 1971 song, "Imagine."

> Imagine there is no heaven
> No hell below us
> Above us only sky
> Imagine there's no countries
> Nothing to kill or die for
> And no religion, too
> Imagine all the people
> Living life in peace
> Imagine no possessions
> No need for greed or hunger
> A brotherhood of man
> Imagine all the people
> Sharing all the world

More formally, the book meets the definition in *The Utopia Reader* by Gregory Claeys and Lyman Tower Sargent of a "eutopia" or "positive utopia." That is, it's a "utopia that the author intended a contemporaneous reader to view as considerably better than the society in which the reader lived." The Greek meaning of "Eutopia" is "good place," from the parts, "eu" for good and "topia" for place.

Since the publication in 1516 of Sir Thomas More's *Utopia*, an ideal image of utopia has developed that is more heavenly and dreamlike, with such characteristics as human immortality and 100% happiness and contentment. Today, to say that something is "utopian" is to say that it is unrealistic or impossible. However, More's *Utopia* was realistic and had several elements which recognized humanity's limitations, such as enslavement of foreigners and criminals and discouragement of atheism.

People in the books, *Jesus and Jesusa* and *2121,* are represented as being similar to people today, just as if an historical figure such as Thomas Jefferson were transplanted into the 21st century. He would fit right in, just as Julian West was quickly acclimated when he awoke in 2000 in Edward Bellamy's *Looking Backward* after 113 years of sleep in his Boston bed.

Humanity in both books has successfully, but not perfectly, responded to its two primary challenges: global warming and nuclear proliferation. If we humans do not imitate art, as expressed in these books, and respond to the challenges facing humanity, we may destroy ourselves and our planet either slowly through global warming, or rapidly by intentional or unintentional nuclear explosions.

Most of the events and international agreements mentioned in *2121,* and in the referenced forward- looking novella, *Jesus and Jesusa*, should occur someday, or the human race will be doomed to a lesser existence.

The novella, *Jesus and Jesusa,* is published in 2014 as the first of a two-book combination with the novel, *2121.* Written also as a utopian history, *Jesus and Jesusa* can be read separately but it's recommended that both books be read in sequence.

I conclude with the closing words of B.F. (Burrhus Frederic) Skinner's preface to the 1976 paperback edition of *Walden Two*:

It is now widely recognized that great changes must be made in the American way of life. Not only can we not face the rest of the world while consuming and polluting as we do, we cannot for long face ourselves while acknowledging the violence and chaos in which we live. The choice is clear: either we do nothing and allow a miserable and probably catastrophic future to overtake us, or we use our knowledge about human behavior to create a social environment in which we shall live productive and creative lives and do so without jeopardizing the chances that those who follow us will be able to do the same.
Something like a *Walden Two* would not be a bad start.

Something like the worlds described in *2121* and *Jesus and Jesusa* would not be a bad start either.

EDITOR'S NOTE (2121)

Names of People and Places

Since 2014, many new words have been introduced into English primarily because of the decision of the Global English Standards Organization (GESO) in 2025 to use the native, local or real spellings of names of people and places. GESO was established by the United Nations in 2018. If the native language didn't use the Latin alfabet, then the best transliteration was used, rather than a translation. With this rule, speakers of other languages could say the name of a place and it would sound to natives almost the same as if spoken in the native language. This usage is intended to respect the integrity of the named people and places. For many or most of the native or real names, the change is barely noticeable, such as Vaticano, and Italia. To assist the reader where the sounds are different, such as for "Deutschland," the names in English are footnoted in the text at their first appearance with their 2014 English names, i.e. "Germany."

Global English Spelling as used in book.

With one exception, the English spelling used in *2121* does not comply with the reforms of the Global English Standards Organization (GESO) as have been thus far implemented in 20 year increments since the establishment of the organization by the United Nations in 2018. The exception is that the 2060 reform, of converting "ph" to "f" when appropriate and not in proper names, is implemented in the text as an occasional reminder to the reader of the book's deviation from English Standard usage in 2121. Otherwise, the spelling in the book is a reminder to current readers of what English looked like to people in the 20th/early 21st century.   These reforms are summarized below in chronological order.

2020, short 'e'

All instances of the sound of the short 'e' as in the word 'bet' shall be spelled with an 'e'. This change was part of the reform known as Spelling Reform 1 as proposed by Australian/British linguist Harry Lindgren. It was adopted in the mid-20th century in Australia, but abandoned.
Examples:
a as in   any to eny
ai as in   said to sed, against to agenst
ea as in   read to redy, breath to breth, measure to mesure, wealth to welth
ei as in   heifer to hefer
eo as in   jeopardy to jepardy
ie as in   friend to frend
u as in   bury to bery
ue as in   guess to gess

2040, drop useless 'e'

Dropped Useless Es (DUE). By this rule, the letter e is dropped from words where it is unneeded or misleading. For example, this means dropping the 'e' at the end of the word 'have' but not at the end of 'behave,' because the 'e' is necessary to make the a sound longer, as in 'bay.'
Examples:
are to ar. were to wer, give to giv, have to hav, some to som, freeze to freez, sleeve to sleev
valley to vally, achieve to achiev
examine to examin, practise to practis, opposite to opposit, involve to involv, heart to hart.
minute to minut, but keep minute when meaning is "small."

2060, 'ph' to 'f'

All occurrences of 'ph' wer to be changed to 'f,' when that was the intended sound.
Examples:
photo to foto
telephone to telefone
physical to fysical

2080 – 'gh' to 'au', 'u', or 'af' or delete

Shorten 'augh' to 'au' when it is pronounced as in the following examples:

caught to caut, fraught to fraut, daughter to dauter.

Shorten 'ough' to 'ou' when it is pronounced as in the following examples:

bough to bou, drought to drout, plough to plou.

Change 'ough' to 'au' when it is pronounced as in the following examples:

bought to baut, ought to aut, thought to thaut.

Change 'ough' to 'of' or 'uf' (depending on pronunciation) when there is the sound for 'f.'

cough to cof, enough to enuf, tough to tuf.

Change 'augh' to 'af' when it is pronounced as 'f' as in the following examples:

laugh to laf, draught to draft.

Shorten 'ough' to 'u' when it is pronounced as in the following examples:

through to thru.

Shorten 'ough' to 'o' when it is pronounced as in the following examples:

though to tho, although to altho, but doh for dough in order to distinguish   from do, as in 'to do.'

2100 – 'ou' to 'o'

Change 'ou' to 'o' when it is pronounced in the following examples:

colour to color, flavour to flavor, harbour to harbor

However, the spelling of 'ou' is unchanged, wherever the 'ou' is pronounced as in the following examples:

contour, velour, paramour and troubadour

2120 – 're' to 'er'

Change 're' to 'er' when pronounced as in the following examples:

calibre to caliber, centre to center, fibre to fiber, litre to liter

2140 'ce' and 'se' (FUTURE)

When words with alternate spellings with 'c' and 's' are homofones, use 'c' for the noun forms and 's' for the verb forms.

Examples:
as nouns: advice, device, licence, practice,
as verbs: advise, devise, license, practise

Otherwise
defense, offense, pretense

2160 'ise' and 'yse' (FUTURE)

Standardize the formerly distinct United States usages of 'yze' and 'ize' to the British version of 'yse' and 'ise'

Change 'yze' to 'yse' as in the following examples:

analyze to analyse, catalyze to catalyse, paralyze to paralyse

Change 'ize' to 'ise' as in the following examples:

organize to organise, organization to organisation.

List of Characters

(Dates are dates of birth unless followed by a hyfen and a date of death.)

Primary Characters

Delano, Chad Forbes - Son of Forbes Franklin Delano & Charlotte Amalie Perkins. 2097

Delano, Forbes Franklin - Father of Charlotte Perkins and Chad Delano. 2069

Grant, Melissa - Wofriend (womanfriend) of Chad Forbes. 2098

Kinselli, Elena Bronte - Mother of Charlotte Amalie Perkins. 2045

Kinselli, Emily Stone - Twin sister of Charlotte Perkins. 2068

Perkins, Eleanor Kinselli - Daughter of Forbes Franklin Delano and Charlotte Amalie Perkins. 2094

Perkins, Charlotte Amalie – (born as Charlotte Amalie Kinselli) Mother of Eleanor Perkins and Chad Delano. 2068

Persepolis, Giorgios Marios - Father of Charlotte Amalie Perkins. 2035

Grant, Michelle - Sister of Melissa Grant. 2100-2121

Trenkler, Maximilian - Manfriend and later husband of Eleanor Perkins. 2094

Wen, Xue - Wofriend of Michelle Grant. 2101

Malaga, Anita Malaga - Wofriend of Juan Carlos, and friend of Melissa Grant

Morales, Juan Carlos - Manfriend of Anita Malaga. 2097-2117

Other characters

Armstrong, Robert - Portland police detective.

Armstrong, Alan Yuri - Astronaut on Moon, together with Liu Sally Yang.

Bailey, Matthew - Cumberland County (Portland, Maine) prosecutor.

Bligh, Christiana - Astronaut, Leader of Mars City, later UtopiaDos.

Blount, Joshua – High school boyfriend and later, husband of Emily Kinselli.

Borenstein, Jacob - Second judge in Chad's state criminal case.

Bradford, Carla Nadeau - Judge at Chad's state criminal case.

Camerada, Laurel – Astronaut on moon during year 2113.

Chavez, Maria – President of the United States, 2117-2125.

Chou, Madeleine – Juror at Chad's trial.

Cook, Cory – police informant.

Corcoran, Tate - Maine Supreme Court judge.

Curie, Nkiru – 2120 astronaut to Mars with Eleanor Perkins and Max Trenkler

Delano, Phillip Warren (later, Philippe De la Noye) - Father of Forbes Franklin Delano.   2031

Delano, Samuel James - Father of Phillip Warren Delano.   2007-2097

Donato, Guglielmo Donato - Cardinal in Vaticano.

Evans, Chad – Good Samaritan in Portland

Gutereise, Wilhelm, - Private investigator in Deutschland

Horton, Robert William – Wrongly convicted of
    burglary in Massachusetts in 2115.

Kline, Angela - Portland police detective.

Lavrov, Amanda - Head of MaineDrug office,
    Portland, Maine.

Marat, Francois – Astronaut on Mars.

Marquis, Donna - U.S. District Court judge,
    Portland

McKelvy, Nina - Chad's attorney.

Mundell, Keith - Friend of Chad Delano

Ondimba, Adisa – 2120 astronaut to Mars with
    Eleanor Perkins and Max Trenkler

Palino, Sarah – Republican candidate for President,
    2120.

Perkins, Elizabeth Alden - Daughter of Eleanor
    Perkins and Max Trenkler 2121

Perkins, Nancy Jay - Daughter of Eleanor Perkins
    and Max Trenkler 2121

Porter, Dorothy – classmate of Eleanor at Brown
    University

Sagan, Carla – Professor of astrofysics at Brown
    University

Sutton, Willie – Manfriend of burglary victim in
    Massachusetts in 2115.

Svensen, Sofie - Attorney for Michelle Grant.

Swayze, Cameron - Private Investigator, Maine

Valesio, Elisa – Resident of Pisa, with acquired
    savant syndrome

Yang, Liu Sally - Astronaut on Moon, together with
    Alan Yuri Armstrong

Chronology

2014 Publication of *Jesus and Jesusa*

2019 Nuclear Explosion at Brownsville, Texas/Matamoros, Tamaulipas

2020 Pope Francesco I issues five encyclicals.

2022 Peace Treaty among Israel and neighbors.

2023 Maldives Action Plan

2026 Adoption of Single Global Currency: the eartha.

2032 Last execution on Earth of a criminal.

2045 United Nations adopts Global Inequality Convention.

2048 Vatican Council III.

2057 Pope Isabella, first woman pope, elected.

2093 Ph.D. dissertations of Forbes Delano and Charlotte Perkins.

2094 Eleanor Kinselli Perkins born.

2097 Chad Forbes Delano born.

2120 Eleanor Perkins and Max Trenkler, and Adisa Ondimba and Nkiru Curie travel to Mars.

2121 Resolution of Chad Delano case; births of Elizabeth and Nancy Perkins.

CHAPTER 1   An Unintentional Death

Judge Carla Bradford asked, "Has the jury reached a verdict in the case of Maine vs. Chad Delano? The jurors all nodded up and down, and a faint, unenthusiastic "yes/uh huh" was heard. Prompted by the judge, the foreperson rose to state that "We, the jury, find the defendant, Chad Forbes Delano, guilty of chemical manslaughter, as charged, beyond any doubt, for the death of Juan Carlos Morales on January 1st, 2117."

This case began on New Year's Eve, Tuesday, December 31, 2116 when 24-year old Chad Forbes Delano and his wofriend, Melissa Grant, were celebrating the New Year's Day holiday[1] at Chad's Portland, Maine apartment with Melissa's sister, Michelle, and her wofriend, Xue Wen. Also there were Juan Carlos Morales and his wofriend, Anita Malaga, who worked with Michelle.

"Why did you have to invite Juan and Anita?" demanded Chad, of Melissa, when he learned of the invitation the previous week.

"They had no other plans. Sorry. My sister asked. That's all," she responded. "I know you don't much care for Juan, but I thought ...."

The guests arrived around 8 p.m. They sat in the living room around the fireplace, in which the electric flame glowed and waved. There had not been a real fire in that fireplace since the 2033 symbolic celebration of the end of most fire, i.e.

---

1. New Year's Day is one of five international holidays pursuant to the 2040 International Holiday Standards Convention. The others are Earth Day, on the third Friday of April, Election Day on the 2nd Monday of June, World Population Day on the 2nd Monday of July, and Peace Day on the 2nd Friday of November. By this convention, member countries agreed to limit their national holidays to five.

combustion, on the Earth.[2] This was only known to Chad and his guests because of the plaque above the mantelpiece. Chad read the text to the group, and their collective response was, "Wow. Who knew?"

Even by that early date, 2033, most fireplaces were obsolete. In 2023, 50 United Nations members ratified Maldives Action Plan(MAP), with was an update of the 1992 Rio Summit Agreement. The Maldives is an island nation southwest of India with an average land elevation of 1.5 meters above sea level. Thus, it's a country substantially threatened by the rising sea levels arising from melting ice caps due to global warming. The Maldives Action plan presented the goal that the concentration of carbon dioxide(CO_2) in the atmosfere would be brought back to 3.0 parts per million by the year 2123. This was approximately the level before the Industrial Revolution which was powered primarily by the burning of fossil fuels. This reduction would be achieved by dramatic reductions, and then elimination, of the burning of fossil fuels together with reductions of all other burning. There were to be significant reforestation programs and projects to sequester carbon dioxide into carbon and bury it, returning it to where it had been for centuries. A significant energy breakthrough came with the development in 2046

2. Edward Bellamy had predicted in his 1888 utopian book, *Looking Backward*, that the chimneys in Boston had disappeared by 2000 because the "crude method of combustion on which you depended for heat had become obsolete." (page 24, Feather Trail Press Edition, 2009) While most of the old pre-2023 chimneys of Portland and Boston were still standing in 2117, the old furnaces were long gone. Still, Bellamy came very close, to predicting the actual chimney-less and furnace-less world that emerged after the 2027 harnessing of fusion.

of an electrically powered process to convert carbon dioxide into the miracle substance, grafene, which is composed entirely of carbon atoms.

Similarly, the MAP sought the reduction of methane levels to pre-Industrial Revolution levels. Though the concentration of methane was less than carbon dioxide, it was 20 times more damaging to the environment because it absorbed more solar radiation. Methane occurs naturally, but it's a primary ingredient of natural gas, and vast amounts of methane were leaked during the 20th and 21st centuries' exploitation of natural gas. The other primary human-related source was the manure of domestic animals raised for food in the 20th and 21st centuries. By the end of the 21st century, both those sources were substantially reduced. The natural release of methane from wetlands was accelerated by global warming itself because of the thawing of millions of square kilometers of frozen tundra.

Prior to the introduction of Solar-POwered Catalytic Conversion (SPOCC) of methane (CH_4) into its constituent five parts (one carbon atom and four hydrogen atoms), the breakdown of methane occurred only through natural processes in the soil and atmosfere. The hydrogen by-product of the SPOCC process was thereafter used in hydrogenfusion("hydrofusion") electric plants and the carbon was converted into grafene.

The Maldives Action Plan also reconfirmed the goal that post-Industrial Revolution global warming should not exceed the goal of 2 degrees Celsius, but the world was, by then, 2023, perilously close to that mark.

It was well-known at the time of the ratification of the Maldives Action Plan that simply allowing wood to decay naturally released the same amounts of CO_2 as occurred by burning. However, it was felt that the symbolism was important, so the burning of renewables became part of the campaign to eliminate the burning of fossil fuels. Also, even when trees which are cut for wood burning are replaced, it still takes years for the replacement trees to grow large enough to consume as much CO_2 as the former trees, cut for burning were previously consuming. Today, the burning of wood or any other non-fossilized material requires a permit, and permits are allocated to countries according to a CO_2 quota system. That quota system was further linked to the global carbon tax which was assessed to every company or organization which burned fossil fuels.

Old-fashioned cremations with wood or naturl gas were permitted if solar cremations were not available. Solar cremations with their temperatures of 700-1000°C were faster and cheaper, and saved the burning of 200-300 kg of wood or 200 liters of propane.

Increased burning of wood might be permitted again when the CO_2 level reaches the equilibrium level of 3.0 per million and remains there for several years.

The symbolism of the wood burning restrictions, despite the net zero effect on CO_2, was also seen in other global restrictions. Despite the development of synthetic gas (syn-gas) in the 2020s and the resulting liberation from crude oil and its derivatives, professional automobile racing was restricted to electric vehicles. These vehicles were powered by a combination of fuel cells and solar cells which created electricity to run the electric motor drives. The Indianapolis 500[3] converted to

3. After the U.S. converted to the metric system in 2040, it was decided to keep the distance of the race the same, i.e. 804.67 kilometers, but continue to call it the "500."

electric cars in 2027 which meant that this year's running of the race would be the 90th electric race. All NASCAR (National Association for Stock Car Auto Racing) was restricted in 2030 to electric and other non-CO_2-producing technologies.

The Maldives Action Plan anticipated the development of nearly unlimited fusion-powered electricity which was made possible by the subsequent 2027 breakthrough at the Cadarache facility of the ITER (International Thermonuclear Experimental Reactor) in France. The by-products of hydrogen fusion included tritium and helium, and neither was radioactive.

The Maldives was admitted to the United Nations in 1965, after nearly 80 years as a British protectorate. As a part of U.N. history, the country is significant because of its threshold status as the smallest nation not asked to merge with others according to the 2027 U.N. Membership Consolidation Convention. The 21 countries with populations less than the Maldives' 310,000 were asked to merge with other member countries by the end of 2030. Among the 21 was the smallest, Tuvalu, in the Pacific Ocean midway between Hawaii and Australia with a population of 10,000. That country chose to merge it U.N. representation into that of New Zealand. The other countries requiring member partners included several Caribbean nations. The movement toward that convention arose after the 2015 admission of Palestine as the 194th U.N. member nation. During its history, several nations had arisen, such as Ukraine, and disappeared, such as the Soviet Union. Others had merged with one another, such as Deutschland and Ost-Deutschland, and Tanganyika and Zanzibar. After the consolidation of the 21 by 2030, the number of U.N. members would settle at 173.

The conversation at Chad's party was awkward, starting with clothes and the weather.

"That's a nice combination, Xue," said Melissa, referring to the colors of Xue's pants and collarless shirt. Everyone at the party wore pants, as skirts and dresses were abandoned long ago, as relics of the male-predator, female-prey game. The informal SAR (skin area ratio) code required that the clothing of men and women should have about the same ratio of exposed skin to covered skin. A clothing manufacturer which produced clothes which were substantially exposing more skin of women or men ran the risk of being labeled as sexist and then being boycotted or sued or both. While accepting the SAR code, 21st century men found it awkward or ridiculous to purchase clothes which showed more of their legs or their chests, so the burden of the movement toward equality was on the women's side. That is, more changes were made with women's clothes, and they stopped baring legs and chests. Gone, too were the women's v-neck lines and other gimmicks to exploit men's seemingly instinctive reflex to follow the lines of the clothes to explore the outlines of women's breasts. The SAR code put a stop to that absurdity. Men and women knew what was underneath the clothes of those to whom they were attracted, and the ease of sexual relationships made obsolete the skin exposure game which was forced upon women. In the warmer climates and warmer months everywhere, men and women wore bathing suits, shorts, T-shirts and other high SAR clothes, but each gender wore them with about equal frequency.

The movement toward unisex clothes with a bias for traditionally men's clothes was balanced by a trend toward more colorful clothing, especially for men. Gone for the stylish men were black or white socks, which were replaced by socks which matched the colors of pants and shirts. In many animal species, e.g. peacocks, the male is the colorful gender.

Leading the way to equality of appearance was the near-50:50 ratio of tattoos on men and women, proving in color that human decoration was not just a feminine virtue or requirement.

The abandonment of skirts and dresses also led to the near disappearance of high-heeled shoes for women, as there was no longer pressure to show the shapes of their legs. Furthering that trend in shoes was the Global Health Initiative which found that high-heeled shoes were unsafe and should no longer be sold. Women were also liberated from the need to shave their legs and underarms. Men didn't; why should women?

Once the desire for equality of appearance took hold, other changes came, such as the reduction of the disparity between the amount of makeup worn by women compared to that of men. While some men began to wear more makeup, the clear trend was toward less makeup for women.

With jewelry, the approach to equality was more evenly weighted. Men have always worn rings and some armbands, necklaces and watches, which made the transformation easier. However, earrings for pierced ears were not popular with men, and their use by women declined after the Global Mutilation Convention grouped ear piercings with genital mutilation and circumcision.

Xue responded to Melissa's compliment, "Thanks, Xue. Michelle picked the colors."

"What's with the lack of snow? asked Anita. "I thought the Global Warming thing had turned around."

"Not for a while," said Melissa, who worked at the Waste Monitoring Division of the University of Maine's climate lab. "The return to pre-Industrial Revolution temperatures probably won't come until long after we are gone. The group in the office next to mine is up to date on that stuff. In my division, we keep track of the efforts to reduce the amounts of waste dumped into the oceans. There are two parts of that work. First, we enforce the U.S. and global rules for solid waste disposal for everything we humans use and discard. Everything is recycled to the maximum extent possible, and that recycling is funded by the 5-20% "external impact tax" (EIT) on every non-biodegradable object sold in the world. The less and slower degradable, the higher is the tax. Second, our office is the northeast U.S. regional center for ocean cleanup. In addition to the annual Atlantic coastal cleanup, we have four Scooper Ships which cross-cross the north Atlantic ocean retrieving non-degraded objects and particles, usually plastic. Would you believe that before our program was initiated in 2055, through the U.N. Global Ocean Waste Convention (GOWC) of that year, there were approximately 10,000-1 million waste particles of debris per square kilometer of ocean, around the world? There are five ocean areas in the world like ours in the North Atlantic, and each of them has four to five scooper ships. That waste is the result of hundreds of years of dumping of millions of tonnes[4] of discarded materials every year into the oceans and rivers. The collected debris of the scooper ships is then brought to Portland for recycling or solid waste disposal. Thanks to the work of those scooper ships over the past 60 years, the density of debris

---

4. A tonne, or metric ton, is 1,000 kilograms. It is also called a megagram, and is equivalent to 2,204.62 pounds.

has declined to about 7,500 particles per square kilometer, which is about the level last seen in the 2000's after the crest of the now-historic "Age of Plastics."

"Hmm," said Xue with mild irritation, "that reminds me of Trivial Pursuit. Let's play."

All agreed, and they moved to the game table. Then, the food was brought out: solar-dried chips, guacamole, afish (short for artificial fish or faux-fish), ameat (short for artificial meat or faux-meat), solar-dried fruits, and non-fat cheese. The afish was, more specifically, afish-salmon and the ameat was afish-chicken. These products were manufactured in biofactories using a process starting with natural stem cells of the desired meat or fish. While none of the partygoers had eaten real salmon or chicken in a long time, they had recalled that the asalmon and achicken tasted the same as their real counterparts. In the mid-21st century, in order to reduce the burdens on the environment and in the interest of treating animals fairly, people moved away from killing animals for food. Natural fish and meat were still available, but very expensive to harvest and it was taxed at a higher rate than ameat and afish. Veganism, with some flexibility at the edges which permitted the eating of products of animals such as eggs and milk and the eating of shellfish, had become the dominant food orientation of the planet. Not everyone had made the transition in all countries, but eaters of natural meat and fish were a diminishing and less healthy minority. They were to vegans as smokers were to non-smokers in the early 21st century.

The group played "Trivial Pursuit" for three hours. They were using a special "100 years of Trivial Pursuit" edition which Chad's father purchased in 2082. The questions in this game focused on the period of those first 100 years. The three teams were tied at the last round, close to midnight, when Chad and Melissa selected "Disasters." His question was, "Where was the world's last nuclear explosion, which occurred in 2019?" As there had been publicity about the 100th year commemoration of that tragedy coming in two years, Chad answered correctly with "Brownsville, Texas." Matamoros, in the Mexican state of Tamaulipas would also have been a correct answer. For 50 extra points, the question was "To the nearest 100,000, how many people died on both sides of the border within the first year of that explosion?" Melissa thought it might be 200,000, but guessed 400,000. The correct answer was 500,000, (actually 523,467) so no extra points were awarded.

"It's hard to believe," said Melissa, "that people were so careless and short sighted about the control and security of radioactive stuff." She and her sister, Michelle, had seen the documentary movie, "Brownsville Bomb," about the disaster. Michelle added, "Did you know that the people who tried to bring the truck with the bomb across the border were actually headed for Washington, D.C.?"

The Brownsville Bomb was one of the most important events of the 21st century. Together with a utopian book, *Jesus and Jesusa,* which was published in 2014, it triggered what was later known as the "Great Transformation," which was the global change in human values which accelerated after the explosion. Finally, after ignoring global warming warnings for years, and after not doing enough about the proliferation of nuclear weapons, the Brownsville Bomb jolted the world into acting proactively to save itself and to make the world a better place. Finally, after centuries of moralists urging more concern about the welfare of others, and less concern about personal wealth and consumption, the beliefs of the people of the world took a turn in ways that surprised many observers.

A global mantra and acronym emerged, NOME, for the Espanol expression, "NO Mas Estupido," ("No More Stupid"). The term was pronounced in English as "No May" which sounded like "No Me." Then it was repeated, "NOME NOME!" meaning "No More Stupid – Not me." In March 2020, Adele, Beyonce, Enya, Madonna and Sade presented their collective song, "NOME NOME" at the Taj Mahal in India. It was the 35th anniversary of the recording of the global hit song, "We are the world" written by Michael Jackson and Lionel Ritchie, and sung with 21 different soloists, including Jackson, Ritchie, Ray Charles and Bob Dylan. The immediate goal of that song was to save the world from hunger. The goal of "NOME NOME" was to save the world, and the venue was chosen to symbolize the need to "Love the Earth" just as Emperor Shah Jahan loved his wife Mumtaz Mahal.

It was not an accident that the song "NOME NOME" was written and sung by women, because a key aspect of the "Great Transformation" was the ascendancy of women worldwide in society and politics. This trend began in the United States when the number of women in college began to outpace the number of men in the 1980s. In 1996 women were awarded more bachelor degrees than men, and by 2011, the total number of U.S. women with post-graduate degrees exceeded the number for men. Around the world, the trend was the same, even if moving more slowly. Women were becoming more educated than men and education was the route to power. Simultaneously, the need for human strength in jobs declined due to increasing automation and the decline of manufacturing and resource extraction work such as coal mining. By 2050, women occupied 60% of the Fortune 500 CEO positions. In a world which required partnerships and collaboration, and women excelled in those roles, the increased prominence of women was assured. Men had finally succumbed to their longstanding testosterone poisoning after centuries of subjecting women and other men to its tragic effects. It was a man, after all, who brought an atomic bomb to Brownsville, while on his way to Washington, D.C. It was men who dropped the atomic bombs on Hiroshima and Nagasaki. It was men who brought the destruction of World Wars I and II.

In the early 21st century, some women thought that the route to power and success lay in joining the military and becoming as warlike and destructive as men. That was a false strategy and was replaced by mid-century with a global boycott by women of military careers for themselves. Many tried to persuade their sons, husbands and significant others from joining the military.

The increased economic power of women led to increased political power and in 2060, women led two-thirds of the nations of the world. There were still a few women who believed, or truly felt, that the male way of aggression and threats was the best way, but soft power and collaboration was better for nations and better for the Earth. The distribution of the urge to aggression and violence between the two genders was illustrated by the classic "double Bell curve" where two Bell curves overlap to some extent. The size of the overlap indicates the proportion of women who have the same level of aggression as men, while most women have less than most men.

One micro-example of the seismic change in the human outlook during the Great Transformation was that cigarette consumption plummeted. In one of the instances where the social behavior of United States citizens led the world, cigarette consumption in that country began declining in 1965 from an average of 3,000 cigarettes per person per year or about 10 per day, to 300 or 1 per day by 2030. Despite the example of this decline, and that of several other "Western" countries, such as Australia, the less-developed world cigarette consumption continued to increase, until Brownsville, and the mantra, "NOME NOME." Clearly, it was stupid to smoke cigarettes, and no one at Chad's party smoked. Chad smoked when he was younger.

Next, Michelle and Xue selected "Legal" and struggled with the question, "Where was the last execution of a criminal in the world?" Xue guessed China, which was correct. That execution was in 2032. For bonus points, they were asked to name the U.S. state and year of the last execution in the U.S. which was Florida in 2026. In fact, it was exactly 90 years ago to the day, on December 31, 2026 that Juan Valdez, a Columbian farmer who had illegally immigrated to the U.S., was executed by lethal injection for murder. Michelle had heard about that anniversary landmark on the radio that afternoon while exercising.

Juan and Anita picked "U.S. sports" and knew the answer to the question of when American professional moveball[5] leagues were forced by

---

5. Moveball was formerly called "football" in the U.S. However, as World Cup Football, formerly called "soccer" in the U.S., became more popular in the U.S., the term "moveball" was developed for the uniquely American game which was declining in popularity due to its violence and injuries. Most schools and colleges had abolished the game, despite the reforms toward non-violence. Also, brand differentiation was deemed significant by the owners of

OSHA (Occupational Safety and Health Administration) order to discontinue their rules which encouraged aggressive and assaultive behavior. It was 2022, a date which Anita remembered as the year her great grandparents came to the U.S. from Mexico. Diehard American moveball fans remembered that year as the year that the game adopted "touch moveball" rules, which changed the premium from size to speed.

The 50 point bonus question was tough: When did American professional hockey teams make a similar change to "no check rules," i.e. no fysical contact? Juan guessed 2028, but the answer was 2025. It was the same year that boxing, ultimate fighting, and other combat extreme sports were abolished.

Thus, Chad and Melissa won for the evening, which Chad secretly savored, as he had a score to settle. His heavy drinking of his home-brew beer was starting to show. He had resented Juan since Juan tried to have sex the previous summer with Melissa while Chad was away. Juan and Anita were only here this evening because Anita was close to Michelle.

It was getting late, and they brought out the champagne around 11:45 p.m. Chad poured full glasses for all six at the game table, but set Juan's glass apart from the others and reached into his pocket. Juan and Anita had gone with a wink to the bedroom for a Q2 (quiet quickie). Michelle went to the bathroom, but paused at Juan's chair and reached out to straighten the candle, and then continued. Juan and Anita returned about 11:50- she with a smile and he with a yawn.

---

moveball franchises. Besides, the players' feet rarely touched the ball or moveball, so continuing to call the game "football" was a misnomer.

All six sat around the table and chatted for a while and then danced. The television was on and the ball was descending from the Facebook Building tower in New York City. Toasts were shared, which Chad initiated.

"May 2117 be the best of times," and then, with his well-known twisted sense of humor, "and may we continue to be spared the worst of times."

Among the songs selected and played was Chad's favorite classic rock song, "In the year 2525" by the 20th century group from Nebraska, Jager and Evans, headed by Denny Jager and Rick Evans. It was an unrealistically pessimistic song, but the rhythm was strong. Chad had memorized the lyrics, to which he karokeyed despite his inebriation,

> In the year 2525, if man is still alive
> If woman can survive, they may find...
>
> In the year 3535
> Ain't gonna need to tell the truth,
> tell no lie.
> Everything you think, do and say
> Is in the pill you took today.
>
> In the year 4545
> You ain't gonna need your teeth,
> won't need your eyes.
> You won't find a thing to chew
> Nobody's gonna look at you.
>
> In the year 5555
> Your arms hangin' limp at your sides.
> Your legs got nothin' to do
> Some machine's doin' that for you.
>
> In the year 6565

Ain't gonna need no husband,
won't need no wife.
You'll pick your son,
pick your daughter too.
From the bottom of a long glass tube.

In the year 7510
If God's a-coming,
he oughta make it by then.
Maybe He'll look around himself and
say,
"Guess it's time for the Judgment Day."

In the year 8510
God is gonna shake His mighty head
He'll either say,
"I'm pleased where man has been."
Or tear it down, and start again.

In the year 9595
I'm kinda wonderin' if man is gonna be
alive
He's taken everything this old earth
can give
And he ain't put back nothing.

Now it's been 10,000 years,
man has cried a billion tears.
For what, he never knew,
now man's reign is through
But through eternal night,
the twinkling of starlight
So very far away,
maybe it's only yesterday.

"You know," said Melissa, who was the most
sober of the group, "it's a little weird thinking about

people in almost 400 years in the future. Will they eat and shit and have sex like us?"

"Yeah," replied Michelle, "and, as my great grandfather used to tell me about the officers in the Army, 'They put their pants on, one leg at a time, like everyone else.' Well, that's how the people in 2525 will dress themselves, too."

"I dunno," mused Melissa. "Four hundred years ago, 1716, there certainly was a lot less sex. It was scary for women, as pregnancy was dangerous. The diet was simpler, though."

The group played more rock classics, some of which are now 150 years old. When rock 'n' roll was just beginning in the 1950's, many of the old-fashioned "classics," such as Beethoven's symfonies which were played on public radio, were 150 years old.

Juan stopped dancing, saying he was feeling groggy and lay down on the couch. Anita continued dancing with the others, except for Chad, who had passed out in a chair. Melissa, Xue and Michelle carried Chad to his bedroom and bed.

"I'm feeling sick," said Juan and said he would walk home, which was in the next building complex, only about 200 meters away. He and Anita said, "Goodnight," to the others and left. Anita walked with him to the apartment door and said to Juan, "Are you ok here?" Despite his occasional stumbles during their walk, she assumed he would be okay walking up to their second floor apartment. She said, "It's still early for my Spanish biological clock, even though it's 12:30 in the morning. I'm going back to the party, but will be home before 3:00." She turned and started to walk back to Chad's.

Juan nodded "Ok, thanks for bringing me this far," and commanded the door, "Open."

He stepped inside, and paused, and slowly climbed a few stairs, and felt nauseous. Then he lost his balance, fell and hit his head on the first granite step.

Chapter 2 Families and Origins

Chad Forbes Delano was born in Chicago on November 22, 2097, the son of Forbes Franklin Delano and Charlotte Amalie Perkins. Forbes and Charlotte met while they were in residence as doctoral degree students at the University of North America. They were taking a non-credit science course in the Astrofisics department, Astronomy 101, affectionately known in the department as "Rocks and Stars." That interest in the cosmos was to change their lives in other ways, too.

Chad's father, Forbes Franklin Delano was born on February 27, 2069 in Poughkeepsie, New York, and was a distant cousin on his father's side of the mother of Franklin Roosevelt, Sara Ann Delano Roosevelt. The name Forbes was his paternal grandmother's surname at birth. The Delanos had a long history in the U.S. beginning with the arrival on November 9, 1621 in Plymouth, now in Massachusetts, aboard the second vessel to that colony, the *Fortune*. The tiny ship, one-third the size of the more famous *Mayflower*, carried only about 30 passengers, mostly men and one woman, the pregnant Martha Ford whose short-lived son was born on the same day.

Among the men were two of French descent, Edouard Bonpasse and Philippe de La Noye. The descendants of both families anglicized their names during the anti-French periods of wars between the England and France in the 18th century. In North America, those conflicts were felt most severely during the French and Indian War of 1754-1763. The de La Noye family anglicized the name to Delano and one descendant, Warren Delano (1809-1898), became a wealthy participant in the China Trade in the 19th century. He married Catherine Robbins Lyman of Massachusetts and they had 11

children, including daughter, Sara Ann, who
married James Roosevelt of Hyde Park, New York in
1880.

It was through Warren's brother that Forbes
Franklin was descended. Many other famous
people were descended from Philippe de La Noye,
including Presidents Calvin Coolidge and Ulysses S.
Grant. Another descendant was Alan Shepard, the
first U.S. astronaut who made a sub-orbital flight
in 1961 and ten years later became the fifth person
and oldest person to walk on the moon. Among his
lesser contributions, he was the only astronaut, so
far, to hit a golf ball on the surface of the moon.
Forbes once calculated that Philippe de La Noye
was 17 generations previous, so Forbes had 2^{17} or
131,072 ancestors at the same level as Philippe.
Nearly all the others are lost to time. Shortly after
Forbes' birth, his father, Phillip Warren Delano,
who had been a genealogy enthusiast, changed his
name back to that of his ancestor, Philippe De la
Noye, but with two capital letters switched, i.e. from
"de La" to "De la."

Born in 1931, Philippe had a talent for the
theatrical, which led to his career interest in
television which was just taking off in the early
1950's when Philippe moved the family to
Montclair, New Jersey. From there, Philippe
commuted to New York to work for RCA, which was
the well-known abbreviation for Radio Corporation
of America and then to CBS (Columbia
Broadcasting System). For three years, he worked
as an assistant to the legendary and courageous
Edward R. Murrow. Philippe's interests were more
with education than with the news of the day and
he asked Murrow for guidance.

Said Murrow, "My early career plan was to be in
education, but in the general sense. I wanted to get
more information to the people, and not just to

those in classrooms. In the early 1930s, I was Assistant Director of the Institute for International Education from which I worked to rescue European scholars from Europe. In that job, I was the liaison to Francs Perkins who was FDR's Secretary of Labor. That was a bit of a stretch from the classroom, but it was important work."

"Forgive me, Ed," said Philippe, "but everybody knows who Frances Perkins was."

"Right," coughed Murrow, "but not everybody, perhaps including you, knew that the Bureau of Immigration was part of the Department of Labor, and Miss Perkins - she was married, but that's another story - was earnestly dedicated to rescuing Jews from Europe, especially those in the arts. In any case, getting back to your request, there's a lot that can be done at the Federal Communications Commission about education."

"How so?" asked Philippe. "I thought that agency was more interested in entertainment."

"Well, that's the problem," said Murrow. "Too many people don't realize that the radio and television airwaves belong to the public and they should be used for education as much as for fun and games. Maybe you could go to Washington and work there to steer the FCC back toward education. I know Ev Dirksen, the Republican Senator from Illinois and maybe he can help you get into the FCC."

"Thanks very much," replied Philippe, and then they went back to work. Philippe didn't think much would come from the conversation, but he had underestimated Murrow's interest in him and the extent of Murrow's influence.

Two weeks later, Philippe received a call from the Chair of the FCC asking if he would be interested in heading the Commission's Education Office.

Philippe agreed and they talked further. The
next week, a start date was determined, and
Philippe moved his family to Chevy Chase,
Maryland, a few kilometers from the FCC offices.

Philippe's father was Samuel James Delano who
was a well-known economist and Nobel laureate.
His wife was Margaret Forbes from another
distinguished China trade family, based in
Massachusetts.

Samuel Delano's interest in economics began at
the breakfast table of his grandfather who told him
of a lecture he had heard in Woolsey Hall at Yale in
1966 by a man whose name he would always
remember, the futurist, Robert Theobald.
Grandfather Delano remembered only one part of
that talk which was that salaries of executives
should be lower than those of people doing menial
work because the work of the executives was so
much more fun. Also, they could exercise power
which was satisfying. Later, Samuel carried the
same reasoning to question the exorbitant salaries
paid to professional athletes who were being paid to
have fun and exercise, which is what all people are
expected to do. These questions led to his later
interest in inequality.

He wrote his Ph.D. thesis in 2030 at the
University of Chicago, which later became the
University of North America, on the appropriate
taxation system to bring income and wealth
inequality into a fair range. "Fairness" was to be
determined in each instance by a democratic
political process.

Measuring inequality easily was a key to
developing the political will to optimize it – that is to
make it large enough to encourage creativity and
work, but small enough to ensure social justice.
One of the easiest to calculate and understand
measurements was the "20:20" ratio for income or

wealth where the income or wealth of the top 20% of the population was compared to the income or wealth of the bottom 20%. Building upon the popularity of that measurement, Delano added to the name the content of the ratio between the two. For income, it became the 20:20:I ratio where the "I" was actual income 20:20 ratio. This nomenclature made the shorthand immediately more clear.

In the early 21st century, income and wealth inequality were as large as they had been before the implementation of income and inheritance taxes in the early 20th century.

In the most egalitarian countries, primarily in Europe and Japan, the ratio of the total incomes of the top 20% averaged about four times the incomes for the bottom 20%, i.e. 20:20:I4. The U.S. ratio was eight, (20:20:I8), with the income of the top 20% of the population being 8.8 trillion earthas and 1.1 trillion for the bottom 20%. This ratio was about the same as some African countries such as Burundi and Cameroon. The countries with the highest ratios were in South America, such as Argentina (20:20:I18), Bolivia (20:20:I42), and Brazil (20:20:I21).

Focusing first on incomes, Delano proposed a unique tax system to keep the politically acceptable ratio constant. Simply, the income tax percentages were indexed to the 20:20:I ratio. When the 20:20:I ratio rose above the country's stated goal, the income taxes for the wealthy rose, and vice versa when the ratio fell. The most important decision for a nation, or relevant taxing unit, was to choose the 20:20:I ratio that was politically acceptable to its voters. Although some conservatives in countries predicted that the voters would pick an unfair and unrealistic goal such as 20:20:I3, or even 20:20:I2, other conservatives argued that when the 20:20:I ratio was higher, there was more incentive for innovation and investment and, therefore, job creation. Voters were, these conservatives argued, interested in jobs. Also, the theory went, many of those voters wanted to be rich someday, and when they arrived at that anticipated holy point, they didn't expect that they would want to give much to governments.

In the mid-20th century, countries sorted out their preferences with the Europeans and Asians averaging 20:20:I4 and the North Americans preferring 20:20:I5 to 20:20:I6. South American and African goals ranged from 20:20:I8 to 20:20:I11.

The inequality of wealth was even more glaring than that of income. One organization, Oxfam, with the goals of reducing poverty, hunger and injustice, calculated in 2014 that the richest 85 people in the world had the same total wealth as the poorest half of humanity, i.e. 3.6 billion people. This is not a typo. That's eighty-five, not 850, 8,500, 85,000 or even 850,000. It's 85. Therefore, each of the 85 had as much wealth as 42.4 million people, or approximately the population of a country like Argentina or Kenya.

In 2044, Delano expanded his proposal to include a 20:20 wealth ratio, or 20:20:W. Although it was widely recognized that income was the generator of wealth, it was also known that not all income was accurately measured and that sometimes, unintended distortions appeared. Delano proposed that inheritance and property taxes be indexed to the 20:20:W ratios as well. Most of the countries indexing their taxes to the 20:20:I ratios also adopted the 20:20:W system of indexing inheritance and property taxes.

In 2045, the United Nations ratified the Global Inequality Convention which set the global goals of at least as low as 20:20:I6 and 20:20:W8. Member countries committed to reaching that goal, or better, by 2055.

The United States implemented the U.N. Convention in 2046 with goals of 20:20:I5 and 20:20:W6. These tax writing goals came easier because of the national LAw Simplification Enabling Reform(LASER) which swept the U.S in the 2020s. The LASER campaign began with a 2021 documentary film by Michael Moore titled "Words Matter?" Among other methods he used to show the length of the U.S. Statutes, the Code of Federal Regulations and the Internal Revenue Tax Code, he printed their total of 477,499 pages (each 21 cm X 27 cm) and laid them end to end from Boston, Massachusetts to Concord, New Hampshire. With the 16 kilometers of pages remaining, he walked with his team nine kilometers to St. Paul's School where he gave a presentation, and then back to the State House. The LASER initiative succeeded in reducing each of those legal documents by 93% to a total of 30,000 pages. The 53 states engaged in similar LASER efforts for their own tax statutes and regulations.

The tax simplification included a progressive flat tax, together with the elimination of most tax credits and tax deductions, except those related to primary goals such as environment protection, earth sustainability and education. One exception to the reforms was the retention of the tax deductibility for contributions to religious organizations, but with a limit of 2,000 earthas[1]

1. After an international polling process conducted by the Single Global Currency Assn. under contract from the United Nations in 2022, the future Single Global Currency was given the name "eartha." which was a natural segue from the widely used euro. In 2024, the Global Central Bank was established and on January 1, 2026, the eartha was launched.

annually. However, as organized religion was declining in popularity, as did organized bowling leagues in the late 20th century, the loss of tax revenue from this deduction was not significant. Together, the tax credits and tax deductions were lumped into the governments' budgets as tax expenditures. All such amounts were automatically entered by the credit card provider or checking account bank. Each quarter the totals for each deduction were published by the Internal Revenue Service and the Congressional Appropriations Committee would evaluate the degree to which the tax expenditures were consistent with national priorities. Every year, the Congress would decide what changes, if any, to make in the deductibility of expenditures for priority objectives. If citizens were spending more, and claiming more deductions for lower priority causes, such as religious organizations, Congress might reduce the deductibility to a smaller percentage such as 50% or place a further limit, beyond the existing 2,000 earthas limit. Similarly, if Congress wanted more money spent on a priority, such as carbon dioxide reduction, or family planning, the deduction could be maximized to 100% and could even be supplemented with a tax credit for a further percentage. The genius of such programs was that citizens and organizations could make their own efficient cost/benefit analyses and manage those expenditures far more closely than a government staffed and operated program.

Coincidentally, the eartha arrived the same year as the mundo arrived in *Jesus and Jesusa*. The eartha had an initial fixed value of one U.S. dollar, .60 euros, 2.5 yuan, and 140 yen, with the values of the remaining 87 participating currencies in the Global Monetary Union set according to the prevailing exchange rates on that date.

Accounting for these tax expenditures was achieved with an automatically balancing entry in the income side of the ledger for every eartha deducted. By so doing, the government and the citizens could see and monitor the money spent for government priorities, but these tax expenditures would always be in "balance" when counted in the calculations of surpluses or deficits.

Another benefit of the (LASER) tax simplification reform was that there was less personal information in individual tax returns, which made easier the movement to open tax information to the public.[2] While some people were adept at hiding their wealth and income by living more simply than they could, most taxpayers lived according to their means and their friends, neighbors and the general public had a general sense of the appropriate level of taxation. If a taxpayer's publicly available tax information did not compare reasonably with his/her lifestyle, then anonymous tips were sent to the Internal Revenue Service, which then initiated audits when appropriate.

For his original income and updated wealth tax indexing proposals, Delano won the Nobel Prize for Economics in 2056.[3]

He was less well-known for his support of the limitation of compensation of CEO's and other

2. This reform, in turn, paralleled the movement in corporations and non-profit organizations to publicize on their websites the total salaries, wages and benefits of all employees. Organizations were no longer able to discipline employees for asking about the wages of other employees. If the totals were deemed disproportionate to the contributions of an employee to the goals of the organization, the word traveled quickly to the organization ombudsman.

3. As with so many Nobel Prize winners, Delano "stood on the shoulders of giants." Others who advocated indexing taxation to measures of inequality were Robert Shiller, Ian Ayres and Aaron Edlin.

executives to 100 times the average wage of hourly/overtime-eligible workers. For example, where the annual compensation, including benefits, of a company's average non-supervisory worker was 10,000 earthas annually, the maximum compensation for a chief executive was to be one million earthas. One difficulty with this approach was the different sizes and missions of organizations with different pay scales. Delano introduced a further multiple which related to the total size of an organization, and another for its mission, but the complexity of the calculations overwhelmed the purpose. The better course was to manage income and wealth inequality through the tax system.

Samuel Delano died at the age of 90 on his own initiative in December 2097, with the assistance of his doctor. He lived in the state of Illinois which had a progressive assisted suicide law that included old-age as a criterion which qualified for medical assistance in terminating one's own life. Delano was also suffering from prostate cancer.

He had lived to see the births of his great-grandchildren Eleanor and Chad, the children of his only grandchild.

That grandson, Forbes Franklin, followed his grandfather's scholarly footsteps. After graduation from Brown University in 2090, Forbes went to the University of North America to seek a Ph.D. in economics. His 2093 thesis[4] was about the costs and benefits of the implementation of a Single Global Currency, the eartha, in 2026, beginning with 146 countries with 83% of the world's GDP. He found that the resulting 8% annual increase in international trade exceeded predictions. In

4. The *Journal of Economic Literature* abstract and summary of Forbes's thesis, are presented in this book as Appendix A.

addition, by the membership terms of the Global
Monetary Union the ability of countries to utilize
their now-unnecessary foreign exchange reserves
for environment-related projects contributed to the
boost in expenditures for family planning and
carbon dioxide mitigation. They were the two
largest contributors to global warming. The other
permitted use of the former reserves, now
denominated in earthas, was to redeem parts of
member nations' debt. For some nations, this was
significant, especially for China. With a 550 billion
eartha national debt and 1.1 trillion eartha foreign
exchange reserve, China was able to redeem its
entire national debt and devote the remaining 550
billion earthas to the authorized environment-
related projects. At the opposite end of the
spectrum, the United States found almost no relief
from the 32 billion eartha FX reserves for its 4.1
trillion eartha national debt. It would take the U.S.
many years of national fiscal surplusses before that
debt would be reduced to the new Global Central
Bank recommended level of 15% of GDP.   In 2026,
the U.S. percentage was 110%, and the worst was
Japan's 225%.

Forbes's future wife, Charlotte Amalie[5] Perkins,
was born as Charlotte Amalie Kinselli on July 4,
2068 in Athens, Georgia to Giorgio Persepolis and
Elena Kinselli. Her twin sister, Emily Stone
Kinselli, was born two minutes later. The family
was in that city because of Elena's work at the
University of Georgia. Giorgio found his way there
from his native Greece on an eclectic journalistic
tour. He had contracted to write an article for

---

5. Charlotte Amalie, named after the queen consort of Danish
King Christian V, is the capital city of the U.S. Virgin Islands.
Neither Giorgio nor Elena had visited the city, but they had
read the name somewhere, and liked it.

Gynaika Magazine about places in the U.S. with Greek names or origins. He first visited the small town of Athens in the geografical center of Maine. Of its population of 1,015, no one in the town spoke Greek, but one citizen had traveled to Greece when she was a college student. The Athens Pizza House was owned by a man whose parents came from Sicilia.

Giorgio then headed for Syracuse, New York, which was named after Syracusa in Sicilia. At the time of his visit, the city government was debating whether to join the "Authentic Name" movement and rename the city as "Syracusa."

Making his way southwest, he visited Sparta, New York which was the last home of Daniel Shays, the leader of the 1786-87 Shays Rebellion. Considering that the rebellion cost the lives of at least five men, it astonished Giorgio that Shays actually was allowed to live to die a natural death at 78. It was especially astonishing because one of Shays' unsuccessful military attacks was on the Federal Armory in Springfield, Massachusetts. Seventy two years later, John Brown would be executed by hanging for his rebellious attack in 1859 on the Federal Armory at Harper's Ferry, Maryland.

In Athens, Ohio, Giorgio made his way to the site of the former Midget Motors Corporation which from 1946 to 1970 made an obscure compact car, the "King Midget." The earlier models were sold as build-it-yourself kits whereby a mechanically skilled person could build his/her car for the modern equivalent of about 200 earthas.

In Nashville, Tennessee, also called the "Athens of the South," Giorgio visited the full-sized, but concrete, copy of the Parthenon which was originally built for the 1897 Tennessee Centennial Exposition. Finally, he made his way to Athens,

Georgia, the home of the University of Georgia, where he met Elena by chance while buying a postcard[6] to send to his family. Elena looked over his shoulder and suggested that he use the Athens/Sparta card which commemorated the friendship between the two Georgia communities, compared to the namesake cities of ancient Greece.

Giorgio's relationship to Elena blossomed and Athens, Georgia was where his journey ended. He completed his articles for *Gynaika* and then began his U.S. career as a correspondent for Al Jazeera-America.

After the birth of Charlotte and Emily. Giorgio had a vasectomy. He had seen enough of the world to know that there were too many humans in it. He had hoped for a son, but he knew that was an old-fashioned idea, and even felt a little embarrassed that he said something to Elena about that desire.

Charlotte Kinselli excelled in school, especially English, and wanted to be a writer. She attended a virtual high school, which was based in Boston, but she lamented the lack of social contact and political activism of that school. After graduation in 2085, she applied to one college, Oberlin, in Ohio, because of its serious socially conscious history. Oberlin was the first college in the United States to regularly admit women and Blacks. When at Oberlin, Charlotte learned about its famous 19th

---

6. A "postcard" was a single thick piece of paper with a fotograf on one side, often sized about 9.5 cm by 14.0 cm that travelers used to send by snail mail to their friends and relative back home with a greeting and a message. They became obsolete with the advent of the computer, email and social media sites.

century alumna, Lucy Stone, who kept her birth name after her 1855 marriage to Henry Blackwell.[7]

Charlotte majored in English and wrote her senior year paper, to use an obsolete term (i.e. "paper") for her electronic product, about the 19th century utopian novel by Edward Bellamy, *Looking Backward*. Given Oberlin's founding as a community and a college, the emfasis there on utopias was part of the college's heritage. She focused on Bellamy's use of coincidence, made more popular by Thomas Hardy in his novels, with specific reference to the women in the split centuries life of the novel's hero, Julian West, both of whom were named Edith.

Inspired by Lucy Stone's example of name-choice-freedom, Charlotte chose her 18th birthday, Independence Day, to change her surname, with which she had always felt uncomfortable. She combined the first part of her father's surname, Persepolis, with the first part of her mother's and her own surname into "Perkins."[8] The decision was assisted by her discovery of the life and work of Frances Perkins, first woman Cabinet Secretary, who was Secretary of Labor under Franklin Delano Roosevelt. Called the "architect" of the New Deal, Perkins was largely responsible for Social Security and national Unemployment Compensation and Workers' Compensation. Before accepting her position in 1933, she required and obtained FDR's support for that legislation and also for national

---

7. This example led to the naming of the name choice freedom organization as The Lucy Stone League. See the Wikipedia entry at http://en.wikipedia.org/wiki/Lucy_Stone_League.
8. Through serendipity came the connection of Charlotte to the 19th century writer, Charlotte Perkins Gilman, who wrote *Herland*, a feminist utopian novel set approximately in 3915, 2,000 years after the disappearance of men from an isolated part of Earth.

health insurance. She died in 1965, just after the passage of the Medicare Amendments to the Social Security Act by the U.S. House of Representatives, which could be said to have been the first step toward Frances Perkins's goal of national health insurance.

After graduating from Oberlin in 2089, Charlotte took a year off from her planned matriculation to the University of North America in Chicago, and explored the sites of the utopian communities of the United States, beginning with Utopia, Ohio. Running short of money, she landed a job in January at the Hancock Shaker Village Museum in Hancock, Massachusetts.

That fall, she computer-hitched a ride to Chicago, through www.ride-hitch.com[9] with a fellow student at the University of North America. Then she began her studies in the University's doctorate program in Utopian Studies.

Emily went to the same primary and intermediate schools as Charlotte in Athens, but chose to attend Clarke Central High School, which was a short walk from home. While both twins were interested in science, Emily was more interested in biology and psychology, and Charlotte was more interested in the inanimate sciences of fysics and chemistry. Emily was also interested in people and had an active social and sexual life, after reaching puberty around her 15th birthday. The age of puberty in western countries, and later throughout the world, declined due to improved nutrition and health in the 19th and 20th centuries. However, early puberty for pre-teens was recognized as dysfunctional as children at that age were not ready to cope with associated social changes.   That reduction was reversed in the 21st

9. As of 2014, not a real website.

century through changes in diet, primarily the lower consumption of meat and dairy products. In some countries, mild puberty inhibitors were introduced into school diets.

Emily learned about sex as a human activity to be optimized rather than feared. Thus, her classes, and her conversations with her mother, were about how to enhance pleasure and ensure orgasm for herself, every time, whether during intercourse or manually. The biology and contraception part was especially easy for her, given her academic interests. Frequent sexual activity was the norm for Emily and some of her classmates. The difficult part was to find times and places which were clean, convenient, comfortable and conducive to female pleasure. Some friends were more active, and most were less. The challenge for these teenagers was to get right the combination of openness that promoted knowledge about optimal sex activity with the privacy that was necessary for trust between partners. In addition, they needed to be open to all the variations of sexuality, including homosexuality, bi-sexuality, asexuality, and those with gender identification issues. The biases of earlier centuries against those who were not solely heterosexual were disappearing due to the large shift during and before the Great Transformation. The world had moved away from pro-population growth perspectives to views which were consistent with one, two or no children. Finally, the world had accepted and implemented the guideline that every child born on Earth was a wanted and planned child. Women were no longer required or encouraged to bear the children of unintended pregnancies. If such a level of reason and responsibility had been achieved in the 1960's when reliable contraception, in the form of the birth control pill, became universally available, at least in theory, the human population would have grown to a zero population growth peak of approximately 4.5 billion. During the 1960's and beyond, women in all countries told pollsters that their planned family sizes were approximately at replacement levels, i.e. an average of two children or fewer. However, the forces of ignorance, led by religious organizations whose missions were ostensibly the improvement of the lot of humanity, prevented the universal availability of birth control, until the mid-21st century. During that 100-year period, the Earth suffered the burdens of an additional four billion human consumers and polluters.

Emily learned a fundamental axiom of the human fecundity problem which was that it wasn't fecundity which was the problem at all, at least not in the beginning of the period of rapid population growth. The problem arose not because of birth control, but because of death control. The advances in nutrition and medicine reduced the world's death rates long before the previously necessary replacement-level birth rates of about 6-7 per woman could be reduced to an average of about 2.1 or fewer, to match those death rate reductions.

Emily's boyfriend of the school year 2084-85 was Joshua Blount and he and Emily made a pact to go to the same college or university. They applied to the same six colleges. Two rejected both Emily and Joshua, and two others rejected one and accepted the other. That left the two which accepted both of them: the University of Georgia in Athens and the University of Notre Dame in South Bend, Indiana. As the Univ. of Georgia was too close to home and was only a safety choice, and to which neither Emily nor Joshua wanted to go, their default choice was Notre Dame.

The first six months of the freshman year at Notre Dame were uniformly conducted at South Bend. After that, students had several choices for international education, because of the global network of catholic universities. However, Joshua's interests emerged differently from Emily's, as their parents quietly, but separately, had forecast back in Athens. Emily went to the University of Firenze[10] to study psychology and fine arts, and Joshua went to the National University of Singapore for its program in GLOWARE (GLobal WArming REversal.)

In March, 2086, they assured each other, and themselves, of their love, and were soon 10,000 kilometers apart, even if separated by only a few keystrokes via Facebook.

Although at ground zero of the Italian Renaissance, Emily immersed herself in the study of psychology. She bridged the gap a few times, as with her paper on the psychological torment of Leonardo Da Vinci, who was widely considered to be homosexual at a time where such a preference was criminal, at least by the letter of civil and religious law.

She discovered the work of Darold Treffert of the University of Wisconsin who became a world-renowned expert on savant syndrome in the late 20th century. More specifically, he studied acquired savant syndrome. People who have savant syndrome focus their brains on one very specific task and perform that task incredibly well. The savant syndrome most familiar to people is the "calendar calculator," where a savant can tell the day of the week or other specific factoid for any day in history. The answer comes quickly and seemingly without effort, even though it would take

10. Florence, Italia.

other people many keystrokes on a computer to find the answer. Other savants have special aptitudes for music or art. The downside of such abilities is that those born as savants are often deficient socially and psychologically in some way, and sometimes to the point of being diagnosed as autistic.

A medical doctor, Dr. Treffert was most fascinated with "acquired savant syndrome" which occurs when a seemingly normal person suffers an accident or a disease which affects a specific portion of his/her brain, and s/he develops savant syndrome. One example was Jason Padgett of the state of Washington, United States, who was a 31 year old father of a daughter when he was attacked and kicked at a karaoke bar in September 2002. Subsequently, he developed an obsession with fysics and math and saw geometric images where others saw other images, such as leaves. Also, however, he was becoming paranoid and obsessive compulsive about the cleanliness of people who touched him, like his daughter. After seeing a BBC documentary about an "acquired savant syndrome" person in the United Kingdom who had an accident and could subsequently recite pi from memory to the 22,514th digit, Padgett contacted Dr. Treffert. After discussions, Padgett learned that he was one of about 40 people in the world who had developed acquired savant syndrome.

Emily was fascinated with such people and searched the internet for more examples. She found one in nearby Pisa. There, in the winter of 2076, Elisa Valesio fell on some rare Pisa sidewalk ice. As a high school graduate, she had some skills with math, but from the fall, she developed the "calculator calendar" syndrome. She learned of her new skill when wondering about the day of the week of her own birth on June 18, 2054. She wrote down "Thursday" and then checked her computer and saw that she was right. She was thereafter able to tell the day of the week of any date which her family and local doctors presented to her.

Emily wondered about how Elisa's savantism dealt with dates using the Julian calendar before the development of the Gregorian calendar in 1582. Part of the reason for Emily's fascination with Elisa's story was that Pisa was only 86 kilometers away by car. Emily contacted Elisa by email and then talked with her using her fone's AT (AutoTranslate) app, and went to visit her.

Emily arrived in Pisa several hours before her visit with Elisa in order to do some sightseeing. With her clip-on "historoglasses" and from specified vantage points in the historic areas, she was able to see the way Pisa looked during eight different time periods: 950 A.D., 1000, 1150, 1300, 1450, 1600, 1750 and 1900. The options were rotating through her glasses and she would blink to select the date she wanted.

Then she told her car sensor the address for Elisa's house and the car prompted her to make the correct turns. She arrived shortly after noon, and Elisa served a meal of gorgonzola and apricot pizza. Emily and Elisa became fast friends and Emily felt ready to begin her acquired savantism interview.

After a few questions, she determined that Elisa knew nothing about the Julian calendar, which was created by Julius Caesar on the advice of his astronomers in 46 B.C. The Julian calendar provided for a year of 365.25 days per year, and thus for a leap year every four years. Over the succeeding centuries, it was determined that years were actually shorter by a fraction of a day, i.e. 365.2425 days. In 1582, during the papacy of Pope Gregorius XIII, a new calendar was developed which corrected the error by slightly reducing the number of leap years every 400 years from 100 to 97. The next "skipped" leap year would be in 2100, leaving eight years between the leap years of 2096 and 2104.

Emily then began her formal interview with Elisa and recorded it on her fone. To provide a valid experiment, she had to be very careful to measure Elisa's responses after providing only bits of information about the Julian calendar. Instead of telling Elisa the general differences between the calendars, she chose three events, the signing of the British Magna Carta in 1215, and the day that Pope Gregorius XI returned to Roma in 1377 to end the Avignon schism, and the Italia Republic Day in 1946. She told Elisa the Julian and Gregorian dates for those three events, as follows:

	Julian	Gregorian
Magna Carta	June 15 1215	June 22, 1215
Gregorius XI	Jan. 13, 1377	Jan. 21, 1377
Republic Day	May 20, 1946	June 2, 1946

Then Emily gave Elisa the Julian dates for several events, e.g. the 1571 Battle of Lepanto and the birth of Jesus of Nazareth, and asked for their Gregorian equivalents. Afterwards, she reversed the exercise by giving Elisa events with their Gregorian dates. Without hesitation, Elisa gave the correct dates in the other calendar and the day of the week of each date. Fortunately, there were only limited social deficits caused by her fall. She found that she could not tolerate more than a few minutes of television, although computer time was unaffected and unlimited.

Emily wrote a paper for her psychology class about Elisa's story, and she also published the article on the internet through the *Savant Syndrome Journal*. "It is likely," she wrote, "that

Elisa's brain's nerve alignments are altered slightly in the cognitive area controlling her calculations. Previous fMRI (functional Magnetic Resonance Imaging) tests of individuals with acquired savant syndrome have precisely identified the brain's changes. This work has vast potential for the enlargement of the capabilities of the brain through electronic stimulation. What blocks such efforts are the still-not-understood asocial side effects of the triggering of acquired savant syndrome. When we understand those side effects and develop the ability to avoid them, we can truly unlock the power of the brain."

This was a direct attack on the view that the saying, "we use only five percent of our brains" was a myth. The "five percent" number may be off by a lot, but Emily presented real proof that the brain has incredible powers of calculation, if the correct neurons are somehow linked at birth, or are shaken into a network by an accident. Most of us can determine, for example, in about a minute of calculation, the day of the week of the first day of the previous month. However, it is inconceivable that a non-savant person could provide the day of the week, in both Julian and Gregorian calendars, for example, of 14 July 1789, the day of the storming of the Bastille and thus the first Bastille Day. Is the brainpower utilized for such a calculation 20 times, or 100 times, more powerful than the normal person who can barely identify a day of the week of the previous month.

Another interest for Emily was religion. During her first term at Notre Dame, she learned more about Christianity and the changes in the Roman Catholic Church since the papacy of Pope Francesco which began in 2013. In 2015, he issued his first major encyclical, "Humanam Oecologiam" (Human Ecology) which set a new course for human interaction with the environment. This encyclical arose from a 2014 workshop conducted by the Pontifical Academy of Sciences entitled, "Sustainable Humanity, Sustainable Planet, Our Responsibility." Instead of emfasizing the historic tradition of the conquest of nature, Pope Francesco wrote that humanity must live with nature, and that would require that humans stop the growth of their population, while respecting human values. He asked for prayers to assist him in seeking ways to promote "sustainable humanity." He cited the life of his namesake, Saint Francesco of Assisi,[11] who, he said, "taught us profound respect for the whole of creation and the protection of our environment." This profound change in Catholic dogma was well-received by Catholics and non-Catholics alike and empowered Pope Francesco to take more steps to move his Church to the forefront of the movement to encourage human ethics and values for the future, rather than being stuck in the anthropocentric past.

In 2020, building on the support he received for the encyclical, "Humanam Oecologiam," Pope Francesco issued five papal encyclicals on issues which had bedeviled the Church for years:

1. "Caelibatus Sacerdotalis" (Celibacy for Priests) It was henceforth the policy that priests could have sexual relationships with men and women as they chose. They were as free as their congregants to be sexual human beings. They were also allowed to marry and have children, consistent with their environmental responsibilities, i.e. one or two children. Since 2014, when Pope Francesco had

---

11. St. Francesco of Assisi was the founder of the Franciscan Order of monks and is known as the patron saint of animals and the environment. In 1979, Pope Ioannes Paulus II declared St. Francesco to be the "Patron of Ecology."

said that the celibacy rule was "not dogma" and that the "door was always open" to changing the rule, this encyclical had been expected.

2. "Mulieres et Sacerdotium" (Women in the Priesthood) Women were now welcome to participate fully in church affairs and were eligible to occupy every Church office, including the papacy. The encyclical presented the historical reasons for the previous exclusion of women, and explained that those reasons had now vanished. For example, there was no longer any concern that the property of the church would be claimed by children of priests. Thanks to the encyclical,"Caelibatus Sacerdotalis," women priests could also marry and have children.

3. "Sexualitatis Humanae" (Human Sexuality) Moving away from the historical foundations of sexual morality which arose from the needs to control disease and illegitimacy, the encyclical recognized the rights of all people to explore and be faithful to their own sexuality. This applied especially to the rights of homosexuals who were henceforth welcomed into the Church and were declared eligible for all of the Church's offices, including the papacy. On a micro-level, Pope Francesco proposed that the Latin word for homosexuality, "impudicitiae," meaning "immoral acts" be changed forever to "sexualitatis isdem," for "sex with same," or the shortened form "sexisdem"

4. "Ortus Imperium et Abortus." (Birth Control and Abortion) Again with the explanation that the historical foundations for old moral rules were no longer applicable, the encyclical approved of all forms of safe birth control. The new moral rule was that people should use effective birth control and not be reckless or careless about it. The encyclical explicitly stated that the 1968 prohibition on artificial birth control in Pope Paulus VI's encyclical

"Humanae Vitae" was no longer applicable. The true interests of "Human Life," wrote Pope Francesco, were in making every child a wanted child and in reducing the size of the human population to a sustainable level, where humans lived in equilibrium with other animals and the environment.

Further, the encyclical reversed the 19th century rule which prohibited abortion. Instead, the encyclical said that abortion was primarily an issue for a pregnant woman to resolve, with the assistance of others, including her doctor. The specific rules on abortion were left to the relevant state or country, but the moral requirements were that they be safe and conducted as early in the pregnancy as possible.

5. "Finem Vitae." (End of Life) Consistent with the Church's changing views of population control and the quality of life, this encyclical provided moral support for Catholics who wished to end their lives with dignity. In several countries and U.S. states, assisted suicide was legalized for people facing a terminal illness. Moving beyond that threshold, Pope Francesco stated that it was moral for a person to commit suicide, and for another person to assist that person, if the burdens of life outweighed the benefits of continuing the struggle. The encyclical provided for a one year "contemplation period," where feasible, and required consultation with a priest.

These changes unleashed a period of growth for the Catholic Church which pleased the conservatives, even if they didn't welcome the specifics of all five encyclicals. The diversity of the College of Cardinals changed dramatically over the next 25 years, and the first woman pope, Isabella, served from 2058-2076. The first openly gay pope, Stephanus XI, served from 2092-2108.

While in Firenze, Emily went to Roma and to the
Vaticano and was impressed. Even though she
realized that the Church was originally founded
upon myths that were no longer part of the
Church's belief system, and that the history of
Church was filled with superstition, cruelty and
discrimination, Emily was attracted to the majesty
of the Vaticano and the Church's newly anchored
optimism for the future of humanity.

Emily returned to the U.S. in the spring of 2087
and was reunited with Joshua. Their videofone sex
had been interesting, and their separate
experiences with others during their time apart
were good and sometimes exciting, but they were
glad to be back together. Sex for each of them was
better together. Their relationship had survived
their time apart, and they vowed to continue the
rest of their life journeys together.

Another big change for Joshua was that he had
become a Mormon. He had shared with Emily the
progress of his conversion while in Singapore, but it
wasn't the same as being with him on a daily basis.
He had been impressed with the discipline and
entrepreneurial energy of two Mormons he had met
in Singapore. The two were on their required
Mormon "mission," but such missions were now
focused on helping educate people about science
and the environment of the earth. Curiously, these
missions resulted in a higher rate of conversion to
Mormonism than was the case with the old-style
missions where young Mormons sought to
persuade non-believers of the historic, though
mythical, foundations of Mormonism.

Assisting Joshua in his conversion, the
missionaries told him that the old Mormon
prohibitions on pre-marital sex had long been
abandoned by that church. The church leaders
learned that the earlier prohibitions had led to

inexperience and ignorance at the time of marriage, and that led to problems such as unplanned pregnancies and sexual unhappiness. Like other religions, the Mormons were changing their beliefs to fit the needs of humanity and one major need was to reduce the number of births and the size of the human population.

Following the lead of the Catholic Church, the Mormon leaders (Presidents and "Quorum of the Twelve") decided in 2030 to allow women to be members of the "Twelve" and to be candidates for the Presidency. In all respects, women were to be full members of the church. This was only 16 years after the excommunication of Kate Kelly of Virginia and Utah for her active efforts to persuade the Church of the Latter Day Saints to ordain women. She was the leader of the organization, "Ordain Women." In the excommunication letter, the church leader had written that Kelly's "actions had threatened to erode the faith of others." Instead, it was the excommunication which eroded the faith of women Mormons. and many left the church forever. Anxious to avoid these losses, the movement to ordain women thereafter gained considerable momentum.

Joshua learned about the history of the Mormons and their 19th century founding by Joseph Smith whose myths rivaled those of mainstream Christians. However, as with the Catholics, the Mormons were able to abandon the myths of the creation of their faith and continue with their well-founded principles of work, community, and abstinence from alcohol.

The demytholization of churches in the U.S. was furthered by the 2053 de-mytholization changes in the section of the Internal Revenue Code which provided for tax exemption for religious organizations. The change eliminated the exemption for religious organizations which relied upon myths for their faith. In a world which relied upon science for survival, the Congress had determined that myths which denied science, such as the Christian myth about the origin of the world in the Garden of Eden with Adam and Eve, were unacceptable. The best known Christian myths were abandoned five years earlier by the Vatican Council III which issued its decisions in 2048. The Council decreed that Catholic faith would be supported not by the myths of virgin birth, the ascension of Jesus into heaven and a God who was father to Jesus, but by the core values arising from humanity's existence on a finite Earth.

Several Christian churches were reluctant to follow the lead of the Roman Catholics. Because of that reluctance, there continued to be a large number of U.S. citizens whose faith in Christian myths outweighed their faith in science, and that anti-intellectual faith was undermining U.S. scientific progress. The Congress determined that it made no sense to provide a tax exemption from income taxes, i.e. a tax expenditure, for organizations which were anti-science while at the same time spending billions of earthas to promote science and science education.

For the Mormons, it was difficult to abandon the mythology surrounding Joseph Smith's claim that he discovered the Book of Mormon inscribed on golden plates in the fields of his farm in Manchester, New York, beginning in 1823.[12]

12. This was not the only instance in Christendom where significance was attached to something dug out of the ground. In Espana, much reverence was attached to a "Black Madonna" statute that was purportedly carved by Luke the Evangelist and buried by priests in 712 when the Moors seized Sevilla. In the 1400s a farmer in Caceres in Extremadura claimed to have been directed by an apparition

However, aware of the impending I.R.S. changes, which were to be effective in 2053, the Presidency of the Mormon Church advised the church members that their faith was no longer based upon the Joseph Smith "stories" as they were called. More important to Mormons were the beliefs in family, as evidenced by the church's unparalleled genealogy records, and in the goodness of people.

The church that attracted Joshua in 2086 was, therefore, far different from the Mormon Church of the 20th century.

Emily and Charlotte communicated about Emily's interest in Catholicism, and Charlotte was fascinated with how that religion had changed so rapidly in the 21st century. She wondered why. She understood that the utopian novella, *Jesus and Jesusa*, played some role in the "Great Transformation," but she wanted to know more. Perhaps it was because that book portrayed a nuclear bomb accident within a year of the actual accident in Brownsville, Texas in 2019.

In the spring of 2090, at the University of North America, Charlotte signed up for the "Rocks and Stars" course where she met Forbes Delano. He was sitting in the row in front of her. During a break in the initial three hour class, he turned around and started a conversation with a forgettable opener.

Once the conversation passed the first stage by his learning Charlotte's name and her *code[13], and

of the Virgin Mary to dig in a certain spot in his fields, where he found the buried statue. The statue is now in the monastery of Santa Maria de Guadalupe in that province.
13. Everyone with a cloud device had the option of adopting a universal I.D. Code, or Starcode. With that code, anyone could locate person's Facebook address, and other contact information as was publicly available. Emergency medical info was there also, for those with authorized access.

knowing about Frances Perkins, he asked if there was any connection. Charlotte explained the creative source of her melded surname. She, in turn, wondered about his name, Delano, and whether there was a connection to FDR. After class then went to the school pub and kept talking until closing time the next morning. In a few weeks they were a couple and moved in together. Initially, they flipped a coin from Forbes's collection, as none was still in circulation as money, and "heads" determined that they would live in Charlotte's apartment. Later, they found a bigger place.

During her studies, Charlotte changed her focus from utopian communities to utopian books and how they influenced the societies around them. Some students in the program favored analyses of the classic utopian books, e.g. *Utopia* by Thomas More. Other students favored the late 19th century bubble of utopian books including William Morris's *News from Nowhere,* which was a libertarian/capitalistic response to Edward Bellamy's *Looking Backward.*

Charlotte chose to write her Ph.D. thesis[14] about the social and political impact of the 21st century utopian novella, *Jesus and Jesusa,*[15] by Maria Maddalena.[16] The book had intrigued her for years. It was published in 2014, and quickly became a *New York Times* global best seller. It was credited

---

14. The summary of Charlotte's Ph.D. thesis is presented here as Appendix B.

15. Published at www.amazon.com in 2014. For the "Mountain Notes" summary of *Jesus and Jesusa,* see Appendix C.

16. Maria Maddalena, Italian for Mary Magdalen, was a pseudonym, and the real author has not been identified. The possibilities include Dan Brown, author of *The Da Vinci Code,* and Reza Aslan, author of *Zealot – The Life and Times of Jesus of Nazareth.*

with being one of the substantial contributors to the great changes in the world between 2014 and 2050.

Those years saw the ratification of two international agreements which were critical to humanity's future. First, the 1970 Non-Proliferation Treaty was strengthened by the 2022 Nuclear Weapons Abolition Convention. By its terms, national nuclear weapons were abolished by the year 2040. The only exception to the total abolition was the continued maintenance and storage of necessary materials for a few nuclear weapons by the United Nations Military Mission for possible use to prevent an impending asteroid crash on the earth, such as the 1908 Tunguska, Siberia event.

The other key change was the 2023 Maldives Action Plan which Chad and his friends discussed on New Year's Eve, 2116. This agreement, together with its rigorous enforcement, ensured that global warming would be reversed during the 21st century.

Beyond the two treaty changes were two inter-related behavioral changes which the *Jesus and Jesusa* fenomenon fostered, directly and indirectly. First, the people of the world and their leaders began thinking as if the earth and humanity mattered, and beyond their short-term national interests. This led, for example, to the 2022 treaty which resolved the interminably long-festering dispute between Israel and her neighbors. Not every human being made the shift, but the change from about 10% of the global population "thinking globally and acting globally" to 60% was enough to make the necessary difference.

Second, there was a turn away from violence at all levels. Peaceful dispute resolution was taught at all levels of the global society, including the

International Peace University, a part of the United Nations University. There had not been a war among U.N. members since the Two-Day war between Kurdistan and Iraq in 2022.[17] That aversion to war, at least between countries, had increased after the 2026 adoption of a Single Global Currency, primarily because money is essential to waging war and the Global Central Bank made it clear that it was not going to help its member countries finance their wars.

After Forbes' and Charlotte's graduations from their Ph.D programs on Saturday, June 6, 2093, they began on Sunday their move to Philadelphia where he had a job with the Federal Reserve Bank of Philadelphia. They first drove to Athens, Georgia, where they were to be married on the 13th. On the way, they voted electronically in the International Election for 13 U.S. Representatives in the 350 member People's Assembly of the United Nations. The rest of North America had seven representatives: Canada, 1; Mexico, 5, and the rest of Central America 1. Forbes and Charlotte had the option of voting for 13 candidates in this Instant Runoff Voting (IRV) election, but chose to maximize the impact of their votes by bullet voting for four Green Party candidates.

The People's Assembly was established by the 2037 International Convention on United Nations Governance, and the election was to be publicly funded by a global .01% sales tax on consumer products. By that Convention, there were to be 350 delegates to the People's Assembly, to be elected every seven years, beginning in 2044. The apportionment of delegates was based on the

---

17. For a more in-depth summary of the global response to the publication of *Jesus and Jesusa*, see the summary of Charlotte Perkins's Ph.D. thesis at Appendix B.

population as of 2037 and would remain fixed to that number for 300 years until the global population reached the predicted U.N. goal of one billion in 2339. The intent of the architects of the 2037 Convention was not to increase or dilute political power based on the predicted population declines in every country.

By the restructured design of the United Nations, the People's Assembly functioned like the U.S. House of Representatives or the United Kingdom's Parliament, leaving the country-based General Assembly to function much like the U.S. Senate or the British House of Lords.   The People's Assembly was based in Geneva, in part to symbolize the intended design that the Representatives were beholden to their voters and not necessarily to their governments.

Chad's older sister, Eleanor Kinselli Perkins, was born in Philadelphia three years before Chad on August 17, 2094. As the first, she reaped the burdens of her parents' mistakes, but also the benefits of being the only child – for three years. Blonde, Eleanor was adorable in the eyes of her parents and four grandparents, and six surviving great-grandparents. She learned to speak her native English just before her second birthday, and began learning Deutsch, the language of her nanny.

Her middle name was the surname of her grandmother, Elena Kinselli. Eleanor Perkins did well in school and liked science. She played with toys that flew, and once sent a drone helicopter into a storefront window.

A year after Eleanor's birth, Charlotte intentionally became pregnant again, as she and Forbes wanted to have children close in age to each

other. By using the Shettles Method[18] and altering
the chemistry in her uterus with an acidic douche,
Charlotte maximized the odds of having a son.
However, the male fetus had several genetic
mutations and Charlotte and Forbes decided
together to abort her pregnancy. It wasn't an easy
decision. Despite all the medical advances,
motherhood was still motherhood, and the sense of
a life forming within one's own body was
irreplaceable.

When Chad was conceived, the old-fashioned
and more fun way, but again with pro-male
chemicals in early 2097, Forbes and Charlotte were
hopeful that the pregnancy would be normal.
However, the 2-week genetic testing showed that
one of the baby's "behavior" genes was mutated in
an unusual way. The pregnancy was difficult and
not certain to continue.

The doctors told Forbes and Charlotte that Chad
could be behaviorally challenged in one of two
ways. He could be secretive, as several famous but
unsuccessful politicians had been with the same
mutation, or he could be overly extroverted and
annoying. Or, given that the nature/nurture mix
wasn't much changed over the past thousand
years, he could be behaviorally normal. The
parents chose to continue the pregnancy.

Chad's first name came from a distant relative in
New Hampshire, and Forbes was weary of the
aristocratic name tradition of staying within the

---

18. The Shettles Method emfasized three aspects of
intercourse to affect gender selection. By timing their
planned- procreation sex to just before ovulation, and by
ejaculating when deep in the vagina and by ensuring the
woman's orgasm, couples increased the chances that male
sperm would fertilize an available egg before a female sperm.
Using a mild alkaline douche also favored the faster
movement of the male sperm.

family's collection of names. He had recalled in his "Rocks and Stars" class of a 20th century astronomer named Chad Trujillo, who was on a team of scientists which had discovered the planet Eris and other celestial objects. Eris has a larger mass than Pluto. If any of Forbes's friends or family asked about Chad's first name, Forbes would think about saying that "Chad" was short for "Chadwick," after the 17th century Duke of Chadwick, who was King George II's brother. Actually, that wasn't true. There was no such brother. The only reference Forbes could find for a "Duke of Chadwick" on the Internet was for a racehorse with that name which raced in the U.S. in 2013-14 for one 3rd place finish and a national ranking of 29,252 out of 41,306 horses. That was before horseracing was abolished as it was disrespectful and harmful, if not lethal, to the horses.

In the Philadelphia schools, both Eleanor and Chad learned to express their emotions through the national Common Emotional Education (CEE!) program. This was part of the nationwide effort to reduce violence by teaching children about emotions and how to deal with their own emotions and those of others. Students were taught healthy ways to deal with anger and how to express frustration, as well as love and other emotions.

The family moved to Portland, Maine in June 2104 where both parents found work that excited them.

Forbes accepted a job as Chief Executive Officer of the State Bank of Maine, now one of 53 such U.S. banks. North Dakota was the first state in the U.S. to establish its state bank in 1919. Since then, it has flourished as a stable part of the state's banking system. It is the repository of all state funds, and it loans money to people, businesses and organizations which promote goals of the state government. The largest loan volume is for environmentally related projects. In the 21st century, student loans were the primary loan category, but the online education revolution had dramatically reduced the cost of education.

In 2024, many banks in the U.S. went through another speculative bubble, similar to the Savings and Loan bust of the 1980s and the banking crisis of the 2000s. Congress finally took notice that North Dakota largely escaped the ravages of both crises, in some substantial part because of the anchor provided by the State Bank of North Dakota. In 2025, Congress passed the National State Bank Enabling Act, as part of the Federal Reserve Act, which authorized states to create their own banks, just as North Dakota had done.

Maine jumped on board in 2026 during a period of progressive politics in Maine and nationally. In 1996, Maine passed its Clean Elections Act which provided for public funding for elections for State Representatives and State Senators. However, it wasn't until 2018 that Maine adopted a computer modeled redistricting system similar to one pioneered in Iowa. The computer was programmed to determine the most equitably sized, contiguous districts with appropriate consideration to be given to existing town, ward and city boundaries. This model was adopted throughout the country in the early 2000s, for local and state elections and for elections to the U.S. Congress. Following this reform, Maine led the nation again, by extending public funding for elections to the races for Congress.

By 2040 all 53 States, with the District of Columbia, Puerto Rico and the Virgin Islands having become states in the 2030's, had their own state banks. One result was that there were fewer bank failures throughout the country, and state and local governments were able to obtain lower interest rates on their debts.

By an odd quirk of legislation, the State Bank of Maine administered the state's Home/Land Restoration Program (HoLaRP). Through this program, no new home was permitted to be constructed on previously farmed or forested land unless an equal amount of previously "improved" land was returned to farm or forest status. As the Maine population was declining, there was less pressure to build homes in virgin territory, but Forbes required remedial conservation mitigation actions in approximately 50 such cases a year.

Charlotte was hired as a professor at the Portland campus of the University of Maine, which had long before absorbed the former University of Southern Maine. She was excited to teach students about 19th and 20th century utopian novels. The university now included all the public colleges and universities in one seamless system. The several mergers led to the reduction in administrative costs.

Maine was a good state for Chad and Eleanor, too. It was a national leader in the resurgence of local farming, so there was ample fresh produce. The number of farms, and their acreage had doubled over the last 100 years. Making room for those farms, thanks to the availability of sex education and free family planning services, the state's population had declined from its peak of about 1.3 million to less than 1 million.

Instead of clearing forests for the resurgent farming sector, farmland was reclaimed from residential areas which had become less populated, in part thanks to the program administered by Forbes. Before an existing or future farmer could clear forests s/he needed to show that other land was not available for farming within a reasonable distance.

Another source of farmland was the cleared land that was no longer needed for the wide swaths of high voltage electric line transmission. With the increased use of local electricity sources, and wireless power transmission, there was less need for long-distance transmission. Where large amounts were required, the current was transformed to high voltage direct current which required only two lines, rather than six. Thus even where the old corridors were still needed, less space was required, which freed land for reforestation and farming.

Maine was also home to a large network of camps for children and families who could return to the recreation experiences of the early 20th century with canoes, sailboats and swimming in the summer and cross-country skiing, snow shoeing and ice-climbing in the winter or to camps with century-based themes, such as 18th century farming or 19th century fishing or logging.

As with many professors, the subject of Charlotte's Ph.D. thesis continued to be the primary intellectual focus for the rest of her career. It had been 90 years since the publication of *Jesus and Jesusa,* and Charlotte was already planning to publish in 2114 a 100-year commemorative edition of the book. Her course was also a licensed GLOOC[19] course. The future book and the course would be based upon her Ph.D. thesis about the

---

19. GLOOC = Global Open Online Courses, which succeeded the successful MOOC (Massive Open Online Courses) which began in the 2010s.

global impact of the publication of *Jesus and Jesusa.*[20]

---

20. See Appendix B for the summary of Charlotte's Ph.D. thesis.

Chapter 3 An Astronaut and a Felon grow up

Eleanor was ten when the family moved to Maine in 2104. She continued her education at the Portland Middle School, which had a year-round program, including global open online courses (GLOOCs). For three months each year, at different seasons, she attended a season-appropriate outdoors camp. The most challenging was the winter "Shaker Camp," which was conducted at the site of the 300 year old former Shaker Village at Sabbathday Lake, in New Gloucester, Maine. Sabbathday Lake was the last active Shaker community in the United States when its last member died in 2023. Participants at that camp lived for three months or more as if they were living in the year 1823, when the community attained its peak population of about 150. Nothing that utilized electricity was allowed in the camp. If people needed to communicate with the outside world, they had to walk or borrow a horse for the five kilometers to the camp's communication center.

Her favorite summer camp was on the campus of Gould Academy in Bethel, Maine where she learned advanced Deutsch in an immersion course. She was surprised at how easily the Deutsch she learned from her childhood nanny came back to her.

In 2107 Eleanor went to boarding school as a ninth grader at Phillips Academy[1] in Andover,

---

1. Among the notable graduates of Phillips Academy are three U.S. Presidents from the Bush family: George H.W. Bush (class of 1942), George W. Bush (1964), and John Ellis Bush ("JEB")(1971). Others include: Samuel Morse (1802), Frederick Law Olmsted (1838), Alice Stone Blackwell (1867),

Massachusetts and the following summer spent three months at the Outward Bound School at Hurricane Island Maine. Through the work of Joshua Miner of Phillips Academy, the Outward Bound movement came to the U.S. from Europe in 1961 to Colorado, and then spread to Maine in 1964. One hundred forty-four years later, it continued the time-tested formulas which emfasized teamwork as well as individual stamina and exercise.

Phillips Academy was one of the international secondary schools which conducted a GLOOC for preparation for the GLOBIT (GLObal Information Test). As it was administered worldwide every five years for people 15 years of age and older, it was administered at the academy to all students at that age or older in 2010, when Eleanor was in 11th grade. The school's average score was 99%. The two most troublesome questions that year were #57 and #83 which read:

#57   How much carbon dioxide would be generated from a liter/kilogram of gasoline?
      A. 2.4 kilograms
      B. 1.0 kilogram
      C. .6 kilogram
(The correct answer is A, because each carbon atom in the gasoline combines with the two oxygen atoms from the atmosfere to create a carbon dioxide atom which weighs more than the original gasoline.)

Henry L. Stimson (1883), Hiram Bingham (1894), Emilio Collado (1927), Jack Lemmon (1943), John F. Kennedy, Jr. (1979), Barack Obama II (2040), Opra Mandela Winfrey (2057).

#83 The Earth's human population in 2109 was 6.5 billion. What were the populations in 1809/1909/2009?

    A. 3.4 billion/4.2 billion/5.1 billion

    B. .9 billion/1.8 billion/7.1 billion

    C. 5.6 billion/6.8 billion/7.1 billion

(The correct answer is B. Answer A should have been eliminated by test-takers because it was expected that every human should know in 2110 that the human population had declined from its high in the mid-21st century, and that there had been exponential growth since the improvement of health in early 20th century which reduced the death rate. Answer C was also incorrect because it failed to show any exponential growth, even though it did show the reduction from 2009 to the present.)

The Phillips Academy scores were 94% on #57 and 97% on #83. The global average scores on these two questions were 25% and 29%, respectively.

In the spring of 2110 Eleanor spent a semester in Peru in order to immerse herself, and twenty fellow students, in Espanol and Peruvian culture. She was especially interested in the Inca civilization which dominated western South America during the 15th and early 16th century. Eleanor wrote home to her parents, "Why did the Spaniards have to conquer, plunder and enslave this civilization, beginning in 1533? What inhumanity we humans, (mostly men!) have committed against each other. " Eleanor tried to make up for that harm in her own way by teaching about the environment in Espanol to sixth graders in Lima.

She explored the Inca ruins of Machu Picchu, which were uncovered by Phillips Academy alumnus Hiram Bingham in 1911. She just missed the upcoming 200-year anniversary celebration of that discovery which was to include an official apology from the government of Espana for the colonization and exploitation by Pizzaro and his successors. The war for Peruvian independence began in 1811 and freedom was won in 1821.

After her graduation from Phillips Academy in 2111, Eleanor went to Brown University in Providence, Rhode Island. Tuition and board at this private college remained very expensive despite the Federal government's expansion of its Pell[2] grant system, and despite the reduction in teaching costs through automation. The Pell grants provided direct grants of 5,000 earthas a year for direct payments to colleges and universities for up to six years.

Eleanor was an excellent football[3] player, but NCAA rules prohibited scholarships based on athletic ability and performance since 2056. Instead, NCAA member colleges were permitted to award scholarships on the basis of financial need. Such needs were quantifiable and subject to audits. After an exhaustive mid-century study, the NCAA had concluded that its previous athletic scholarship system had contributed significantly to the international decline in U.S. education standards. Simply, the study found that China, Korea and Europe were not offering athletic scholarships, and the graduates of universities in those countries were earning Nobel Prizes more frequently than Americans and they were founding more companies.

Because Eleanor's parents earned substantial salaries, they did not qualify for any scholarships or other financial aid beyond the Pell grants. They

2. Pell grants were named, coincidentally, for Rhode Island U.S. Senator Claiborne Pell (1918-2009) who was dedicated to making higher education more available to all.
3. Football was formerly called "soccer" in the United States.

and Eleanor were, however, able to borrow money at a subsidized low interest rate.

At Brown, Eleanor majored in fysics and developed a specialty in astrofysics, the study of the universe. She was especially interested in the origins of the observable universe and the latest enhancements to the Big Bang theory. It fascinated her that the "Big Bang" theory was not just about the creation of our own galaxy approximately 13.8 billion years ago. It's thought that a "Big Bang" is the same way that all the other galaxies and universes were created and are still being created. The total universe is obviously larger than the observed universe, just as the observed universe is much larger than what was observed only 100 or 1,000 years ago. Since no end can be found, the universe must be assumed to be infinitely old and infinitely large, with an infinite number of big bangs occurring every infinitessimal unit of time (i.e. shorter than a nanosecond, which is one billionth of a second) of every day, moving infinitely into the future.

Looking more closely at the observable universe, i.e. within the territory filled with the remnants of our own "Big Bang," the numbers are still staggering. The most distant detected stellar structure named Erehtraf ("Far there" reversed), and formerly named UDFj-39546284, is 13.4 billion light years away. A light year, representing the distance that light can travel in a year at the rate of 299,792 km per second, is 9,460,730,472,581 km, or, in shortened form, 9.46 trillion km. The distance to Erehtraf is 126,773,788,332,583,000,000,000 km or in verbal form, 126 sextillion, 773 quintillion, 788 quadrillion, 332 trillion, 583 billion kilometers. Among other reasons, there is little point in humans considering travel to Erehtraf because it no longer exists. It probably died about a trillion years after Erehtraf's light began its long journey in all directions. Our own sun is expected to die in about a trillion years. However, long before that, in about 3.5 billion years, it will be about 40% hotter than it is now, and the Earth will be as hot and as inhospitable and dry as the planet Venus is now. By then, humans will inhabit other planets and spaceships.

Back on Earth in astrofysics class, Eleanor had to consider that our sun is one of approximately 100 billion stars in our galaxy, and that our galaxy is only one of at least 300 billion in the universe observable by human instruments. "Then," as her class was urged by Professor Carla Sagan, "imagine that our observable universe is reduced to the size of a marble within another similarly sized universe, and shrink THAT universe to the size of marble, and then repeat the process again, and again. NOW, do you get a sense of how BIG is the total universe?"

Eleanor shared a shrug with a nearby classmate and said, "This is ridiculous, but....here we are."

"Now, asked Professor Sagan, "how many seconds have there been since the approximate birth of Jesus of Nazareth? For the sake of discussion, let's say that it occurred on January 1, 1."

Students groaned. One student, Dorothy Porter, knew from a math paper she had done in high school that McDonald's stopped in 1994 its official counts of the number of hamburgers it sold when the number reached 99 billion. She had also remembered that when McDonald's stopped selling hamburgers, cheeseburgers and Big Macs in 2032 during its transition to a vegan diet, someone had calculated that the grand total sold was approximately 440 billion. So Dorothy volunteered, "a trillion?" By that time, Eleanor was able to do the calculation on her computer: 60 X 60 X 24 X 365.242 X 2112. The answer was 66.6 billion.

"Wait a minute," said Dorothy. "You mean that McDonald's sold more - many more - beef hamburgers in the 77 years from 1955 to 2032 than the total number of seconds since the year 1?" Eleanor projected her calculations onto the wall, and then she divided 440 by 66.6 and said "Yeah. Like 6.6 times as many." Such numbers are barely comprehensible.

The professor made another effort to make the numbers comprehensible.
"Take the estimated age of just our observable universe," he said. "Let's suppose that each billion years is represented by 100 kilometers, or 10 million years per kilometer, so the distance from our universe's big bang to the present is 1,400 km, or roughly the distance from Providence to Charleston, South Carolina. Now, let's assume that humans became recognizable as tool-wielding animals approximately 500,000 years ago. Everybody with me?"

She continued after seeing some students nodding up and down. "Ok. Eleanor, let's suppose you are a bird flying from Providence to Charleston. How far do you think you would fly on the 14 billion year timeline before your 500,000 years was used up?"

"Hmm," she gestured, and struggled to get her fone to do the math. "Ten kilometers?"

"Well, you're close," she said, with a smile. "It would be 50 meters, which would get you from this classroom to the front door of this building. Let me just add here that the image gets more dramatic when you consider the length of the holocene, the most recent and current geological epoch which could be said to have begun about 12,000 years ago. It's also been called the anthropocence, as it encompasses the entirely of human civilization, if that is defined by human writing. Anyway, I digress."

"Yes," said Eleanor quietly to Dorothy, "She digresses a lot."

"Anyway," concluded Professor Sagan, "If you flew on that universe timeline for the length of the holocene, you would fly for 1.2 meters. Thus, in terms of the age of our universe, we humans don't count for much."

Later that year, Eleanor conducted an experiment, together with an astronaut on the moon, Laurel Camarada, which gave her first-hand contact with the space program. The experiment was a test of the ability of a laser beam to transmit computer messages. She measured the degree of degradation of a message when the beam was off-center by degrees and millimeters. The experiment led Laurel to ask Eleanor about her interest in the space program.

"Have you considered becoming an astronaut?" she asked.

"Not really, but there is a family connection to Alan Shepard," responded Eleanor. Her father had once told her that about the distant cousin relationship through the Delano family with Alan B Shepard, the first U.S. astronaut, so the idea of becoming an astronaut was not new.

"Wow. He was my hero when I was a child," said Laurel. "I did a 6th grade paper about him. We have it so much easier, now. You can become an astronaut after six months of training."

"Really?" asked Eleanor. "I thought you had to be in the military first."

"Not for a long time," she said. "I went to Stanford and studied math."

That afternoon, Eleanor completed the preliminary online application, and was hooked.

After graduation from Brown in 2115, she took a year off from formal education, and used her savings for a trip to see several volcanoes around the world, including Mt. Etna in Sicilia, still the only active volcano in Europa, and the dormant Mt. Vesuvius, and the five active volcanoes in Hawaii.

While in Sicilia, she visited members of her maternal grandmother's family, the Kinselli's, and also the estate 13 kilometers outside the city of Bronte, known as Castello di Nelson. This estate was given in 1799 by King Ferdinand of Napoli and Sicilia, to Lord Horatio Nelson, the Napoleonic era British naval captain and commander, in appreciation for Nelson's support of the king's government. The connection to Eleanor was that her mother, Charlotte, was named after Charlotte Bronte, and Bronte's name came from the Nelson estate. As the locals tell the story, Charlotte Bronte's father, Patrick, visited Castello Di Nelson, and had an entirely different surname, and was so enamoured with the estate that he changed his name to Bronte. More accurately, as Eleanor later learned, Patrick was born with the surname Brunty, and he felt that Bronte was more elegant and assumed that spelling of the name. In any case, Eleanor's grandmother, Elena Bronte Kinselli, knew the story, and had read Charlotte Bronte's *Jane Eyre* and Emily Bronte's *Wuthering Heights* and named her daughters after the authors.

By the fall of 2116, Eleanor was 23 and back in the U.S. and she completed her formal application to be an astronaut. NASA's previous de facto minimum age for astronauts was 26, but NASA officially established a minimum age of 22 in 2034, after the decision was made to cease most round trips to the moon and plan future human space travel as one-way colonization expeditions. That age limit was accepted by the new Global Aeronautic Space Organization (GLASO) when NASA was merged in 2036 with the space programs of the other leading space exploration nations and brought under the jurisdiction of the United Nations.

The competition to become an astronaut was severe as there were 243 other applications from around the world for the 30 openings. Despite the odds, Eleanor was accepted. The next step was a three year formal training program emfasizing fysical fitness, flight training and more academic studies. The first base for training was in Houston, Texas at the Manned Space Center, to which Eleanor reported in early December 2116.

She took the MAGtrain[4] home for a one-week Christmas break, even though no one in her family was Christian. In fact, there were very few Christians left in the country, so the holiday was essentially a day to celebrate winter. In the 21st century it became a holiday to celebrate consumption, but that goal was displaced by the changes enacted during the Great Transformation. That is, it was realized that global consumption was a problem for human happiness and survival and not a solution. Advertising was regulated and required to provide factual information about products and services, without appeals to the emotions. Thus, advertisements with beautiful people standing next to products, or skits with

---

4. Short for Magnetic Levitation Train, the MAGtrain used electricity both for propulsion and for powering the electromagnets that kept the train about 15 millimeters from the surface of the tracks. It takes far less energy to keep a vehicle that distance from the ground than to power an airplane, which were now mostly restricted to cross-ocean travel due to the availability of MAGtrains over land.

friendly dogs next to or inside products, vanished.
The goal for reformers was to have consumption
based on need rather than want, or worse, rather
than artificially stimulated want.

Economists had learned that it was not required
that people continue to purchase "things" in order
to maintain full employment. Instead, it was
necessary for governments around the world to
contract with their citizens to be "employers of last
resort." With the savings from the substantial
reduction of the military forces in all nations,
especially in the U.S., and from the significant
reduction in the cost of their criminal justice
systems, and from other savings, most
governments were able to reduce their
indebtedness. Further, they created "rainy day"
funds to provide for employment for those who were
not able to find employment in the private sector.
Governments of the world had similar priorities for
what needed to be done in the public sector, e.g.
restore the world's forests, and there was more
than enough work to do.

Upon the emergence of the work of John
Maynard Keynes, it had been gospel for economists
for the next 80 years that increased government
spending, including borrowing money to create jobs
was a legitimate and economically sound practice.
One problem with that theory was that, with rare
exceptions, countries found it far easier to borrow
money in bad times, and in good times, than to pay
off those debts during good times. For example, the
U.S. transformed itself from being the world's
largest creditor nation after World War II to the
largest debtor nation in the early 21st century.
While this change had a beneficial result of
providing dollar liquidity for the international
currency markets, the transition to debtor status
also showed the world how tenuous was the

justification of keeping the U.S. dollars as the primary international currency, and thus accelerated the transition to a Single Global Currency. The indebtedness also led to the relative decline in the U.S. standard of living.

Instead, a school of economists at the Indira Gandhi National Open University (IGNOU) determined that the savings from "going green," demilitarization and the movement to online education, were more than enough to fund the reduction of debt and future commitments for full employment. The IGNOU school found that the Keynesians had overlooked the West's reliance upon defense spending as a primary cause of indebtedness, rather than the commitments for full employment.

The childhood and youth of Eleanor's younger brother, Chad, was less eventful or successful. He was seven when the family moved to Portland, so he went first to a Portland Montessori school for second grade. His parents looked for signs that his genetic mutation was causing any behavioral problems. That was a challenge, as he seemed to alternate between behaving well and not well in about the same ratio as other boys. Was his decision to get up at dawn at 5:47 one October morning[5] and explore Portland on his "Solar Scooter" a product of gene mutation, or was it

---

5. It was Friday, October 9, 2105. Chad was seven, and would be eight in less than two months. Sunrise was at 5:47 a.m., instead of 6:47 a.m., because the U.S. had abolished "Daylight Savings Time" in 2046. It had been a holdover practice from the days when farming was a major part of the economy and it was somehow easier to change clocks than change their schedules. In the interest of "straight talk," everyone knew long before 2046 that there were no "savings" of daylight, as the lengths of the days remained the same regardless of where people set their clocks.

because he was a curious kid? The "Solar Scooter" battery provided the necessary power until the sunrise. That adventure ended when a Good Samaritan, coincidentally named Chad Evans, saw Chad on the Induction Lane of the superhighway. Evans then alerted the police with his cellfone and then alerted other cars in the vicinity to slow down while he recovered Chad. From Chad's "body chip" the police were able to locate his home and they accompanied Evans as he brought Chad home. The sun was just rising and Forbes was in the kitchen getting coffee when Evans and the police arrived with Chad.

"Well, good morning, Chad, and good morning to you, officers," said a bemused Forbes. The officers were smiling and Chad seemed healthy and mobile, so Forbes's natural instincts to be optimistic and cheerful led to his warm greeting.

"Hi Dad," said Chad. "I went for a little trip on my scooter and got lost."

Forbes called up to Charlotte, "Honey, there's no need to try to wake up Chad for school this morning. I have him here in the kitchen – together with his new friends."

The officer and Evans explained how Chad was found, and Forbes offered to give Evans 100 earthas as a reward, but Evans declined, saying, "Thanks very much. It's a pleasure to meet you, but I have to return this Zip Car. Bye. Bye, Chad!"

Zip Cars were part of the 21st century fenomenon of sharing cars, boats and homes, which arose as part of the computer age, which had significantly reduced the transaction costs of sharing. With computers, it was vastly easier to verify the character, experience and responsibility of potential share partners, and much easier to complete a transaction.

Chad made it to school on time and had a "Show and Tell" adventure to present to his classmates. During the school day, Forbes took the "Solar Scooter" to the repair shop and had a "GPS-Block" installed which first triggered a buzzer when the scooter went more than 50 meters from the GPS-repeater station near the Delano back door. When the scooter went 25 meters farther, the electric motor would automatically shut down.

Chad's being in the Induction Lane with a scooter was the clue that told Chad Evans that something was wrong. The Induction Lane was normally reserved for specially equipped vehicles which received their power by the conversion of electromagnetic energy from the road coils into a coil in the vehicles, which then converted the energy back into electric energy to power the motors. The system worked, as Chad Delano was told, the same way that his electric toothbrush was recharged, without any direct metal contacts. In any case, he shouldn't have been on the highway, and was lucky he wasn't killed.

The Induction Lane was a variation of the overall solar construction of highways around the world. Since 2043, all high-use roads in the U.S. were required to be constructed with solar collectors, the power from which could be fed into nearby networks, as well as provide power for their Induction Lanes. Similarly, all buildings and other structures were required to have solar collectors for every external surface exposed to the sun. The construction of new buildings was also affected by the requirement that their steel and aluminum and other metals be fabricated using electric arc furnaces which required no coal or other fossil fuel for heating the raw materials.

The low-use roads, formerly paved with asphalt, were left to decompose into gravel/dirt roads, which allowed rain to filter through to the subsoil without the pollution from the asphalt. These gravel/dirt roads were maintained with grading and renewed layers of gravel/dirt, together with a compound which minimized dust during dry periods. With the conversion to gravel/dirt roads, together with the upgrading of the high-use paved roads to solar collectors, the U.S. ratio of paved/unpaved roads went from 2:1 to 1:1. There were approximately three million kilometers of each type of road.

In the third through sixth grades, Chad seemed to progress as an average student, and not as a star like his sister. One of his favorite memories was the trip in the summer after sixth grade to Plymouth, Massachusetts to the Pilgrim Hall Museum, the country's oldest continuously operating museum, where he learned more about his de La Noye ancestor. That was the time when his father taught him about mathematical exponents with this exchange.

"Ok, Chad," Forbes began during the two hour drive back from Plymouth, "how many generations, dads and moms having children, do you think there have been since Philippe de La Noye came to Plymouth in 1621?"

"I don't know, Dad. I'm not so good with math," said Chad. "Maybe ten?"

"Ok, you're close. There have been 18 generations, including yours. That's not many, considering the U.S. Delano family goes back to 1621."

"Where were the Delano's or de La Noye's, whatever, before that?" asked Chad.

"They were originally from France. De La Noye, means in francais, "of the drowned." I don't know what that means, though. Maybe it was a family of sailors or fishermen," said Forbes.

"When did the family change the spelling to D-E-L-A-N-O?" asked Chad.

"I think it was the original Philippe's grandson who changed it."

"Why?" asked Chad.

"Well, I guess because it was easier to spell. Also, the Pilgrims and the Puritans, who arrived later, were especially oriented to England, and the grandson wanted a name that didn't sound so French."

"Hmmm. Dad. So why did granddad change his name back to De la Noye?"

"Good question. My mother wondered about that. She thought that maybe Philippe was hiding from something. Anyway, I guess he just thought De la Noye was more authentic, and that we were long past the need to hide the fact that the family came from France."

"Hmm. Lots of my friends' parents have different names. That's cool. Ok. What about those numbers you wanted to quiz me about?" asked Chad.

"Ok," remembered Forbes. "How many parents do you have?"

"That's easy. Two."

"And how many grandparents?"

"Four."

"And how many great grandparents, in the third generation away from you?" asked Forbes.

"Six?" asked Chad.

"No. It's eight. To get the number of parents for each generation you multiply by two, and four times two is eight. In the next generation, there were 16 great grandparents. Now, here's the big question. How many great, great, greats were there going back to the original Philippe de La Noye?"

"No idea. Maybe a thousand?" guessed Chad.

"Well, this is where you use exponents, which you'll learn next year in school. There are 18 generations, so that's two to the 18th power, so that's about 250,000. I forget. Can you get out your calculator? Without knowing how to operate the exponent key, just key in two times two and then press the EQUAL button 18 times."

"Ok. Dad. It's 262,144. Whew! That's a lot of ancestors," said Chad.

"That's the funny thing about genealogy. Because of the old naming system, where children all had their father's last name, and daughters adopted the names of their husbands, we're only familiar with a small part of one-half of our family. We only know of one ancestor in that 18th generation, the first Philippe, and his wife. Who knows who the other 262,000 were?" said Forbes.

That fall, Chad went to Portland Middle School. Like Eleanor, he took the required Emotional Education courses and learned how to better express himself, and be more sensitive to the feelings of others. He was often the student who waded into situations where a girl or boy bully was starting to intimidate a fellow student.

After eighth grade he told his parents that he did not want to attend a boarding school. His experiences with boarding camps were enough to convince him that staying home, with familiar girlfriends and with an ample supply food in the convenient home refrigerator, was more his style. Even if he didn't have a good relationship with his parents, who seemed to be more devoted to the successful, older Eleanor, the parents he knew were preferable to the "in loco" parents he didn't know. Later, he continued with Portland High School.

Chad played football[6] for the high school team. At 1.8 meters and 111 kilograms in his sofomore year, he was big enough to play moveball,[7] but the school had canceled its moveball program in 2096. Since the 2022 adoption of "touch moveball" rules, moveball had been less dangerous for boys, but it was still primarily a male game and that wasn't fair. However, the Portland School Committee was more concerned about the cost of equipment and the relatively small amount of exercise which was actually gained during a moveball game. Football was far safer, especially after the abandonment of the ability to "head" a ball, and it provided much more cardiac-valuable exercise – except for the goalie, and that was the position that Chad played.

He liked working with computers and with wood, but didn't feel the need to excel at school. The message at home was that Eleanor was the "star" and there was no need to bother to compete for her position.

Blonde and blue-eyed, despite his part southern Italian heritage, Chad was a sought-after partner, and Melissa Grant, also blonde, considered herself lucky to have him. She had moved to Portland for her 11th grade year in 2112 and was in love with Chad by November. She, too, had low self-esteem.

They did much together, including skipping school when the time seemed right and they would go to his house or hers, primarily for sex. They graduated in 2115 and planned to go to Cumberland County Community College for the two year program in computer science. That summer, they jointly took a GLOOC course in computer history – all 169 years since the U.S. ENIAC vacuum tube computer was developed in 1946.

---

6. Formerly called soccer in the U.S.
7. Formerly called football in the U.S.

The next year, Melissa continued to learn programming and computer applications, while Chad drifted into other subjects, including Maine history, environmental studies I, and computer grafics. Chad had inherited a trust fund from his great-grandfather and Nobel laureate in economics, Samuel James Delano. The trust proceeds, payable monthly for the rest of his life, became available to Chad when he turned 18 in November 2115. With that money, and some to spare, Chad and Melissa moved together to an apartment on Munjoy Hill, at the north end of the city.

It was ironic that Samuel James left money to his second generation descendants, as that contributed to the income and wealth inequality that bothered Samuel James Delano so much. He apparently thought that by providing a modest income for each descendant, rather than a large fixed amount, he was helping more than he was hurting. After the death of each second generation descendant, i.e. his great grandchildren, the principal of the trusts would be given to several charitable organizations including Zero Population Growth.

In his writings, he opposed the long term passing of family wealth from generation to generation. With longer lifespans, many people knew their great grandchildren, so that was the appropriate cutoff.

Eleanor had dinner with Chad and Melissa on December 26, 2116 at a restaurant in the Old Port area, now more protected from the still-rising ocean. Over the last century, it had risen two and half meters. Chad knew about the ocean rising from his environmental course and it was apparent that the Portland sea walls were newer and higher than those which could be seen at low tide.

"You know, Sis," said Chad, "it was a little tough following your act as a top student, as you were.

Now, with you being an astronaut, it's even tougher."

"Sorry," returned Eleanor. "I can only pursue my dreams. Whenever the parents start comparing you to me, I cut them off. 'Wrong discussion,' I tell them. By the way, what happened to your dream of kayaking up to Greenland and then to the Siberian straits last summer?"

"Well," said Chad, "Melissa didn't want to go, and it was too long a trip to be without her. Still, I did kayak to Labrador, but ran out of money while there and needed some help from Mom and Dad. That was just before Great Gramp's trust came into effect."

"Right. Heard about that. You and Melissa are welcome to come to Houston sometime. Better in the winter than summer, of course."

"Ok. Maybe. Thanks," said Chad. "Speaking of dreams, did you ever read Mom's book about that utopian book, *Jesus and Jesusa*? I think she came close to finding out the true author's name."

"Yeah," answered Eleanor. "That was one of 'life's persistent mysteries,' to use the overused family expression. I read it. I actually did a school project on the original utopian book, rather than Mom's comments. It was amazing how events in the actual 21st century actually followed what the book seemed to predict. All the changes, which seem to have saved humanity from disaster, were called the 'Great Transformation.' Mom said she recently received an email from someone who read her paper and who wants to write a utopian novel about a future society where there are no wrongful convictions or close to none."

"Yeah," said Chad. "She told me about that guy. Don't know about the wrongful conviction part. Sounds weird to me. I didn't know there ever were any wrongful convictions. How could that happen?"

"Well," recalled Eleanor, "people can get pretty convinced about the truth of something, even if it's untrue. In school, we studied the history of justice in the U.S. and I wrote a paper about wrongful convictions. It was frankly unbelievable how many innocent people we sent to prison in this country, and even executed, before the reforms of the mid-21st century reduced the wrongful conviction rate to a tenth of a percent or less. The problem touched a lot of people including the families of the wrongly convicted and the victims of crime and their families. When the wrong person was convicted, the victims began to reassemble their lives with the expectation of closure. However, in those cases, the defendants kept on insisting on their innocence and seeking publicity for their causes, which blocked the closure that the victims and their families sought. In those cases where exonerations of the wrongly convicted were finally achieved, sometimes 20-30 years later, it was too late for searching for or convicting the real perpetrators. Also, too many police and prosecutors were so vested in their original theories of cases, that they were unable to renew an investigation and prosecution. Thus, the victims suffered double losses and rarely achieved the recommended closure with the apprehension and conviction of the real perpetrator.

In fact, Max had a relative who was wrongly convicted in Massachusetts and sent to prison for life for building a bomb which killed a policeman – but the relative had nothing to do with the bomb. Zero. Nada."

Melissa asked, "Wow, but first things first. So, tell us about Max, what's his name."

"It's Max Trenkler," answered Eleanor. "He's from Deutschland.[8] I love him, and we're thinking about getting married. What about you and Chad? Are you thinking about marriage?"

Melissa looked at Chad and chose to answer first. "We've talked about marriage, but I've wanted to have children. Or at least one. But Chad says he doesn't want children. Too much stress, and the Earth doesn't need more people. So we're a little stuck. Still, I've known others who have had similar differences and they worked it out, so we're staying together – at least for now."

Chad added, "Yup. That's about it. It's hard enough trying to get my own life together, so it's hard to imagine bringing someone else into this world and helping him or her figure it all out. Dunno."

The next day, Eleanor took the return five-hour MAGtrain to Houston. "Have a good time at your New Year's Party," she said as she departed.

8. Germany

Chapter 4   Investigating a death

At Chad's apartment, the New Year's party continued, but without Chad. He had passed out from the champagne he continued to drink after Juan and Anita left.

Michelle and Xue brought a batch of marijuana cookies they had made with a new variation of THC (Delta-9-tetrahydrocannabinol), the primary ingredient of marijuana, which she had received from Xue's relatives in China. Such mailing of drugs was completely legal after China agreed to abide the U.N.'s 2034 Global Drug Convention. That international law closely paralleled the U.S.'s dramatic changes in its Controlled Substances Act in 2028, which legalized all drugs formerly denominated as Schedule 1-5 drugs. Since then, U.S. doctors were able to prescribe such drugs as needed and requested. To reduce abuse, patients were requested to submit to random urine or saliva tests so doctors could determine if the drugs they were prescribing for their clients were the only such drugs their clients were using. If not, there were civil and criminal penalties.

At 3:30 a.m., Anita left Chad's to return to the apartment she shared with Juan. She told the door to open and then saw Juan sprawled on the stairs, face down, with blood oozing from his head. He didn't seem to be breathing.

Anita screamed and yelled, "911!" into her wrist fone. The EMT's arrived within six minutes, but quickly confirmed Anita's sense that Juan was dead. His "Body Talk" chip, or more simply, body chip, said so.

Beginning in the mid-21st century, every newborn child in the Western world had a body chip implanted underneath the right arm. The tiny chips were approximately one millimeter in diameter and they were rechargable by electromagnetic induction at the entrances to public buildings, including schools and hospitals. If the charge was nearly depleted, an email was sent to the owner, and to the owner's doctor to advise of the low charge status. The chips were reprogrammable for special individual issues for each person.

Body chips were equipped initially with several health and safety options. First, they had a GPS option which could be used to find someone, for example, a lost child. Second, they had a heart monitoring function which would trigger a house alarm and send a message to a pre-designated fone if there was a problem, such as if a child was experiencing the initial stages of SIDS (Sudden Infant Death Syndrome). It was that heart monitoring option that enabled police to determine that Juan was dead and that the exact time of death was 12:32 a.m.

Two policepeople arrived just after the EMTs. Bob Armstrong and Angela Kline were experienced investigators. Their initial assessment was of a New Year's Eve Party intoxicant who had an unfortunate accident. However, according to regulations, blood was extracted by the EMT's for tests. Then Juan's body was taken to the morgue.

Juan's family was devastated. Juan was an only child, and one of only two grandchildren of both sets of grandparents. His 20-year old body was cremated and the ashes were scattered in Portland harbor. There was only one other choice, other than cremation, since the 2051 Federal regulations on dispositions of bodies, and that was a natural burial in a sheet in a designated cemetery. The location was marked by GPS coordinates, but permanent markers were not permitted.

Two days later Armstrong and Kline received the blood test results by email and they showed the presence of the chemical eszopiclone which is the active ingredient in a Canadian drug marketed as EZsleep. Kline learned further that EZsleep's primary U.S. distributor is MaineDrug, which was based in Portland. That was a coincidence that had to be pursued. Perhaps it wasn't just a coincidence.

They visited the MaineDrug offices with the CEO, Amanda Lavrov. She was trained as a farmacist and had joined MaineDrug after a scandal in 2111 involving embezzlement of drugs. She assured Armstrong and Kline that since 2114 every single pill that her company manufactured or imported was fully accounted for by the AMC system. AMC, for Atomic Marker Count, was a system that relied upon the unique count of atoms on the surface, one atom deep, of each pill's coating. As the count was in the billions the level of uniqueness extended to the nearest 10,000 atoms.

However, that system didn't help Armstrong and Kline as the pill or pills they were searching for had already been consumed. There was no way, Amanda told them, that the eszopiclone in Juan's body, or rather in the retained tissue samples, could be distinguished from that chemical's derivation from other sources. Even more difficult would be the challenge of distinguishing between different batches of the same marketable product, in this case, EZsleep, with its distinctive dark blue coating. Nonetheless, she told the officers, "I'll check with the manufacturer."

Now Armstrong and Kline knew that there was a local possibility that there was a ready and unmarked, supply of EZsleep, at least before 2114. They asked Amanda to email them a list of all of MaineDrug's employees over the past ten years.

Armstrong and Kline had already interviewed
Anita and had the names of the other attendees at
the New Year's Eve party. They interviewed Chad
and he seemed nervous. He was sorry about
Juan's death, but didn't care much for him. Chad
knew each Juan from high school and they
socialized with different groups. He said, "I prefer
not to say why I didn't like him." Chad said that he
didn't use sleep-inducing drugs, preferring frequent
sex with Melissa instead to assist his sleep. He said
that he had not heard of the drug, EZsleep. He had
an uneven employment history, and couldn't
remember all the places he had worked over the
past five years. Much of that was through a
temporary labor agency, Maine Staffing Co-op.

His current job was driving an express package
delivery truck. He liked it, as there were few
hassles with supervisors. However, with the
continuous video-GPS monitoring, the supervisors
were never far away. His company was able to
quickly deliver packages with a smile, and little
chance of crash landing, as had happened with
several recent drone deliveries in Portland. His
electric powered truck was a better environmental
sell than the liquid fuel on the drones. It wasn't
fossil fuel, but the biological waste-generated
methane was still a generator of carbon dioxide,
even if the net total CO_2 count was zero.

The "net zero" argument about the consumption
of the creation of carbon dioxide from the burning
of non-fossil fuel was an annoyance to
environmentalists and advocates of reversing global
warming. Whether the source of CO_2 was fossil
fuels or sustainably manufactured fuels, it was still
CO_2. Humans and their domestic animals didn't eat
coal or drink oil, but they still created CO_2 from
their sustainably sourced food. Regardless of the
source, the exhaled air still contained carbon

dioxide. Every human produces approximately one kilogram of CO_2 per day, or 365 kg/ .365 metric tonnes per year. As carbon constitutes approximately 37% of the weight of carbon dioxide, each human exhales approximately .14 tonne of carbon. With a global population of 6.3 billion, even if shrinking slowly, human breathing produced .9 billion metric tonnes of carbon per year.   If there were many fewer people and many fewer domestic animals, there would be less generation of CO_2, and the land that was used to create food for humans and their animals could be used for trees which consume far more CO_2 than is consumed by vegetable plants and grains.

A healthy tree can store 6 kilograms of carbon per year, while providing daily oxygen for a single person. A hectare of trees, with approximately 175 trees, can store a tonne of carbon in a year, or enough to absorb the exhaled CO_2 of eight people. With 100 hectares in a square kilometer, the exhaled CO_2 of the Earth's 6.3 billion human population could be absorbed by trees on 8.2 million square kilometers, or a land mass slightly less than the size of Brazil. That, in turn, is approximately five percent of the Earth's land mass.

On the land mass in Portland, work and a career didn't seem to be high priorities for Chad. When he didn't have a job, but needed money, he would go to the National Employment Agency (NEA) office and get a guaranteed job. The work of the NEA was to achieve a constant zero, or less than .5 percent, unemployment rate. That is, if there was a person who was available to work part-time or full-time and wanted to work, the NEA would find appropriate work for that person.

This agency was established in the 21st century to ensure that every American had work. The idea was based on the Civilian Conservation Corps (CCC) which was developed during the Great Depression in the 1930's to give work to the unemployed. Similarly, the NEA put people to work for the priorities that required national attention including environmental cleanup and restoration of natural vegetation to areas previously inhabited by people. With a declining population, it was important to restore land to its pre-industrial/residential state. There was other work, too, the assignment to which depended upon the skills and experience of the unemployed. As with temporary employment agencies, sometimes those jobs led to regular employment.

Chad had worked at a Portland suburban site where there was formerly a shopping center but which was being restored to its natural forested habitat. His job was to separate the manmade from the natural materials in the ground. At times, it was almost like an archeological dig. At another site he helped identify and clear an area of an invasive plant species, Japanese barberry.

Armstrong and Kline met with Melissa at her apartment, in their effort to make her as comfortable as possible with the interview. Melissa said that she was distraught over Juan's death and explained that she had been attracted to him, before meeting Chad. Juan seemed normal at the party, until he and Anita slipped away for a Q2. Later, Kline said to Armstrong, "Anita didn't mention the Q2 when we talked with her."

Later that day, the officers met with Melissa's sister, Michelle, who had had several hookups with Juan before his steady relationship with Anita. Michelle was feeling closer to him, but then she became pregnant. Juan, who fancied himself as a descendant of Don Juan, had told Michelle that he had turned off the nanovalve on his vas deferens, the sperm tube, and that it had been turned off for several days. Maybe that wasn't enough time to ensure that no lingering sperm could be transferred during sex. The switch was an app on his watch fone. By unfortunate coincidence, she was changing her method of contraceptive and was in-between protection methods. Accidental pregnancy didn't happen often in the 22nd century, but like many parts of life, avoiding pregnancy depended partially upon mutual honesty, trust and attention to detail. Michelle detected the pregnancy within a week as she was enrolled in a weekly urine testing regimen as part of a University of Maine health study. She had her abortion the next day, and learned by the required DNA testing that the father was Juan, rather than one of her other partners. The abortion was relatively painless, but she wasn't happy about it, as it was embarrassing to look stupid in the eyes of her medical team and her friends.

When she confronted Juan about the pregnancy, he laughed at first, but then said he was sorry, after learning more about what happens with unwanted pregnancies.

Armstrong asked Michelle, "Do you use any prescription sleep medication?" and she said, "No," without hesitation.

Kline asked, "I saw there were champagne glasses at Chad's. Did you all drink a toast together?"

Michelle agreed, "Yes, we did, just at midnight."

Kline pressed further, "Who set the glasses out and who poured the champagne?"

Michelle answered, "Chad did."

Kline felt she was getting somewhere with this line of questioning, "Did you see anything unusual when the glasses were set out or when they were filled?"

Michelle paused, "Well, I didn't think anything of it at the time, but Chad set Juan's glass slightly apart from the others."

"Anything else?" asked Kline.

"Well," answered Michelle, "one other odd thing that didn't make sense at the time. I thought that he was tossing the cork of the champagne bottle into the wastebasket, but after the motion of his right hand toward the basket, I didn't hear anything hit the basket. It was odd. Then Chad turned around and he still had the cork in his left hand. I was just then going to the bathroom, so I didn't think further about it."

Armstrong re-entered the conversation, "Anything else?" he asked.

"No, I guess that's it," answered Michelle.

The officers interviewed the others from the party, but their focus was on Chad. Of the six, he was the only one with an arrest record. Three years before, he had been arrested for assaulting a man with whom he had had words about Melissa. There was no conviction because the man would not testify against Chad, as he didn't want to admit what he had said to Melissa.

Another arrest was for "theft by eating" when he was 16 and subject to the juvenile laws. As a child he had learned from his parents how to eat bites of food while at the grocery store. They hadn't actually intended to teach Chad this skill, but he watched during family grocery shopping trips as they shared a few olives stuffed with gorgonzola or a few dark chocolate-covered almonds before purchasing a few hundred grams of each. The difficulty for Chad arose because his parents had done their earlier shopping in Philadelphia at a local friendly store, whereas Chad purchased his food at the local supermarket, which had multiple cameras and sensors. On several occasions Chad was caught on video eating about half as many chocolate almonds and olives as he purchased. When the cameras recorded the sixth such "food theft," there were civilian-clothed detectives observing too, and they arrested Chad. He pled guilty and was sentenced to work in a food pantry for three months.

A third arrest came a year later for littering. In a world more focused on saving the Earth, littering was treated as a more serious problem than before the Great Transformation. The subject of the litter charge was a discarded cigarette filter. Even though all movies, which showed the formerly cavalier ways that spies, cowboys and even doctors tossed their cigarette butts to the ground, were required to show subtitled warnings that such behavior was no longer tolerated; Chad had stupidly discarded at least one butt. While it may have been stupid when the old movies were made, because of the apparent contempt for the environment, it was more stupid now because of the national DNA database, which contained everyone's DNA. Chad was easily identified and he pled guilty, paid a fine, and had to perform 100 hours of community service picking up litter.

The most relevant crime occurred in 2115, when Chad had been convicted, by guilty plea, of "chemical sexual assault" after dropping flunitrazepam (FUZ), a so-called "date-rape drug" into a woman's drink, and then having sex with her. Following their hunch, Armstrong and Kline searched the internet for anything that Chad may have written about himself or others. They found a 2116 comment in his own "self-blog" about the anger that he felt when Melissa had told him about Juan's sexual aggression toward her the previous year. When Chad's older sister, Eleanor, saw those comments shortly after they were made, she strongly recommended to Chad that he remove them, but it was too late. Once something is posted on the internet, it could be saved somewhere, somehow, for years. Thus, the officers found the comment in the backup copies, including subsequently deleted materials, of the blog which they had accumulated.

The officers obtained a search warrant for Chad's apartment and his car. They seized several items, including the few bottles of pills in his bathroom. None of the pills resembled the distinctive dark blue round EZ pills. In other bags, they dumped the contents of Chad's trash baskets into their clear plastic bags. Chad wasn't home, initially, but returned when the search was almost completed.

Angela Kline asked Chad, as the host of the party, if he had any idea why Juan Carlos became so tired and disoriented so quickly. Chad said, "No idea," but said it a little too quickly and flippantly for the officers.

Armstrong asked Chad if he would be willing to take a polygraf or voice-stress test, or lie-MRI test. From cumulative research done in the 2030's, each of the three tests had similar reliability records, about 90%. Subsequent studies of the hybrid combination polyvoicegraf test, developed in the 2020's, showed even better reliability. The officers also told him that he was a suspect in the death of Juan, and that he had the right to consult an attorney and to decline to talk with them further. Because Chad knew about his own previous record with dropping a drug into a woman's drink, and because he knew of his dislike for Juan, he didn't think taking a truth test was a good idea.

Also, he had a better reason for not taking the truth test, as he disclosed later to his attorney, Nina McKelvy, whom he called right away. She told him, "I'll be right there."

While Chad waited for Nina to walk to his apartment, which was only a few blocks from her office, he called his mother. She had just finished conducting the final exams for her special fall course on the original *Utopia*, by St. Thomas More. It was outside her usual course load of 19th and 20th century utopian literature, but 2116 was the 600th anniversary of the 1516 publication of *Utopia*, and she had been asked to conduct a GLOOC course for the occasion. Fifteen thousand, three hundred students took the course. The exams were graded by a computer using digital literary analysis, and Charlotte's role was to read the relatively few exams for which the students appealed the computer grading.

Charlotte was troubled by Chad's call. She asked him, "Well, did you do it?" and he told her the truth, "I don't know." Then he explained some details until Nina arrived at his apartment.

There were not many criminal defense attorneys in Portland because of the overall decrease in crime during the 21st century. That reduction was primarily due to the legalization of recreational drugs, Emotional Education in schools and gun control.

The legalization of recreational drugs in the U.S. began with the legalization of medical marijuana in California in 1996. When the predicted benefits emerged without the costs predicted by opponents, other states followed California's lead. The movement's second major boost came in 2012 when Colorado and Washington State approved by referendum the sale of recreational marijuana. The "Yes" votes came from potential users and from libertarians who supported most personal freedoms and from fiscal conservatives who sought the tax revenues from the regulated businesses. Further, those conservatives anticipated the savings from avoidance of police, prosecution, judicial and corrections costs from the decriminalization of marijuana.

The next wave of drug decriminalization came with the legalization of heroin in New York in 2022. The rationale behind legalization was that, despite the availability of prescribed non-addictive alternatives to heroin, it was still the drug of choice for tens of thousands of addicts. By legalizing heroin, New York reduced the price to addicts and, through taxation, raised tens of millions of earthas to assist users in managing their addictions. By requiring prescriptions from doctors, the new law brought a substantial proportion of the previously hidden world of heroin use into the open. Drug-related crime dropped significantly, as did the number of drug overdoses. Further, an unforeseen benefit was on the international stage in Afghanistan where the growing of opium poppies was legalized, taxed and regulated. That brought prosperity to that country's farmers, and it knocked a revenue source out of the hands of organized crime, just as it did in New York. The success of New York's law was a repeat of previous drug legalization efforts. Rather than continue the piecemeal state-by-state efforts, the campaign focused on national reform, which led to the 2028 amendments to the Controlled Substances Act.

The Emotional Education role in the reduction in crime came from the efforts of the anti-domestic violence movement. It was there where researchers found that 80% of the people, usually men, who were convicted of assault had severely limited abilities to show emotion in a reasonable way. Rather than learning how to respond with words to show anger or frustration, these individuals learned to be violent and attack others. Other criminologists noticed this finding and found similar statistics for people convicted in other violent crimes. Many of the people in prison for violence were there not for some long-planned activity, but for a thoughtless, often inebriated moment that they would regret for the rest of their lives. The resulting success of pilot programs was a new emfasis on emotional education in schools, which contributed to a significant reduction in violence.

The Emotional Education movement arose in partial response to the 1948 utopian novel, *Walden Two* by B.F. Skinner. In that book, the director of the Walden Two community, T.E. Frazier, had said that the goals of the schools were to teach "learning and thinking."[1] After that, the children could learn by themselves. Frazier mistakenly thought that disruptive emotions such as jealousy and fear could be eliminated by removing the causes of such feelings. Students were taught to cooperate, rather than to be competitive. The Emotional Education movement corrected Frazier's, and hence, Skinner's, mistake, by fully incorporating emotional education into the curriculum of schools throughout the world. The better approach was not to try to eliminate human emotions, which was unrealistic, but to teach methods to encourage safe and constructive expressions of those emotions.

Gun control was the Achilles heel for the U.S. criminal justice system in the 19th, 20th and early 21st centuries. Not only did the U.S. have the highest crime rates for the industrialized/cyber-world countries, but it also had the highest ownership rate of guns, at almost one gun per person, including children. This was almost twice the rate of the second highest gun ownership

1. Burrhus Frederic Skinner, *Walden Two*, 1948, Prentice Hall, New Jersey, 1976 Edition, page 110.

country, Serbia. The U.S. obsession with guns persisted even though the U.S. had seen the assassinations of Presidents McKinley and Kennedy and several other assassination attempts on presidents in the 20th century. Then came the 2014 publication of *Jesus and Jesusa,* with its depiction of the apparent attempted assassination of the Co-Popes, and responsible people asked themselves, "What were we thinking? Do we really want another assassination attempt in this country? Do we really want to continue to see 83 people killed every day in the U.S. by guns?" Two thirds of those deaths were by suicide.

Spurred by the Federal Government's establishment in 2015 of an independent repository for fone records, which would be subject to inquiry or searches only by court order, gun control advocates proposed a similar repository for information about every gun in the country. The information would include serial number, manufacturer, caliber, and special bore characteristics which would be determined by firing a round into a container and saving it for the repository. The National Repository Organization (NRO) was established through a grant from the James Brady Foundation and gun owners across the country were encouraged to voluntarily register their guns. Millions did so, but most did not. That led to legislative efforts to strengthen the NRO.

Vermont enacted a law in 2017 which required its gun owners to register their guns with the NRO. Seeking to test and invalidate the law, a gun owner named John Frank Kennedy from Dorset refused to register his hunting and sports guns and was fined the current equivalent of 1,000 earthas. He appealed his conviction and lost in the Vermont courts. Kennedy appealed to the U.S. Supreme Court that Vermont's statute violated his Second

Amendment rights. Not without some sense of
irony about defending a conviction of a man named
John F. Kennedy for gun violations, the State of
Vermont aggressively argued that the NRO did not
infringe on Kennedy's right to bear arms. The
Supreme Court ruled against Vermont in 2019 in
Kennedy vs. Vermont.

The growing outcry from citizens who saw that
guns were dangerous and must be regulated led to
the 2022 ratification of the 30th Amendment to the
U.S. Constitution, which stated that states and the
Federal Government had the power to regulate the
use of guns. Soon afterwards, every state required
guns to be registered with the NRO, and deaths by
guns dropped dramatically, including the large
category of suicides by gun. These reductions were
not fully understood, but one hunch was that it
was due to a type of "Hawthorne Effect" where
something changes because people are paying
attention to it.

Within a few years, the repository was helping to
solve most gun homicides and other gun-related
crimes and that success served to reduce the
frequency of gun violence.

Overall, the drug legalization, Emotional
Education campaign, and gun control initiatives
significantly reduced the amount of crime, and
thereby reduced the need for criminal lawyers.

Chad had originally learned of Nina McKelvy
through a friend of a friend. She had represented a
man who was accused of assaulting and killing the
21-month old daughter of his wofriend. McKelvy
quickly investigated that case and sought a
meeting with the police and her client, instead of
waiting for the police to form the assumption that
her client was hiding from the truth. She brought
to that meeting fotografs of her client and the
deceased child and she brought his office calendar

showing how little time he was home with the child alone during the weeks and months before her death. After that meeting the police turned to other theories, including the possibility that the child died of one or more accidents, which compounded the effects of pre-existing conditions. Chad was impressed when he heard about Nina's work in that case, so he contacted her about his earlier charges.

When Nina arrived at his apartment after the departure of officers Armstrong and Kline, Chad told her that he had planned to drop an EZsleep pill into Juan's champagne that night, but couldn't remember doing so. This was true despite his use of memory-enhancing chemicals and the MEMRY electrical implant his parents had requested to be surgically placed in his brain as a boy. They were advised that it would help counteract his genetic behavior mutations.

Worse, he had told a friend, Keith Mundell, that he had planned a joke for New Year's Eve. Chad remembered putting the single pill, wrapped in foil into his pocket early in the evening of New Year's Eve, and he remembered checking his pocket the next day and noticing that the foil was no longer there. On Nina's advice, Chad declined to take any of the offered truth tests.

The next day, Armstrong and Kline received the report of the 310 employees at MaineDrug over the past ten years. On the list, within the Maine Staffing Co-op sublist, was Chad Delano for three days in September, 2115.

With that information, Armstrong and Kline went to the District Attorney to ask for an indictment of Chad Delano. The D.A. then submitted the request to the Grand Jury, which later heard from several witnesses, including Chad's friend, Keith. Chad was invited to testify, but on the advice of his attorney, he declined.

On Friday, January 10, 2117 the Grand Jury indicted Chad on the charge of "chemical manslaughter" for the death of Juan Carlos Morales. The crime of "chemical manslaughter" was defined as when someone "...recklessly, or with criminal negligence, causes another person to ingest a chemical which directly leads, or substantially contributes, to the death of that person."

After consulting with Nina, Chad reported to the police station for the bail process on Saturday morning for the reprogramming of his body chip to allow law enforcement to continuously monitor his location. Arrestees on bail were required to visit the jail monthly for a visual checkup, in case the bail program of the body chip was malfunctioning, and also to obtain a wireless recharge.

The only required payment was the daily rental for the use of the bail program, which can be waived for those unable to pay. The "bail program" was given its name as it usually displaced the historic legal process of arrestees giving money to a bondsperson or law officer in order to secure attendance at trial. However, when a judge determined that there was some likelihood that an arrested person would try to subvert the bail program on the body chip, or take other steps to avoid coming to trial, a large deposit of money, usually in the thousands of earthas, would be required.

After receiving his bail programming, Chad was free to resume his normal life, plus newly necessary visits to his attorney. However, his previously "normal" life was changing rapidly. Melissa ended her relationship with Chad as she felt that the charge about Juan was true, in part because Chad did not deny that he had intended to do "something like that." Other friends also abandoned Chad, especially those who were close to Juan Carlos.

The investigation by Bob Armstrong and Angela Kline continued. Through Chad's lawyer, they asked for another interview with Chad, but Chad declined the request. In their experience, the innocent suspects welcome such invitations. Armstrong and Kline searched the internet for articles and an international expert on the effects of eszopiclone on people generally. They learned that the drug was generally effective and non-toxic as an inducer of sleep, but for a small minority of consumers, the results were more debilitating. In fact, that information was in the "infopak" on the box.

The trial was scheduled for Monday, April 12, 2117.

Chapter 5 The Trial

Chad chose to be tried by a jury. The JuryComputerMatch system picked 20 likely jurors, 12 men and 8 women, and they all appeared in court on Monday, April 12. If for no other reason, the compensation was reasonable, as each juror was paid at the rate of 20 earthas an hour, or five times the minimum wage, if not otherwise compensated by employers for the time away from work. The criminal trial rules gave each side three objections, so as to bring the number of jurors to 14, i.e. 12 jurors and two alternates. Chad's attorney objected to one woman juror because she had once been a victim of a sexual crime, and was therefore not likely to be sympathetic to Chad. Two other defense objections were to a man and a woman who had Ph.D. degrees. Chad's lawyer did not want intellectuals on the jury.

"Given my mother's work, that's a little ironic, isn't it," Chad asked Nina.

The prosecution objected to a man who had played professional sports and was thus likely to be sympathetic to men, and to a woman whose son was a criminal defense lawyer. The third objection was more obscure, and it was used to remove a man, Jeff Bloodsworth, who worked at the hydrofusion power plant. The prosecutor, Matthew Bailey,[1] simply had a hunch that the man, by virtue of his masculine looks, would be sympathetic

---

1. Ironically, Matthew was a relation of the famed defense attorney, and supporter of polygraf testing, F. Lee Bailey, who had moved to Maine in the early 21st century. As the lawyer of one of the most famous 20th century claimants of wrongful conviction, Dr. Sam Sheppard, F. Lee Bailey knew well of the problem. In Maine, he became a supporter of Dennis Dechaine's ultimately successful claim of wrongful conviction.

to Chad. Bailey was right about the decision, because Bloodsworth would likely have been sympathetic to Chad; but Bailey was lucky with his reasoning. The real reason for the anticipated sympathy for Chad was that Bloodsworth had an ancestor, Kirk Bloodsworth in Maryland, who was convicted of murder in 1985 and sentenced to death. After a nearly accidental discovery of DNA evidence, he was finally exonerated, but it destroyed several years of his life. A relative of such a man was less likely to convict a defendant except in the most certain circumstances.

By the end of the day, the jury was selected, and they were excused. "Tomorrow," Judge Carla Bradford told them, "you will begin your two days of juror training, which will include videos with excerpts of two trials."

After the jury left, Bailey motioned to Nina to request her to move to the side of the courtroom where they could talk privately.

"What's up?" she asked.

"We have an unusual development." said Bailey. "I just learned that a potential witness has come forward to say that Chad had told him that he had dropped the pill into Juan Carlos' drink on New Year's Eve. I've arranged to interview him tomorrow morning during the jury's continued training, and I'm asking you if you would like to join me in the interview."

"This smells funny," answered Nina. "What's the person's name?"

"It's Cory Cook," said Bailey. "He worked with Chad for a few days last year on an NEA project digging up invasive trees. He said that he just learned about the trial, and wanted to help."

"Right," sneered Nina. "Just wanted to help truth and justice and the American Way. That's what many informants say. I'll obviously talk with Chad about this Cory person, but sure, I'll be there tomorrow morning. At 8:30 in your office?"

"Yes, my office. You got it. 8:30." said Bailey.

By the time that conversation ended, Chad had left the courthouse, so Nina called him.

Chad answered his wrist fone and Nina asked, "Chad, do you know a Cory Cook?"

Chad answered, "I don't recall anyone by that name. How would I know him?"

"Well, this person knows you from a temporary job removing invasive trees," said Nina.

"Hmmm," thought Chad, and then he remembered, "Might he have a nickname, 'Cookie'?"

"That's probably him," said Nina. "Let's meet at the 'Chocolate Caliente'" shop around the corner, assuming that you haven't made it too far, walking from the courthouse. I love that thick hot chocolate drink. Among other things, you can tell me what he looks like, as it looks like I'm meeting him tomorrow morning."

In a few minutes, they met at "Chocolate Caliente" in the Old Port on Exchange Street. The Quick Stop Shop specializes in thick hot chocolate from Espana, Italia and Mexico."

"Ok," said Nina, "What do you remember telling this man you call Cookie about your case. I thought I told you not to talk about your case with anyone."

"You did," confirmed Chad. "I don't recall telling him anything more than was in the newspapers, which was about my upcoming trial and about the death of Juan Carlos and the claimed pill. Well, maybe I told him what I've told others. Sorry. That I thought that I might have done it."

"Well," signed Nina, "he apparently thinks that you said that you actually did put the pill into Juan's drink."

"Not true. Not true. I didn't, but we both can see what he could have done with what I did say."

Sipping her last swallow, and then scraping the rest from the cup and sliding it into her mouth, Nina concluded, "Well. We'll see what he says, tomorrow."

The next morning, Nina came to the interview of Cory Cook by Matthew Bailey. After introductions, Bailey asked Cook, "Let's start at the beginning. When did you first meet Chad Delano?"

"Well," said Cook, "He and I were working on a tree removal group last year in Falmouth. He told me about his case and he told me that he put the sleeping pill into that guy's drink at the party, when the guy died."

Nina interjected, and even though she saw the tattoo that Chad had described, she asked, "Before we go any further, do you go by a nickname?"

"Sure," said Cook, "I go by 'Cookie' to people who know me."

"Ok, thanks," said Nina.

Bailey continued, "Ok, but I'll call you Cory. What led you to come to tell me what you know?"

"Well," said Cook, "I figured that you would want to know the truth."

Both Bailey and Nina had heard that line before, and Bailey asked, "Why didn't you come to us sooner?"

"Aaah. I didn't think Delano would be going to trial. Thought he would take a plea. Then I heard that he didn't."

Nina had done some checking on her databases the night before. Cook had a record of crimes against women, and he had two convictions for which he had served two years in prison. He was still on parole for the second conviction.

She asked Cook, "Your coming forward wouldn't have anything to do with your arrest for sexual assault of a minor two weeks ago, would it?"

"How'd you find out about that? I mean, No." babbled Cook.

Actually, Nina didn't learn about that incident from the computer. She had called a friend who said that Angela Kline had investigated a case involving a "Cookie." Of interest to Nina was the absence of that incident from the arrest database.

Nina said to Bailey, "Can we talk outside?"

Bailey anticipated what was coming. "Look, Nina," he said, "I didn't know anything about an incident two weeks ago. I knew we had a credibility problem with his former convictions, but I didn't know about this."

"Actually, Matt," said Nina, "the real problem isn't another sex crime as that's not what Chad is charged with. The real problem is Kline's role in this. It seems pretty obvious, and Judge Bradford, has seen this before, that Kline somehow learned about Cook's contact with Chad, and she made a deal with Cook. The deal surely was that if he testified that Chad admitted to Cook the dropping of the sleeping pill at the New Year's party, Kline wouldn't, with a wink and a nod, file an arrest report on the incident two weeks ago."

Bailey wasn't happy about this turn in the interview. He thought he had a witness who could help convince the jury that Chad was guilty. Not a perfect witness, but a witness nonetheless. He said to Nina, "I'll check into this. It may be that Kline had other reasons for not filing an arrest report. We'll see."

At the courthouse, Tuesday's training began with a video presentation by the Maine Chief Justice, and then video presentations by a prosecutor, defense attorney and a law professor. The jury then saw the first of the two trial videos, "Jury Justice," which lasted three hours. At the two and one-half hour mark came the closing statements by the prosecutor and defense and the charge to the jury by the judge. The video then stopped, and the jurors were asked to vote on guilt or innocence. The vote was 7-5 for guilt. Then the video continued and showed the actual jury finding the defendant guilty.

For the closing training period, the jury was shown a 2107 remake of the classic jury film, "12 Angry Men." Filmed 150 years after the 1957 classic starring Henry Fonda, Lee J. Cobb, Jack Klugman, and nine others, "12 Jurors" had a balanced jury by race, gender and age. Like the original 1957 12 jurors, the jurors in the 2107 version brought their beliefs and biases into the jury room. In the customized version for Chad's jurors, the film was stopped when the film's jurors first adjourned to the deliberations room. The break allowed trainers to poll Chad's jurors by secret ballot, on their initial votes for a verdict.

On Wednesday, there was a discussion session about Tuesday's "Jury Justice" video, with jurors explaining why they voted as they did. Then came the first two hours of the second video, and the vote was 6-6. After the third hour of the video, the vote was 12-0 for acquittal. The jurors were pleased to hear that the defendant in the video was acquitted. The jury received copies of the Maine document, "Juror Guidelines," and discussed the section, "Juror Do's and Don't's." In particular, jurors were advised not to visit the scene of the alleged crime on their own and not to talk to anyone about the trial, including other jurors, during the trial. After further discussion, the jury was dismissed for the day.

On Thursday morning, the jury, and Chad, went to his former apartment for a site view, and then they went to the lobby of the apartment building of Juan Carlos; and then returned for the opening of the trial.

As has long been the custom, the prosecution presented its case first, after the opening statements. Anita was the first witness. She described how she walked Juan home and how tired he was. She cried when she described her regret of not staying with him to take him up the stairs.

"If I had just walked with him up a few stairs, he would still be alive today," she moaned.

Chad's friend, Keith Mundell, testified that Chad had told him of his idea to drop a sleep drug into Juan's drink. He told him of other ideas for that night, too, including sex with Melissa and Michelle together.

Officer Angela Kline testified that she had asked Chad at the time of the search warrant if he had any idea why Juan became drowsy and that he quickly denied any such idea. She described how she and Bob Armstrong carefully searched Chad's apartment and removed items which might lead to relevant evidence.

After she and Armstrong had left the apartment, Kline testified, "We felt stuck. There was nothing."

Knowing the answer as he did for most questions, Bailey asked, "What did you do with the seized items?" Kline then explained how she handled the contents of each of the wastebaskets at Chad's apartment, first by dumping them into a clear plastic bag. Back at the police station, she emptied each of the police clear plastic bags onto a sterile glass table. Within each bag were the contents of a single wastebasket, plus the black plastic bag that formerly lined Chad's wastebaskets. Using a sample exemplar black plastic bag purchased by the prosecution, she showed the jury how she emptied the contents of each of Chad's bags into a police clear bag, by grabbing the bottom of each bag and holding it upside down. She explained that from the bag from the wastebasket near the "Trivial Pursuit" table fell a small piece of crumpled aluminum foil. Using two sets of sterile, rubber tipped tweezers, Kline said she unfolded the piece to its two dimensional size, which was about one centimeter^2 square. She took fotografs of the material at several stages of the unfolding, and it appeared that the foil previously contained only one pill. Kline testified that she inserted the foil into a plastic container and sent it to the laboratory for testing.

By pressing a button at her seat, a juror, Madeleine Chou, notified the judge that she wanted to ask a question. As part of the criminal justice reforms of the 21st century, jurors were encouraged to participate in the trial process. The intent of the reform was to restore trials to their role as fountains for the truth, rather than battlegrounds for adversarial lawyers where truth was often a casualty rather than a goal. Judge Bradford then asked prosecutor Bailey to hold his questions while the judge communicated with the

2. In 2030, the U.S. formally announced its decision to fully adopt the metric system, now called the ISQ (International System for Quantities) and to abandon the foot/pound English system. President Ford had signed the Metric Conversion Act in 1975 which committed the U.S. to metrication, but subsequent presidents and Congresses blocked full implementation. The U.S. decision included a 10-year implementation plan, which was not a major burden for the country because many products, such as medicines and equipment destined for export were already using the metric system.

juror about her question. Chou then keyed the judge, "Can you please ask Ms. Kline how she knew that the foil contained only one pill."

Judge Bradford then asked Detective Kline that question and she answered, "We looked at the folds in the foil. Then we compared them to samples we had prepared in the office of the same foil being folded so as to enclose one, two and three pills. The folds in the foil taken from Mr. Delano's wastebasket corresponded closest to those of the single pill sample in our office."

She then testified that the laboratory report about the foil came back with two significant results. First, there were traces of eszopiclone, the active ingredient of EZsleep. Second, there were sufficient skin cells left on the foil to test for DNA. The DNA was then compared to the DNA for Chad Delano, whose fetal DNA was on file; and there was a 99.99% match.

As the use of the DNA universal database, for the U.S. at least, had become routine since its adoption in 2037 an expert witness was not required to explain it to the jury. Instead, the prosecutor asked Kline about the database. Kline testified that pursuant to the law, now 80 years old, DNA samples were taken from every child born in the U.S. and from all immigrants and people traveling to the U.S. The U.S. standard was adopted by the U.N.'s DNA Database Convention in 2044.

Kline's testimony was the high point of the prosecution's case. Nina McKelvy's cross-examination focused on the possibility that someone else could have touched the foil, and left no DNA, but Kline persuasively discounted that possibility. "I've never seen that happen," she said.

Xue Wen, wofriend of Michelle Grant, testified next. She was a software programmer for the Environmental Stabilization Project and, like an artist, she was sensitive to fysical patterns. She testified that she saw Chad bring the champagne glasses to the table and move one glass closer to Juan's seat, whereas the other glasses were left in a group in the center.

Nina cross-examined, "Did you see Chad drop a pill into Juan's glass?" and Wen responded, "No."

The last witness was to be Cory Cook, but Bailey decided not to call him, as Cook's credibility was subject to considerable challenge in Nina's potential cross-examination. Nina would also recall Angela Kline as a witness and that testimony would not only undermine Cook's credibility; it would also reduce the credibility of Kline's own previous testimony in the case.

The prosecution rested its case on Thursday afternoon, April 15, without calling its final witness, Melissa Grant, Chad's former wofriend. The prosecution knew that she would testify that Chad had told her of his plan to embarrass Juan at the party. He also knew that Michelle had told officers Kline and Armstrong that she had seen Chad make some kind of a motion toward the wastebasket after pouring the champagne, but Bailey decided to hold her testimony in reserve. He calculated that Chad would testify and that he would lie about his previous plans regarding Juan. Then, Bailey would present Melissa to impeach his credibility with her own recollection of what he told her. Once Chad's credibility was further impaired, in addition to the damage done by his lie to the police about not having any idea about why Juan might have become drowsy, the prosecution felt confident about a guilty verdict.

The timing of the close of the prosecution's case was good for Chad, as the next day was one of the five international holidays, Earth Day, on the third Friday of April. Thus, Nina McKelvy had the weekend to think about her trial strategy for the next steps.

On Monday, Nina sought a directed verdict, meaning that she asked the judge to rule that there was insufficient evidence presented by the prosecution to even warrant sending the case to the jury. Judge Bradford denied the motion.

McKelvy then consulted with Chad and announced that the defense would present no witnesses and rest its case. She would gamble that the jury would find the evidence insufficient to find Chad guilty beyond any doubt. Actually, it was a gamble with Chad's life and not hers.

The "beyond any doubt" standard was relatively new, in the long history of Anglo-American jurisprudence. In the late 20th and early 21st centuries it was proven by the then-new DNA technology that a significant number of people convicted in U.S. courts were actually innocent. The percentage of wrongful convictions was estimated to be between 1-5 percent. At its peak, the U.S. prison population in 2012 was about two million, which meant that between 20,000 and 100,000 innocent people were in prison. Those numbers represented a staggering amount of suffering by the wrongly convicted as well as their families and supporters. In addition the victims and their families suffered through the struggles of the wrongly convicted. Further, the numbers meant that there was an equal number of "wrongly free" people, and many of them went on to commit more crimes after innocent people were arrested and convicted in their place.

A civil rights movement, called the Innocence Movement, arose to assist those who were wrongly convicted, but even by the year 2014, which was 25 years after the first DNA exoneration of a wrongly convicted man, Gary Dotson in Illinois in 1989, there were still fewer than 100 wrongly convicted inmates being exonerated each year. At the same time, it was estimated that thousands of people were being wrongly convicted annually. The proverbial super tanker was turning around, but it was still going away from the intended destination.

The Innocence Movement had become an international campaign with the creation in 2012 in Ohio of the Center for the Global Study of Wrongful Conviction. When the Center began comparing the statistics on wrongful convictions around the world, it became increasingly clear to U.S. lawyers and citizens that the U.S system was not the "best in the world" as was claimed by many lawyers. Instead, it was the foremost generator of injustice, including wrongful convictions. The U.S.'s retention of the death penalty made the U.S. justice system look even worse in the eyes of the world.

As the plight of the wrongly convicted was one of the most poignant stories in the world of justice, the International Criminal Court announced in 2015 that it would hear claims of wrongful conviction from citizens of any country.

Also in 2015, the Innocence Movement in the U.S. elected for the first time, an exoneree as its leader. He was Scott Prade, a former Chicago policeman who had been convicted in 1992 of murdering a bothersome neighbor. From the time of his initial police interview and arrest, Prade proclaimed his innocence. However, his former peers were confident that their initial hunch was correct and were reassured by the subsequent confirmation of the facts and by inmate informants who told them that Prade had confessed to them.

"He deserved it," one inmate recalled that Prade had said. Another inmate said that Prade had said, "That asshole said he wanted to have sex with my wife." Prade sought the help of a private investigator and found an attorney who was willing to work for almost nothing, as that's all Prade had left.

In 2013, a court finally determined that he was innocent, and that the Chicago Police Dept. had withheld important evidence about an alternate suspect. Also uncovered was a police memo which said that convicting Prade was a necessary price to pay to show the people of Chicago that the police had the integrity to even arrest and prosecute one of their own.

After his election, Prade persuaded the other leaders of the Innocence Movement that two national goals were required. First, there needed to be a goal for the minimization of wrongful conviction to .1% of criminal convictions. Second, he sought a national campaign to both reduce the frequency of wrongful convictions in ongoing trials to that percentage, but also to reduce the number of wrongly convicted people in prison to that same .1%. He sought to achieve both goals within five years.

Prade testified before the televised hearings of the Senate Judiciary Committee which was considering the $100 billion Act to Reduce Wrongful Convictions. Said Prade, "How can you ask a person to be the last wrongly convicted person to remain in prison because of a mistake?[3]

3. This plea by Prade echoed one made in 1971 by then-anti-war activist, and Vietnam Veteran, John Forbes Kerry, who testified before the Senate Foreign Relations Committee. He asked, "...how do you ask a man to be the last man to die in Vietnam? How do you ask a man to be the last man to die for a mistake?" John Kerry later became a Massachusetts Lt. Governor, U.S. Senator, Democratic Candidate for President and Secretary of State. Prade had become aware of Kerry's speech through his contact with Kerry's former Senate Office manager who was a criminal defense lawyer and member of the Innocence Movement.

Even at the seemingly low rate wrongful conviction at .1%, that still meant at the time that there would be approximately 1,900 innocent people in prison in the U.S. At a time when there were a few highly publicized airplane accidents, including one where a plane with 300+ passengers disappeared completely, Prade noted that a person's chances of being wrongly convicted were more than a hundred times greater than the chance of dying in a plane crash. This was especially true for men of racial minorities.

Part of the campaign to reduce the frequency of wrongful convictions to .1%, or as close to zero as possible, was to change the courtroom standard of guilt. Historically, courts in the U.S. required a showing of guilt "beyond a reasonable doubt." However, the powerful evidence of thousands of exonerations in the 20th and early 21st centuries showed that juries often misunderstood that standard to mean "**probably** committed the crime" or even "**might have** committed the crime."

Appalled by the tidal wave of suffering which was inflicted upon these wrongly convicted people, and by the growing cost of the exonerations, often more than several million dollars each, the states initiated a Constitutional Amendment which became the 29th, when ratified in 2020. That Amendment states, "No person shall be convicted of a crime unless the evidence establishes guilt beyond any doubt."

During the campaign for the state-by-state passage of the Amendment, the most effective media presentation explicitly defined the numerical value of "beyond a reasonable doubt" and "beyond any doubt." The first part of the campaign was to conduct polling each state to ask the following two questions:

If you were on a jury in a criminal case and you were asked to determine whether there was guilt "beyond a reasonable doubt" what percentage of guilt do you think that would mean, on a scale of zero to 100 percent? The average for the United States was 76% with the high being 89% in Oregon and the low being 65% in Texas.

The second question was the same except the standard was "beyond any doubt." The U.S. average was 91% with the low and high among the states being 78% and 97%. Legal experts expected the average percentages for the two questions to be 95% and 99.5%. The 95% standard for "beyond reasonable doubt" came from a senior Federal Judge in New York, Jack Weinstein, who wrote, "In my opinion, a probability of guilt of no less than 95% should be necessary to support a conviction."[4] However, he wrote that in 2006 before the full impact of the high frequency of wrongful convictions was seen in the U.S. It was before, for example, the May, 2012 creation of the National Registry of Exonerations[5] when it startled the U.S. legal system with an initial compilation of 891 exonerations since 1989.[6] Judge Weinstein's 95% standard would have led to at least a 5% wrongful conviction rate, which was intolerable. Hence, the national move to the "beyond any doubt" standard gathered momentum.

---

4. J.B. Weinstein and I. Dewsbury, "Comment on the meaning of 'proof beyond a reasonable doubt" in *Law Probability and Risk*, 5, pp 167-173, 2006.
5. National Registry of Exonerations at https://www.law.umich.edu/special/exoneration/
6. By 2027, the Registry of Exonerations count for the U.S. exonerations had risen to 24,632, but since then, the annual rate had declined dramatically. On 1 January 2117, 90 years later, the count was 28,836.

After the passage of this "beyond any doubt" Amendment, it was estimated that the wrongful conviction rate dropped to one percent or below. It brought back to the public consciousness the often misquoted adage known as Blackstone's Formulation that "it is better that ten guilty persons escape than that one innocent suffer."[7] Conservatives argued that guilty people were going free because of the new standard, but there was little effort to quantify the claim. Like the trial lawyers who are purportedly taught not to ask a question at a trial if they didn't know the answer, the conservatives wisely did not sponsor a study of the claim of guilty people being set free because they understood that it would likely be found to be infrequent and hard to prove.

Another reason for the dramatic decrease in both the number of wrongly convicted people in prison and the number being wrongly convicted each year was the increased use of the polygraf and its hybrid successor, the polyvoicegraf. A 2013 study[8] found that polygrafs were accurate in 80% of the cases where there had been exonerations from wrongful convictions. The article argued that in those instances where either side claimed a polygraf was inaccurate, a second examination could be given to the same person, or to another person in a similar position to know the same set of facts. The argument for such a second examination was that the odds of a machine, which is 80% accurate, and

7. See Blackstone's Formulation, Wikipedia, at http://en.wikipedia.org/wiki/Blackstone's_formulation.
8. "Polygraphs and 250 Wrongful Conviction Exonerations," by Morrison Bonpasse, at http://www.bonpasseexonerationservices.com/about.html An earlier version of the article was published in the July, 2013 edition of *Polygraph*, the magazine of the American Polygraph Association.

20% inaccurate, being inaccurate twice on the same issue was 4% (.20 X .20). Since then, the technology had improved, which brought the accuracy up to the 90% range. With that accuracy, the odds of a double inaccuracy dropped to 1% (.10 X .10).

This accuracy rate was higher than the rate for most other types of approved courtroom testimony. For example, eye witness testimony was formerly thought to be the most valid type of truth, but it was found in several studies to be wrong 35-60% of the time.[9] Further, the National Registry of Exonerations found that 37% of wrongful convictions were caused by mistaken eye witness identifications.

Finally, the overall reduction in crime due to legalization of drugs, gun control and Emotional Education allowed more law enforcement resources to be allocated to the crime that remained. That increase of per-crime resources, led to better investigations and fewer wrongful convictions.

If Nina had presented a defense, Chad would have been required to testify, unless he could persuade Judge Bradford that he had a good reason, apart from a desire not to tell the truth, not to testify. Usually such a reason would include aspects of other previous behavior by a defendant which a jury might find distasteful, and which feeling might outweigh the utility of the evidence of such behavior to the prosecution.

This requirement for defendants to testify was another mid-21st century reform in the U.S. criminal justice system, which culminated in the

9. Wrongful Convictions Blog,
http://wrongfulconvictionsblog.org/2012/04/11/eyewitness-identification-how-reliable-is-it/

31st Amendment[10] to the U.S. Constitution, which became law in 2030. Prior to the reform, defendants had the right not to testify, as guaranteed by the 5th Amendment to the Constitution, which states that defendants, among other protections, "...nor shall be compelled in any criminal case to be a witness against himself,..." This right against self-incrimination was inserted into the 5th Amendment as a way of allowing defense counsel to test the prosecution's case, without forcing the defendant to testify. The theory was that if the prosecution's case could not stand on its own feet without the defendant's testimony, then it should fail. The purpose of the protection was to prevent law enforcement officials from using mental or fysical force to extract testimony and confessions from defendants.

This shield against the testimony of defendants was not always thought to be necessary. Prior to the rise of the role of defense counsels in the late 18th century and the rise of the adversarial trial system, it was the obligation of defendants to speak at their own trials in order to defend themselves.[11] The 31st Amendment restored the obligation of defendants to speak in the interest of presenting the truth to the fact finder in a trial, whether it be a judge or jury. This change reduced the risk that a jury or fact-finding judge would not have the

---

10. The 31st Amendment reads, "Defendants in criminal cases shall testify as to what they know about the facts of the case against them, unless a disinterested judge shall determine, after an appropriate hearing, that the risk of prejudice outweighs the prospective value of the defendant's testimony.

11. See John Langbein, "The Historical Origins of the Privilege Against Self-Incrimination at Common Law," 92 *Michigan Law Review* 1047 (1994) at http://digitalcommons.law.yale.edu/fss_papers/550/n

benefit of hearing the defendant's side of the story, if his/her defense counsel had a trial strategy which did not include the defendant's testimony.

In Chad's case, the absence of the defendant's testimony was still the result, because his attorney chose a radically risky strategy of presenting no evidence at all, in the belief that her cross-examination of the prosecution witnesses and the inherent weakness of the prosecution's case were enough to require the jury to find the defendant "Not Guilty." Nina knew that if Chad had testified, he would have admitted that he told Melissa of a general plan to embarrass Juan and that he did have an EZ pill in his possession on the night of December 31, 2116. He would have admitted what he told Melissa in court for three reasons. First, it was the truth. Second, he knew that the prosecution had Melissa ready to testify about the relevant conversation. Third, that's what he had told his lawyer, and she was bound by her oath as an attorney not to permit a client to commit perjury on the witness stand.

While Nina understood that her strategy represented the old style of criminal defense lawyering, where trials were first a game and second a search for truth, her first duty was still to her client. Both he and she were not sure that he actually did, or didn't, drop the pill into Juan's drink. She was confident, however, that if Chad testified, the jury would conclude that there was no doubt that he actually did do what he contemplated doing.

After closing arguments by the prosecution and the defense, the judge gave the case to the jury after instructing the jurors on the standard of guilt beyond any doubt and on several other aspects of the case, including the reliability of police witnesses as compared with civilian witnesses.

She told them, "Beyond any doubt means what it says. You may think that the defendant might have committed the crime. You may even think that the defendant probably committed the crime. However, that is not enough to convict him and subject him to criminal punishment. The standard is 'beyond any doubt.' This is not the place for a U.S. legal history lesson, but please understand that many Americans, including one or two in this very courtroom in the 21st century, were convicted of crimes they did not commit. The standard then was 'beyond a reasonable doubt,' rather than the current, and higher, standard of 'beyond any doubt.' "

The jurors left the courtroom and began their deliberations. That evening, the jurors went home, after hearing instructions, once again, that they were not to discuss with anyone the facts of the case or their views of the case.

The deliberations continued all day Tuesday.

On Wednesday morning, April 21, at 11:30, the jury returned to the courtroom and announced that it had a verdict. Judge Bradford asked the foreperson what that verdict was in the charge of chemical manslaughter against Chad Forbes Delano and the foreperson responded, "Guilty." The judge asked, "And did you reach that verdict beyond any doubt," and the foreperson answered, "Yes, your honor." Judge Bradford then asked each of the other 11 jurors the same question about "any doubt" and each said, "Yes." She thanked the jurors and told them they were free to discuss the case and their deliberations with anyone, but urged them to be careful to be as accurate as possible. She told them, "If, at any time, you have doubts about your votes in this case, please contact me, and we can discuss your concerns, and take appropriate action. There has not been a wrongful conviction in this court for many years, but there is always the possibility of a mistake."

Pursuant to Rule 24J of the Maine Rules of Criminal Procedure, Nina McKelvy asked the judge to make available to her the sound recordings of the jury's deliberations. This rule was added almost a century earlier to ensure that juries properly discussed the facts and law of the case. Before the passage of the rule defense attorneys had to rely upon the voluntary recollections of jurors about their deliberations. It was an expensive process to interview 12 jurors and probe for violations. It was usually a wasteful game of "Gotcha." Now, with Rule 24J, defense lawyers could listen to the deliberations and if s/he found violations of rules, the prosecutor would be asked to listen to the applicable portion of the recordings. Then the prosecutor and defense attorney would ask the judge for guidance. Sometimes, verdicts were vacated because of this rule. In this case, Nina's subsequent review of the recordings of the jury deliberations found nothing irregular.

Judge Bradford announced that a sentencing hearing would be held the following Monday and closed the court. Chad was taken to the county jail and his body chip was reprogrammed for sentence monitoring, which provided more precise GPS locator information and readings of heart rates and breathing. As the possible sentence included incarceration, he was held at the jail until sentencing.

Chad and his parents were devastated. Eleanor did not attend the trial because she was in Houston and she was assured that Chad would be found Not Guilty. The family didn't want to interfere with her astronaut work, and didn't want the publicity about Chad to taint Eleanor's achievements.

One reality which was never mentioned in court was the sheer luck or bad luck involved in Juan Carlos's death. He could have made it safely home and into his bed without falling down the stairs. He could have fallen and simply hurt his head or bruised or even broken a bone. Less likely, he could have hit his head and become an acquired savant syndrome person. Such people develop remarkable artistic, musical or mathematical abilities after an injury or serious illness. None of this could be presented to the jury, because the law is that if a person's actions have some causal relationship to subsequent bodily harm to another person, then that person is criminally responsible for those actions. This is true even if the same actions, such as dropping a sleeping pill into a person's drink lead to no subsequent harm in nine out of ten, or 99 out of 100, other instances.

Another person might habitually drive through stop signs. If detected by a policeman or an automatic detector, the driver would be charged with a traffic offense and would likely pay a fine, and even lose his/her driver's license for multiple offenses. However, if another car comes into the same intersection at the same time and the driver is killed, then the habitual stop sign runner would be charged with vehicular homicide, even though his/her intent and actions are exactly the same in all the instances of sign running. It was luck that led to the homicide charge, even if the odds were high that such a collision might occur eventually with multiple stop sign running.

The next Monday, the 26th, Judge Bradford heard details about Chad's life and about the life of Juan Carlos Morales. Chad did speak on his behalf and said,

"It is true, your honor, that I had planned to do something to embarrass Juan on that New Year's

Eve night, but I have no active recollection of actually putting anything into Juan's champagne glass. It certainly was not my intent to harm Juan fysically. I cannot explain why the pill I apparently put into the crumpled foil container was no longer in that foil when it was found in the wastebasket in my apartment. He was a creep, but that was not a reason for him to die so young. I'm very sorry that he died, and I apologize here to his family."

Chad's mother testified about Chad's birth and the pre-natal testing and how she and Chad's father decided to go ahead with the birth despite the DNA abnormalities that were detected. Nina McKelvy had told Charlotte that such intimate information, which had not previously been shared with Chad until the previous night, might be useful in reducing the punishment.

Charlotte thought she did well as a witness, but she was preoccupied with the class discussion of *Jesus and Jesusa* the day before in her class.   One student, Jill Bonhoeffer, had asked why the book had such a powerful effect on the real world, as Charlotte had argued in class and in her Ph.D. thesis.

"I'm not sure," answered Charlotte. "It wasn't often that books made a difference, especially utopian books. In the 21st century, most futuristic books were dystopian, and the kinder, gentler utopian books seemed to have gone into disfavor. In other subject areas, the public just didn't seem to take notice of the truth in books. Rachel Carson's *Silent Spring*, published in 1962, seemed to be the last book before *Jesus and Jesusa* that had launched a movement. For example, there were many books about claims of wrongful convictions in the 21st century with considerable data to back up the claims, but society paid little attention until a court ordered that the incarceration be terminated, and that a new trial be initiated if the prosecution felt it had enough evidence to proceed. Where the courts didn't act, the public didn't seem to care. But why *Jesus and Jesusa*? I'm still not sure."

Jill responded that she thought that it was just luck that this unusual book, *Jesus and Jesusa*, by the pseudonymous Maria Maddalena came along at the time when the people of the world had had "enough," as in the expression, "Enough is enough." Then came the actual Brownsville explosion and people became scared and energized.

"I think," said Jill, "that people really did have enough, and that then they organized. It wasn't rocket science, and it seemed to be up to women to step up and seize their rightful place in the world order; and then make it right."

"Do you think," asked Charlotte, "that it was a complete coincidence that the fictional Kahuta explosion in *Jesus and Jesusa* was in 2020 and the real explosion in Brownsville was a year earlier, in 2019, with almost the same result? Do you think that it was a coincidence that the fictional 'Great Transformation' in *Jesus and Jesusa* from 2020 to 2070 and then forward to 2120, was paralleled by the work of the "Great Transformation Network in real life?" How about the popes' names? Francesco I and Francesco II?"

"I don't know," said Jill. "It doesn't seem real that a book could have such a powerful effect. Makes you wonder what would have happened if *Jesus and Jesus* hadn't been published."

Forbes looked at Charlotte's glassy eyes. "Are you okay?" he asked.

"Yes," said Charlotte, I drifted off into thinking about a discussion in one of my classes today."

The prosecution spoke last, and asked for six months incarceration, or "Restricted Life, Level 5," for Chad, primarily because of the earlier guilty verdict for "chemical assault." The incarceration was to be followed by two years of "Restricted Life, Level 4," which meant living in a group setting in a community and monitored with a reprogrammed body chip.

It was nearing lunchtime, and Judge Bradford ordered a court recess for lunch and to allow her to think further about a just sentence.

At 2:30 p.m., the court reconvened. Judge Bradford asked Chad to stand, and said,

"I've thought a lot about this case. You are not the first young person to have caused great harm to a person and a family because of criminally negligent thoughtlessness. I've heard the testimony about your birth and upbringing, but you are still a responsible adult.

You are hereby sentenced to ten years of Restricted Life, Level 3. Your lawyer will explain to you how that sentence will change your life enough to make you reflect further on the harm you caused to Juan Carlos Morales and his family. Good day."

As part of the criminal justice reforms of the early-to-mid 21st century, the punishments for crimes were dramatically altered, and standardized across the country. The death penalty was abolished in 2029 when the U.S. Supreme Court held in a Missouri case, that execution was finally prohibited by the Constitution as "cruel and unusual." This was three years after the last execution in the U.S. which was in Florida. It was three years before the last execution in the world, which had been carried out in China. Both facts were known to the Trivial Pursuit players at Chad's New Year's Party.

All convicted felons were required to have their body chips reprogrammed during their "restricted life" sentences which not only tracked their locations, but also monitored their blood pressure, adrenaline level and other bodily functions that might indicate impending violence. When pre-determined threshold levels were detected in a felon, s/he would be contacted by an RMO (Restriction Monitoring Officer) by triggering a noticeable vibration in the body chip. The RMO would then talk with the felon on a videofone, or request that the felon come to the RMO's office.

Incarceration, which was Restricted Life, Level 5, was used only for people who were likely to harm others with minimal warning that could not be acted upon rapidly enough by an RMO. Society benefitted especially through the sentencing of white collar criminals to community service where they were able to provide significant assistance to non-profit organizations. Through the use of the Level 1-5 system, and through the legalization and regulation of gambling and drugs, gun control, and provision of emotional education, the U.S. prison population was reduced during the mid-21st century to from two million to less than 400,000.

By 2117, the prison population for the entire U.S. was 155,000. This was only 16,500 short of the goal of 138,500 as calculated when applying the .05% goal set in 2034 by the Federal Prison Population Reform Act (FPPRA) to the 2117 U.S. population of 277 million. Another way to express that goal was 50 people per 100,000 population. At the time of the FPPRA, that rate was very close to the actual current rates for Iceland and Japan. When the goal was set, it seemed nearly impossible and was compared to President John Kennedy's 1962 setting the goal for the United States to land a person on the moon by the end of the 1960's.[12]

---

12. At the time of the setting of that moon landing goal in a speech in 1962, the end of the decade was a maximum of

The country did achieve that goal, and it has come close to achieving the .05% incarceration goal as well.

Coincidentally, this goal was numerically close to the .1% goal for the percentage of wrongful convictions. With the current prison population of 155,000, that would mean that there are 155 wrongly convicted people in prison in the U.S. However, most legal professionals feel the .1% goal had been exceeded, i.e. with lower numbers, long ago, and that the problem of wrongful conviction had ceased to exist.

Within prisons, there were also five levels, A thru E. At the 5A level, inmates with good behavior records were permitted monthly sex visits[13] from significant others (SO's). Prisons were no longer totally sexually segregated, so that men and women with their varying sexual preferences were housed in the same units or pods, but not the same floors. If a 5A inmate requested, his/her monthly sexual visits could be with another inmate, male or female. As prostitution was entirely legal outside prison, it followed that inmates could pay other inmates for

seven years and three months in the future. When Kennedy spoke, the United States had launched only two people into orbit, beginning with John Glenn in January and Scott Carpenter in May 1962, and neither flight lasted longer than five hours.

13. In the 20th and 21st centuries, these visits were called "conjugal visits" as there was still considerable reluctance to address the sexual needs of inmates. It was felt by many that sexual deprivation was part of the punishment. For those willing to address the issue more carefully, it was felt that masturbation was sufficient sexual release, but it was shown by psychological research that the need for sex was partly social, too. By depriving most inmates of sexual relationships, and without any incentives for more sociable behavior, the authorities were increasing the likelihood of violence in the prison and of recidivism upon release.

those weekly visits if there was not mutual affection to eliminate the need for payment. If these arrangements were abused, then inmates were moved to lower levels, with the lowest level being 5E, or solitary confinement.

Outside prisons, for a Restricted Life, Level 3 felon like Chad, the monitoring was restricted only to location. He was not permitted to leave Maine without prior approval from his RMO. He was required to do community service 10 hours a month. As he liked the outdoors and felt good about his previous work in eradicating Japanese barberry from Maine, he requested that his community service be similar to that work. The request was successful and he was assigned to a team which searched for and dug up the plant called "Japanese knotweed" or "Mexican bamboo." After careful removal from the soil so as to avoid leaving regeneratable root fragments, the woody plants died and they were used for long term compost. Like the invasive Kudzu in the southeastern United States, these two plants were brought to the U.S. from Asia by people who had short term decorative plans for them. Such invasive species illustrate the laws of unintended consequences, and are frequently mentioned in presentations by the forthinkers[14] of the Global Transformation Network.

Chad was not permitted to take GLOOC[15] courses for the first five years of his sentence. By 21st century standards, these punishments would not seem sufficient as compared to the crime and result of his crime, i.e. the death of Juan. However, Chad was ostracized by the community which led

---

14. Forthinkers is slang, or an informal abbreviation, for Forward Thinkers.
15. GLOOC = Global Open Online Course.

to the loss of most of his friends including his wofriend, Melissa. The prohibition from GLOOC courses, in a society which prized education and intellectual growth, was significant.

Chad knew that he wasn't perfect, but neither he nor his parents, and certainly not his devoted sister, expected him to be a convicted felon at the age of 24.

Chapter 6 Help from Houston

During a call home in February, 2117, Eleanor's mother told her that a friend of Chad's had died after a New Year's Eve party at Chad's. The friend had fallen on the stairs at his apartment. Charlotte didn't tell Eleanor that Chad had been arrested, and that Chad and his parents had found a lawyer for him, and that the trial would begin in April. Charlotte didn't want to disturb Eleanor, but she was also in a state of denial. "My son? Guilty of manslaughter?" Charlotte thought. "That's ridiculous."

Chad and Eleanor exchanged emails, but he didn't mention the crisis at hand. On advice of his lawyer, he didn't put anything on the internet about the case. Still, Eleanor sensed that something was wrong at home and she asked her father during an early March call, "C'mon, Dad, what's going on?" she asked.

Forbes never liked the decision, mostly determined by his wife, to keep the problem away from Eleanor. She was the older child and she might even have some helpful advice. So he told her, when she asked.

Eleanor was shocked. "Did he actually do it?" she asked. The problem was that Forbes didn't know. In fact, he said, "Chad doesn't really know if he did it. He has said that he thought about dropping a pill into Carlos's drink, but he cannot remember actually doing it. The trouble is that he was so out of it himself from beer and champagne, that he can't take a reliable lie detector test whether it be a polygraf, voice-stress test, polyvoicegraf or fMRI. The new fMRI (Functional Magnetic Resonance Imaging) technology is especially accurate, because it can tell when a person is using his or her "creative" part of the brain to tell a lie, or the "memory" part of the brain to recall the truth. However, even that technology won't help Chad because he says he simply cannot remember. His lawyer tells us that she's confident she can obtain a "Not Guilty" verdict. The jury has to find guilt beyond ANY doubt, and that's a tough standard. I don't know that there is anything that that I know beyond ANY doubt. Well. Maybe. I know, for example, beyond any doubt that I'm talking with you right now."

Eleanor was appalled, without even considering what the GLASO program might think. Her own brother on trial for manslaughter? "When's the trial?" she asked, and Forbes said it was scheduled for Tuesday, April 15. Monday was a holiday: Patriots' Day, which was still celebrated in Massachusetts and Maine, a former colony of Massachusetts.

 After that call, Eleanor called her parents almost every day. She called Chad, but he was not interested in talking. Angry at himself, he guessed that he really did drop that EZsleep tablet into Juan's drink. He didn't think it would do anything more than make Juan sleepy and want to go home – which is exactly what happened.

Eleanor also called her aunt Emily Kinselli who was now living in Washington, D.C. where she was the director of the National Zoo, or more formally, the National Zoological Park of the Smithsonian Institution. Emily didn't know of Chad's problem, and supported Eleanor's active concern. This was a time to mobilize support for Chad, rather than worry about decorum and family secrets.

Emily was an activist who was hired at the zoo with the specific goal of implementing its "return to the wild" program. That program shifted the focus of the zoo from pulling wild animals from their natural habitats for the viewing pleasure of zoo visitors to preserving endangered species. This was now the predominant goal of zoos and aquariums around the world. Once a species was restored and taken off the endangered species list, specimens in zoos around the world were returned to their natural habitats. The giant panda bear was the most popular animal at the zoo and Emily worked with the Government of China to return the three pandas to their native habitat in central China. The giant panda was no longer endangered, in part because Chinese government and international funds had successfully been used to purchase and/or protect additional panda habitat land.

The flip side of Emily's "return to the wild" program was that she sought to make the National Zoo a leader in production, restoration, distribution and broadcast of videos of animals in their natural habitats. There were thousands of old films, videotapes, digital and grafene recordings that needed to be gathered into one archive, whether electronically or fysically.

The opening for broadcasting the Zoo's videos was the FCC's "Delano Amendment"[1] requirement that 20% of all television time, and the equivalent of 20% of internet time be devoted to educational programs. The FCC regulations specifically referred to programs about "Earth and its natural and animal environments." Emily had a special connection to the requirement as it was named after Charlotte's father-in-law, who was still alive. He had persuaded the Congress and President

1. Originally, this amendment to the Federal Communications Commission Act was to be called the "de la Noye Amendment," but the FCC Commissioners persuaded Philippe that with Franklin Delano Roosevelt as the still-revered very recent President, it made more political sense to call it the "Delano Amendment." It sounded more "American," too.

Eisenhower that the national security of the
country depended upon an educated public, and
that education must have a large part of the
programming to the people. He argued for a 40%
requirement for education, with 30% for news and
sports and 30% for entertainment, but the political
reality was that the public wanted more
entertainment. The result was the 20% standard,
which reminded Philippe in a weird way of his
father's 20:20:I and 20:20:W standards of
inequality.

The "Delano Amendment" requirements were
copied by countries around the world and were
endorsed by the U.N. GLEO (Global Literacy and
Education Organization). With people around the
world exposed to more educational programming,
the scores on the quinquennial GLOBITs (GLObal
Basic Information Test) improved and were now
approaching the long held goal of 80%.

At home, Emily was concluding her call with her
niece, Eleanor, "I support your efforts, and will call
sister Charlotte. She never liked controversy, and
prefers to think of things as they should be, and I
emfasize the 'should' part. You know, utopias and
all that."

That night, Emily discussed the problem with
her husband, Joshua, who was head of the "Voter
Participation Office" of the Department of Justice.
Before obtaining this position, he had been working
in St. Louis for the "Global Voter Foundation,"
which sought universal voter participation in state
and Federal elections. At that time, Emily was the
manager of the St. Louis Zoo, where she reduced
the number of species of animals at that zoo from
700 to 250, all of which were on the global
endangered species list.

The Global Voter Foundation had two primary
projects: promoting electronic voting and public

financing of elections at all levels. Electronic voting was now permitted in 30 countries, including the U.S. Voter participation in state and Federal elections in the U.S. had increased to 90%.   Voters self-authenticated by logging in with a "selfie" foto and the fingerprint app. The incentive for voting was a free hour of cell fone time and it was sponsored by the cell fone providers as a public service.

The other major project was prompted in the U.S. by the 2034 adoption of the 32nd amendment to the U.S. Constitution which had two parts. First it reversed the Supreme Court's 2010 decision in Citizens vs. United, which had found that corporations had some constitutional rights of speech. The Amendment declared that "artificial entities" were not citizens and only had the rights and responsibilities which were assigned to them by statutes of local and state governments and the Federal Government.

The second part of the Amendment gave governments the ability to regulate campaigns and the money spent on them. In short, money was declared not to be speech. This provision also enabled the further growth of public financing of elections, which the Voter Foundation was supporting. Maine had provided public funding of elections since 2000 and its law was a model for the rest of the country. When applying for public funding, candidates agreed to decline all campaign contributions from other sources. As few candidates wanted to be labeled as being in the pockets of private contributors or corporations, the participation rate in the Maine "Clean Elections" system was 95%. Now, by 2117, forty-five states had public financing of elections for state offices.

The Federal Government was slow to introduce public financing for elections for the House of

Representatives and the Senate and the President and Vice-President. Using money contributed by Federal taxpayers using a one-dollar checkoff on tax returns, the Federal Government first funded part of the 1976 Presidential election. However, most subsequent Presidential candidates declined public funding as they were able to raise larger amounts of money privately. In the 2060 election, the voluntary deduction system was changed to funding Congressional and Presidential elections with taxpayer money. The funding formulas were based on multiples of the average funding for the elections in the states. For the Presidency, the formula was for 53 times the average public funding for governors of the 45 states with publicly funded elections.

One by-product of the 32nd Amendment was that governments could regulate the contributions by individuals to their own campaigns. In states which had passed laws implementing this provision, the reform eliminated a major source of abuse whereby wealthy people had essentially purchased their primary and regular elections by contributing to their own campaigns.

Joshua was planning to call his brother-in-law, Forbes Delano about the Maine election laws when Emily told him about Chad's trial. Also, Joshua wanted to talk with Forbes about his vasectomy and how it felt, during the operation and the years afterwards. He and Emily had finally decided not to have children. They had been engrossed in their careers and had put off the decision for many years. Now, in their early 40's, they had decided on sterilization, and Joshua "won" the coin toss. After the husbands talked, Emily talked with Charlotte about Chad and offered her support.

The trial lasted longer than Eleanor expected and she called many times when the jury was deliberating. Like others, she thought the length of the deliberations was a good sign. "If they're talking about problems with the case, they must think there is SOME doubt," she thought.

On the afternoon of Thursday, April 29th, she called again, hoping for good news, but there was no answer. Then she sent a text, "What happened?"

Her father called her back to say that Chad had been found guilty, "beyond any doubt." The sentencing hearing was scheduled for the following Monday.

Eleanor was stunned. She asked herself, "How could this have happened? My brother's not a criminal. Even if he dropped a pill into the drink of that guy, he didn't mean to start a chain reaction leading to his death."

On Monday afternoon, Eleanor called again for the sentence and heard the news, "10 years: Life Restriction 3." She was surely the only astronaut with a brother found guilty of manslaughter, whether it be "chemical" or any other variation.

"This isn't right," she thought to herself. "There's something wrong with this."

During her astronaut training, Eleanor read a biografy of Sally Ride, the first American woman astronaut who orbited the earth. At the time of her flight on board the shuttle Challenger in 1983 at the age of 32, she was also the youngest American astronaut to orbit the earth. As important as that part of Sally Ride's story was to her career, the part of the book that struck Eleanor the most was the reported role of Ride's mother in correcting a wrongful conviction back on earth.

Eleanor read that McGeorge School of Law student Gloria Killian was convicted of murder in California in 1986. The deaths of a man and his wife came at the hands of two male robbers who were allegedly acting upon a plan devised by Killian. After 13 years in prison, Killian met Sally Ride's mother, Joyce Ride, who was visiting Killian's prison pursuant to her interest in helping victims of domestic abuse. That was Killian's interest as well. In large part due to Ms. Ride's provision of investigative and legal services worth over 25,000 earthas, Killian was exonerated in 2002. Without that fortunate assistance, Killian might have had to serve out her term until her scheduled release, if she lived to see it, in 2018 at the age of 67. She retains the distinction of being the only law student to ever have been exonerated from a wrongful conviction for murder.

In early May, for the first time, Eleanor talked with her manfriend, Max, about Chad's case. She had met Maximilian Trenkler on the first day of astronaut training in the fall of 2116. Tall and blonde, which characteristics were almost a disadvantage to him as he was considered a caricature of a Deutsche man, Max was one of two astronaut trainees from Deutschland.[2] He spoke English well, but it was a helpful surprise to him that Eleanor spoke Deutsch as well as she did. Max had little knowledge of the law, but he had heard of a member of the American branch of his family, who had been wrongly convicted of murder, or its Federal court equivalent, in the late 20th century in Boston.

The American branch of the family was begun in the 1930s when Alfred Maximilian Trenkler, later known as Freddie, emigrated to the U.S. from Austria. He had been a champion ice skater in Austria and the U.S. had several traveling professional ice skating shows. He met fellow skater Josephine Johnson Barnum, a descendant

2. Germany

of P.T. Barnum's brother, William, and they married and had a son, Alfred William. Alfred grew up in Milton, Massachusetts, went to private schools and became an electrical engineer. One night in 1991, he gave a young man, Tom Shay, a ride home and Tom liked Alfred and tried to keep in contact with him. That fall, a bomb exploded in the face of a Boston Bomb Squad officer who was called to inspect a suspicious device at the home of Tom's father. The officer died shortly thereafter and Alfred and Tom were convicted in separate trials in Federal Court of malicious destruction of property and life by means of explosives. The Government's theory was that Alfred, the electrical engineer, had built the bomb for Tom, who allegedly wanted to kill his father. Actually, Tom loved his father, despite his ill-treatment and lack of reciprocal feeling. Shay was released in 2010 after serving his term, but Trenkler had been sentenced to life in prison.

Alfred served 22 years in Federal prison before being exonerated through the efforts of his family, a volunteer investigator and writer, and Tom's former attorney who become a Federal judge after Tom's trial. Always believing in Tom's and Alfred's innocence, she joined Alfred's defense team upon her retirement. Alfred was exonerated in 2014.[3]

Max told Eleanor his general summary of this story and Eleanor was surprised that she could be so close, one degree of separation, to such a horrible case of injustice. Before reading about Joyce Ride, she had never heard of such a thing as a wrongful conviction, and now she knew about

---

3. The full story of the Alfred Trenkler case can be found at the Internet Archive website, www.alfredtrenklerinnocent.org and in the book, *Perfectly Innocent – The Wrongful Conviction of Alfred Trenkler.*

two. She also knew that even Chad thought that he probably did put the EZsleep into Juan's drink. Still, she had a feeling that he didn't do it.

Eleanor talked with her parents, and they and Chad were resigned to the ten year sentence. "After all," said her father, Forbes, there hasn't been a wrongful conviction for a long time in Maine, and Chad thought he might have done it – if only he had not drunk so much that night."

Forbes had another issue on his mind which distracted him from a more vigorous defense of Chad. He had been diagnosed with liver cancer the previous month, and he needed a transplant. His doctors had tried virotherapies, whereby viruses from measles and other vaccines were loaded in massive doses into his body, where they were expected to kill the cancer cells. Despite the widespread success of virotherapies in other patients with liver cancer, they didn't work for Forbes. The other bad news was that he was ineligible for a liver transplant from a live donor or a cadaver because his immune system was abnormally weak.

In the mid-21st century, livers and other organs were developed within the bodies of pigs and other animals, using stem cells from the patient. That practice went into disfavor and decline for two reasons. First, it involved the killing of animals and second, there was a newer technique whereby the patient would be his/her own "host" body for the stem cell-organ-to-be. Forbes was scheduled the following week to have a section of his liver removed in order to create clean stem cells, i.e. liver stem cells without the cancer. Then the cells were to be grown in a laboratory until a three-quarter size liver was developed in about three months. Then the regenerated liver was to be transplanted back into his body where it would grow further to full size. In the meantime, Forbes had to undergo chemo and radiation therapy, and that prospect was undermining his energy for Chad's case.

Fortunately, Forbes and his family did not have to bear the cost of these expensive medical procedures because health care was provided by the government, with private supplemental health insurance through Forbes' employer, the State of Maine. Coincidentally, 2117 was the 100th anniversary of the adoption by the U.S. of a single-payer, government funded system for all citizens. It was modeled after the previously successful Medicare system. The change from the previous employer-based system, which had been extended by some improvements in 2014 called "Obamacare," was occasioned by the support of the U.S. Chamber of Commerce and the National Association of Manufacturers. Those two organizations finally decided to align their political position on the issue of payment for health care with their business needs and away from their previous anti-government funding ideology. In fact, as businesses realized, they needed government to regulate the capitalism that allowed them to prosper and compete fairly. For many business people, it was an "Ah Haa" moment to see that business regulation was actually in their interest.

The business reality was that in a system where health costs are borne by employers, those employers pass the costs onto the prices of their goods and services which are paid by their customers. That, in turn, means that the prices of the goods and services of those employers are higher than those from countries where health care is provided by government taxation. It was estimated in 2015, for example, that $1,500, or 5%, of the cost of a $30,000 new car was entirely due to the costs of health insurance for automobile manufacturer employees. In the increasingly globalized economy of the early 21st century, the international competition forced U.S. corporations to finally seek to move the health insurance system entirely onto the lap of the government. Congress and the new President were persuaded to make the change in 2017.

Charlotte was also focused on her work and the implementation of the idea she proposed to the Utopia Soon Society (USS) to conduct annual evaluations of every United Nations member country according to "best practices" in six categories. She had become tired of teaching about past visions of utopia, and wanted to help move the country and the world toward real reform.

The countries were ranked on a "Global Utopia Soon Index" (GUSI). The six categories, as proposed by Charlotte, and with a brief overview of the sub-categories, were:

1. Sustainability. (degree to which society was reducing the human net footprint to zero, and even moving to "plus side" where human activity had a net positive role for Earth.

2. Health (compiled from data from many sources including: lifespan, infant mortality, nutrition, obesity, etc.)

3. Justice (percentage of incarcerated citizens, wrongful conviction rate, crime rates, compensation for victims, etc.)

4. Inequality (positions on the 20:20:I and 20:20:W indices)

5. Diversity (degree of representation of multiple races

and genders in society compared to representation in government and other organizations.)

6. Education (scoring on the GLOBIT [GLOBal Information Test], for selected age groups.)

7. Employment (as measured by employment rate, job satisfaction indices, etc.)

The 2117 GUSI showed Denmark, Canada, Japan, Costa Rica and Liberia with the top scores, respectively. Did this mean that Denmark was a utopian country? Well, almost. It was utopian as was humanly, and humanely, possible as of that date, given the current state of technology.

Back in Houston, Eleanor and Max talked about Chad's case and Max found a private investigator who might be able to help. Wilhelm Gutereise lived in Deutschland, and had been successful in finding the families of original owners of property seized by the Nazis. From Deutschland, he could do some investigating for Chad on the internet, and he knew investigators in the U.S. who could investigate the case locally.

Chapter 7 – Investigating Again

Max Trenkler contacted Wilhelm Gutereise, and he was available, but his hourly rate was high, at 80 earthas an hour.[1] Max was pleased to learn that in addition to the successful work tracing the original owners of art, Gutereise had worked on several wrongful convictions in Europe and had done some historical research on a claimed wrongful execution in 2011 of Troy Davis of Georgia. Davis was convicted in 1991 of the murder of an off-duty policeman, Mark MacPhail in Savannah. During the years after the conviction, seven of the nine witnesses against Davis recanted their courtroom testimonies. One of the remaining witnesses who declined to recant his testimony was the primary alternate suspect in the crime. The case attracted international attention, hence Gutereise's interest. Many international leaders, including Pope Benedictus XVI, appealed to the U.S. and Georgia governments to stop the execution. Gutereise's research took him to Savannah in 2079 where he interviewed descendants of the witnesses who had testified against Davis, and learned even more details of

---

1. With the adoption of a Single Global Currency in 2026, the eartha was worth approximately 1 US dollar(USD). In 2041, the Global Central Bank announced its goal to reduce inflation to zero, after it was finally determined that the old goal of 2% annual inflation was harming people's long term savings. Previously, it was thought that material consumption had to be maintained. In 2050, the eartha was revalued by a multiple of 10, so that prices were cut to 10% of their former nominative value. As prices had roughly doubled from 2026 to 2050, this meant, in USD terms, that 2050 prices in earthas were approximately 20% of their 2026 amount. Thus, in 2050, and thereafter, with zero inflation, an 80 eartha hourly rate, for example, was equivalent to $400 in 2026.

how their original testimonies were fabricated, often at the intimidating request of the police.

His breakthrough in the case came from his approach to the great grandchildren of Officer Mark MacPhail. As the great grandchildren learned, their forbears had been boxed into an adversarial "we-they" position by the justice system. Instead of meeting with the supporters of Troy Davis, the early 2000s supporters of his execution issued press releases and believed those press releases as being the truth, rather than reading the actual documents, such as the recantations of most of the witnesses.

By 2079, it was time to find common ground and the MacPhail family convinced the State of Georgia to establish a Davis-MacPhail Justice Commission to fully explore what happened to Mark MacPhail and to Troy Davis. With its subpoena power, the commission learned about a secret "Last Testament" of the primary alternate suspect in the case. However, by the terms of the "Testament" it was not to be opened until 100 years after the death of the suspect, which was in 2022. It was expected that when opened in 2122, the "Testament" will have a confession to the killing of Officer MacPhail.

After Max had determined that Gutereise was available, he referred Eleanor's parents to him and Charlotte contracted with him in September, 2017 for a renewed investigation of Chad's case. Forbes was nearly immobilized by the liver therapy, in preparation for his transplant operation scheduled for late October.

Through his international private investigator network, Gutereise found a private investigator in Maine, Cameron Swayze, who had excellent references and there was good coverage of her work on the internet. She agreed to work on Chad's case. Cameron had written her senior thesis at Bates College about the Dennis Dechaine case, which was, until the 2056 case of Jeffery Krone, Maine's best known wrongful conviction case.

Krone was convicted in 2050 of sexually assaulting his stepdaughter, Denise Hearn, primarily upon her testimony, a rape kit showing Krone's DNA, and evidence of bruising on her arms. Krone testified that he was drunk and did not remember sex with Denise. After the trial, she recanted several times and said that she had masturbated her stepfather to an erection and then climbed onto him, which explained the presence of his sperm in her body. However, the police, prosecutors and two judges would not believe her recantation, even after she passed a polygraf exam. A volunteer private investigator wrote a book about the case, *Please Believe Me!*, which showed Krone's innocence and gave Denise another polygraf examination with the same, "no deception indicated" result. This time, a retired judge read the book and was convinced of Krone's innocence, even if not convinced of the correctness of his lifestyle. The judge's concerns were openly presented by Krone's lawyers to an appellate court, and Krone won his habeas corpus petition in 2056.

Cameron looked more closely at this case because it involved a fact pattern that had one similarity to Chad's case, which was that Krone didn't remember what had actually happened on the night of the alleged crime.

She also re-examined her e-files of the Dechaine case, as it also involved a problem with memory during the time of the alleged crime.

Dechaine was convicted in 1989 of sexually assaulting and murdering a 12-year old girl, Sarah Cherry, of Bowdoin, Maine. The trial was in the same year as the first U.S. DNA exoneration, of

Gary Dotson in Illinois. Fortunately, Dechaine's attorney had heard of DNA's potential for forensic truth. Dechaine had asked Judge Carl Bradford, the great great great uncle of Judge Carla Bradford in Chad's case, to delay the trial for several months so Dechaine could have DNA tests done at his own expense. Judge Carl Bradford declined and said that the trial should not be delayed. The memory issue for Dechaine was that his alibi for the apparent time of the kidnapping of Sarah Cherry was that he was high on amphetamines ("speed") and was walking in the woods and couldn't remember exactly what had transpired during his day. The time of her actual murder was another disputed fact in the case. His advocates calculated that she was killed after Dechaine was located and under surveillance.

Dechaine was convicted and sentenced to life in prison. Four years later, the first Innocence Project, in New York, accepted his case. In 1993, the DNA underneath the victim's thumbnails was tested and found to be exculpatory, but not conclusively so. That is, another person's DNA was found, but that person was not immediately identified. The State of Maine fought the obvious conclusions of most Maine citizens, and of the author of the book about the case, *Human Sacrifice*. This governmental obstinance forced Dechaine to continue his struggle for exoneration for 21 more years. Judge Carl Bradford continued to be assigned to the case and denied most of Dennis's claims of injustice, despite the appearance that he, Bradford, was more interested in saving his own reputation than in achieving justice for

Dennis Dechaine.[2] It wasn't until 2015 that
Dechaine was finally exonerated by a decision of
the Maine Supreme Judicial Court.

That decision was precipitated by a new state
law in 2014 which amended the Rules of Evidence
in criminal cases by requiring a judicial
presumption that evidence which is gathered by the
police and later lost was exculpatory. In
Dechaine's case, there was an unidentified
fingerprint on the front door at the home where
Sarah Cherry was babysitting. Because it was lost
before Dechaine's 1989 trial, his first jury did not
know about it. His attorney was not permitted by
the former rules of evidence to mention it. With the
new law of evidence his attorney at his new trial
would be permitted to tell the jury that there was
an unidentified fingerprint and that the jury must
assume, because of the new law, that it did not
belong to Dechaine.

Similarly, there were human hairs found on or
near Sarah Cherry's body, but those hairs were
never tested for DNA. While his case was still
under active appeal, the prosecution destroyed the
hairs, ostensibly as part of a routine cleanup
practice. Those hairs were not mentioned at
Dechaine's first trial, but the Maine Supreme Court
confirmed that the defense could mention those
hairs at a second trial, and that they must be
presumed to be exculpatory to Dechaine.

Given those two required evidentiary
presumptions, and the likelihood that a new jury
would find him not guilty, the Maine Supreme
Court ordered that Dechaine's initial conviction be
vacated and that the prosecution be given 90 days

2. For more information about Dechaine's case, see the
website in the Internet archives at
www.trialanderrordennis.org.

to decide whether to request a new trial. No new trial was requested, so Dechaine was released.

After Judge Carl Bradford's full retirement a few years later, Maine changed its rules on the assignments of judges to subsequent proceedings in the cases of defendants claiming further judicial relief. The risk of prejudice and injustice was thought by the legislature to far outweigh the state's previously declared interest in efficiency, by having the same judge continue with cases.

Turning her attention to Chad's case, Cameron first looked at the documents available on the Internet to get a basic understanding of the case. On Tuesday, October 12,[3] she interviewed Chad at his apartment, which was not the same apartment as he had for the 2116-17 New Year's party. He had lost his job as an express package driver and could no longer afford that apartment. He shared with Cameron the same details he had shared with his attorney about how he had planned to drop an EZsleep pill into Juan's champagne, but couldn't remember actually doing so.

Then Cameron went to the police station and met Bob Armstrong and Angela Kline, who were

---

3. This day used to be celebrated in the U.S. as Columbus Day, to commemorate the birthday of the Italian sailor who led the Europeans to the Americas. However, after the enactment of the International Holiday Convention in 2040, with its requirements of five global holidays and up to five national holidays, Columbus Day was dropped in the U.S. One problem with the holiday was that Columbus's "discovery" led eventually to the decimation of the native American populations. The U.S. chose the following days for its five national holidays: Presidents' Day on the second Friday of February, Memorial Day on the last Friday in May, Independence Day on the first Friday in July, Labor Day on the first Friday in September and Religions Day on the fourth Friday in December.

confident that there was no problem with their
case. Together, they had worked on more than 100
investigations. Said Angela, "when we are confident
of a suspect's guilt, we have secured a conviction
by trial or guilty plea every time." Cameron asked
to see the fysical evidence, and Angela said, "Sure,
but you are wasting your time." Armstrong was not
so sure.

Cameron looked first at Juan's clothing and the
lab reports of his blood tests, and then Anita's
deposition and trial testimony. Then she viewed the
fotografs of Chad's apartment and examined each
of the police clear bags which contained each of the
black plastic bags with the contents of Chad's four
trash baskets. The most important black bag was
the one from which the one centimeter square
aluminum foil fragment came. Cameron emptied it
the same way Angela Kline described at Chad's
trial, holding by the bottom corners upside down.
Then Cameron took one additional step. She
pushed the bag inside out, without contaminating
any of the inside walls of the bag, and there it was:
a blue pill stuck to an interior fold at the bottom of
the bag.

She said to herself, "Whew. That was lucky," and
took a deep breath. Her heart pounded with
excitement and apprehension, first that she almost
missed it, and second that it might not be what she
hoped it was. All she could do now was take the
correct next steps and see what played out.

She set the bag down on the table and took
several fotografs. Then she went to retrieve Angela
Kline. Before she arrived at Angela's office,
Cameron changed course and sought Bob
Armstrong who was likely to be a little more
understanding. Then, together, they found Kline.

The three returned to the evidence room and
Cameron explained exactly what she had done

before finding the blue pill. Angela immediately understood what had happened, and she felt anguished. First, she felt terrible that her technique of emptying the black plastic bag had a flaw, i.e. that items stuck to the inside of the bag and not obviously heavy or visible from the outside, could escape detection. Second, she feared that this would harm her own career if it developed that Chad Delano were to be found innocent.

As Cameron watched carefully, Armstrong put the other contents of the plastic bag back into its container, and then put the bag itself into a plastic cannister. He had Cameron and Angela sign the submittal slip to the lab.

Cameron then returned to the evidence room and looked at the remaining items from Chad's apartment. However, she knew that the pill, by itself, would profoundly affect the case. "Sometimes in this work," she thought, "we get lucky." Especially if you are meticulous, as Cameron was.

After leaving the police station, she called Wilhelm with the news, and afterwards he called Nina McKelvy. Then they waited for the lab results which were expected by Friday, the 15th. Cameron and Nina were prepared to challenge the lab results, but the lab had a good reputation, especially since the 21st century movement of the lab from the prosecutors' department to the State's Department of Science. As it turned out, they did not need to challenge the lab's work.

Nina called Matthew Bailey and advised him of what Cameron had found, but he had already been contacted by Armstrong. Bailey said he would ensure that the lab results were sent as quickly as possible to Nina, and they agreed to meet the following Wednesday. Nina also called Chad who was mystified, but greatly relieved.

"Could it have happened," he asked, "that I dropped or threw the pill into the wastebasket at the last minute, instead of putting it into Juan's champagne?" Chad and Nina discussed the legal steps which would be necessary to secure his release from Restricted Life 3.0. Maybe he could get his old job as a software code writer back. On the other hand, he knew what others knew, which was that he actually did intend, at least at one point, to do what he was convicted of doing.

The lab results came by email from Bailey on Friday afternoon, and they confirmed the hopes of Chad's team, which was that the blue pill was an EZsleep pill. The lab also explained how the pill was likely stuck to the bag so strongly that it didn't fall out when Angela Kline shook it, upside down. There was a film of champagne on at least one side of the pill which partially dissolved the pill's coating. That film likely came from a spill onto Chad's fingers from his pouring the champagne. Surprisingly, when the pill was tossed into the wastebasket, the champagne and the pill's coating then combined chemically with the polymer surface of the plastic bag to form an epoxy-like adhesive between the bag and the pill. As it was not possible for the lab to fysically pull the pill from the bag, the lab technicians cut out a circle of the bag, about the size of an eartha coin, i.e. 2.3 centimeters.

Nina was optimistic about her upcoming meeting with Matthew Bailey, as she thought this new evidence showed that the EZsleep pill that was associated with the foil wrapper that had been introduced into court was the one found inside the bag. That meant to Nina that the EZsleep chemical that Juan had ingested must have come from another source, and not from Chad. Bailey, however, was not overly impressed with the new evidence. Nina asked Bailey to join her in a motion to the court to vacate Chad's conviction and dismiss the charges.

"At the least," she continued, "you could join me in vacating the conviction and then you could move for a new trial. If the jury had known that Chad had actually discarded the pill, there would have been some doubt, and the jury would not have convicted him."

Bailey saw it differently, saying, "There are several possible interpretations of the newly-found pill, and only one of them would indicate Chad's innocence." One simple answer, for Bailey, was that Chad had two pills, despite the court testimony that the foil formerly had one pill in it. Another answer was that Chad had two foil containers in his pocket that night, and used one and threw the other away somewhere outside his apartment.

After some discussion, they agreed that a judge would have to make the decision on the next steps. As the case was still within the one-year filing period for an appeal, Nina said she would amend her existing appeal which was filed in June and which had not yet been acted upon. On December 15, Nina filed the Amendment to her appeal.

The Supreme Court of Maine held the two-hour hearing on the appeal in January, 2118. Of the five judges, Judge Tate Corcoran was the most skeptical of Nina's claims for Chad. He asked, after her oral argument, "How do we know that your client didn't have two pills in two foil wrappers?" Nina conceded that she didn't know, but she said that the question was not as important (better not to tell a judge that his question was irrelevant) as the question of whether the existence of the "wastebasket pill" would have introduced any doubt about Chad's guilt. By their questions, two

other judges seemed to see that enough doubt had
been introduced so an appellate judge could say
that a reasonable juror could not have concluded
that there was not "any doubt" of guilt. The
remaining two judges seemed, by the nods of their
heads, and their questions, to be leaning in the
direction of Judge Corcoran.

Two months later, the 3-2 verdict affirming the
conviction was announced by email.

Nina told Chad that she thought there was a
good chance that the U.S. District Court of Maine
would agree with Chad's position and rule that the
Maine state courts had denied Chad his federal
constitutional rights. The biggest problem was
that the Federal Courts still used the "beyond a
reasonable doubt" standard. Thus, the Federal
District Court Judge would have to see that the
finding of the single EZsleep pill introduced enough
doubt for a reasonable juror to conclude that there
was reasonable doubt about Chad's actions.

Matthew Bailey and Nina squared off again in
Federal Court at the May 25, 2118 hearing, before
Judge Donna Marquis and the arguments were the
same, with one exception. Nina cited the 2015
Federal case of <u>Chad Evans v New Hampshire</u>
where a First Circuit Court of Appeals Judge
overturned Evans's 2001 conviction for murder.[4]
The judge found that the new evidence in that case,
and the use of previously ignored New Hampshire
Statutes, would have led a reasonable juror in a
retrial to find enough reasonable doubt to require a

4. The defendant, Chad Evans, was the great-great-great
grandfather of the Good Samaritan by the same name who
may have saved Chad Delano's life when finding him on his
"Solar Scooter" about 13 years earlier.

verdict of "Not Guilty."[5] Bailey argued that the case was too old, and not relevant.

In September, Judge Marquis' opinion was emailed to the attorneys and it was against Chad. As Nina's legal bills to Chad, but mostly to his parents, now exceeded 55,000 earthas, she suggested that there would be no further value in appealing to the U.S. Supreme Court, which would cost another 10,000 earthas. Chad and his parents agreed, but from Houston, Eleanor argued that it wasn't right to quit now. She was sure that, despite the off-and-on intent, Chad didn't drop the EZsleep into Juan's champagne. Eleanor then offered to split the cost of the appeal with her parents, so the appeal to the U.S. Supreme Court, actually called a Petition for a Writ of Certiorari, went forward.

Nina prepared the appeal and actually came to think that it might be successful. She filed it on Monday, January 10, 2119. The Supreme Court's denial came quickly, two weeks later.

Nina advised Chad, Eleanor and their parents that this was the end of the legal road, unless some new dramatic form of evidence appeared.

5. For more information about the Chad Evans case see the Internet Archives at www.chadevanswronglyconvicted.org.

Chapter 8 Marriage and Mars

Eleanor and Maximilian finished their astronaut training on Friday, March 25th, 2118. The previous winter, the candidates were asked for their assignment preferences for their astronaut careers. There were three basic alternatives. First was the International Space Station(ISS), the original modules for which were launched over a century earlier, in 1998. Since then, some modules had been jettisoned, and others had been substantially repaired; but the core remained. There were ten astronauts on this spacecraft, and their primary tasks included the maintenance of the earth monitoring equipment on the ISS.

The second choice was joining the colony on the Moon.[1] In 2028 a man and woman astronaut, who were married to each other, went to the moon for a six-month stay. It had been long before decided that sexual deprivation was not a healthy way to treat astronauts, who were at least as deserving of satisfactory sex lives as prison inmates, so pairings of astronauts were designed for their sexual satisfaction as well as achievement of other goals. It had been many years since NASA learned that sexual dissatisfaction among astronauts was not productive, and most astronauts were not interested in even short term space trips without a partner. In the 2020s, NASA recruited a cadre of

---

1. The Moon was given a new official name of Lunaterra, i.e. Earth moon, in 2024 by the International Astronomical Union. Previously, it had been noted that the moons of other planets in our own and other solar systems were given names, e.g. Titan, which is the largest of Saturn's 62 moons. While "Lunaterra" was increasingly used in scientific journals, most earthlings still refer to Lunaterra as "the Moon," which is how it's referenced in this book. It's capitalized due to its importance.

asexual candidates for astronaut positions, but legal problems arose due to the obvious discrimination for reasons of sexual orientation. NASA's claim of justification for a necessary purpose was insufficient to persuade the courts, and even less sufficient to persuade the Congress which was, by then, majority female.

The moon base, called Goddard, after the American forefather of rocketry, had been previously constructed by robots, and had been stocked with supplies to support the six month exploration. The male astronaut was Alan Yuri Armstrong, a great-great grandson of Neil Armstrong, the first human to walk on the moon. His first names were after the first American to venture into space, Alan Shepard, and the first human to orbit the earth, Yuri Gagarin. For some children, their names and their family histories are insurmountable burdens, but for Alan, his heritage was a helpful escalator to the life he wanted, i.e. to be an astronaut.

His wife was Liu Sally Yang who grew up not wanting to be an astronaut, despite having a middle name for the first American woman astronaut, Sally Ride. Liu's mother, named Lui Yang, was the first Chinese woman astronaut, but the allure of space did not interest Liu Sally Yang as a child. Instead, she was interested in biology and GLOWARE (GLobal WArming REversal). However, she attended a "families-of-astronauts" gathering in Moscow in 2021, the 60th anniversary of the orbiting of Yuri Gagarin. At that conference, Liu Yang met Alan Armstrong and they fell in love. She then decided to modify her perspectives of biology and GLOWARE to focus on the vantage point of outer space.

They traveled to the moon in 2028 and were the first astronauts since the Chinese one-week expedition in 2022. They were launched by a joint project between NASA and RKA, the Russian space agency.

Alan and Liu's most important activity on the Moon was simply to experiment with their own bodies to test the key unknown regarding future colonization of the moon. That was whether the moon's weak gravity, 16% of the G-force on earth, was enough to overcome the deleterious effects of long periods of weightless space travel. It was known by then that three hours a day on a centrifuge in the ISS, in various sitting, standing, and lying positions, was enough to counteract the absence of gravity and keep their bodies in approximately the same condition as if they were on earth. The centrifuge's spinning created a force equivalent to two times the pressure of gravity, or 2G. It was not known what proportion of the body's need for gravity would be filled by the moon's gravity. Alan and Liu's moon stay showed that what the body needed was some gravity, and the moon's 16% was enough to avoid the effects of weightlessness. For reasons not yet fully understood, the natural gravity had a beneficial effect that exceeded what was artificially created with the centrifuges.

After Armstrong's and Yang's stay, the next moon venture was to establish a colony on the moon in 2040 when three women and five men were sent for permanent settlement. It was the first major space expedition by the newly formed GLASO. The moon colony gradually expanded to 20 people in 2060 and then to 40 by 2072. Since then, 40 has been the equilibrium count.

The effect of that 16% gravity on infants in utero and after birth and as children was not known. Instead of testing the question over a period of years with infant animals, which was

blocked out of concern for the safety of the
nominated chimpanzees, it was the practice that
pregnant astronauts were brought back to earth for
duration of their pregnancies. As there were
resupply missions flying back and forth to earth
every two months, the return to earth of pregnant
astronauts was feasible. However, it was expensive
and not recommended, as a returning astronaut
took the place of valuable manufactured cargoes.
The preferred stay for the moon-residing astronauts
was permanent. Since the Moon colony was
established, two pregnant astronauts, and one
prospective father, and three very sick astronauts
had been returned to earth. Three others had died
on the Moon but their bodies were not returned to
Earth. Instead, they were placed into used oxygen
capsules, especially split and rejoined. At the
requests of the deceased, each of the capsules was
launched from the Moon into infinite space.

Eleanor's and Max's third option was to travel
to Mars, our solar system's second most hospitable
planet, or second least inhospitable, to future
human life. Beginning in the 19th century, there
had been serious speculation that there had once
been human-like life on Mars. In 1877, the Italian
astronomer, Giovanni Schiaparelli, reported that he
had seen canals on Mars. In 1895, the U.S.
astronomer, Percival Lowell, supported that theory
with more fotografs and speculation. However by
the early 20th century, further observations and
calculations discounted the possibility of
humanoid-made canals on Mars. Still, the
fascinated persisted, and a large proportion of the
research about Mars was to search for traces of
previous life of any kind.

In the 1960's orbiters were sent around Mars,
and in 1971, the first vehicles from Earth were
successfully landed on Mars. The Soviet Union's

'Mars 2' crash landed in September, but the December landing of 'Mars 3' was soft enough to permit radio transmissions for 14 seconds before it died. The U.S.'s 'Viking 1' and 'Viking 2' arrived five years later in 1976. Each was a combination orbiter and lander. Both landers landed safely and transmitted for several years, with 'Viking 2' lasting until 1982 when a human error caused the antenna to malfunction.

The better word to describe the "travel" to Mars that Eleanor and Max were considering was "emigration" as it was a one-way journey. The gravity on Mars, roughly double that of the Moon and 40% of the Earth, was sufficient for a long-term colony. The first human Mars colony was established in 2071, one hundred years after the Soviet 'Mars 2' and 'Mars 3' unmanned landings. During the ten years prior to 2071, twelve missions to Mars had shipped robots and materials for the future colony. As a reminder of the hazards of space travel, a thirteenth mission crash landed with such force that if humans were on board they would have been killed. Nonetheless, robots were able to salvage many of the materials for future use, including potential reconstituting in the future colony's 3-D printing systems. The robots were so successful in building the pre-colony on Mars, complete with underground housing units to protect colonists from radiation, that GLASO launched a full review of its Mars program to evaluate whether it wanted to continue with a human expedition. Proponents argued that Mars was only the bridge to future human space travel. The opponents feared that perhaps Mars was "a bridge too far." The overwhelming consensus at GLASO, and in the global insta-polling of 220 million people on the question, was to continue the plan for human colonization of Mars.

The first Mars colonists were two heterosexual couples in their early 40s.[2] The decision had been made long before that any space travel to Mars would be a one-way trip. Initially, the idea seemed shocking when first proposed by the private organization, Mars Alive!, in 2012. It seemed like planned suicide. However, several of the astronauts at the time were descended from immigrants from another country or continent, and for most of their ancestors there was never a plan for a return trip. Few of those immigrants ever returned to their native countries. In the 21st century, with videofones, emigrants were far closer in time to their home families and friends that the pre-electronic-era migrants ever were.

Mars Alive! had planned to send supplies to Mars in 2018, and biennially thereafter, and then its first group of four humans in 2028, and then three more humans each year for three years. However, the initial 2018 journey failed and a second supply ship had to be prepared, launched and landed on Mars in 2020. That effort was successful, and was followed by three subsequent supply missions. The four humans were launched in 2028. However, they all died during the landing on Mars. Those deaths were the second set of deaths of any astronauts in outer space. The first three occurred in 1971 when the Soyuz 11 capsule lost its oxygen when beginning the re-entry

---

2. The first married couple to fly in space together was Mark Lee and Nancy Jan Davis, who flew on the 50th U.S. Space Shuttle mission in 1992. They fell in love during training for the flight and married secretly. By the time they told NASA of their marriage it was too late to rearrange the crew. Thereafter, NASA formalized the rule against spouses flying together, which rule was not repealed until the preparation for the first six-month Moon expedition in 2028 with Liu Yang and Alan Armstrong.

process. Most of the subsequent deaths had been of the U.S. space shuttle astronauts aboard the Challenger (7) on takeoff in 1986 and the Columbia (7) upon re-entry in 2003.   There were no fatalities in outer space during Apollo Moon program, although Apollo 13 came dangerously close.

None of these deaths were of the type feared by astronauts and their space programs, which was the "Major Tom" scenario. Named after an astronaut in David Bowie's 1969 album, "Space Oddity," the feared scenario was that the astronaut would lose fysical and communications contact with his/her spaceship and drift off into space to die. Without direct communications, the public was spared Major Tom's last conscious moments. A similar death occurred to astronaut Francis Poole in Arthur Clarke's *2001 – A Space Odyssey*, where Poole's spacesuit was punctured by command of the malevolent computer, HAL, and Poole was lost into space.

Even if not of the feared, lingering type, the 2028 Mars Alive! deaths were a devastating shock to that organization, from which it did not recover. The cause was never clearly revealed by Mars Alive!, but it was thought to have been human error by the ground control team. In part, the accident brought unwanted additional attention to the organization's hubris-laden name, "Mars Alive!"

Errors by ground control were especially poignant in missions beyond Earth orbit and the Moon because of the time delay in communications. Once the fatal message was sent, it would take several minutes to reach its destination. In 1999, the Mars-bound "Climate Orbiter" was lost due to the mistaken use by one of the engineering teams of foot/pound measurements when the rest of the vehicle was designed according to the metric system.

After the Mars Alive! fatalities, GLASO imposed requirements for private space ventures with human passengers. The most important requirement was that there must be a backup plan in the event of one or more catastrofes. For example, subsequent privately-funded human spaceships to Mars had to be accompanied by an unmanned spacecraft which might be utilized as a supply ship or rescue vehicle. In addition, for trips to Mars, at least one year's supply of oxygen and food needed to be stockpiled at a future landing zone on the planet before a private organization could send humans.

These requirements explained the 50-year gap between the failed efforts of the 2020s and the eventual GLASO settlement on Mars in 2071. Before the merger into GLASO, the U.S. NASA had planned to put humans on Mars in the 2030s, but that nation's reckless fiscal management doomed the project for lack of funds. The precedent for such a time gap was the period between the last Apollo landing of astronauts on the Moon in 1972 and the two Chinese astronauts who arrived 50 years later in 2022. That latter year was picked by the Chinese to commemorate the recognition that their economy had outpaced the U.S. and had become the largest in the world. Ironically, the importance of this achievement was dampened because the world GDP standards were changed from a national total measurement to a national per capita measurement. On this scale, China still ranked eleventh in the world. The Chinese sent another two-week expedition to the Moon in 2034, which was the last human expedition to the Moon until the GLASO permanent colony expedition in 2040.

In 2115, the age limits for men and women Martian astronauts were reduced to 22. After forty-plus years of experience with the Martian colony, GLASO decided that the human-made environment at Mars City, as it came to be known, was sufficiently stable to permit and encourage younger astronauts to emigrate. The obvious next step was for the colony to raise its own children and become self-sufficient.

Eleanor knew that the earlier high threshold age for women astronauts was a guide as accidental pregnancy was less likely for them. In those earlier years GLASO considered sending women who had been voluntarily sterilized, but then backed away, as that might have appeared to be an entrance requirement and exert undue influence on women to make that choice against their own personal interests.

In 2079, six more astronauts emigrated to Mars. There were two gay men, two gay women and an asexual man and a heterosexual man, Jose Aparacio, who was replacing one of the earlier Martian astronauts who had died. Jose's compatibility with the women astronauts already on Mars was well-established before lift-off by personality tests and video conversations.

The primary purpose of the Martian colony was to extend human knowledge of its universe. More specifically, the colony was responsible for identifying asteroids which might endanger both the humans on Earth and those on Mars. The 2013 explosion of the Chelyabinsk asteroid in Siberia was an eye opener, as it was not previously detected because it was coming from the direction of the sun. It was a 65-foot wide rock traveling at 68,000 km per hour when it exploded with the blast equivalent of about 20-30 times the power of the 1945 Hiroshima atomic bomb. After that surprise explosion, GLASO launched "Sentinel" and other spacecraft to detect potential collision-course asteroids.

When risky asteroids were detected, a rocket, or more than one, was sent to that asteroid to deflect its course. One method was to place a reflective sheet on the surface of the asteroid, so that the rays from the sun would nudge it slightly away from its current course, just like the reaction of a toy radiometer. Another method was to place a plasma engine on the asteroid with the same goal of altering the rock's course. The third method was to explode a nuclear weapon on or near the asteroid if the other methods were not effective. The nuclear option had never been necessary.

Eleanor and Max talked a lot about their options, and decided several months earlier to ask to be considered for placement into the Mars colony. The future of their family was a big issue. They wanted to have children and they wondered what a life would be like on Mars where there would be very few other children. Would their children be happy on Mars, or would they be resentful they were not born on Earth? Eleanor and Max thought the latter feeling to be like an Earth-bound child wishing s/he was born to a neighbor's parents, or to a mother when she was living with her first lover, a very rich man. Wishing you were born somewhere else to someone else would not be a feeling unique to children born on Mars.

"What's weird," said Eleanor, "is that all my life I've heard about the need to reduce the human population. Girls and women have been encouraged for about 100 years to have fewer or no children. Now, I'm applying for a job, or really a life, and it seems that a requirement is that I agree to have children. And the more, the better. I was even told by my interviewer that the fact that my mother was a twin assisted my application for the Mars program."

"Yah," I was wondering what you thought about that pressure," responded Max. "Actually, while we both are interested in having children, it seems awkward to me, too, as the future father."

At the June, 2118 astronaut training graduation, it was announced that Eleanor and Max, and another heterosexual astronaut couple had been chosen for the Mars spaceship to be launched in two years. October 10, 2119 was the next optimal day, as such days occur every 26 months, to catch the time when the orbits of Earth and Mars are closest to each other, albeit still about 92 million kilometers apart. At these optimal launch times, the trip to Mars can take approximately 60 days, depending upon the speed of the spaceship. The trip to Mars used to be a six-month journey until the development of hydrofusion power and a spaceship model that enabled plasma propulsion. After leaving Earth's gravity, plasma propulsion is used to accelerate a spaceship to speeds up to 100,000 km/hr, which brought the length of the journey down to two months.

Eleanor's and Max's parents and families were in the audience and they had mixed emotions about Eleanor and Max emigrating to Mars. It was not a surprise as both children were excellent performers in the training program, and they had told their parents and families of their applications for the Mars colony. The news was softened by the knowledge that there would be frequent communications by holografic video fone, where it would seem that their children and future grandchildren would be fysically present. Coping with the 4-36 minute time delay for electronic signals to travel to and from Mars, for a total of 8 to

72 minutes, would be a challenge, but
surmountable.

As their families were already in Houston, as
were all their astronaut friends and their families,
Eleanor and Max had scheduled their wedding for
the next day, Saturday. For those who could not
fysically attend, there were several two-way web
cameras.

Special training for the 60 day Mars trip
included fysical exercises to prepare astronauts'
bodies for weightlessness. Eleanor specialized in
learning the techniques of print 3-D manufacturing
that were already in use in Mars City. Max's
specialty became the food growth and recycling
systems, and how to better use the minerals on
Mars for food production.

Over the next year, Eleanor and Max and the
other two married astronauts for the next mission
to Mars, Adisa Ondimba of Gabon and Nkiru Curie
of Congo, trained together for their future roles as
travelers to Mars and as Martian parents. All four
underwent additional genetic testing to be as
certain as possible that their children would be
born without genetic infirmity or disposition to a
disease. As part of their agreement to have children
on Mars, they also agreed not to have children on
earth before their journey to Mars. GLASO was not
yet ready to send toddlers into space.

In January 2119, the four astronauts traveled
to the International Space Station for their
initiation into space travel. It was always the
preference of GLASO to have astronauts undertake
at least one Earth-orbit space trip before traveling
permanently to the Moon or Mars. Despite all the
Earth-based training, some astronauts still found
that their appetite for space travel was not what
was anticipated, once they leave the Earth for the
first time.

On September 20, 2119, the four astronauts traveled to the South American launch site in Para, Brazil. In 2044, GLASO selected three new launch sites which were closest to the equator, and thus could best take advantage of the equatorial speed of the Earth's surface at that latitude at 1,670 km/hour. The other two were in Gabon, Africa and the island of Sumatra in Indonesia. Rockets which took off from those three sites needed less energy to launch their cargoes into orbit, or on their way elsewhere, than those used at other sites closer to the poles. For example, it takes approximately eight percent more fuel per pound of cargo to launch from the Russian spaceport in Kazakhstan, or Cape Canaveral, Florida, than from any of the three new GLASO sites.

Even though Eleanor and the other astronauts were very knowledgeable about the universe and space travel, the idea that people standing on the equator were actually moving at the speed of 1,670 km/hour was still a bit staggering. That's more than the 1,250 km/hour speed of a 9 mm bullet when fired from a Glock 17 pistol. Similarly, the water around them and the air above them were also moving at that speed. Also confounding was the idea that people standing at the North and South Poles were not moving at all, at least not due to the rotation of the Earth. They would only be rotating in a counter-clockwise direction if at the North Pole and clockwise if at the South Pole.

In addition to the rotation speed of the Earth, which depended upon one's distance from the equator, everyone on the earth was traveling around the sun every 365.2425 days at the rate of 108,000 km/hour. Borrowing from the familiar slogan about Superman's flying speed, that's 86.4 times the speed of "a speeding bullet," in this case, a 9 mm bullet fired from a Glock 17.

When on Mars, Eleanor calculated that she and Max and all of Mars City would be traveling at 86,871 km/hr as Mars takes 687 Earth days to travel around the sun.

Finally, all these speed calculations must be incorporated into the perspective of the orbits of our sun, together with our solar system, and neighboring stars around the center of our galaxy. Each orbit, at the speed of 792,000 km/hr takes 255 million years. That speed is approximately seven times the Earth's speed as it orbits around our sun.

These were just a few of the background calculations that astronauts still find challenging, if not stupefying.

On October 10, 2119, Eleanor, Max, Adisa and Nkiru launched atop their 118 meter tall rocket from Para and began their 60 day journey to Mars.

Chapter 9 – A Tip and Followup

Chad and his parents watched the October 10 launch of Eleanor's rocket by videocloud at their Portland home, and were much relieved when the image disappeared from the live screen and then appeared on radar. After about 12 minutes, the ship achieved the necessary speed of 40,000 km/hr to escape the Earth's gravity. It was still accelerating when the hot plasma engine started, using a hydrofusion power source. The plasma engine would then take the ship to Mars in 60 days. Back in Portland, life moved more slowly.

Michelle Grant was still living with her wofriend, Xue Wen, but she was becoming less happy with the relationship and with herself. Xue sensed that the changes began after Chad's trial two years before, and increased after he lost all his appeals almost exactly a year ago. They went to a party on New Year's Eve 2118-19 which seemed eerily like the party at Chad's two years earlier. Michelle had a few of her favorite drinks, Moxie[1] and bourbon, and then took a few tokes[2] from Xue's joint.

While talking with someone else about GLOWARE and the 85 centimeter rise in the ocean level during the previous hundred years, Michelle interrupted herself and said, "You know, two years ago, I did something stupid." Xue overheard her and thought she finally understood Michelle's declining spirits and affection for her. Xue guessed

1. Moxie has been a popular Maine "soft drink," i.e. carbonated drink, since its development in 1876 by a Massachusetts doctor, Dr. Augustin Thompson. He was originally from Union, Maine, and the drink was originally a patent medicine, "Moxie Nerve Food." Cocaine was one ingredient, as it was for the early mixtures of Coca Cola.
2. A "toke" is an inhalation, or drawing of a puff, of a cigarette, or marijuana joint.

that it was related to what happened to Juan Carlos. During the past two years, Michelle had mentioned his death several times, but it wasn't a discussion about loss and sadness. The context was typically about fate or luck or justice. By her statements, she seemed more confident than others of Chad's innocence.

The next day, Xue asked, "What did you mean when you said last night that you had done something stupid two years ago? Did it relate to me?" She was confident that it didn't relate to her, but she framed the question that way in order to deflect Michelle's understanding of her suspicion that it related to Juan Carlos's death.

Michelle understood Xue's question exactly as she meant it, and her response was a lie, "Oh, I spilled champagne on Melissa's pants at Chad's party, don't you remember?" Xue didn't because she was confident that the incident didn't occur. Neither Michelle nor Melissa had mentioned it at the time, or shortly thereafter.

For Xue, this exchange meant the end of her relationship with Michelle. Before now, she could accept or tolerate her moodiness and depression, but now she thought she understood. "Still," she thought to herself, "I might be wrong." She now had a choice. She could confront Michelle directly, and show her suspicion, which, if she was wrong, would ruin their relationship. Or, she could contact the private investigator for the Delano family, Cameron Swayze, and see what she could do with this information.

A week later, Xue found Cameron Swayze on the Internet, as Chad's case was widely covered in the media. Xue sent her an anonymous tip. At least she thought it was anonymous. She wrote, "You should explore the possibility that Michelle Grant put something into Juan's drink."

Cameron saw the tip, and immediately realized, "Of course. There was another pill from someone else at the party." In order not to give a hint that she had received a tip, Cameron began what was intended to look like a routine, "Try again," series of interviews with Chad and his friends of New Year's Eve, 2116-17, but with a little unacknowledged emfasis on Michelle.

Cameron learned from Juan's wofriend, Anita, that Juan had dated Michelle three years ago, or one year before the party, and that the relationship came to a sudden end. Anita had assumed that Michelle had told Cameron that information, but it didn't come out at the trial.

Chad's former wofriend, Melissa, also knew that information, but her reason for not telling Cameron during the first interview was that she, like Chad, assumed that Chad had committed the crime, and didn't want to further complicate the case and dig up her sister's history when it wasn't necessary.

Cameron interviewed Xue and neither acknowledged to the other anything about an emailed tip. However, Xue did say, after assurances of confidentiality, what she had heard Michelle say at the most recent New Year's Eve party, i.e. that she did something stupid two years earlier.

Chad could recall nothing more than he had already told Cameron. He challenged the investigator to explain why she was wasting more of his parents' money on this additional round of interviews. He was sick of the legal system and the high costs.

Now armed with more information, Cameron contacted Michelle to schedule an interview, but Michelle said she didn't have time and hung up. That was like waving a red banner in front of a bull, to use an old-fashioned frase that was slipping into disuse because of the 2031 global outlawing of bullfighting in Espana and in Mexico and other Latin America countries before that. Even the non-lethal bullfighting was outlawed by the U.N. Treaty because of its disrespect of the bulls. Cameron called again and Michelle identified the number on her fone ID, a wonderful 20th century invention, and declined to answer. Then Cameron sent an email, which was received, but not answered.

Cameron contacted Chad's attorney, Nina McKelvy, and updated her on the re-investigation status. Nina said, "I'd given up on this one, but shouldn't have. I'll contact the prosecutor, Matt Bailey, and see if his interest in justice outweighs his interest in winning." She called Matt and they agreed to meet the next day.

At their meeting, Nina told Matt what she had learned and of her suspicion that Michelle was the person who put the pill into Juan's champagne. She reminded Bailey of his options, which included bringing Michelle to his office for questioning and potentially charging her with "obstruction of a claim of innocence." This was a statutory crime created in most states in the early 21st century in order to cleanse the justice system of previous wrongful convictions and to prevent new injustices. The penalty for such obstruction was twice the severity of the crime for which the person refusing to cooperate might be charged. In Michelle's case, she could be charged with obstructing a claim of innocence from someone convicted of "chemical manslaughter," which had a standard sentence of 10 years of "Restricted Life 3.0" for first time offenders. Thus, the potential penalty for her for being convicted of "obstructing an innocence claim" was 20 years of "Restricted Life 3.0."

Matthew believed that his case against Chad was extremely strong, and that Nina's efforts were a waste of time. On the other hand, he was well aware of the plague of injustice that afflicted the U.S. in the late 20th and early 21st centuries when the nation's prisons were tripled in size, and too often contained innocent people. He knew that many prosecutors had been forced from office for failing to take seriously claims of innocence brought to them by lawyers and even inmates themselves, pro se. After the infamous Michael Morton case in Texas which led to the jailing in 2013 of the former prosecutor and later judge, Ken Anderson, the public revulsion at the scourge of wrongful convictions finally percolated up to the attention of political leaders and judges. Morton had been convicted in 1987 of murdering his wife and spent 25 years in prison until finally released in 2011. Prosecutor Anderson had withheld exculpatory evidence from Morton's lawyers and he and the police had failed to use that information to find the real killer of Morton's wife. That real killer, Mark Norwood, was finally identified after Morton's release, and convicted.

Bailey agreed with Nina that he should take the next step of asking Michelle Grant to come to his office for an interview. "Do you know if she is represented by counsel?" he asked Nina. "Don't know," she responded.

Bailey called Michelle and left a message on her fone identifying himself and asking her to call. In case anyone else might hear the message, such as a roommate, he said nothing in the message that was incriminating or defamatory.

The next day, Bailey was called by Michelle's attorney, Sofie Svenson, and she asked what Bailey's call to Michelle was about. He replied, "We have some questions about the Chad Delano case, and would like to talk with Michelle."

Realizing the risk and price of non-cooperation, Svenson agreed to bring Michelle to a meeting with Bailey the next week.

At the meeting, Michelle said that she didn't remember too much about the 2116-17 New Year's Eve party. She was asked whether she had ever taken EZsleep, and she said she wasn't sure. Bailey asked specifically about whether she had any involvement in putting EZsleep, or any drug into Juan's champagne. She said, "No." She did acknowledge, however, that she did have a troubled romantic relationship with Juan Carlos a year before the party and that it ended when she became pregnant, accidentally, and had an abortion. Juan Carlos was not very considerate about the problem, despite his obvious share of responsibility. In fact, he accused her of having sex with several other partners who could have been the father. Since that relationship with Juan, Michelle closely examined her own previously ambiguous sexual preference, and then met Xue.

After the meeting, Bailey called Nina to tell her that he learned nothing new from Michelle. However, that wasn't entirely true.

He then called Svenson and told her that he was going to subpoena Michelle's medical records. Svenson raised concerns about Michelle's privacy, and that she would call Michelle's doctor to advise her to refuse to give Bailey those records, in the absence of a court order.

Bailey assured her that he had a permissibly narrow reason for obtaining the records, and he was not interested in anything else about Michelle, but that wasn't enough to gain Svenson's consent.

The next week, Bailey filed a motion in Superior Court for Michelle Grant's medical records. A hearing was scheduled for Tuesday, February 13, 2120. The case was no longer assigned to Judge Carla Bradford because this new proceeding questioned the validity of the conviction of Chad over which she presided. The "Dechaine rule" required that a different judge preside over any subsequent proceeding where an earlier verdict in the same case was being challenged. The new judge was Jacob Borenstein and he heard the arguments for and against the subpoena by Bailey and Svenson. Also, speaking in support of the subpoena was Nina McKelvy. She and Bailey had continued their communications throughout the re-investigation. Nina, in turn, kept Chad and his family informed, including Eleanor who had been in Mars City for two months.

In mid-March, Judge Borenstein issued his opinion that the subpoena was to be issued and that it must be obeyed by Michelle's doctor. The judge wrote that Michelle Grant's privacy concerns were outweighed by the interests of justice for Chad Delano.

Sofie Svenson consulted with Michelle on the merits of appealing Judge Borenstein's decision. Svenson thought it was a close call for whether an appellate court, a little removed from the nits and grits of criminal justice, might have more regard for Michelle's privacy concerns. Despite the cost, at 100 earthas an hour, which was three times Michelle's pay rate, she asked Sofie to appeal.

The appeal was filed in July and the hearing was conducted on August 14. There were no surprises from either side, and none from the three judges, either. On September 9, 2120 the court issued its opinion affirming Judge Borenstein's order.

A month later, Bailey had the records and they had what he was looking for, which were prescriptions by Michelle's doctor for EZsleep in

2116. He wanted to call Sofie Svenson again and have her bring Michelle in for another interview, but he knew it would be futile because Michelle would again deny dropping any of her EZsleep medicine into Juan's champagne glass, or anyone else's.

Bailey learned, or re-learned, something else from the medical records, which was that EZsleep was marketed by MaineDrugs. This had been part of the testimony at Chad's trial, but somehow Bailey now saw the coincidence in a different light. As drug cases had declined precipitously since the overall legalization of recreational drugs in 2028, about 90 years ago, he had very little knowledge of the drug business in Portland or elsewhere.

He called MaineDrug and arranged an appointment with Amanda Lavrov. She told him of the new technology about the measurement of the atoms in the coating of EZsleep pills, just as she had told Armstrong and Kline three years earlier. It was hi-tech and she was proud of it. However, he had the same view as Armstrong and Kline, which was that the pill or pills he was concerned about had already been consumed, so the new technology didn't help him.

He asked Amanda, "Were there any chemical changes to the insides of the pills over the past few years?" She said she didn't know but would call the manufacturer and get back to him. It was now the fall of 2120 and Bailey was thinking about deer hunting season, and left for the weekend in northern Maine. Hunting was no longer the lethal sport of the past but an electronic version of paintball. Hunters would find deer and lock them into their telescopic sights, which posted a simulated laser X on the deer's body, and snap – take the foto. The only deer which could be killed were those which had been certified as sick by the Maine Warden Service.

The next week, Amanda called Bailey and said, "I have interesting news. There was a change in the composition of EZsleep in October 2115. I'll mail you the documents from the manufacturer. I further checked to find that our own office began selling the new version in February 2116, after the supplies of the old version were exhausted."

"Ok, thanks very much," said Bailey who had mixed feelings about the news. It was not a badge of honor to have convicted an innocent person.

According to the documents Amanda sent to Bailey, the new version of EZsleep had a combination of 80 percent eszopiclone and 20 percent temazepam. He now needed three more pieces to the puzzle. First, he wrote an order to the laboratory for further testing of Juan Carlos Morales' blood for the presence of temazepam. The presence of that drug wasn't indicated in the first reports. Second, he asked the lab to do a complete analysis of the ingredients of the blue EZsleep pill that was glued to the skin of the black plastic evidence bag. Third, he reviewed the transcript of Chad's trial to see when Chad worked at MaineDrug as a temporary employee.

The transcript search was completed quickly, with a few keystrokes. Detective Armstrong had testified that he had received from MaineDrug an employment report which showed that Chad worked there in September, 2115 through the temporary employment agency, Maine Staffing Co-Op. Included with the testimony was the reference to "State Exhibit #5" which was the report, and Bailey had that, too. One down, two to go.

Tuesday, November 5, was Election Day in the U.S. and the Democratic Party, now with its official color changed from blue to green, was poised to retain control of Congress and the Presidency. From her inauguration in 2117, President Maria Chavez had remained a popular leader in the continuing struggle to reverse global warming, reduce population growth and ensure that the wrongful conviction rate stayed below .1%.   She led by example, by making the White House entirely self-sufficient for electricity, thanks to the 98% surface coverage for solar panels and collectors, and additional solar panels and batteries on the White House grounds. Even the bulletproof fotochromic windows collected solar energy, while they also automatically adjusted their absorption of light according to the season. It sold its excess power to the National Grid. The backup system was a micro-hydrofusion powered electric generator.

The Republican candidate, Sarah Palino, made her strongest case for election when arguing for tougher criminal laws. "The pendulum has swung too far in favor of criminals," she stated in the first of five presidential debates on September 5th. "Too many criminals are being acquitted for crimes they obviously committed." Relying on her staff, she cited a case of Robert William Horton, a Black man, who was found not guilty in Massachusetts of burglary and rape in 2113. Several policepeople insisted, off the record, that Horton was guilty, despite the fact that he had passed a voicepolygraf. In 2115 he was arrested again for burglary and found guilty later that year "beyond any doubt." His fingerprints were on a window at the scene, but he argued that was because he knew the victim and had been in her house. He claimed that he had raised the window to cool the house, and not to break into it. Again, he had passed a voicepolygraf, and was becoming a poster child for those skeptics who still opposed the use of lie detectors in judicial proceedings.

On September 10, Horton's lawyer filed a motion for a new trial on the basis of new evidence, which was that the victim's manfriend, Willie Sutton, had recorded a statement that he had stolen the items from the purportedly burglarized house. He stated that before the crime, he had taken a signed receipt for autobody work from Horton's truck and left it in the victim's driveway. After the crime, he had put a few of the less valuable items in Horton's truck in order to incriminate him. He had thought that Horton had his eyes on Sutton's wofriend. Sutton had come forward with the truth in September because he had seen the Chavez-Palino Presidential debate, including Palino's claim regarding Horton's case. He said in his statement, "You know, even thieves have some code of honor, and it just got to me that Horton was taking the rap for what I did. Even worse, some White politician was dumping on him for it." What he didn't say was that he had been arrested in August, 2120 for robbery and his defense attorney had approached the Democratic District Attorney with a proposed plea agreement. In return for the information about the 2115 "Horton" burglary, the D.A. would agree to reduce the robbery charges to a misdemeanor trespassing charge. Horton was exonerated and filed a claim for compensation for his wrongful conviction.

With Palino's "tough-on-crime" position demolished, her campaign never recovered and she lost the popular vote 43%-51%. The remaining six percent was split among other candidates. The Electoral College vote for the 53 states, was 279 for Chavez and 235 for Palino, with 273 being needed to be the majority out of 547, thanks to the 2045 passage of the National Popular Vote Law by 49 of the states. The remaining four states cast their ballots according to their previous formulas.

In Chad's case, the lab test results came back in early December 2120 and they showed the presence of temazepam in Juan Carlos's blood in sufficient quantity to support the view that it came from an EZsleep pill. The likely source was MaineDrug which had begun selling that modified version in 2116, which was after Chad's employment there. Second, the lab report said that the pill from Chad's wastebasket tested zero for temazepam.

Thus, as far as Matthew Bailey could determine, Chad had somehow acquired an EZsleep pill when he was employed for three days at MaineDrug in September, 2115 and the pill he tossed or dropped into his wastebasket on New Year's Eve, 2116-17 came from that earlier batch. There was no evidence that Chad had ever acquired any EZsleep pills after that, so Bailey made a note to obtain Chad's medical records. Actually, he thought, "I should have done this long ago."

He also made a note to give Chad a polygraf examination on the question of where he obtained the "wastebasket pill" and whether where were any others from that batch of pills in his apartment in 2116. The lie detector tests would be valid for those questions as he was presumably not under the influence of those drugs or alcohol or any other substance during the relevant 2115 and 2116 time periods.

Chad willingly authorized his doctor to give Matthew Bailey his medical records. They showed no prescriptions for EZsleep, or any other sleep medication. Chad also agreed easily to taking a polygraf examination, voice stress exam, voicepolygraf, or an fMRI brain scan or all four. It was agreed to first conduct a polygraf, and, if necessary, either or all of the other tests later. In early January 2121, Chad tested "no deception indicated(NDI)" on the polygraf when he said that he had stolen EZsleep pills from MaineDrug when he worked there in 2115. Similarly, he tested "NDI" when he stated that the "wastebasket pill" was the last of the batch and that he had used the others much earlier in 2116. Bailey felt there was no need for Chad to take any other lie detector tests.

Now Matthew Bailey and Nina McKelvy had all they needed to return to Judge Borenstein's court and ask together for a dismissal of the charges against Chad. They argued at the hearing on February 16, 2121, that it was extremely unlikely that Chad had dropped an EZsleep pill into Juan Carlos's drink at his 2116-17 New Year's Eve party. Chad was in the courtroom and he testified to the facts he had told his attorney, Matthew Bailey, and the polygraf examiner. Thus, while it wasn't yet certain that Michelle had dropped an EZsleep into Juan's drink, it was nearly certain that no jury would have found Chad guilty beyond any doubt if that jury had known what was now known by Bailey and other key players. It was nearly certain that Chad never had an EZsleep pill with the ingredient temazepam, and that the pill from his foil wrapper was the pill found glued to the plastic wastebasket liner. That pill had no temazepam.

Judge Borenstein was prepared for the hearing, and, barring an unforeseen presentation or fact, he was planning to vacate Chad's conviction and order that he be released from "Restricted Life 3.0."

After the presentations by counsel, the judge did exactly as planned, and addressed Chad directly,

"Mr. Delano. Having heard the evidence presented in this case, and hearing the same request from both the prosecutor and your attorney, I hereby set your conviction aside. On behalf of the State of Maine, I apologize to you and your family for what you have been through. Although nothing can bring back to you the years of "Restricted Life" you are fortunate that Maine still has a statute providing for compensation for wrongful conviction. I will support your application for such compensation should you apply."

As with so many of the 21st century exonerations, there was bad luck involved in the original conviction and good luck involved in the exoneration. The bad luck was Juan's fall, which was not just a fall, but a fatal fall. The good luck, assisted by preparation, was first that Cameron used a careful technique in searching through the fysical evidence. Second, Chad was lucky with the tip from Xue Wen. It's not often that a friend will sacrifice a relationship in order to provide justice to a wrongly convicted person.

Chad and his family and Nina were exultant and went together to their favorite restaurant, "Fresh," for lunch to celebrate. The restaurant warrants that 95% of its food comes from the state of Maine. Even before the very low-cost hydrofusion electricity became available after the 2027 technological breakthrough, the cost of electricity was reduced by re-engineered nuclear fission plants which used previously discarded radioactive fuel rods from the older plants. With low-cost electricity, it became economical to grow warm-climate vegetables and fruits in Maine, rather than ship them to Maine from the American south or from another country. En route to the restaurant, the family stopped at the Portland Police Department, with a copy of Judge Borenstein's order. There, they had Chad's body chip reprogrammed to remove the monitoring program. That night, the news of Chad's release was covered by the media and the internet.

Matthew Bailey stayed behind in the courtroom for an offline conversation with Judge Borenstein.

He told the judge that he was planning to issue an arrest order for Michelle Grant the next day and ask a Grand Jury that she be indicted for "chemical manslaughter" and "obstruction of a claim of innocence."

The next morning, officers came to Michelle's apartment and she did not answer their knocking. They tried calling her fone number and they sent an email and text. There was no response. Using their specially authorized keys, they opened the apartment door and searched the apartment. In the bedroom, they found Michelle's fully-clothed body, a half-full glass of water, and an empty bottle of EZsleep.

Chapter 10 Eleanor and Max in Mars City

Eleanor, Max, Adisa and Nkiru arrived on Mars on December 10th, 2119. The approximate per person cost for the trip was 30 million earthas, so humans were still a long way away from convenient interplanetary travel. Most of that cost arose from the effort to escape Earth's gravity. For every kilogram of a spacecraft and its cargo, about 25 kilograms of rocket structure and fuel were required. For a spacecraft weighing 150 metric tonnes, a fueled rocket weighing 3,750 tonnes was required. By comparison, the net weight of an A550 Airbus plane which can carry that same cargo is about 400 tonnes.

They were escorted to their rooms and then introduced to each of the 65 citizens of Mars City, now increased to 69.

The colony on Mars had evolved since the first four astronauts arrived in 2071, almost 50 years earlier. Three of the original four were now in their 80's and still functioning well, but the inevitable signs of aging were appearing. One had died in 2114, after an accident punctured her spacesuit while outside the city's buildings. Subsequent spaceships, including Eleanor's, had brought 70 astronauts, of whom four more had died. Two had died of cancer before the colony's medical facilities were equipped to handle advanced treatment, and two had died of heart failure.

When GLASO decided in 2118 it was time for Mars City to create and raise its own children, and hence the recruitment of Eleanor and Liu, GLASO also decided to limit future emigration to Mars from Earth to replacements for those who died, when necessary. The Mars City population was expected to stabilize at around 70 until Martian births began to exceed Martian deaths, and the population was then expected to grow on its own, without the need of immigrants from Earth.

GLASO reached its decision to reduce the flow of emigrant astronauts to Mars for several reasons. First was the general expense of about 30 million earthas per astronaut, just for the travel cost. Second, GLASO had other space exploration priorities, including the search for intelligent life in other galaxies. Third, the public had less interest in the Mars colony now that it was almost 50 years old. It was no longer "new." Like the settlers of other colonies, such as Plymouth in North America in 1620, there comes a time for a colony to stand on its own, apart from continued subsidies from the mother country, or, in this case, mother planet.

The arrival of the two heterosexual couples, with their explicit goals of having children on Mars, prompted a predictable amount of humor and conversation among the citizens of Mars and the newcomers. For Eleanor and Max, the new one-room apartment was a welcome change from the public confines and weightlessness of their spaceship. Sex in the spaceship was okay, but not the same as in one's own bed stabilized by gravity in a private apartment.

"You know," pondered Eleanor, "we were never told much about previous sexual activity in space or on Lunaterra." She liked the formal name for the Moon. After a period of about 80 years of space flight, from 1961 until groups of men and women were landed on the Moon and Mars, there was little discussion of sex in space. For the unfortunate few astronauts who orbited the Earth solo for prolonged periods, sex with oneself was the only realistic alternative. Videofone sex with loved ones on Earth was psychologically hazardous, given the difficulty in guaranteeing the security of encrypted communication. The time delay of long distance signals was awkward, too. However, once planning began for the colony on Mars which was finally established in 2071, it was clear that sexual activity had to be programmed into the plan. Hence the first astronauts to Mars were two heterosexual couples. Gay, lesbian and asexual citizens and astronauts complained quietly about the apparent priority for the heterosexuals, but the LGBT astronauts later gained their fair share of space flight and colonization.

Since 2071, there had been much more discussion about sex in space, especially after two pregnant astronauts returned to Earth from the Moon. For Eleanor, Max, Adisa and Nkiru, the plans and discussion were explicit: sex and childbirth were expected.

Eleanor and Max embraced in their apartment and soon learned that the 38% gravity ratio to Earth made sex more active and less of a fysical burden, regardless of who was on top.

Eleanor was confident that she was fertile, even without the fertility drug she agreed to take. The intent of the drug was to encourage a multiple birth, but no more than three. Max, too, was confident of his fertility, as his sperm count was on the high end of the Bell curve for his age group.

The two couples agreed with their doctors that they would continue to use birth control for a year after coming to Mars. Like every couple moving to a new neighborhood, and a new job and work environment at the same time, all four astronauts wanted to be sure that they had made the right decisions. There was no turning back for them, but they wanted to be extra sure before they brought children into this new world they chose for them.

On December 10, 2120 by their one-year agreement with the doctors, the couples stopped using birth control, with the expected effects to diminish gradually over the next few weeks. For Eleanor and Max, the predicted result came late in January, with a saliva-based pregnancy test. They waited, however, before communicating the news to their families, as they wanted to be sure. Two weeks later, in mid-February, 2121 Eleanor learned that she was carrying twin girls, with a due date of approximately October 21, 2121. A month later, Adisa and Nkiru learned they were pregnant, with twin boys and a girl, with the expected birth on November 2.

Eleanor and Max went to the communications center and called her parents first. On the screen was displayed the current distance between Earth and Mars, and the lasercomm time delay, which were 73,000,000 km and 6.5 minutes. Laser waves replaced radio long ago as they can carry more content than radio. They spoke for about six minutes for the transmission to her parents in Portland, and then in about 20 seconds, transmitted another six minute call to his parents in Frankfurt, Deutschland. Then they had about a seven minute break while waiting for each set of parents to receive their respective six minute messages and then respond with their own six minute messages. Since Eleanor's and Max's arrival at Mars City, the delay had once been its shortest for the year which was 4.9 minutes. During the coming year, the longest time delay would be as long as 36 minutes.

At last, the Delanos' response came through. The call had come to Forbes's cell fone and he had the signal transferred to a wall at the restaurant. They spoke happily of Chad's exoneration on that same day and thanked Eleanor for her moral and financial support. Without it, he would still be on "Restricted Life 3.0" and would continue in that disgraceful position for seven more years. It was 1:00 p.m. Eastern Time on Earth in Portland, and the family was still at the restaurant. They hadn't yet sent a text or email to Eleanor with their news.

Then came the signal from Max's parents. It was 7:00 p.m. in Frankfurt, so they were able to receive the Mars call at home and respond immediately. At the end of their broadcast, they said there was no need to call back as they were going out to celebrate.

Then Eleanor and Max sent a final message to the Delanos, with Eleanor crying, "What a wonderful day for both of us!" Eleanor said that she would send updates on her pregnancy from time to time, and copies of the sonograms.

Then Eleanor and Max went back to work.

With 69 citizens, politics in Mars City was a little different from 69-person communities on Earth. It could be compared with Beddington, Maine, with its population of 68, which is the smallest incorporated town in Maine. Every one of the 61 adults in Beddington has a vote, and that's what the people of Mars City demanded in 2121. From its initial settlement, Mars City was governed by astronauts appointed by GLASO, according to a quasi-military system, but few of the residents were in their country's military services. Even for those with military rank, sometimes the GLASO-designated leaders were outranked by other astronauts from other countries of origin.

In May 2121, Commander Christiana Bligh capped her unpopular administration with an order that a labor tax be assessed on each resident of Mars City to clean the community room. A labor tax was a unit of time of work. The problem was that only a few men used the community room for playing cards, and the rest of the men, and all the women, didn't like being told to clean up after others. Led by Francois Marat, formerly of French Guiana, the majority of the residents advised Commander Bligh that there was to be a new government in Mars City.

As there were no weapons in the colony, power was held in several ways. The "red planet revolutionaries," or "Reds" for short, controlled the Mars food supply, which was entirely grown on site, and the communications system. Without those, Commander Bligh could not function. This was a serious protest.

Without violence, the two sides negotiated a solution which led to the establishment of the human community of UtopiaDos,[1] as a complete corporate successor to Mars City. Most citizens agreed that "Mars City" sounded more like a shopping mall on Earth than a new colony on Mars. UtopiaDos was organized as a utopian democracy with annual elections of officers and representatives. Military ranks were abolished, making every person in the community a civilian.

A committee was delegated to create a Declaration of Independence on July 4, and a Constitution for their future governance. Both were modeled after the United States documents of the same name, as the U.S. was the best known and oldest representative democracy on Earth.

The Declaration of Independence began,

July 4, 2121.

The majority Declaration of the people of UtopiaDos,

---

1. Translation from Spanish is Utopia Two. Since the publication of St. Thomas More's Utopia in 1516, there had been few efforts to create a sequel. In fact, the most frequent ten results for a Google search for "Utopia II" or "Utopia Two" were about a super yacht by that name. Similarly, a search for "Utopia III" produced another yacht.

When in the course of human
events, it becomes necessary for one
people to assume among the powers
of the universe, the separate and
equal station to which the Universal
Declaration of Human Rights entitles
them, a decent respect to the opinions
of humanity on Earth requires that
they should declare the causes which
impel them to independence and the
establishment of the political
community of UtopiaDos.

We hold these truths to be self-
evident, that all people are created
equal, that they are endowed at birth
with certain unalienable Rights, that
among these are Life, Liberty and the
pursuit of Happiness. –That to secure
these rights, Governments are
instituted among people, deriving their
just powers from the consent of the
governed,...

Simultaneously, the citizens issued the draft of
their Constitution which began,

We the People of UtopiaDos, in Order
to form a more perfect community or
utopia, establish Justice, insure
domestic Tranquility, promote the
general Welfare, and secure the
Blessings of Liberty to ourselves and
our Posterity, do ordain and establish
this Constitution for UtopiaDos....

Left out of the goals was the need for a "common
defense," as that was not necessary on Mars.

The Declaration of Independence and
Constitution were communicated to GLASO and
also to the United Nations, where they were
received with astonishment, but acceptance.

The UtopiaDos (U.D.) had a Bill of Rights which incorporated the protections of liberty of the U.S. Bill of Rights and the United Nations Universal Declaration of Human Rights.

Some residents were hesitant to call their community "UtopiaDos" as they had learned in school that utopias were impossible, dreamlike communities where everyone was happy. In fact, a utopia is simply a place where human beings can be, to borrow from a 20th century U.S. Army recruiting slogan, "all they could be." UtopiaDos was truly a place where all fysical needs were met and where there was true equality of opportunity.

Importantly, the community elected Christiana Bligh as its first President, because that would make the new government for UtopiaDos more acceptable to GLASO and to the United Nations. The situation was awkward, but the people of the GLASO member countries understood the principles of self-representation and democracy, so the new arrangement was permitted to continue. As the Director of GLASO said to his staff, "What were we going to do? Stop sending people and supplies to UtopiaDos?"

Even that threat would have meant little, as the colony's need for supplies had decreased dramatically over the 50 years due to three major developments. First, it managed to produce its own food, using genetically modified variations of Earth vegetables and fruits. Of course, there are no eaters of natural meats on Mars, but there was an ample supply of ameat and afish. Second, it made good use of its several 3-D printers, which enabled the colony to produce every working fysical part that was needed by the community. They were especially useful for products which incorporated the miracle material, grafene, for electricity-related items. The raw materials for other products sometimes had to be different from the recommended material on Earth, but the manufacturing system worked. Third, the development of safe hydrofusion in 2027, coming up now on 100 years, propelled the world forward to a continuous energy surplus.

On Earth, it enabled the sharp decline in the generation of greenhouse gasses, primarily carbon dioxide from the burning of fossil fuels as all such power plants were decommissioned rapidly after 2027. The production of hydrofusion power plants, both large and small, was made a global priority, just as the production of military vehicles was made a priority in Detroit in the U.S. after December 7, 1941. The United States and other countries mobilized their economies to manufacture safe hydrofusion power plants.

The two hydrofusion power plants on Mars provided enough electricity for the extensive computers, HVAC systems and the Carbon Cycle process which provided the oxygen for human breathing, together with what was generated by the green plants.

It also powered the UtopiaDos hospital, which consisted of one operating room and one lab. It was there that Eleanor came for the birth of her twins on October 20. Her pregnancy had gone smoothly and for the first time scientists on Earth and on Mars were able to watch the gestation of a human in a less-than-full gravity environment. They wouldn't know the effects, for sure, until the births, but the signs were promising.

On October 21, Elizabeth Alden Perkins and Nancy Jan Perkins arrived on schedule. They were the first humans born extra-terrestrially, i.e. not on Earth. The family joke was, "Baby steps for us. Giant steps for humanity." Elizabeth was named after Elizabeth Alden, who reportedly was the first girl born in the Pilgrim colony at Plymouth. She lived until the age of approximately 93, leaving 82 grandchildren and 556 great grandchildren. That fecundity was perhaps a precedent that Eleanor had no ambition to better. Nancy Jan was named after Nancy Jan Davis who was the wife of Mark Lee when in 1991 they became the first astronaut married couple to fly in space.

Eleanor and Max had considered naming one of the girls Virginia Dare Perkins, after the first European child born in North America, at the Lost Roanoke colony in 1587. However, when her grandfather, John White, returned to Virginia three years later, the Roanoke Colony had vanished, and presumably Virginia Dare was dead. It was not a happy story, and not one to share with your child when she becomes curious about the origin of her name.

Prior to the births, and even prior to Eleanor's pregnancy and their knowledge of the genders of their children, she and Max agreed on a naming process for whatever children they created. The girls would have her surname and the sons would have his surname.[2] Hence, both girls were named Perkins. Eleanor had talked with her mother about the origin of her surname and it seemed to make sense. She and Max talked about melding their surname into either Perkler, or Trenkins, for themselves and their children. However, neither of those names sounded appealing, and they couldn't think of another surname they wanted to use, such as Washington. Also, they both felt committed to

2. This was one of several non-sexist child-naming conventions recommended by the Lucy Stone League, named after the 19th feminist, Lucy Stone, who kept her birth name, after her marriage in 1855 to Henry Blackwell. Other conventions are to agree to name the first child after one spouse and the second child after the other, and so on.

their names for which they had worked hard to
bring respect and credibility.

Eleanor and Max called their respective families
with a patch-in from Eleanor's hospital room, this
time with a 34 minute delay, so they sent their
calls and hung up. They would check in about an
hour for the responses.

During the pregnancy, they knew of their
upcoming role in the history of the human species.
Nonetheless, it only reached their deep consciousness as they held their two children. These were
the first human children in history who would
never live on Earth. In two weeks, Adisa's and
Nkiru's twin boys and a girl would arrive, and
someday perhaps love would break out among the
five, leading to the next generation and the next.

Appendix A –

Dissertation of Forbes Franklin Delano
For the degree of Doctorate of Filosofy
University of North America
Dissertation Advisor: Dr. John Milton Friedman III
May 1, 2093

The Costs & Benefits of the 2026 Implementation of the Single Global Currency

Abstract
    The 2026 implementation of the Single Global Currency, with 146 member countries of the Global Monetary Union, saved the world trillions of earthas.[1] The initial success, with member countries producing 83% of the world's GDP, was followed by all of the remaining United Nations members joining by 2028. Simply, there was no longer an alternative. The benefits far exceeded the costs, and the benefits exceeded the expected benefits.

Summary
    It was feared by many economists, especially those in the United States, that the Single Global Currency would excessively impair the abilities of countries to respond to "shocks," i.e. bad economic events, such as an asset bubble crash. The classic, multicurrency remedy for such shocks was to lower interest rates to encourage investment and to depreciate the currency in order to make exports

---

1. The statements of values here are stated in terms of earthas as they are valued in 2121. With zero inflation since around 2050, an eartha is now worth about five 2026 US dollars.

more attractive abroad, but those remedies had more costs than benefits.

First, here are tallied the benefits.

BENEFITS OF THE SINGLE GLOBAL CURRENCY

International Trade. During the years of preparation for the eartha, proponents expected a 3-5% increase in international trade. Instead, there was an 8% increase in international trade in 2026, the first year after the launch of the eartha. This especially benefitted the poorer countries of the world which were previously subject to large fluctuations in currency exchange rates.

Foreign Exchange Reserves. By 2026, the central banks of countries and monetary unions had accumulated 1.4 trillion earthas in currency and financial assets of foreign countries. Another trillion was held as gold stockpiled in underground vaults.[2] Those reserves were doing little good for anyone, except to protect against the disasters which sometimes befell the multicurrency system.

With the implementation of the eartha, these reserves became denominated in earthas, and were available to be spent either in reducing national or monetary union debt or environment-related projects as agreed in the Global Monetary Union charter. These projects contributed to the global boost in expenditures for family planning and carbon dioxide mitigation.

2. Milton Friedman, great great great uncle of John Milton Friedman III, memorably wrote, "People must work hard to dig gold out of the ground in South Africa--in order to rebury it in Fort Knox or some similar place." Milton Friedman, *Capitalism and Freedom*. Chicago, IL: University of Chicago Press, 1962, p. 40.

Increase in Asset Values. Before the eartha, the values of financial assets of many countries were diminished in value because of the currency risk. Currency risk, a term no longer known to many young economists, was the risk that a national or monetary union currency could fail during a currency crisis. A currency crisis would occur when foreigners and national citizens would lose faith or trust that a currency would hold its value, so they would sell the currency on the global foreign exchange markets. Rational selling would become panic selling when it reached about a 10% loss threshold, and then there would be a crash to near worthlessness. Once currency risk was eliminated, the values of financial assets around the world were allowed to reach their natural value, without regard to the risk that owners would be subjected to a currency crisis.

Debt Repayment Risk. A part of currency risk was the risk of a country defaulting on its foreign debt. When countries had their own currencies, any hint that they would reduce or stop payments on national debt would result in a devaluation of the value of the currency, and sometimes cause a currency crisis. However, as the debts were usually denominated in a more stable foreign currency, such as the U.S. dollar, a devalued domestic currency meant that the debt repayments would become even more costly. With the use of earthas, there was no risk to a debtor nation that its debt would become more costly to maintain due to currency fluctuations.

Lower Global Interest Rates. With greater monetary stability, creditors were able to lend money at lower interest rates. The existence of the globally publicized Global Central Bank interest rates made local variations less tolerable to borrowers.

End of Balance of Payments Issues. One of the immeasurable benefits of the eartha arose from the elimination of the need to rectify imbalances of payments. Though often misunderstood, such imbalances were currency issues and not economic issues. If a country or section of the Global Monetary Union was importing more than it was exporting, its economy would eventually decline relative to the surplus exporting countries. However, there would not be a risk of currency failure, and rising interest rates to prevent currency outflows.

End of Currency Fluctuations. Another benefit was the saving of an estimated 60 billion earthas a year which were previously spent in coping with the fluctuating foreign exchange markets, primarily transaction costs. Some of those savings were achieved by the elimination of the need to purchase foreign currency hedges against currency loss, but most came from the elimination of the requirement to conduct business in a currency other than one's own, which required the purchase of another currency – which always triggered a transaction cost.

COSTS OF THE SINGLE GLOBAL CURRENCY

National Loss of Control over Monetary Policy. While the loss was certain, it was not certain how well countries would have solved their economic problems if they had kept the ability to adjust interest rates and exchange rates. Having the tools is not the same as using them effectively. However, in the years since the development of the euro, countries learned how to stimulate investment and exports without the often-abused tools of interest rate setting and exchange rate manipulation.

Loss of Jobs in Currency Management. Thanks to a Global Central Bank retraining program, currency traders and others dislocated by the Single Global Currency were able to find other work. However, most people formerly employed in the currency management business naturally moved to related work, such as banking or insurance or trading in commodities.

Text (for the full text see, "Links: Academic Articles" at www.singleglobalcurrency.org.)

Appendix B

Dissertation of Charlotte Amalie Perkins
For the degree of Doctorate of Filosofy
University of North America
Dissertation Advisor: Dr. Sargent Hill Lyman
April 10, 2093

The Global Social and Political Impact of the
Utopian Novella *Jesus and Jesusa*

ABSTRACT

The 2014 publication of *Jesus and Jesusa* by Maria Maddalena contributed significantly to the global "Great Transformation" which can be said to have started in 2020. The Brownsville, Texas atomic bomb explosion in 2019 can be said to have been the precipitating event which accelerated the changes begun by the Great Transformation Network. Without the associated changes, the nations of the world may have descended into vortex of competition and environmental and nuclear catastrofe. As it was, the world came close to both.

SUMMARY

Religion and Jesus and Jesusa

In 2014, there were three major theist religions, Christianity, Islam and Hinduism, with populations of approximately 1.6, 1.1 and 1.0 billion people respectively. Although each religion espoused humanistic morality, their leadership or membership bore significant responsibility for slowing, if not blocking, the movement toward the modern world of political and social reason and environmental responsibility. Other much smaller religions shared in that responsibility, or irresponsibility. For example, with only 14 million adherents, judaism was able to divert the attention of many Muslims away from their economic needs and toward seemingly endless conflict with the state of Israel. That conflict contributed significantly to the nuclear explosion in Brownsville, Texas in 2019, which was curiously parallel to the fictional 2020 explosion in Kahuta, Pakistan in *Jesus and Jesusa.*

Some religions, such as Baha'i, with only 7 million followers, openly endorsed progress. For example, long before 2026 its leaders supported the adoption of a Single Global Currency as the appropriate money for all humans.

When *Jesus and Jesusa* was published, there were an estimated 1.1 billion humanists or secularists or non-believers. As most were not members of a church, the calculations of their numbers were more subject to polling and estimates than for those religions with active adherents. Another by-product of their not participating in organized services was that they were not active politically, at least not until the 21st century. After the 2014 publication of *Jesus and Jesusa*, there were dramatic shifts from the member populations of all religions to the secular humanists.

The publication of *Jesus and Jesusa* had an especially strong effect on the members of the Catholic Church. The reasoning of many Catholics seemed to be, "if the Catholic Church in a novel can lead humanity toward a better world, why can't we do it in real life, real time?" Thus motivated, the women of the church, and the equality-minded men increased their efforts for the ordination of women. In the book, the ordination of women came only after the 2022-23 Vatican Council III, but in a case of life improving upon the imitation of art, Pope Francesco promulgated the change in 2020 with a broad Papal Encyclical which pronounced that women were welcomed to the priesthood, effective July 22, the Feast Day of Maria Maddalena. She was recognized as one of the two most important women in Christianity, along with the mother of Jesus of Nazareth. She traveled with Jesus and his male disciples and may even have been his wife. She is a saint in the Catholic, Orthodox, Anglican and Lutheran churches. Further, decreed the Vatican Council III, all priests may experience human sexuality, as do their congregants, and they may marry as well, whether as heterosexuals or homosexuals or with any other sexual preference.

As change has moved slowly in the giant Catholic Church in the past, it took several years for the Church to transition to a gender neutral organization. Pope Francesco elevated the first woman cardinal in 2025 and three more in 2028. It was estimated that if Pope Francesco and his successors appointed female and male cardinals in equal numbers, it would take until 2050 before there would be an equal number of women and men wearing the red biretta. The average tenure of a cardinal, usually appointed in later middle age, was about 20 years.

Great Transformation Network

In 2014 and thereafter, readers of *Jesus and Jesusa* gathered electronically through all the global social networks, including Facebook, Google, Qzone and Sina Weibo. They saw many ideas in the book that seemed reasonable, and which required considerable political activism. Calling themselves the "Great Transformation Network," (GTN) and using the slogan, "What would Jesus and Jesusa do?" millions of people around the globe worked on a forward thinking agenda that would ensure humanity's survival and equilibrium with the Earth.

The mobilization of people for GTN was the largest showing to date of the power of social media to utilize the "cognitive surplus"[1] of people around the world who sought to assist humanity. In colloquial terms, they were seeking to help save the world. It was estimated that the 7+ billion people in the world when the GTN was started had about one trillion hours of leisure time, including 200 billion hours of television watching time, and that some of that time was available for GTN work. Before GTN, the most successful example of using the internet to mobilize volunteers around the world was Wikipedia. During its first ten years, approximately 150 million hours of labor was contributed, without monetary compensation, to the creation of Wikipedia content.

In addition to *Jesus and Jesusa*, B.F. Skinner's *Walden Two* was another utopian book which inspired the GTN. Widely criticized at its 1948 publication and thereafter for being elitist and undemocratic, the basic message of *Walden Two* was largely ignored by governments. That basic message was that using the well-known techniques of positive reinforcement and the principles of behavioral psychology, humans could become better people. That is, they could behave better. They could be educated and trained to care more about each other and the fate of their earth and pay less attention to the consumption of goods, entertainment, fashion and professional sports. In the 1960's thousands of individuals created communities or communes to seek to replicate the

---

1. The term "cognitive surplus" was developed by Clay Sherkey in 2014, when he published a book by that name.

world of *Walden Two*, but without government support, they failed, or didn't expand enough to influence the rest of society.

The GTN approach was that democratic governments could take the lead, replacing the role played by T.E. Frazier, the creator of the Walden Two, Three, Four, et al. communities. Instead of the "Planners" and "Managers" of *Walden Two*, all parts of governments would be devoted to positively reinforcing the values necessary to restore the Earth and alter humanity's role on the Earth from destruction to equilibrium. The GTN organizers relied heavily on B.F. Skinner's subsequent non-fiction book, *Beyond Freedom and Dignity*.

A 21st century inventor, Dean Kamen, famously said, "Free cultures get what they celebrate." In Skinnerian terms, such cultures get what they positively reinforce. Incentives were developed around the world to encourage achievement of the GTN goals below. In parallel, the previous incentives to non-Earth centered values were reduced or eliminated.

The GTN's primary goals were:

1. Military Spending. Reduction of military spending by all nations, first to a level approximately equal to 1% of national GDP and then to zero. (Note, however, that the GTN recommended, per #13 below, that actual military spending not be included in the calculation of GDP.) The zero level would be achieved as countries adopted the Costa Rica model for spending for national security, which it developed in 1948 when its army was abolished. The early 21st century global average for military spending was 2.4% of GDP, with the United States leading with 3.8%. By dropping from 2.4% to 1%, the world would release

approximately 280 billion earthas annually for earth-centered work. This far exceeded what the IPCC (Intergovernmental Panel on Climate Change) determined in 2014 would be needed to reduce carbon dioxide emissions to levels required to reverse global warming.

The 1% of national GDP goal included the .025% allocation by each U.N. member to the United Nations Military Mission which included two parts. The first priority was peacekeeping among and within member nations. The second was to provide defense against objects posing a risk of hitting Earth. This second responsibility was shared with GLASO (GLobal Aeronautic Space Organization).

2. <u>Nuclear non-proliferation and abolition of nuclear weapons</u>. The Non-Proliferation Treaty, which became effective in 1970, had a basic bargain which was that the existing nuclear powers would reduce and later eliminate their nuclear weapons in return for the agreements by the non-nuclear powers not to acquire nuclear weapons. During the 44 years to 2014, there had been some slippage as a few more countries acquired nuclear weapons, and the original nuclear countries had sidestepped their part of the bargain, but the essential limits of the treaty held fast. The GTN sought implementation of the original bargain and the reduction of stockpiles to 10 nuclear weapons for each of the remaining nuclear weapons countries by 2025 and their abolition by 2040. Spurred by the 2019 Brownsville, Texas nuclear disaster, those goals were achieved, on schedule.

3. <u>Global warming</u>. The GTN sought the eventual reduction of the primary greenhouse gas, carbon dioxide, to 3.0 parts per million by the year 2120.

In 2014, the world passed the 4.0 threshold, and the GTN's goal was that the peak should be no more than 4.5, and then there must be a decline. Thanks to improvements in technology, including the rapid development of hydrofusion-powered electricity production, the actual CO_2 peak of 4.1 ppm was achieved in 2046. Then it declined to 4.0 by 2055 and to 3.0 by 2114, exactly 100 years after reaching the previously dreaded 4.0 mark, and six years ahead of its 2120 goal.

This goal was part of the larger goal to transform humanity into the conservators of nature, rather than its destructive masters.

4. Population Growth. The GTN sought the eventual reduction of human population to some still-to-be-negotiated equilibrium level between 1-2 billion. In the meantime, its goal was that human population should reach a peak of no more than 9 billion by 2050 and decline thereafter. The actual peak of 8.7 billion was achieved in 2048 due to a combination of trends:

 a. While some homosexuals, the transgendered and asexual individuals chose to have children, most did not. As there was an increased global acceptance of non-heterosexuality, this dynamic became more important.

 b. The number of unwanted and unplanned births dropped to close to zero due to increased global acceptance of women's rights and family planning and the need to reduce the size of the human population.

 c. More women chose to remain childless, and most of those who did choose to bear children chose to have one child, or one pregnancy, with two children.

Finally, after 2048, the desired decline began. The citizens of countries whose populations had already declined, e.g. Japan, had shown the world that their happiness was more important than national population-size competition. Japan's population had peaked in 2010 at 128 million, and by 2050, it had declined to 100 million and 80 million in 2090. It is expected to reach 70 million by 2100, which will be a drop of 55% in only 90 years.

Thus, Japan has led the world in population reduction and has shown the world that individual happiness and prosperity can accompany such a decline, as well as the obvious environmental benefits. By 2093, the global population had dropped to 7.3 billion, which was the count in 2014. If the world were to achieve the population reduction successes of the Japanese, the global population would drop to 4.8 billion by 2138, 90 years after the 8.7 billion peak in 2048. The Earth last saw that 4.8 billion burden in 1984.

Remarkably, these declines occurred during a period of longer lifespans. The records for longest living man and woman inched upwards during the 21st century from about 116 and 122 years of age, respectively, to 120 and 124, and the number of people who reached 100 grew by a multiple of 10 to .05% of the global population. In 2093, there were 3.6 million centenarians, making the odds of reaching that age about 1 in 2,000.

The lives of the elderly were significantly enhanced with the availability of the synthetic protein klotho, which stimulates brain activity, and sirtuins which help control the aging process. While age-related diseases were reduced in frequency and severity with these proteins, and more people were able to reach the general aging limits, the ultimate biological clock was not substantially altered beyond the few additional years noted above.

5. <u>Education</u>. One key to the "Great Transformation" was an educated populace. Thomas Jefferson said it many times, e.g. ""I know no safe depositary of the ultimate powers of the society but the people themselves; and if we think them not enlightened enough to exercise their control with a wholesome discretion, the remedy is not to take it from them, but to inform their discretion by education."[2] The United Nations established the Global Literacy and Education Organization (GLEO) in 2018 with the fixed goal of 100% literacy by 2030 for every human being above the age of 15. That gave member nations 12 years to bring the worldwide average from 84% to 100%. A larger challenge was to achieve substantial comprehension, i.e. 80%, of the facts presented in the Global Basic Information Test (GLOBIT) by 2040. The test was to be prepared and administered every five years, and the first prototype sample was conducted on the Internet in 2023. For the 8.2 million volunteers, with a high school education or equivalent or greater, who took the GLOBIT, the average score was 46% correct answers out of 100 questions.[3] For college or university graduates, the average was 76%.

In that spirit, the GTN sought at least 240 days a year of education for all children through the age of 18. In 2020, only three countries, China, Japan and Deutschland, had school years of that length

---

2. See "Thomas Jefferson on Educating the People," collected by Reid Cornwell, at http://tcfir.org/Our_Opinion.cfm.
3. The 2023 GLOBIT questions and answers are on the internet at http://www.bonpasseexonerationservices.com/2121.html

or longer. By 2090, the number of countries meeting the 240 standard had risen to 64.

6. Inequality. Seeing that global income and wealth inequality were becoming more unequal in the early 21st century, GTN sought to reverse that trend. The adoption of the Delano Indexed Inequality Taxation system (20:20:I and 20:20:W) by the U.S. and later by the United Nations with the 2045 Global Inequality Convention, helped to restore inequality to fair and tolerable levels, while still providing incentives for innovation and wealth accumulation.

7. Violence. Related to the reduction of military budgets was the GTN goal of reducing overall human violence. For several reasons, including the vast variety of human violence, there was no global goal. Instead there were goals for reducing some of the inducements to violence, such as goals for imposing appropriate externality taxes on various types of entertainment which were shown to increase human violence. Television programs, movies and video games were taxed according to the amount of gratuitous violence which was contained in their offerings. The base standard was the United Nations decennial assessment of how much actual violence occurred around the world. The violence tax was then assessed progressively higher when the amount of particular types of violence was one, two, three or more times the base level average actual amount.

The GTN sought the reduction of harmful fysical contact during sports activities. Sometimes, this involved the banning of a sport, such as boxing or extreme or ultimate fighting, and all martial arts that involved harmful hitting of another person. Those banned sports were correctly compared to the gladiator spectacles of the Roman Colosseum. Usually, however, the GTN sought rule changes such as the eliminating of "heading" in football[4] and elimination of "checking" in ice hockey.

Also related to the above goal of reducing military budgets was the GTN goal to increase to 21 years the age of eligibility to join the military of countries or the United Nations. It was the worldwide consensus that while lower threshold ages were acceptable for sexual activity, driving and voting, training a person to kill required a higher level of maturity. The Geneva Conventions required that soldiers disobey wrongful orders, and asking a person younger than 21 to undertake such a challenge to authority was deemed too unrealistic.

8. <u>Animal Rights</u>. The concept of non-violence was extended to the treatment of animals, with the moral imperative, "Thou shall not kill." As the justifications for war and criminal penalty executions diminished, it became more clear to the GTN that all killing of other animals with brains must stop. While food was a special case (see below), the killing of animals for other reasons, such as for clothing or for research was proscribed.

However, there continued to be an exception for "justified killing" of animals which was when it was in the interest of the species, such as the need to thin out a herd which had become too large for its natural space. Another type of "justified killing" was analogous to the now-accepted practice of voluntary euthanasia for humans when life was nearing a natural end. A similar standard was applied to animals with terminal illnesses. Without

4. Formerly called "soccer" in the United States.

human consciousness, the concept of voluntariness was set aside.

Further, the GTN sought to protect and shield animals from human-induced pain. This applied especially to the use of animals in the testing of medicines and cosmetics. The ethical rule for such testing became, if the product is not good enough, or safe enough, to test on humans, it should not be tested on animals.

9. <u>Nutrition, Food from Plants, not Animals</u>. The GTN sought to return humans to their historic, and pre-historic place in the animal world as herbivores. Humans are naturally herbivores, and have the teeth to prove it, even if they have gone through a period of history as omnivores and eating fish and meat. Among the "great apes," only chimpanzees and humans became meat eaters. With the advances in food technology, and the need to respect other animals, it was time to revert back to the more natural herbivore practices, except for those humans for which there was limited access to plants, such as Eskimos. However, even in the northern climates, solar agriculture in enclosed spaces was increasing the availability of fruits and vegetables. Not only was it important to eat fruits, vegetables and nuts, instead of meats and processed foods, it was important to eat those foods as much as possible without cooking. Cooking destroys much of the nutritional value of food.

As a substantial portion of the protein utilized by humanity until the mid-21st century came from animals and fish, there was going to be an inevitable time lag before all peoples could understand and adopt the environmentally moral vegan diet. For some people, fish and meat would never be totally eliminated as their food, but the lower the percentage, the higher became the moral and nutritional value of their diets.

The GTN recommended and lobbied for taxation for unhealthy food, with the tax percentage increasing in direct proportion to the food's harm to health. That harm was weighed as a ratio of unhealthy ingredients to healthy ingredients, per gram. For example, red meats were taxed, and more than pork. Donuts were taxed more than white bread.

10. <u>Criminal Justice</u>. As far too many people were in prisons around the world, the GTN goal was to reduce the global number to no more than 50 per 100,000 population, or .05%, by the year 2050. The United States, as the most prison-oriented society in the early 21st century, made the most significant reduction pursuant to GTN initiatives. The country's rate of imprisonment dramatically dropped from 716 per 100,000 to 67 per 100,000 by that goal year, 2050.

What really stung the U.S. was the charge of hypocrisy, which is a first-order sin of a society or government. The world was no longer willing to accept the U.S. pronouncements that its justice system was the best, etc. The GTN quoted Jesus and Jesusa, as they had quoted Jesus of Nazareth, "Judge not, that you be not judged. For with what judgment you judge, you will be judged; and with the measure you use, it will be measured back to you. And why do you look at the speck in your brother's eye, but do not consider the plank in your own eye? Or how can you say to your brother, 'Let me remove the speck from your eye'; and look, a plank is in your own eye? Hypocrite! First remove the plank from your own eye, and then you will see clearly to remove the speck from your brother's eye."[5]

11. <u>International Justice</u>. Although the International Court of Justice had been established in 1946, as the replacement for the earlier Permanent International Court of Justice, 1922-46, it had not achieved the respect and power which originally expected. The problem was that too many nations were allowed to exempt themselves from the jurisdiction of the court. With the rallying cry of "justice for all" the advocates for the "Great Transformation" sought the elimination of that ability of nations to avoid international judgment.

Even though it was one of the founding countries for the International Criminal Court, the United States initially precluded the court's jurisdiction over its citizens. At the time, the U.S. saw itself as the "policeman" of the world, but as the legacies of World War II faded, and other nations rose in wealth while the U.S. descended into debt, that "policeman" role disappeared. International pressure increased in 2020 when the United Nations General Assembly threatened to move its venue from New York to Geneva, Monrovia, or Hong Kong unless the U.S. agreed to drop its claim to "exceptional" status. In 2021, the U.S. agreed to accept the jurisdiction of the I.C.C. over its citizens and its military forces.

12. <u>Toxic Products</u>. Because too much of what humanity manufactured was toxic to humans and to animals and plants, taxes on sales of products were modified to reflect their external costs, which included the costs of safe disposal. For example, the extra cost of finding, collecting and disposing of

5. The Book of Matthew 7:1–5

plastic pieces added approximately 20% to the cost of items made with plastic. With that extra income, governments were able to scour land and sea for plastic pieces. The disheartening videos of animals trapped by plastic items they either ate or simply explored out of curiosity were finally having an effect. Where imposing taxes to compensate for the external costs did not provide enough incentive, some products were simply designated to be banned. For example, the plastic can and bottle holders which trapped birds and other animals were banned. They were replaced by their predecessor paperboard/cardboard equivalents, which were far more bio-degradable. Also their production did not require the use of petro-chemicals.

Pesticides and herbicides which killed the pests and plants through chemicals were banned. Since the 1962 publication of Rachel Carson's *Silent Spring* it was clear that toxic chemicals worked their way up the food chain into the human diet. However, it was not until the 2062 publication of *100 Years Since Silent Spring*, that the world finally understood the full extent of the poisoning of the earth. By then it had become clear that whether through direct exposure to those chemicals or through diet, the dramatic increase of several neurological diseases, including Parkinson's disease and Alzheimer's disease, was directly attributed to pesticides and herbicides and related chemicals. Instead of their use, non-toxic genetic alterations were used to reduce the threats of pests and unwanted plants.

By 2080 the incidence of Alzheimer's disease had dropped to 50% of its rate in 2020.

13. <u>Altering of GDP standards</u>. There were two major recommendations for the universally utilized

GPD standard. First, goods and services which were inconsistent with environmental standards and with human emotional growth were not to be included in future GDP measurements. The proponents of this change were following the 21st century adage, "you get what you measure." The reasoning was that if you want to discourage military spending, then it shouldn't be included in a measurement that most people want to see grow. Hence military spending on salaries and all the goods and services utilized by the military was no longer to be included in GDP. Another spending category no longer to be included in GPD measurements was prisons, as increased spending for prisons was not a sign of a good society, but of a dysfunctional society.

The second recommended change was that the primary calculation of GDP no longer be measured as a national total, but as a per capita measurement. Of course, observers could do the math once they knew the per capita number and the population of a country or other political unit, but the medium was the message. Per capita measurement was the medium. This change reversed the previous incentive for countries to encourage population growth into one that encouraged family planning and the decline of population numbers.

Economists in the 20th and early 21st centuries had been so obsessed with the growth of GDP that they forced themselves into the embarrassing position of continuing to support population growth long after it was clear that such growth was ruining the planet and the well-being of its human and other populations.

14. Sports and Exercise. In addition to the removal of violence from sports, the GTN saw the need to restore exercise to sports. Primarily, this was to be

achieved by supporting games and sports which empfasized exercise, football, and reducing support for sports which involved less exercise, such as baseball. Bicycling and walking as forms of transportation were encouraged.

Related to this campaign was the need to reduce the purchases and use of devices which discouraged exercise, except where necessary. It was a hard standard to develop and impose, but examples made it easier to understand. For example, it made no sense for a society to manufacture lawnmowers which people could ride and thereby avoid exercise, while simultaneously encouraging them to drive their automobiles to exercise centers to exercise. The GTN recommended that governments require that operators of sit-down lawnmowers have a certificate of disability from a doctor. Otherwise, people were expected to walk behind their lawnmowers. This change was not as burdensome as it might have been if implemented in the early 20th century, because genetically modified grass had been developed to grow to specified heights. Depending upon climate and individual preferences, landowners could purchase seed for grass 7 cm, 9 cm or 11 cm in full growth length. Thus, the need for lawnmowers dropped by 80%.

Similarly, golfers were required to have disability permits to drive golf carts, and operators of ATVs (All Terrain Vehicles) needed the same unless they were carrying cargo that was too heavy to carry on foot.

The laws were as important as incentives for attitude change as they were tools of behavior re-enforcement. It was not a productive use of a policeperson's time to give tickets to golfers for not exercising enough.

The book, *Jesus and Jesusa*, did not achieve these changes by itself. However, it gave a sense of possibility to the otherwise dismal chances of moving the Roman Catholic Church and humanity forward. Other books in history which have had dramatic effects include Harriet Beecher Stowe's *Uncle Tom*. When President Lincoln met her during the Civil War, he is reputed to have said, "So you're the little woman who wrote the book that started this great war."[6] Another powerful book was the *Communist Manifesto*, which led to what might have been called the 20th century's great mal-transformation. Perhaps the best parallel came from the feminist books by Simone de Beauvoir, *The Second Sex*, and by Betty Friedan, *The Feminine Mystique*. Those books helped launch a new wave of feminism, which, in turn, led to further pressure on the Catholic Church to ordain women.

CONCLUSION

The publication of *Jesus and Jesus* was critically important to the future of humanity. The period when the benefits became widely recognized was called the "Great Transformation," after the same designation of a specified period in the book. The term "Great Transformation" was applied to the period of time from 2020 until 2120 just as other terms, such as "Industrial Revolution" were applied, post hoc, to periods of time.

6. See Wikipedia, "Harriet Beecher Stowe," at http://en.wikipedia.org/wiki/Harriet_Beecher_Stowe.

Appendix C – "Mountain Notes"
Summary of book, *Jesus and Jesusa* by
Maria Maddalena

The Calcata Foreskin

The story of *Jesus and Jesusa* (Jay-sooz' a) began in Calcata, Italia, a small town north of Roma. In January 1983, the town's sacred relic, the foreskin of Jesus, also called the "Holy Prepuce," was removed by an unknown person from under the bed of the village priest in Calcata, Don Dario Magnoni. Actually, it was in Calcata Nuova as the old town, Calcata Vecchia had been abandoned in the 1930's due to earthquake risks. Nearly the entire population of about 400 people had moved up the hill to the newly built town. However, the foreskin had been left in the old church, which was named for Saints Cornelius and Cyprian. Sometime before leaving for a church-related trip to Roma, Don Dario brought the relic from the old church to his bedroom. When he returned from Roma the next week, he found his house had been burglarized. No money was taken, but the "Holy Prepuce" was gone.

As the body of Jesus had ascended, by Christian belief, into heaven, the foreskin from his Jewish circumcision was one of only two remnants of his body which remained on earth. The relic had been in the town since 1527 when a Deutsche soldier was captured in the town with the relic in his possession. He had participated in the "Sack of Roma," and was returning north, when captured. He hid the relic in his cell, and it wasn't rediscovered for 30 years, in 1557. It remained in the church in Calcata, enduring centuries of disputes with other churches which also claimed possession of the "Holy Prepuce." As the Calcata claim to sole authenticity grew, pilgrimages to Calcata increased, until 1983. This is the period when the novella begins.

DNA and Cloning

In the 1950's James Watson and Francis Crick, with the inspiration and unrecognized assistance of Rosalind Franklin, presented to the world the structure of DNA, the key to the design and propagation of life. Speculation began in the ensuing decades about how DNA could be used to artificially recreate cells, and then organs and finally people, which was described in several science fiction books. Gradually, reality caught up to those books.

In *Jesus and Jesusa*, Pope Ioannes Paulus II[1] was advised in 1982 that scientists could, in the foreseeable future, take the DNA from one of the only two known remnants of the body of Jesus, his foreskin, and use that DNA to recreate a human being. Pope Ioannes Paulus II saw potential danger to the church, and Christianity, too, that the relic could be stolen by others. So he took the prudent step of having the foreskin relic removed in 1983 from the church in Calcata and brought to the Sacred Archives in the Vaticano for safekeeping. It was a secret operation, and speculation arose later that the local priest and/or others had stolen the relic, but no one in the town knew the real story.

At the Vaticano, controversy swirled about the future of the Catholic Church and what role the Holy Prepuce could play in its revival. In November, 2011 Cardinal Guglielmo Donato, the newly appointed President of the Pontifical Commission

1. Pope John Paul II, (1978-2005). He was the third longest serving pope up to that time, after St. Petrus (33-67) and Pope Pius IX (1846-1878).

for Vaticano City State, authorized a Catholic scientist to remove a .5 centimeter square of the foreskin relic and evaluate whether the DNA in that fragment could be used to recreate a human being. The scientist, Angelo Pappalardo, of the Universita degli Studi di Salerno, recruited a five person team to assist him in this project. All were sworn to secrecy.

After six weeks of analysis, the team agreed that it was possible to recreate a human being from the DNA in the Holy Prepuce. However, they also agreed not to tell Cardinal Donato the truth. They were scientists first and Catholics second, and they believed that the current pope, Benedictus XVI, would suppress any report of feasibility that the team might issue. Further, they feared for their own safety if they told the Vaticano the truth.

After the report of "no feasibility" was sent to Cardinal Donato, the team of five was not sure what to do. The team had kept the .5 cm square sample, after telling the Vaticano that it had been consumed in the analysis process. Professor Pappalardo then proposed that as scientists they must pursue what they believed to be possible. He recommended that sufficient DNA be extracted to clone not one but two human beings: with one of each sex. The sexual change could be achieved by taking one of the cloned embryos and switching "off" the Y sex chromosome and doubling the X sex chromosome so as to create a female.

He argued, "In this world of gender equality, it would not be fair to produce just a male child from the Jesus foreskin." Prof. Pappalardo proposed that an infertile woman volunteer, who is seeking to have children be found to bear the two children and raise them to adulthood. The other four scientists were astonished, but the plan was possible and it would advance the science of reproduction, if not the Catholic religion.

The other four members of the team agreed unanimously to proceed with the project. It was agreed that members of the team would tell no one else of the source of their human DNA, including the prospective mother and father until an appropriate time.

With careful screening, the prospective parents were found, Giuseppe and Maria Prescelto of Paestum, in the province of Salerno, Italia. Giuseppe was a mason and stone cutter, specializing in Greek temple preservation, and Maria was an attorney. Paestum was one of the outposts of ancient "Magna Graecia" (Greater Greece) and managed to preserve, by geografical luck, three of its magnificent temples. Two were dedicated to the goddess Hera and one to Athena.

Giuseppe and Maria agreed to raise the two children until adulthood, and agreed not to seek the identities of the biological parents, according to standard practices of in-vitro fertilization.   The implantation of the two embryos was successful, and Maria's pregnancy was easy and she was happy. As was the normal practice for expecting parents, Maria underwent pre-natal genetic testing, and the fetuses were entirely normal.

Births of Jesus and Jesusa

The twins were born on 30 May 2014. Although they were known to the scientists as being "identical" in the usual sense of defining twins, except for the altered gender gene, there were accepted as fraternal twins by their parents and everyone else. Without prompting from the scientific team, Giuseppe and Maria named them Jesus Giuseppe Prescelto and Jesusa Maria Prescelto. They chose the English spelling for

Jesus because of Maria's high school year in the
United States, and the Espanol spelling for Jesusa
because it was the most common in their Google
search for feminine equivalents for Jesus.
Relatives and friends saw the children and called
them "angelic," but such terms were commonly
used to flatter the parents of attractive children, so
no further weight was given to such labels.

The Early Years

As Jesus and Jesusa grew, it became more
evident that they were different from other children.
They spoke in measured cadences, in order that
everyone could understand them. In their teens,
the twins were said to have had "wisdom beyond
their years." They had an unusual affection for
each other as well.

Recognizing that their children were special,
Giuseppe and Maria enrolled them in the Da Vinci
School, a secular humanist private boarding school
run by the Italian Secular Humanist Foundation, a
member of the Global Secular Humanist Movement. The school was in the former Benedictine
Abbey in Santa Maria di Castellabate, about 70
kilometers south of Salerno. They wanted their
twins to learn about the world through the lens of
every religion and not just one.

In June 2032, at the age of 18, Jesus and
Jesusa Prescelto graduated from the Da Vinci
School. They chose this day to drop their surname
and be known only by their first names. In music
history, they had learned how Madonna Louise
Ciccone renamed herself "Madonna." They felt they
had a mission on Earth and their names were their
destiny.

Their intellectual and spiritual passion was to
learn more about the religions of the world, in the
hope that there was common ground among them.

From the Bellagio Center foundation, they obtained a travel grant for 15 months, until their entry into the multinational campus program at Universitat Heidelberg in Deutschland.

Universitat Heidelberg

Their first year was spent at the Deutschland campus, with subsequent years in Johannesburg, Boston, and Beijing. They studied as much science as possible, together with courses about ethics and utopias. While at Beijing, they led the march against the death penalty along the Great Wall of China, leading to the final global abolition of executions.

Graduation was scheduled for Saturday, August 29, 2037 at the Heidelberg, Deutschland campus.

Early in the summer of 2037, Professor Emeritus Pappalardo and two other members of the Salerno team, the others having been deceased, visited Giuseppe and Maria and told them about the origin of their children. From the available information on the internet, Dr. Pappalardo and the team had been watching the development of Jesus and Jesusa. First, of course, they were stunned to see the names that Guiseppe and Maria had given to them – without knowledge of their origin. Second, they were impressed with the twins' spiritual growth. Third, they were concerned about what the knowledge of their origin would do to the twins and their family.

The fourth issue was the question of publicity. During the 23 years since the births of the twins, there had been several efforts at cloning humans from long dead tissue, but no one had successfully used the technique secretly used by the Salerno team. In fact, the Salerno team had tried to reproduce its own work with other human tissue from deceased members of families, but it hadn't worked. Some team members still wondered whether they should have conducted their live experiment, just because they thought they could do it, and they wondered why the Jesus and Jesusa project worked, whereas the others did not. One member even wondered if there had been some kind of a religious miracle. Still, the opportunity had been there to change science and the world.

Yet the team members were sworn to secrecy, as they agreed, until the twins turned 21 or graduated from college, whichever came later. The team's plan was to write a paper about what they did, but keep the names of the twins' secret, unless the twins agreed. It was a plan that was out of touch with the modern reality of communications, including social networks.

Telling Jesus and Jesusa

Jesus and Jesusa were coming home before the beginning of the final two month college session in the summer of 2037, when they were 23, and their parents decided that this was the time to tell them about their origin, beyond what they already knew.

The twins knew they were special, but they didn't know why. They used to be the objects of jokes about their names, but they were not the first children to feel the sting of the cruelty of their peers.

With their knowledge of religion and of people around the world, Jesus and Jesusa knew that the news of their origin would be of great importance, but they sought to keep it secret, while they had some time to think about it.

On August 26, the Salerno team published their article, "Nature-Nurture in Human Cloning," in an academic publication, *The Journal of Human Genetics.* Despite the team's efforts at anonymity for Jesus and Jesusa, there were calls from journalists to their parents' home on the 27th and to their college dormitory rooms by the 28th. They knew they had to present the truth, as they knew it, but they begged the reporters for time.

They scheduled a media conference in Salerno for Monday, the 31st and asked reporters not to ask them questions until then. Of course, that didn't prevent the Heidelberg graduation from being the most widely publicized college graduation in history. Even without the participation of the twins, the story went viral and non-stop around the world.

At the media conference in Salerno, the twins began to feel the full impact of who they were and what they represented.

"Were they the Second Coming?" asked one reporter. Jesusa responded, "We are here to serve others."

"Which of them was the Messiah?" asked another, to which Jesus answered, "If one of us is, then we both are."

A Muslim reporter asked about their potential roles as Muslim proffets, and Jesusa answered, "We are here for all humanity and religions."

At age 23, they were not the youngest people to ever experience the thrill of international youthful fame and the temptations and challenges that come with it. Shirley Temple was famous at age five in 1933 and continued to live a productive life. Princess Diana of England struggled with her fame, but became the best-known supporter of the 1999 International Mine Ban Treaty, before her accidental death in 1997. Austrian Crown Prince Rudolph was heir to the Austro-Hungarian Empire, and all its apparent power and wealth, but he committed suicide at age 31 in 1889. The 20th century was littered with rock-and-roll stars who

lost their balance and lives quickly, such as Janis
Joplin and Jim Morrison.

Early Careers

However, Jesus and Jesusa had already
developed perspectives on life and humanity and
they chose, not unlike many of their peers, to use
their fame to change the world for the better. They
spoke of peace and of the need to severely reduce
military budgets. They campaigned for an
International Peace Day as part of the general
campaign for an International Holiday Treaty,
which later became international law in 2040, upon
the ratification by 50 countries. They added their
voices to the movement to provide family planning
services to all men and women. While global
population growth was slowing down and would
soon stabilize, it was still over 8.5 billion.

They visited religious leaders around the world
and asked that those leaders encourage their
members to seek and find common ground with
members of other religions, rather than differences.
They had developed a following, much like that the
Dalai Lama who, like themselves, was placed by the
decisions of others into the forefront of his or her
religion.

With all their speaking and traveling, they had
little time for their relationships with friends and
peers, and thus they had few. It seemed that they
were, like their namesake, giving their lives for their
fellow humans. They despaired that the human
population was destroying their earth with its
fertility and with its toxic gasses and substances.

The burden of their heritage and names
haunted them and they decided not to pass on that
heritage to others, at least not biologically. Jesus
had a vasectomy and Jesusa had a tubal ligation,
and they made their decisions public. "It was

time," they said, to care about the earth and for the long term future of humanity. They were not asking, they said, for everyone to have themselves sterilized before having any children, but they recommended the operation for all who had made that decision, with or without children.

Fame and Power

Now, the major religions of the world took notice of these courageous twins, for they understood the meaning of sacrifice, and sacrifice was part of the core of those religions. Now, the questions came more frequently from the Jews, "Are you the messiahs?" And from the Christians, "Are you the second coming of Christ?" Such questions and hyperbole annoyed Jesus and Jesusa because they focused on their perceived divinity rather than their ideas.

However, like others born into outsized roles, such as the heirs to the British crown, they understood the reality of their fame. They knew that scientists created them from the skin tissue of a long-long-deceased human who most assuredly was not the man called Jesus of Nazareth. They also knew that the primary reason that anyone listened to them, was because, like their namesake, their unusual birth. It was a dilemma of dilemmas.

They knew they loved each other, but they kept that fysical relationship secret and infrequent. When traveling together, they always had separate rooms. They thought that the public would never tolerate their sexual relationship. They knew that incest was prohibited in civilized societies as a pre-modern way to prevent unwanted genetic mutations. However, even though their sterilizations doubly assured the prevention of pregnancy and thus of such mutations, the taboo was too strong to test openly.

Jesus found himself to be part asexual and part bisexual. He had quiet relationships with men and women, but everyone knew that his first loyalty was to his sister. Similarly, Jesusa was bisexual, but mostly loved women, except for Jesus.

As their fame and influence spread, they understood that it was not what their namesake said and did that led to the creation of a religion in his name. It was the mythology of who he was and what his followers, especially Paul, said about him after his crucifixion. Further, it was his sacrifice and the sacrifices of his followers which gave momentum to Christianity.

International Humanist and Ethical Union

Still, they looked for the best opportunity for their unique voice. At a conference in Istanbul, they met the former leader of the International Humanist and Ethical Union, Sonja Eggerickx, and they explored their mutual interests. She encouraged Jesus and Jesusa to take a leadership role in the IHEU. Jesus and Jesusa wanted people to focus on earth-oriented values and discard the mythology, in many religions, of where someone came from or where their body went after death. To them, fertilized eggs become embryos in mothers' bodies and people are born, and when they die, their bodies are all that remain and not for long.

"From dust unto dust," they would remind their audiences.

They knew about the IHEU from their studies and they remembered learning that the brother of Aldous Huxley, author of *Brave New World*, was Julian Huxley who was one of the founders of the IHEU. The Huxley family was distinguished for many reasons, and the brothers were the grandsons of Thomas Henry Huxley, a friend and supporter of Charles Darwin.

In 2038, Jesus and Jesusa were elected as co-presidents of the IHEU and the organization prospered. Many new members cited the "children" of Jesus as the reason for their support of humanism. "If a child of Jesus can dismantle the mythology of Jesus's purported birth and death, then it's safe for all of us," wrote one new member on an IHEU blog.

As Jesus and Jesusa were seeking to promote a better life for all humans on earth, their earlier interest in utopias blossomed into support for advocates of a future, more rational society. They joined in the endorsement of the "Great Transformation," the 50-year campaign which was announced in 2020. The number of people who openly declared themselves to be atheists or humanists grew dramatically after their election.

Plan for Vaticano Council IV

In 2039, Jesus and Jesusa met with Pope Francesco II, who succeeded to the papacy in 2027 after the resignation of Pope Francesco I on his birthday, December 17, 2026 at the age of 90. The Pope told them of his plan to convene a Vaticano Council IV in 2042, 20 years after the convening of the reform Vaticano Council III, which had endorsed the ordination of women, the abandon-ment of celibacy and the welcoming of marriage for all priests.

Pope Francesco II was planning to recommend the de-mythologization of the Catholic Church, meaning that the Church should abandon the long-held views in such impossible myths as a virgin birth, ascension into a heaven that does not exist, and the existence of a personal God. Instead, he would urge the Church to focus its mission on what Jesus said and did as a human being. His messages of love and forgiveness were especially important to Pope Francesco. For these dramatic changes he believed he had the support of most of the Cardinals.

Despite the ordination of women, the member population of the Catholic Church was continuing its long decline, as education in sciences continued to grow. Polls had shown to Pope Francesco II that former Catholics and potential Catholics viewed the myths of the traditional Church as the barriers to their future religious participation.

Ordination of Jesus and Jesusa

Most of the new women priests, bishops and cardinals supported this change, and they were lobbying their cardinal superiors. At the conclusion of their visit, Pope Francesco II announced the simultaneous ordinations of Jesus and Jesusa as Catholic priests, together with their elevation as cardinals. Jesusa thus became the sixth woman Catholic cardinal. The Pope explained how the IHEU and the Catholic Church would be working together over the next three years to promote their mutual interests. By this time the IHEU claimed over two billion members or passive sympathizers, which put it at about the same size as all of Christianity. For the Catholic Church to align with such a large group would help the Church survive into the next centuries.

Jesus and Jesusa reached out to the Jews of the world and traveled to Israel and other Jewish centers. They actively, but quietly, sought recognition as messiahs, but that was not yet attainable.

Similarly they went to Medina and Mecca and sought the support of Islamic leaders for them both as proffets in the Muslim faith, just as Jesus of Nazareth was recognized as an Islamic proffet.

Vaticano Council IV

In 2042, Jesus and Jesusa joined the Vaticano Council IV and lobbied their peer cardinals to join in declarations that the source of Christian faith was not in the divinity of Christ, just as they were not divine, but in the messages to the work that he left with his disciples.

In 2043, the Vaticano Council IV released its findings, the most important of which was the demytholization of Catholicism. The Catholic Church was now a humanist church. There were dissenters, to be sure, but now the Church would move forward to assist its members in the real moral issues of the day which related to the care of the Earth and the need to reduce the size of the human population, and increase the spiritual and fysicial welfare of all.

Supporting that focus on the true moral issues, the Vaticano Council IV endorsed Pope Francesco II's proposal for the Vaticano to abandon its status as a political unit. There was no modern reason for the Catholic Church to be the only religion in the world which also was a political state. The change meant large savings for the dismantling of the Vaticano diplomatic corps, including its mission to the United Nations. Instead of being a state, the territory of the Vaticano would be included within Municipio I, one of the 15 municipalities of the City of Roma. The approximately 900 citizens of the Vaticano City became citizens of Roma and Italia. The pope had one vote, like every other citizen of Roma.

Pursuant to the Council's determination, Pope Francesco II announced that the Catholic Church would be joining the IHEU.

Co-Popes Jesus and Jesusa

Pope Francesco II also announced his intention to resign in 2044, and he took the unusual step of designating Jesus and Jesusa as co-popes-elect. He expected the College of Cardinals to convene later that year to confirm his selections.

Jesus and Jesusa thus became the first co-popes, and Jesusa was the first woman pope. Also, at age 30, they were the youngest popes.

In May of 2045, the Co-Popes began a world tour going eastward, beginning with Istanbul. There, they signed an agreement authorizing the mutual exploration of re-unification of the Catholic Church with the Eastern Orthodox Church, from which it split in 1054. The agreement specifically set 2054 as the target date for re-unification, which would mark the end of the 1,000 year schism.

Jesus and Jesusa then traveled to Jerusalem, but they took an indirect route. They first took a MAGtrain to Aleppo, Syria, and then a car to the three peaks of Mount Hermon, a symbol of the earlier divisions and wars among the Syrians, Lebanese and Israelis. Thanks to the 2021 Alexandria Treaty among the Israelis and their Muslim neighbors, Mount Hermon and the Golan Heights were returned to full Syrian sovereignty.

From there, the Co-Popes chose to walk the approximate 320 kilometers to Jerusalem, stopping at sites along the way where Jesus and proffets of Islam had been. They walked along the Jordan River and swam in the Sea of Galilee. Arriving in Jerusalem they spent an equal amount of time at Christian, Jewish and Muslim holy sites and in meetings with the leaders of the three faiths.

Temple Mount Accord

At the Temple Mount, a place holy to the three faiths, the Co-Popes signed an accord with leaders of the several Jewish and Muslim sects. Also invited and signing were the leaders of the ten largest Christian denominations, including the Eastern Orthodox, Protestants and Anglicans.   The accord held forth the goal of merging their faiths into a single faith based not on the divinity of any of their ancestor leaders, but on the view of humanity they held in common. The accord, later known as the Temple Mount Accord of 2045 also expressed a desire to join with the faiths of Asia and Africa.

Continuing eastward, the Co-Popes flew to India and met with Hindu leaders and to Thailand to meet with Asian Buddhist leaders. "We must do what we can to save humanity," said Jesusa, "and working together with a common spiritual vision will help all of us do that work."

Then they went to South America and visited the major countries southerly along the Pacific coast and then back north along the Atlantic, and then to Cuba. In Havana, Jesus and Jesusa dedicated the renovated Havana Cathedral of Mother Mary, formerly called the Cathedral of the Virgin Mary. As with other churches and places with references to the now-discarded myth of a virgin birth, the name of the Havana Cathedral was changed. The mother of Jesus of Nazareth was still much revered in the Catholic Church for the values that she instilled in her son, but Christianity no longer needed to rely upon myths for its spiritual strength.

Before heading to Western Europe and Roma, the Co-Popes flew to Miami for a New Year's Eve celebration and Mass. The Church continued the rituals of Mass. with the sharing of bread and wine as symbols of the bodily and spiritual sharing of the food and drink sustenance for humanity.

Not everyone in the Catholic Church welcomed the changes brought by Vaticano Councils III and IV and by the ascendancy of Co-Popes Jesus and Jesusa. Before the trip began, Church leaders in the U.S. advised against coming to the U.S. for fear of an assassination attempt by disgruntled Catholics. Citizens in the United States were still heavily armed. There was some relief as the trip to Miami concluded without serious incident, aside from some heckling and threatening words on the Internet. "See," said Jesus to Jesusa, "despite some bitterness in the U.S. about its relative decline in the world, and despite some Catholic opposition to what we have done and what we symbolize, our messages of love and optimism are still welcome here."

Dallas

Jesus and Jesus had also learned about President John Kennedy, as his name was given to several streets in Italia and to a building at their school. When at the University of Heidelberg, they had traveled to Berlin and saw a video of Kennedy's trip to that city in June, 1963. Given their interest in John Kennedy, Dallas was added to their itinerary, before going to New York and then to Notre Dame Cathedral in Paris and then home.

In Dallas, reality struck in the form of a kamikaze drone that struck their popemobile while on the way from the airport to the Dallas Book Depository and Dealey Plaza. Taking a slightly different route than the 1963 Kennedy motorcade, the co-popes traveled west on Elm Street and came into Deavey Plaza where Kennedy was shot. Just after passing through the intersection with Houston Street a drone plane fired six 9 mm caliber rifle shots into the popemobile before crashing into it at 130 km/hour. Hitting the windshield, the drone further injured the driver, who had already been hit by two of the bullets, and the car burst into flame. Three other bullets hit the bullet proof glass protector between the driver and the Co-Popes.

The sixth bullet went through the front seat and hit Jesusa's left hand as she was ducking behind that seat. "Oh, my God!" she screamed. The popemobile crashed into a building on Elm Street whereupon police and EMTs descended upon the vehicle and removed Jesus and Jesusa and drove them to the new Parkland Hospital which was built in 2015, replacing the hospital where John Kennedy was taken and died.

The wound to Jesusa's hand was serious, in the sense that any bullet traveling through a human body is serious, but not life-threatening. There were no broken or shattered bones and no nerves were severed. The radial artery was cut, and it was repaired after the loss of .5 liter of blood. She stayed in the hospital for a day and then she and Jesus continued their tour to New York, Paris and finally Roma.

The assassination attempt in Dallas caused worldwide revulsion at the continued widespread availability of guns and weapons in the United States.

2084 resignations

Jesus and Jesusa continued their reigns until their own resignations on their 70th birthday on May 30, 2084. At 40 years, their reigns were the second longest in Church history.

During their reign, the Catholic Church supported the "Great Transformation" until its formal pre-determined end in 2070. In its place, the "Great Transformation II," was proposed by the United Nations Secretary-General Malia Obama and later ratified by the General Assembly. The Catholic Church, as the Holy See, rather than in its former status as the city-state, Vaticano, was a co-sponsor.

Jesus and Jesusa retired as popes emerita to their childhood home in Salerno. As was the experience of other cloned animals, their bodies declined faster than others, after the age of approximately 65. Earlier in their lives, they made a pact to leave this world together, just as they had come into the world together. If they had a choice, and were not otherwise taken by accident or unstoppable disease, they would commit suicide together. In March, 2089, Jesus had a stroke, causing a fall in the garden and he was partially paralyzed. In April, Jesusa was diagnosed with a new form of Alzheimers, i.e. one that defied the previously developed cures.

Mutual Suicide

They knew their time to die was coming, and it did not scare them. They decided to take their lives on their 75th birthday, on May 30, 2089, in the presence of their closest friends. Instead of using a helium "exit bag" which imposed some obligation on those accompanying suicides during their last moments, Jesus and Jesusa chose to drink a suicide medicine. With the help of a doctor, and the previous successful experiences of millions around the world, they chose red wine with codeine, pentobartitol, and seconal.

On the 30th, they toasted each other and their friends, and then "to the eternal survival and goodness of humanity." Their bodies were cremated and then the ashes were taken to the Vaticano and entombed in the Sacristy.

Afterword

The companion utopian novels, *Jesus and Jesusa* and *2121* present an optimistic view of humanity's future. Whether enough of their purported content will come true in time to save the Earth from barely reversible harm remains to be seen.

With some predictions, I hope that the pace of change was overly conservative, as with the predicted global end of capital punishment in 2032. Perhaps that time will come sooner. Not soon enough for Troy Davis, Rocco Barnabei and Cameron Todd Willingham, but soon enough to avoid such future tragedies as were their arguably wrongful executions.

Another prediction which may be too conservative is the birth of the first human on Mars in 2121. Maybe it will come much earlier.

Conversely, some predictions, such as the development of hydrogenfusion("hydrofusion") electric power plants by 2027 may be too optimistic.

The pace of political and social change varies according to many factors and is often unpredictable. There were few people who predicted in the 1980s that the Soviet Union, the largest country in the world and home to over 280 million people, would disappear by 1991.

In the United States, the emotional issue of gay marriage was barely on the radar screens of social and political leaders during the years of upheaval in the 1960s. In 1972, the U.S. Supreme Court refused to hear an equal protection challenge to the refusal in Minnesota to grant a marriage license to a gay couple. Alarmed at the possibilities, many conservative states, primarily in the South, enacted laws and constitutional amendments to stop gay marriage by declaring that marriage was to be available only to one man and one woman. The Federal Defense of Marriage Act (DOMA) was passed in 1996. Maybe the opponents protested too much.

The publicity of the opposition seemed to beg the question and the tide soon turned, beginning with the legislative legalization of civil unions in Vermont in 2000. Then came the court-ordered legalization of gay marriage in Massachusetts, California, Connecticut and Iowa and then Vermont forged ahead with the first statutory legalization of gay marriage in 2009.

In 2013 the U.S. Supreme Court found the DOMA to be unconstitutional in U.S. v. Windsor. In the following years, the remaining laws and state constitutional provisions were swept aside. In 1996, the first national poll on the issue showed 27% support for gay marriage. By 2010, that number had increased to 50% and to 55% by 2014. Each new poll seemed to show increased support.

Thus, in less than 15 years, a major social change had occurred despite fervent opposition which based its case on history and religious doctrine.

If such a change could occur so rapidly in the sensitive area of gay marriage, then there is room for hope that humanity will soon grasp the same tools for social change to reverse global warming and stop nuclear proliferation, and remedy other problems described in *Jesus and Jesusa* and *2121*.

Author Acknowledgments

I thank Angelo Pappagallo for his encouragement, comments and suggestions for *Jesus and Jesusa* and *2121,* and for his interest in the subjects and themes of the two books.

Jennifer Bunting's initial comments were appreciated, as has been her considerable assistance with my previous books.

Carol Scofield's and Chad Evans's careful and enthusiastic reading and general encouragement were helpful at the end of this utopian journey.

I thank my wife, Leah, for her love and patience.